Talulla Rising

GLEN DUNCAN

CANONGATE

Edinburgh · London

Published in Great Britain in 2012
by Canongate Books Ltd, 14 High Street, Edinburgh EH1 1TE

www.canongate.tv

1

British Library Cataloguing-in-Publication Data
A catalogue record for this book is available on
request from the British Library

ISBN 978 1 84767 947 5
Export ISBN 978 1 84767 948 2

Typeset in Perpetua by Palimpsest Book Production Ltd,
Falkirk, Stirlingshire

Printed and bound in Great Britain
by CPI Group (UK) Ltd, Croydon CR0 4YY

This book is printed on FSC certified paper

For Isobel

ACKNOWLEDGEMENTS

My thanks to all at Canongate in the UK, Knopf in the US and Text Publishing in Australia, especially: Francis Bickmore, Jamie Byng, Jenny Todd, Norah Perkins, Lorraine McCann, Angela Robertson, Cate Cannon, Jaz Lacey-Campbell, Polly Collingridge, Andrea Joyce, Morven Dooner, Marty Asher, Sonny Mehta, Diana Coglianese, Kim Thornton, Ruth Liebmann, Peter Mendelsund, Mandy Brett and Jane Novak. Once again I'm indebted to my brilliant agents, Jonny Geller in London and Jane Gelfman in New York, and to my friends and family, without whose support and occasional salutary ridicule I would have long ago gone off my nut. They are: Louise Maker, Mark Duncan, Marina Hardiman, Stephen Coates, Nicola Stewart, Jon Field, Vicky Hutchinson, Pete Sollett, Eva Vives, Andrea Freeman, Glen & Dave Teasdale, Bryn & Sally Teasdale, Sarah Forest, Ben Ball, Paige Simpson, Alice Naylor, Jon Cairns, Gavin Butt, Nicola Harwood, Tracy Ryan, Mike Loteryman and Anna Baker Jones. Special thanks to my inspirational Ma and Pa, and finally to Kim Teasdale, for all the usual reasons, but chiefly for allowing me to steal her best ideas and take credit for them.

PROLOGUE

SUGAR AND SPICE AND ALL THINGS NICE

*T*alulla Demetriou, you have been a Very (pause) *Bad* (pause) *Girl*.

My mother always said this with a glimmer of delight in her eyes. She was a Very Bad Girl herself. What she hated above all was weakness. Especially in women. She'd rather pure evil. *She* was pure evil, when she had to be. She acknowledged an elite: our family, a handful of friends, certain celebrities. The rest of the world was made up of idiots and mediocrities. *The Humans*, she called them.

(God being dead, irony still rollickingly alive...)

Later, courtesy of my psycho-terrorist Catholic Aunt Theresa, I discovered I was also a Dirty Little Girl. A Dirty, *Filthy* Little Girl, to be precise. When I was eight she caught me and Toby Greely in the basement examining each other's private parts. One minute Toby and I were alone, watched by the room's stunned miscellany – cardboard boxes and a broken ping-pong table and some rolled-up sunshades – the next the silence shifted and I knew someone else was there. Aunt Theresa stood on the bottom step. Her face was always moist from Pond's Cold Cream but right then it shone with what looked like newly minted divinity. *My* face, when I turned it to her, was hot and overfull. I had a rich soft feeling because of my pants round my ankles and Toby on his knees and the silence that had cocooned us while

3

he'd taken his long, careful – and indeed tender – look. I'd been close to some big revelation, I believed, and along with horror at being discovered was queenly annoyance at being interrupted. Even then I was thinking Toby and I would have to get back to this, soon.

'Talulla Demetriou,' Aunt Theresa said, 'you are a dirty little girl.' And then, since that didn't quite cover it: 'A dirty, *filthy* little girl.'

The Dirty Filthy Little Girl was pretty and liked bad things. In Tenth Grade she was friends with Lauren Miller, who was also pretty and also liked bad things. For example there was a drippy and permanently cold-sored girl they tormented and nicknamed NODOR (No Danger of Rape). One day the Dirty Filthy Little Girl was sitting on Jason Wells's lap at recess and Lauren called out something awful to NODOR as she went by and you could see from NODOR's face it really hurt her, hurt her in her *heart*, and at the same time Jason's hard-on was pressing against the Dirty Filthy Little Girl's ass and the Dirty Filthy Little Girl got the rich soft feeling again and knew there was a connection. It was like the Devil putting his arms around you from behind and you leaning back into it and enjoying the lovely surprising warmth.

At college the Very Bad Dirty Filthy Little Girl knew once and for all she was an agent for the forces of darkness. She was the worst kind of young woman: one who recognised the pro-actively politicised female she ought to become, then didn't become it, but instead carried on being attracted to evil guys and having the wrong kind of sexual fantasies and making herself look as attractive as possible and ultimately accepting that she was too selfish and good-looking and lazy and perverted to ever live the kind of life she knew she ought to. By the end of her sophomore year she was openly reading the wrong authors and

4

no longer going through Gethsemane every time she wore a sexy dress or a pair of politically bankrupt shoes or let a guy fuck her in the ass, which, to be fair to her, was a privilege she granted very (pause) *very* (pause) selectively, and often with mixed feelings or when completely hammered.

Finally, the Very Bad Dirty Filthy Little Girl capped her career of moral slippage by dropping out of her Masters in Literature and becoming a businesswoman. A servant of Mammon! With no great surprise – in fact with loose-limbed satisfaction – she discovered she had a penchant for what a later lover (the lover to end all lovers) would call 'the smut and savvy of American Trade'. Her mother was both disappointed and sufficiently vain to be flattered by how much like her her daughter had turned out.

Given the Very Bad Dirty Filthy Little Girl's record, it was astonishing that when her marriage collapsed it wasn't because she was cheating on her husband, but because he was cheating on her. She enjoyed a brief sojourn on the moral high ground.

'Brief' being the operative word. No sooner had she got used to the toothsome satisfaction of being *all sorts of lousy things but at least I'm not a fucking liar you miserable fuck* than she got bitten by a werewolf one night in the Arizona desert, and was forced to say goodbye to the moral high ground for ever. She discovered that not only could she kill and eat people once a month, but she could kill and eat people once a month and *love* it.

Until she found out she was pregnant. Then a whole new species of trouble began.

PART ONE

NATIVITY

'Whatever else is unsure in this stinking dunghill of a world a mother's love is not.'

James Joyce — *A Portrait of the Artist as a Young Man*

1

'*Oh, mon Dieu*,' Cloquet said, when he opened the lodge door and saw me on the floor. 'Fuck.'

I was on my side, knees drawn up, face wet with sweat. Pregnancy and the hunger didn't get along. Hated each other, in fact. I pictured the baby pressing werewolf fingernails against my womb, five bits of broken glass on the skin of a balloon. And only myself to blame: when I could've got rid of it I didn't want to. Now that I wanted to it was too late. Conscience from the old life said: *Serves you right.* I'd fired conscience months back, but it was still hanging around, miserable, unshaven, nowhere else to go.

'Did you get it?' I gasped. Behind Cloquet the open door showed deep snow, the edge of the pine forest, frail constellations. Beauty mauled me even in this state. Aesthetic hypersensitivity was a by-product of slaughter. Life was full of these amoral relations, it turned out.

Cloquet rushed to my side, tugging off his thermal gloves. 'Lie still,' he said. 'Don't try to speak.' He smelled of outdoors, dense evergreens and the far north air like something purified by the flight of angels. 'You have a temperature. Did you drink enough water?'

For the umpteenth time I wished my mother were alive. For the umpteenth time I thought how unspeakably happy I'd be if she and Jake walked in the door right now, grinning, the pair of them. My mother would dump her purse on the table in a puff of Chanel and say, For God's sake, Lulu, look at your *hair* – and the weight would lift and everything would be all right. Jake wouldn't have to say anything. He'd look at me and it would be there in his eyes, that he was for me, always, *always* – and the nightmare would reduce to a handful of solvable problems. (I'd expected their ghosts, naturally. I'd *demanded* their ghosts. I got nothing. The universe, it also turned out, was no more interested in werewolf demands than it was in human ones.)

'Talulla?'

Pain thickened under my toenails, warmed my eyeballs. *Wulf* smirked and kicked and cajoled in my blood. Come on, what's a few hours between friends? Let me out. Let me *out*. Every month the same delirious bullying, the same pointless impatience. I closed my eyes.

Bad idea. The footage ran, immediately: Delilah Snow's room, the wardrobe door swinging open, its long mirror introducing me to myself in all my grotesque glory, what I was, what I could do, the full range of my options. Monster. Murderer. Mother-to-be.

I opened my eyes.

'Let me get you some water,' Cloquet said.

'No, stay here.'

I had hold of his coat and was twisting it. My dead moaned and throbbed. My dead. My restless tenants. My forced family of thirteen. *Those* ghosts, yes, of course, as many as you like. The only way to be sure of never losing the ones you love. The Dahmer Method. Extreme, but effective.

'Breathe, *chérie*, breathe.'

Chérie. Mon ange. Ma belle. Lovers' endearments, though we weren't, and never would be, lovers.

One by one the broken-glass fingernails withdrew. The pain furled shut, like time-lapse film of a flower closing. By degrees, with Cloquet's help, I made it to the armchair. *Wulf* smiled. The prisoner's smile at the guard, knowing the breakout gang's already on its way.

'Did you get it?' I asked again, when I'd caught my breath. 'At least tell me you got it.'

Cloquet shook his head. 'There was a screw-up. It's stuck in freight clearing at Anchorage. It'll be in Fairbanks Saturday morning. There's more snow coming, though. I'll have to take the Ski-Doo and trailer.'

I didn't say anything. I was remembering an artwork I saw once at MOMA: a foetus made entirely of barbed wire. Lauren and I had just stood there looking at it, silenced.

'Don't worry,' Cloquet said. 'It's two days. You're not due for six weeks. I'll go back to Fairbanks Saturday first-thing. They promise it'll be there. It has to be.'

'It' was a consignment of obstetrics equipment, including oxygen machine, forceps, foetal and adult stethoscopes, heart monitor, PCA pump, sphygmomanometer and sutures. 'Fairbanks' was Fairbanks, Alaska. Necessary obscurity: WOCOP – World Organization for the Control of Occult Phenomena (*think CIA meets Keystone Kops meets Spanish Inquisition*, Jake had said) – knew I'd survived Jake's death and was carrying his child. Its hunters wanted my head and its scientists wanted me strapped down in a lab. It didn't stop there. Having found a correlation between survived werewolf bites and increased sunlight tolerance, vampires were after – what else? – my blood. More than all that, my straw-clutching subconscious had seen the snow as a sterile environment, a natural hospital. Conventional medicine was out of the question – *Well, Miss Demetriou, as you can see on the monitor, here's the umbilicus, and here's a very healthy-looking placenta, and of course here's the—JESUS FUCKING CHRIST WHAT IS THAT? –* so Cloquet had found the converted hunting lodge, with its exposed beams and wood-burning stove and wardrobes that smelled of camphor. Three thousand dollars a week, no other residents within fifteen miles, no phone reception, a half-mile of dirt road through the Christmas trees' thrilled hush to the highway, from which Fairbanks was a ninety-minute drive southwest. I could scream as loud as I liked. No one would hear. I had a recurring vision of myself lying on the dining table in a pool of blood, screaming as loud as I liked. I had a lot of recurring visions.

'It doesn't matter,' I said. 'This thing's going to kill me anyway.' Gratuitous. Post-Delilah Snow I was full of random cruelties. I knew how the fear of me dying gnawed him now he was an accessory to murder. Murders, plural. Looking after a werewolf uniquely disqualified you from doing anything else. As Jake's poor minder Harley could have confirmed, if he hadn't had his head cut off. That Cloquet had become *my* minder still occasionally mesmerised me, the giant absurdity of the fact. Yet I remembered the feeling of dreamy inevitability that night in the forest five months before, when I'd put out my hand – my changed hand, clawed, wet and heavy with blood – and he, after a cracked laugh, had taken it. What had happened moments before – carnage, death, vengeance, loss – had left the two of us with a raw permissive consciousness, and into it this new relationship insinuated itself. *Expect the absurd,* Jake had warned me. *Expect the risible twist, the ludicrous denouement. Expect the perverse. It's the werewolf's lot.*

Cloquet shut the door, took out a big white hanky and blew his nose. The cold had given him a look of surprised innocence. Sometimes I saw him like this, humanly, the mangled person and the road back to his childhood strewn with wrong turns and ugly coincidences. Long ago he'd been a little boy, side-parted hair and a volatile world of loved toys and stormy adults. Now, as he snuffled and swiped, nostrils raw, eyebrows raised, I had an image of this dark-eyed child standing alone on a jetty looking out over black water, waiting for the reunion that would never come. Tenderness stirred in me – and like an awkward reflex the new force obscured it, said it didn't fit the grammar, wasn't the done thing. There was too much else going on in me to argue, but I'd already made it known I didn't like rules. God only knows to *whom* I'd made it known. Some vague werewolf scheme of things I didn't even believe in.

'How is it?' he asked.

'Better.'

'I wish you'd take the drugs.'

Just say no. So far I had. Acetaminophen, pseudoephedrine, codeine, Demerol, morphine. All with potential side-effects my imagination made certainties. *Administration of this drug during the first trimester can cause behavioural abnormalities in the infant.*

Behavioural abnormalities. Jake and I would've exchanged a look. But ironies were like secrets: unshared they died. Jake and I would've. Jake and I. Jake. I. There were these moments when there was nothing between me and the reality of his death, when the future without him yawned, a vast space of sheer drops and wrong perspectives. There'd be more and more of these moments, I knew, until eventually they wouldn't be moments at all, just the continuous, crushing way things were. The way things were that having our child was supposed to alleviate.

'Save the drugs for when I really need them,' I said.

We both knew I really needed them already, what with *wulf* jamming the room with its stink and the cattle-wire shocks in my fingernails and ringing iron in my eye-teeth and *outside* whispering the dirty talk of the wild. Transformation was less than twenty-four hours away.

'You don't have to be brave, you know,' he said.

'I'm not. I'm just thinking ahead.' I didn't want to think ahead. (I didn't want to think back, either. There was horror in both directions.) Rufus, my fish supplier for the Brooklyn diners, had described watching his wife having their baby. *I want to tell you it was beautiful*, he said, *but basically it looked like someone had taken a twelve-gauge to her pussy*. This image kept coming back, as did the Sex Ed video they showed us in high school, yellowed footage of a big-thighed woman sweatily giving birth. Unanimous teen revulsion. Lauren had said to me: Fuck the miracle of life, where do I sign up for a hysterectomy?

'I'll go and check downstairs,' Cloquet said.

'No, I'll go.'

'You should rest.'

'I need to move. *Ow*. Fuck.' The baby shimmied, scraped something in me. It sent these violent communiqués. The same communiqué, every time: *I saw you. In the mirror. You and Delilah Snow*. Mother.

I waited for the pain to fold itself away again.

'You sure you don't want something?' Cloquet asked.

I shook my head, no. Then held out my hand to him. 'But I don't think I can get out of this chair by myself.'

2

One minute you're little Lula, eight years old, sitting on the counter in the Tenth Street diner drinking a vanilla shake under the pink Coors neon – the next this, the stink of liver under your fingernails and the water in the shower running red around your feet. In the thought experiment you commit suicide. *I wouldn't do it. I'd kill myself.* In reality you don't. In reality you kill and eat someone else. You start at one end of the experience, go through it, come out the other side. You've killed and eaten a human being. Blood winks on your fingers, mats the hair on your arms and snout. The gobbled life flails and struggles in what it touchingly mistakes for a bad dream. The moon sets. The next day you wake up in sheets that smell of fabric conditioner. There is CNN. There is coffee. There is weather. There is your human face in the mirror. The world, you discover, is a place of appalling continuity. *I ate his heart.* It seems incredible the words don't refuse, don't revolt. But why should they? *You* didn't. There's your horror, yes. But your horror's a tide going out: every wave stops a little further away. Eventually the tide doesn't come in any more. Eventually there's just the sighing delta, the new you, the werewolf. The last werewolf, as it happens.

Jake had thought he was the last. He'd thought he was ready to go, too. *One by one I've exhausted the modes*, he wrote:

17

hedonism, asceticism, spontaneity, reflection, everything from miserable Socrates to the happy pig. My mechanism's worn out. I don't have what it takes. I still have feelings but I'm sick of having them. Which is another feeling I'm sick of having. I just . . . I just don't want any more life.

Then he'd met me. Courtesy of the risible twist, the ludicrous coincidence. *Love has come*, he wrote.

Full, incendiary, unarguable with. Love has come, and with it the renewed pricelessness of time. I think of an hour with her — then of my hundreds of thousands of hours before knowing her was possible, wasted hours, by definition. The life we could've had if she'd been around a century ago (or fifty years, or ten, or Jesus Christ five) is an obscenity in my imagination. The bigger obscenity, of course, is the question of how much life we've got. There's no God but I know his style: he wouldn't teach you the value of time unless you had fuck-all time left . . .

He was right. We had two months. *Careful what you wish for*, he'd sent me, dying, in my arms. Before we'd met he'd wished for death. Death had listened. Death had made a note. Unerasable, it turned out.

A century and a half of loneliness coda'd by sixty days and nights of love. Not much of an equation. Reversed, it looked a lot worse: sixty days and nights of love followed by hundreds of years of loneliness. No wonder I missed every abortion appointment I made.

I had three recurring daydreams. One was of me with a twelve-year-old daughter living in a Los Angeles villa. Turquoise pool, cactus garden, sunlight, Cloquet in a straw hat and white bermudas teaching us French.

Another was of a little werewolf boy in a shredded school uniform covered in blood, a leftover eyeball in his lunchbox, a human tongue flopping out of his blazer pocket. Of course it was darkly hilarious. Dark hilarity's always an option, if there's no God.

I said *three* recurring daydreams.

I know.

Not yet.

·

Halfway down the basement stairs my legs buckled. I grabbed the banister, slid to my knees and vomited. Bile and water, since I hadn't had solid food in twelve days. It hadn't always been this way. I'd swanned through the first eighteen weeks of pregnancy symptom-free. Then, without warning, everything had changed. Cramps, vomiting, night sweats, visual disturbances, nosebleeds, back ache, diarrhoea, breathtaking uterine pains. Overnight, biology made me its punchbag. If I was lucky I got about a week's grace post-transformation, when the bodily violence subsided, but when the moon hit first quarter it started up again, and the fiercer the hunger, the more maternity beat the shit out of me. A curse on top of the Curse: you're starving, but your appetite makes you sick. (My last victim, an onion-and-whiskey-flavoured pimp in Mexico City, had brought on x-rated vomiting less than an hour after I'd eaten him. A pointless death. Now he was an oddity among my dead, confused and wraithy from having not been taken in properly – or from having been taken in and then half forced out again.) For a while I'd clung to a moral theory, that motherhood abhorred murder. But things had happened. Things had happened, and the theory had gone.

'It's okay,' I croaked down to Kaitlyn. 'It's just me.'

The stuff you come out with: It's just me. Your other kidnapper.

How reassuring. Kaitlyn didn't reply. She was on her feet by the camp-bed, holding the restraining cable. Twenty-three, according to her driver's licence. Pale skin, greasy blonde hair, slightly bulbous blue eyes and a blow-up dollish mouth. Overall a look of not being quite clean (I imagined a grimy navel and a bedroom like the site of a poltergeist freak-out) but slim and pretty enough not to have suspected anything worse than a one-night stand when Cloquet picked her up in Fairbanks. She'd resigned early into the belief that sex was the only thing she had to offer, spent a lot of time docilely doing things in bed she really didn't want to do, but hey, you know, that was guys, that was the world. There were millions of young women just like her all over America. I'd never been one of them. Because as a child I'd had love and winter nights with my dad talking me through the constellations. Because I'd had catastrophic drunk uncles who'd blearily sought my eight-year-old opinion and sharp aunts (Theresa excluded) who'd marched against the war in Vietnam. Because I'd had *The Iliad* and Emily Dickinson and the fabulous spectacle of my mother's ego, her outrageous sense of entitlement.

'It's a lie about the ransom, isn't it?' Kaitlyn said, when I reached the bottom step. 'I mean I'm not stupid. No one who gives a shit about me's got any money.' She was through the crying phase. She was through all the dramatic phases: shock, terror, rage, grief. It had taken seventy-two hours. Now there was mechanical misery. If we held her long enough it would become boredom. Eventually acceptance. But of course we weren't going to hold her long enough. Why do you keep going down there? Cloquet wanted to know. You don't have to have contact with her. Why don't you let me deal with it?

'It's bullshit,' Kaitlyn said. 'I know it is. There's no fucking ransom.'

The ransom story had been a kindness. To fill the hole. Which would otherwise have filled with terrible things. Though never in a hundred years the correct terrible thing. I felt sorry for her. The Curse didn't purge empathy. It waited for transformation to alchemise it into cruelty. That was why I kept coming down here, to measure how much of my human remained. Too much. Always too much. That was the genius of lycanthropy: species divorce was never finalised. No matter what you did to humans their claim on your feelings endured. (*Wulf* rolled its eyes. Of *course* their claim on your feelings endures. If it didn't, killing and eating them wouldn't feel so unbelievably good, would it?)

'*Tell* me,' Kaitlyn pleaded.

Her jeans smelled appetisingly sour. My hands were full of busy weakness. Three months back I'd eaten a twenty-four-year-old hiker in the Alleghenies. He was covered in russet fuzz and full of startling supple strength, the way a rabbit or a goose is when you grab it. He hadn't ever been in love. He had a lot of love, waiting, undischarged. Courtesy of the dark hilarity, I thought Kaitlyn would be good for him. They'd be good for each other. When they met. In me. Talulla the matchmaker. This was the thing with dark hilarity: once you started, there was no end to it.

'Don't,' she said, when I took a step closer. Without warning *wulf* had flared and bulged, pressed on her intuition like a thumb on a bruise. Fresh fear opened her pores, released fraught pheromones, a mouth-watering mix with the acrid denim. The animal moved in my jaws, rippled, swelled, for a second seemed to have torn through – that familiar trick, so convincing I put my hand up to where the giant muzzle should be. Nothing. Of course. Not yet.

'*Tell me why you're doing this,*' Kaitlyn wailed, at the edge of tears.

I didn't answer, but I knew when I raised my head the monster was looking out from behind my eyes. Kaitlyn's face crimped and trembled. The low room suddenly obvious and me like no woman she'd ever met. She put her hand up to cover her throat, where her skin was as pale as the flesh of an apple. The ghost claws tugged the nerves under my nails. They knew the body's soft tensions and the joy of rupture. For a moment she sensed what was coming off me and thought *not human* – but nausea mugged me again and I turned away, heaved-up more bile. My fingers and toes strained in their sockets. My canines needled. A wall went up in Kaitlyn against what she'd thought because *not human* was, after all, crazy.

'How can you do this?' she said, not quite knowing what she meant. 'I mean you're fucking *pregnant.*'

I'd thought she was going to say: I mean you're a fucking *woman*.

Technically I wasn't a woman, but even I, dirty, *filthy* little girl that I was, had wondered if the Curse wasn't an opportunity to offer the Sisterhood some belated help, by taking male victims only. *Asshole* male victims, wherever possible. But *wulf*'s tastes were aggressively catholic, demanded the good, the bad, the ugly, the beautiful – and everything in between. Jake had tried it, the forced diet of villains (he once ate five murderers on the trot) but the monster had backlashed, pushed him into a reactive run of innocents. *Wulf*'s got God's appetite, Lu, he'd said. Or literature's. It wants the full human range, from saints to psychos. You try to weight the scales, trust me, the fucker won't have it. He'd had the dark hilarity. Dark hilarity had been his MO – but it wasn't enough on its own. He'd needed a purpose, too. That was the werewolf survival kit, dark hilarity plus purpose. For a hundred and sixty-seven years his purpose had been penance. Then he met me – and his purpose was love.

'Did you hear me?' Kaitlyn said.

I straightened, wiped my mouth, waited for the sickness to subside. 'It'll be over soon,' I said. 'I just came to see if you needed anything. He'll bring you some food down in a little while.'

3

Richard, my ex-husband, once said: I hate that smug look a woman gets when she's pregnant, as if her cunt's gone on to the higher calling. It was the sort of thing he came out with to offend the po-faced, but deep down we both knew he meant it. I'd seen it in pregnant women myself, the new centre of gravity, the benign autism. Then, when I'd started to show, I'd seen people seeing it in me: a woman rich or dumb with certainty, glowing with inane self-containment. Even grief couldn't touch it. I'd be lying curled-up on a hotel bathroom floor, face a mess of tears and snot because my idiot heart couldn't stop reaching into the emptiness where Jake should have been – but a part of me always remained sealed, inviolate, wrapped like a force field around the new life I carried.

Until the night I met Delilah Snow. After that the force field pretty much unravelled.

•

By the time I got upstairs to my room the cramps were so bad I couldn't make it to the bed. My face was a neuralgic map. My teeth chattered. I got down slowly onto my hands and knees and forehead. The thin Inupiat rug had a friendly smell of dust and patchouli and mould. Thanks to pain I'd rediscovered the humble

23

rewards of lying down in unlikely places. I could hear Cloquet weapons-checking downstairs. It was what he did to reassure himself. We had hardware stashed all over the lodge. Machine gun in the laundry hamper. Flamethrower under the sink. Crossbows in the closets. A dozen grenades. Tucked beneath my pillow were four wooden stakes and a Glock nine-millimetre. (Glocks, Colts, Springfields, Walthers, Tri-Stars, Magnums, Berettas. Until the Curse I'd been no more likely to own a gun than I would've been to own an elephant. Now I could've opened my own store.)

It took me a long time to crawl to the en suite and begin running a bath. (I'd taken a lot of baths, less for physical relief than psychological comfort: they reminded me of my teenage self, the little white bathroom on the third floor of the Park Slope house, where I'd go and soak and read and brood and scheme and take stock of my body and jerk-off.) Undressing was a dreamlike ordeal. For a moment, I knelt in front of the mirror. Stone breasts webbed with veins I'd never seen before. Belly as big as a cauldron. Navel sticking out like a lewd gesture. It's disgusting, Lauren had said of her sister's enormous pregnancy. She used to be pretty. Now she's just this fat, shambling *cow*. Lauren would rather not have had a body. As far as she was concerned her body was engaged in a full-time campaign to gross her out or embarrass her in public. I remember the way she reacted when I told her – a while before either of us had begun it – what menstruation was. What do you mean you bleed an egg out? An *egg*? Jesus *Christ*, Lu, that is so repugnant. Why do you make this stuff up? But even while she was objecting I knew she knew I *wasn't* making it up. I missed her. She'd ended up siliconed and divorced from a Los Angeles gangster. It had been years since we'd caught up, and now, no matter how long we talked, we'd never really catch up again.

I hauled myself onto the toilet and slumped there, exhausted.

I never saw a wild thing sorry for itself, my mother used to quote, lifting my chin with her fingertips, drying my tears with her sleeve. *A small bird will drop frozen from a bough without ever having felt sorry for itself.* It worked every time, until one day when I was seventeen and hungover and heartbroken and I turned on her and said that wild things were incapable, by fucking definition, of feeling sorry for themselves and it was a stupid bogus poem and D.H. Lawrence was an asshole. And she'd said, Oh, I didn't know you'd become so literal. I guess you've joined The Humans. That's too bad.

A single big cramp dragged something out of me. I got, trembling, to my feet, and looked into the toilet bowl.

Blood. Mine. A lot. For a moment I thought I'd had a miscarriage. Relief, panic, excitement, anger – then the realisation that of course I hadn't, that a seven-and-a-half-month foetus couldn't just slip out like that, that there were no limits to the sort of moron I could be. Meanwhile the toilet held my blood with a kind of pathos, something sad and ugly it was condemned to show me. Standing there looking down at it I felt sorry for the little girl I used to be, who'd had no idea of the terrible changes to be visited on her.

I never saw a wild thing sorry... My mother said it one last time, between morphine fugues in hospital on her final day. My dad had gone to the bathroom. I was alone with her. I took her hand.

What's that, Ma?

The disease and the drugs had given her a traumatized version of her beauty. When I was small one of my favourite things was watching her getting ready to go out, which she always did ironically, as if it was beneath her, until the very last moment, when she was ready and would give me a look of female collusion, woman to woman, in the mirror. I loved that look.

You're like me, she said.

We stared at each other. For a distended moment it was as if we'd become one person. She said: I don't want to go. Then the drug descended again and her eyes closed. It was the last time she spoke. Four hours later she was dead.

I flushed the blood away. Goosefleshed, scalp aching, I stepped into the tub, lowered myself, eased my shoulders under the water. The heat took the edge off the pain, and the change in temperature surprised the baby into stillness. I thought of Kaitlyn saying, How can you do this? I mean you're fucking *pregnant*.

Then something heavy and alive passed across the roof, very close, travelling fast.

4

WOCOP. Vampires. Didn't matter which. They'd found us.

Adrenalin zero to sixty – instantly. (And a flash of surprising relief: they'll kill me and it'll all be over and I'll be dead and with Jake or at least with Mom. I had a vision of the three of us in a beautiful Roman forum version of the afterlife, olive trees, blue sky, me carrying the baby, laughing.)

I slipped getting out of the tub and chipped a bone in my knee. Ignored it. Dressed quickly, grabbed the Glock and a stake and went downstairs to wake Cloquet.

'Did you see anything?' he whispered. His face was pouchy from drunk sleep and his breath rotten with Jack Daniels but he had the Cobra's safety off and was waking up fast.

'Felt,' I said. 'Didn't see.' He understood: this close to transformation *wulf* made big inroads.

'Here,' he said, 'take this.' A crossbow and quiver of wooden bolts pulled from the drinks cabinet. 'Anyone comes through the door, you know what to do.'

'You need me with you,' I said. He started to protest, but I cut him off. 'If it's a vampire you'll need my nose. I'm not asking.'

He knew I was right. 'Okay,' he said, 'but please stay close.'

We opened the door and stepped outside. Cold assaulted us.

Moonlit snow scintillated as if with delight. The drive, cleared by Cloquet days earlier, ran straight to the dirt road beneath the trees thirty yards away. At right-angles to the house was a stone outbuilding housing Ski-Doos, snowcat, mini-plough, emergency generator and miscellaneous tools. The Cherokee was dug-out and snow-tyred, ready to go. I put my hand on its flank as we passed, the way a girl would casually reaffirm the bond with her horse. We scanned the roof's edge in silence. Cloquet looked at me. Is it still here? I nodded. Yes, but not close. Vampire? I couldn't be sure. *We don't get on with vampires*, Jake had warned me. *Mutually assured revulsion. We're inimical to boochies at the genetic level*. Genetic or not, we couldn't stand the smell of each other. If there was one nearby the reek would soon have me reeling. My dead pins-and-needled in my arms and legs. Cloquet mouthed, emphatically: *You stay here*.

I mouthed back: *No fucking way*.

It must have taken us fifteen or twenty minutes to go around the lodge, stopping, listening. In places the snow was so deep we had to wade. There was frantic cellular activity in my chipped knee. Cloquet used night-vision binoculars for a sweep of the trees. Nothing. Nevertheless the ether trembled. Whatever it was it was still here, moving as we moved, preserving the distance between us, an odour or vibe maddeningly just out of range.

We made it back to the driveway, exhausted, without incident. Cloquet's face looked scrubbed awake. A dewdrop hung from the tip of his nose. I knew what he was thinking: if I'd sensed a vampire then a vampire had sensed me. Our cover was gone. We'd have to move. Right now. That thought – flight, *again*, the energy it would demand – filled me with fervent weakness. I tried to see myself rushing upstairs and throwing essentials into a bag. The image drained me. I closed my eyes and rested my head gently against the Cherokee's passenger window. I wanted to sleep. For ever. Lie down in the snow and go out. *Go out, go out beyond all doubt—*

Then the scent hit me full force, and I knew what it was.

I opened my mouth to tell Cloquet – didn't need to: a wolf, lean and dark and silent, dropped like a long dollop of molasses from the roof to the pitched porch, sprang from there onto the bonnet of the Jeep, paused, didn't look at me, then leaped down and took off along the drive.

We watched without a word until it disappeared into the trees.

Smiling, I realised it was the first time I'd smiled in days, maybe weeks. I'd got one glimpse of his green mineral eyes and a big pulse of his alert masculine allegiance. I'd felt myself extending into him, seeing through his eyes and (paradox like a zen koan) my own, simultaneously. An invisible nervous system stretched through and beyond him to an unseen wolf pack. They were with him, with me, we were part of the same tense consciousness.

'Is that why we're out here?' Cloquet whispered.

'Yes.'

'*Mon Dieu*, he was big.'

'You won't believe this,' I said, 'but I've never seen one in real life before. Not even in a zoo.'

'How did it feel?'

With the smile a few tears had welled, fallen, stopped. Not sentiment. Just the effect of respite from the pain, which, now the animal had gone, was returning. I blinked. It was a deep reassurance that he hadn't really looked at me. He hadn't needed to. His will had dissolved into mine, then out again.

'I wasn't quick enough,' I said. 'It's like something going past in a fast-flowing stream.'

'What?'

29

'I could have controlled him.'

'Really?'

'Yes.'

The baby, who'd gone quiet, now kicked again. I jammed my jaws together, closed my eyes, rode it out. Cloquet was still looking at the place in the trees where the wolf had disappeared. 'Do me a favour, *chérie*,' he said. 'Make sure he knows I'm on your side, okay?'

5

There was a TV ad for diapers I'd kept seeing. A succession of ludicrously cute babies laughing or gurgling or crawling or lying on their backs kicking and flailing to a soundtrack of fruity clarinets. The last frame dissolved to a pretty young mother, blonde and fabulously wholesome in pale blue cardigan and white blouse, holding her freshly diapered infant in her arms, while the clarinets harmonised on a surprising, tender, intense note, to signify the bond of love between madonna and child, who stared into each other's eyes, sacrosanct and eternal. There was no doubt this healthy young woman full of American calcium would kill to protect her baby, nor that she'd be greeted with a righteous species cheer if she did. I'd kept seeing this ad, couldn't get away from it. Every time I heard those first clarinet notes fear surged from my scalp to my fingertips and the baby inside me took on ominous mass. But there was no changing channels. I was compelled to watch, even in the days before I met Delilah Snow – though it was only after I met her that I understood why.

•

Two hours before full moonrise I sat with a stack of Jake's diaries in my bedroom window seat, wrapped in a blanket, sweating and shivering and being casually picked up then dropped by pain and wondering how much worse than this giving birth could possibly be. *My cousin Janine said it's like taking a rock-hard shit the size of a baby*, Lauren had claimed. *Imagine that. And it could be a huge baby. I looked it up. In 1879 a woman had a baby that weighed twenty-three pounds. That's like twelve bags of sugar all stuck together in a lump...* As kids Lauren and I had loved our dolls. But we'd pulled their arms and legs off too, or stuck pins in their eyes, fascinated by their trapped sentience, their utter paralysis in the face of our will. And when we'd tired of torture we went back to caring for them as if the abuses had never happened.

Wulf adjusted its position, squeezed my spine, momentarily split my elbows. My teeth chattered, then stopped. I took one of Jake's diaries from the pile next to me.

Meanwhile Bloomingdale's and Desperate Housewives *and Christmas and the government carried on*, I read.

> *She was carrying on herself, in extraordinary fusion. I could see it in her tense shoulders and flushed face and the care with which she'd applied her make-up. It hurt my heart, the unrewarded courage of it, the particular degree of her determination not to fold in spite of everything. In spite of becoming a monster. It hurt my heart (oh, the heart was awake now, the heart was* bolt *upright) that she'd had to be brave all alone.*

But she never believed she *was* all alone. She was enough of a romantic to suppose she couldn't be.

And she wasn't.

Now she is.

I had all the journals. Six weeks after Jake's death my dad had called to tell me there was a letter marked private addressed to me at the restaurant. (My dad. The necessary lies. Obviously I couldn't stay with him. Anyone close to me was in danger. So

I told him I was going back to school at UCLA to finish my Masters. Sweetened it by giving him the job of finding a third restaurant, of which he'd be in sole charge. But the money, Lu, for Christ's sake, where's the money coming from? Two friends in Palm Springs looking to invest. What, those two gay guys? No, not them. You don't know these two. I was at college with them... And so on, an ever-expanding fiction struggling to cover the mad truth that would otherwise kill him: Nikolai, your daughter's a werewolf. Hair, claws, fangs, the whole B-movie deal. Twelve victims. You don't want to know. Little Lula whose diapers you changed and whose rapt face listening to *Facts About the Planets* or *Tales of Ancient Greece* was one of your purest pleasures. Oh, yeah, and she's got a bun in the oven. The father was a werewolf too, but he's dead. He left her rich, mind you. That's where the dough's coming from...) The letter, which I sent Cloquet to pick up, was from Miles Porter, President of the Coralton-Verne International Private Bank on Fifth Avenue and 45th Street. Jake had left instructions: if, after a certain date, the bank had received no *further* instruction, Mr Porter was to contact me. I'd been authorised to access the safe deposit box held in Jake's name. I had Porter's direct line and, as per Jake's instruction, 'should call when I had the six-digit security code.'

Which I didn't have. Which I had no clue how to get.

A vampire ruse? A WOCOP trap? During our first week in Manhattan together Jake had told me he'd made arrangements aside from the twenty million, but the subject was so morbid we never went into details. Now he was gone and I didn't know what to do.

I called Miles Porter and told him I was travelling (in fact I was at a small overpriced hotel with too much dark wood in Cold Spring, having let my apartment go) but that I'd be in touch when I got back to the city. Then I hired a private detective to make sure 'Miles Porter' was who he said he was. He checked out. Unfortunately this guaranteed nothing. WOCOP used civilians and vampires used familiars. In any case, I didn't have the six-digit code.

A week passed. I rang the new tenant of my old apartment to see if there were messages or mail as yet unforwarded. Nothing. Then Ambidextrous Alison called. St Mark's Bookshop had telephoned the restaurant. My copy of *Heart of Darkness* was ready for collection. Ask for Stevie.

I hadn't ordered any books.

Heart of Darkness.

Marlowe.

Jake.

Conrad, not Chandler. Literary snob to the end. I sneaked back into Manhattan in a blonde wig and red-framed sunglasses. Stevie was a pudgy young guy with bleached hair and rosacea and a stare that said whatever your particular brand of assholery he'd seen it a thousand times before. He wore a Pearl Jam t-shirt and a white nose-stud I mistook at first for an enormous zit. *Customer paid for this five months back and told us to call you on the specified date. As in yesterday. Didn't leave a name but said you'd know.*

Pages three, eight, fourteen and seventy with corners turned down and digits circled. 3,8,1,4,7,0.

A big risk, but I took it.

Alone in one of the bank's secure rooms I opened the metal case. Fifty-three journals, crammed with Jake's tiny italic hand-writing. Little black Moleskines in the recent years, further back calfskin or cloth bindings, half a dozen with broken jackets bound together with elastic or string, two or three water-buckled and freckled with mould. Some entries dated, others not. Long periods – decades, sometimes – when he gave up writing altogether.

There was a sealed envelope placed to be the first thing I'd see on opening the box. On the envelope it said:

In case we didn't have enough time.

Love you.

Jake.

Inside were instructions on how to access six Security Code Only bank accounts in Switzerland, plus a list of half a dozen names, phone numbers and services, headed: *People You Can Trust.* I didn't recognise any of them.

In case we didn't have enough time.

Love you.

Jake.

Until that moment I'd been in bereavement's phase of smiling idiocy: I'd see him again and we could laugh about all this together. Now, suddenly, it was over. I sat down on the floor of the booth with a feeling of fracture in my chest. Life tolerated weeks, months, years of your denial – then snapped out of it and turned on you with contempt: You dumb shit. He's *gone.* You're never going to see him again. You think there's a reward for not crying? You think if you hold grief in long enough death'll be moved to let him back in to life? Wake up, sister. Last werewolf or not he was one more scrap of paper on its way to the furnace – and so are you. So shed the tears and get up and stop kidding yourself that death – or life, for that matter – gives a fuck.

It was a bleak, detailed time in there under the fluorescents, inhaling the chemical smell of the carpet and the sad old odour of the books. Jake had made life bearable. Jake was gone. Draw the obvious conclusion.

Every time I thought, Right, get up, stupid, I found I couldn't, but instead closed my eyes and wrapped my arms around myself again.

Eventually, I did get up. I had to, or wet myself where I sat. Biology's indifferent to your big moments. Knocked-up biology doubly so. I had nothing to carry the journals in. Had to put them back and return with a wheelie case to collect them. (Silver-suited Miles Porter reacted to all these manoeuvres with barely restrained delight at their sanity.) You'd think I would have locked myself away and read the lot chronologically, but somehow I couldn't. Going from start to finish would confirm that I'd had all of him there was to have. Instead, over the months, I'd dipped in at random. More like having a conversation. More like having him there with me.

I keep thinking I should give Harley sex before I go, I read.

I have, after all, had sex with men. Two hundred years, you get around to it, along with everything else you get around to. By the end of the 1800s I'd done what I could to render myself completely AC/DC (Oscar Wilde was in the dock, so my buggery acquired political credentials) and I pride myself as few men can on having given it the old college try. But by the dawn of the twentieth century I was forced to concede, nobly elastic of anus though I was, that I had an abiding soft spot, which is to say hard spot, for the girls...

Until the second trimester turned my body into a war zone it had been sexual business as usual. A dirty business of diminishing returns. There was no arguing with Curse libido (really, *no* arguing with it) but most of the time it was like drinking when you couldn't get any more drunk. I got sick of come-stains and the loveless smell of condoms and curtains drawn in the afternoon and guys who either didn't know what to say or couldn't shut up. Aunt Theresa's pronouncement nudged me like a dog who didn't understand I wasn't its owner any more. Even as a

36

child of the post-moral age I felt slutty and miserable a lot of the time, visited at moments — face twisted on the pillow, ass in the air, mouth slurring *fuck me... fuck me... fuck me* — by a vision of my doe-eyed dad (never my mom) standing in the corner shaking his head in sad disbelief. As a substitute, presumably, for him standing there shaking his head in sad disbelief when I yanked someone's kidneys out and swallowed them like vol-au-vents. It didn't take long for me to start relying on escorts, who at least didn't expect smalltalk and left when they were told; but even that wasn't straightforward. For one thing I didn't have Jake's knack of getting turned on by someone I thought was a moron. For another, the male nastiness that used to get me guiltily wet lost its erotic clout when I pictured these men meeting me in my other form. It was tough to take a guy's cock-swagger ser-iously when you knew just the whimpering baby you could reduce him to come next full moon. Along with fear of what excessive screwing might do to *my* baby all this meant I ended up mastur-bating. A lot. Enough for a black comedy, if it hadn't made me so lonely and miserable. At least, I told myself, when I could dredge up wryness, I wasn't in any danger of falling in love.

Jake never slept with Harley, as I knew now I wouldn't with Cloquet. I'd found out the hard way, caught by Curse lust one evening only a couple of weeks after Jake's death. Cloquet was taking a shower and the bathroom door was ajar. I was passing. I stopped. I looked. He stood in profile with his palms against the cubicle wall, head bowed, eyes closed, water pounding his back. Tall, pale, thinly muscled body, a tattoo I couldn't decipher on his left hip. His cock (circumcised) wasn't erect, but it wasn't fully flaccid either. *Wulf* grinned and licked her lips. I pictured myself walking in, opening the cubicle door, his face, surprised, the moment of mutual visibility, my hand reaching through the steam and him rising, rising for me——

No.

Verboten.

I knew it intuitively, and, since these were the days before Delilah Snow, I took it as evidence of a werewolf scheme of things, an unspoken catechism. *A werewolf shall not enjoy carnal relations with her familiar.* The bond had to be unequal, maybe specifically required unrequited—

Just at that moment Cloquet looked up and saw me.

We didn't speak. He didn't turn or try to conceal himself, but I knew from his look – part sadness for what was dead in himself, part relief to be free of it – that werewolf Commandments or not, he wasn't going to be my lover. Someone had killed or broken the sexual man in him, though not, I knew, the need to submit to something he believed bigger than himself. (I knew who 'someone' was, too: Jacqueline Delon, gamine billionaire occultist femme fatale who'd stopped at nothing to get what she wanted. What she wanted was immortality. The non-figurative kind. She wanted to live forever and never look a day older. To which end she snared (and bedded) Jake Marlowe with a view to turning him and his prized sunlight-resistant blood over to the vampires, in exchange for their brand of eternal life. Cloquet had been her unhinged lover. He knew if she got what she wanted he'd lose her. So he'd tried to kill Jake. Twice, with farcical results. He needn't have bothered. Jacqueline's deal with the vamps never went down. Mid-transaction at her Biarritz retreat, WOCOP, who'd been tracking proceedings, launched an assault. Madame's corpse was last seen playing human shield to one of her Undead business partners. From then on Cloquet stopped trying to kill Jake and started trying to kill the man responsible for Jacqueline's death, WOCOP werewolf hunter, Eric Grainer. *Life's generally artless*, Jake wrote, *but it does get these occasional hard-ons for plot. It connects things, nefariously, behind your back, and before you know it*

you're in the final act of a lousy movie. A lousy horror movie, usually...
Cloquet did kill Grainer – but not before Grainer killed Jake. On
a night of full moon, five months ago, in a Welsh forest, where,
when the carnage and death and vengeance and loss had done
their thing to us, I offered him my hand . . .)

I turned from the bathroom doorway and walked away, embarrassed. Phoned an escort agency and selected a guy who received
in-call clients and took a cab to his apartment (we were in San
Francisco at the time) and had two hours of depressing muscularly
efficient professional sex, sans conversation. The next morning I
went to Cloquet's room. He was up and dressed, standing by the
window, apparently doing nothing, apparently waiting for me. I
said: I'm sorry. He looked at the floor and said: I'm your friend.
It's a great thing in my life, to have a friend. Then he looked up
at me and suddenly he seemed the saddest, gentlest man I'd ever
seen. There was a suspended moment in which we both knew
this was a chance to separate as well as a chance to continue,
then the awkwardness dissolved between us and we knew we
were past what had happened. I said: I'm glad we're friends. I
understand. Now let's go have coffee.

After that I'd got organised, brought to libido the same
management skills I'd applied to the restaurants and delis –
until pregnancy and the Hunger started their war and my
sex-drive died, albeit with the warning that it wouldn't stay
dead for ever.

Two hundred years, you get around to it... Would I? I'd never had
sex with a woman, though it worked often enough as a fantasy.
Women together in porn turned me on too, although in the
desperate days *jellyfish* together would have turned me on. (I
knew what was wrong with pornography. But the part of me
that knew was weaker than the part of me that didn't care as
long as it worked. Of course it was depressing – and responsible

for making the question every twenty-first century female was sooner or later faced with *Will you put in your mouth something that's just been in your ass?* Back when I might have wanted the cheap thrill of a guy's contempt or the dreary high of self-degradation, maybe; but since the Curse I found I wanted different things... But when you needed to get yourself off it was hard to take the long view. Harder still when the long view in question was four hundred years.) I might have slept with a woman already if ubiquitous male coercion hadn't put me off. (Richard, my ex-husband, made a monotonous art of it, allegedly mitigated by what he thought of as glamorously brutal honesty: I don't want you to *want* to do it, for God's sake. I want you to go down on a woman in spite of *not* wanting to. Jesus, where's the fun in it for me if you *want* to? I thought everyone knew that.) Jake would've added his share, if he'd lived. He was *wulf*, but sufficiently *wer* so that he'd soon enough have been angling for a two-girl-one-guy fuckkilleat if my being the only female lycanthrope on earth hadn't made it impossible.

Fuckkilleat.

I don't just like it, I'd confessed to Jake. I don't just like it. I *love* it. (And his hand between my legs had rewarded me. We'd exchanged horrors like wedding vows. Love and a shared nature could make any ugliness beautiful. Which left what was left when your lover was dead.) That was the inconvenient truth: killing and eating a victim felt very (pause) *very* (pause) good. And killing and eating a victim with someone you loved? It was as the heroin addicts said of their drug: if God made anything better, He kept it for Himself. The memory of the kill with Jake at Big Sur bubbled stickily around everything else in my head, caramelizing my brain. It had been bliss. That was the word: bliss. You don't forget bliss. Especially when you know you'll never have it again. Even if I got my appetite back it wouldn't be the same.

The Curse insisted there was no solo route to heaven. You needed a partner in crime. *Better to have loved and lost than never to have loved at all.* Really? It didn't feel like it facing four centuries of never draining the filthy Grail again. My mother once told me she thought hell would be nothing more than being given a glimpse of God – then having it taken away, for ever.

Which thought led me back to the question I'd forbidden myself from asking, and which I couldn't stop asking, and which I'd *been* asking since the first days after Jake's death: Couldn't I make myself a companion?

Werewolves don't reproduce sexually, the journal said:

Howler girls are eggless, howler boys dud of spunk. If you haven't had kids by the time you're turned you're not having any, get used to it. Lycanthropic reproduction is via infection: survive the bite and the Curse is yours.

But here's the thing, the old news, the stale headline: no one is surviving the bite any more.

Thanks to a virus. For which WOCOP had found a cure. A cure they'd shot into me the night I was bitten. (The organisation had had an internal crisis: with werewolves at the brink of extinction the Hunt had all but cancelled its own paycheck; the guys who did their job so well they did themselves out of a job. Certain members had realised this and resolved on getting monster numbers back up. The World Organisation for the Control of Occult Phenomena found itself facing an insurgent offspring, the World Organisation for the *Creation* of Occult Phenomena. The ideologues and old-schoolers, horrified, reacted by coming down hard on the rebel faction, but in the interim I'd been darted – accidentally – with what turned out to be an efficacious version of the anti-virus. I was bitten, I didn't die, I changed.)

So if any of my victims survived, wouldn't they become were-wolves too, the old-fashioned way? In theory it was as simple as finding a guy I liked then taking him for a moonlit stroll at that time of the month. *If you go down in the woods today...* Except of course for the minor snag of how his feelings towards me would change once he realised that every full moon he'd have to trans-form into a monster and rip someone to pieces and eat them. *I know you hate me for doing this to you, but trust me, once you've experienced fuckkilleat you'll be glad I did...* Not a good start to a relationship. But what was the alternative? My libido was dead now but resurrection was only a matter of time. There was no kidding myself I was going to make it through the next four hundred years effectively – by werewolf standards – celibate.

That isn't going to be the problem, Lulu, I imagined my mother saying. The problem is going to be finding a man worth Turning...

I was shivering so badly now I couldn't hold the journal steady. I set it aside and crawled onto the bed, hands swollen, body jabbering with cramps. Random memories detonated: lying with my face on the Brooklyn stoop watching a bee sipping a puddle of spilled Pepsi; my mother laughing at something grown-up; my first period, that warm trickle like a big teardrop but I put my fingers there and it was blood and Mrs Herschel saying in a smokey sisterly way you're a young *lady* now Talulla, which just made me think of Lady Diana and creepy big-eared Prince Charles.

'It's time,' Cloquet said from the doorway.

'I know.'

'As we decided?'

'Yes.'

As we decided. We hadn't decided anything. We'd made hypo-thetical observations. *Outside would be easier to deal with. We shouldn't forget we have sedatives. It would be better if I went out first.*

42

Behind these were bald specifics: Cloquet would give her a sedative. I would go into the forest. He would bring her out and tie
her up. I would come out of the dark and take her life, quickly.
Or as quickly as the hunger's tastes allowed.

At the thought of which *wulf* gave me a jolt of demand that
nearly threw me from the bed.

'You better go,' I said. My watch showed 16.42. Moonrise
was 17.11. Twenty-nine minutes. I wondered if Kaitlyn was
awake. What sort of life she'd be leaving behind. No one who
gives a shit about me's got any money. The sour-smelling jeans
and the chipped nail polish and the trying not to see the contempt
the guys had for her even when they were holding her head and
going Oh yeah baby, that's it, just like that, you could still tell
it was contempt just beneath – but the hunger interrupted with
a flash of her midriff punctured and the soft white meat opening
with helpless obedience (the word 'flensing' suggested itself,
though I wasn't even sure I knew what it meant) and I couldn't
lie still any longer but got up and staggered with unstrung knees
downstairs and watched Cloquet draw the sedative into the
syringe and we couldn't quite look each other in the eye.

'Are you okay?' he asked. I stood in the doorway, flesh heavy
with the sordid basics of my needs. My old voice inside still
sometimes objected: You can't do this. It's the worst thing. You
have to stop. My old voice was a machine that didn't realise its
own obsolescence. Because while it went on the new voice
eloquently didn't say anything, knew it didn't have to, knew the
argument was already won. And in any case, this wasn't the
worst thing, killing Kaitlyn. I knew what the *real* worst thing
was. I'd known since the night I met Delilah Snow.

'I'm fine,' I said. He'd left me blankets on the couch. So I'd
have something between me and the cold when I stripped.
Practicalities, like biology, endured.

'I'll go downstairs now,' he said. Gentle. For my benefit. So I'd be kind to myself and not mind the murder.

When I change I change fast. The moon drags the whatever-it-is up from the earth and it goes through me with crazy wriggling impatience. I picture it as an electrical discharge, entering at my soles and racing upwards in haywire detonations that shock the bones and explode the neurons. The magic's dark red, violent, compressed. I get random flashes of mundane memory – pushing a shopping cart around Met Foods; opening my apartment window; standing on a subway platform; saying to someone, *No, that's carbohydrates in the evenings* – intercut with images of the kills: a white male body on an oil-stained warehouse floor; a solitary trailer with a storm lamp burning; a female thigh releasing a dark arc of blood; my clawed hand scooping out a still-hot heart. This is the Curse's neatest trick: one type of memory doesn't destroy the other. It's still you. It's still *all you*. You wouldn't think you were built to bear such opposites, but you are. You'd think the system would crash, but it doesn't.

Meanwhile, the freak biology show. My lungs expand, threaten to burst against the ribs – but never do. My spine elongates in three, four, five spasms and the claws come all at once, like speeded-up film of shoots sprouting. I'm twisted, torn, churned, throttled – then rushed through a blind chicane into ludicrous power. Muscular and skeletal wrongness at an elusive stroke put right. A heel settles. A last canine hurries through. A shoulder blade pops. The woman is a werewolf.

And she's starving.

I stood, transformed (jaws open, tongue as thick as a baby's arm, breath going up in signals of dreadful life), half a dozen trees back from the edge of the drive. Moments ago I hadn't wanted this.

44

Now I wanted nothing else. Same every time: you forgot the Curse was an exchange, took your speech and your mercy but gave you in return the planet's dumb throb and your own share in it. Lilac shadows on the snow, the fine-tuned trees, the Eucharist moon and the victim's heart like a song calling you home.

Kaitlyn wouldn't see me waiting here. She wouldn't see me until the last moment, but in all the moments before the last moment she'd know what she didn't want to know, that the worst thing had come to her. The worst thing was a simple thing, an old thing, an ordinary thing – and here it was. She'd look for God, guardian angels, miraculous intervention – and get nothing. Just the trees and the snow and the moon – nothing from them either. She'd get the real universe, once, before the end.

The two of them emerged from the front doorway, Kaitlyn tranquilised, Cloquet struggling to hold her up. He'd dressed her warmly, hat, gloves, fleece. Reflex kindness. Or else he didn't want the cold to undermine the sedative. A few steps past the Cherokee her left knee buckled and she went down, crookedly. I could see him considering fireman's-lifting her, the effort it would take to carry her all the way to the trees. He settled for uncuffing her and taking her arm over his shoulder, wrapping his other arm around her waist, her head lolling. As they staggered towards me, I thought, Like a guy and his drunk girlfriend.

A voice with a weird accent said: 'Twenty thousand years, you think you've seen it all.'

I jumped. It was right behind me (*how the fuck?*) – but when I turned there was no one there.

For a moment I stood still, breath moist and warm around my muzzle.

Then my waters broke.

6

As with all dreaded things, once it happened it felt inevitable.

Of course I'd known it was a possibility. Simple math determined an approximately one in thirty chance labour would coincide with a full moon. Cloquet and I had prepared. We had labour-inducing drugs: Pitocin, dinoprostone, misoprostol. We had (or would have had, if the consignment hadn't been stuck at Anchorage) half a dozen amniohooks – little plastic crochet-needle type instruments used if the drugs don't work to rupture the membrane of the amniotic sac – though the thought of having to resort to these terrified both of us. The plan had been to wait until the thirty-sixth or -seventh week then make a decision: induce and risk slight prematurity or leave it and risk having to give birth... like this. *Radical* prematurity I'd refused to prepare for. Radical prematurity would just mean – in the old universe where things meant things – that the baby wasn't meant to survive.

Well, now we'd find out.

Ghost voice shoved aside, I looked down at the steaming splash my waters had made in the snow. *The passing of the mucus plug from the cervix is known as the show. It is a sign that labour is soon to start, but it goes unnoticed by many women.* Many women and one idiot werewolf. *The amniotic sac ruptures either shortly before or at any time during the first stage of labour. The first stage of labour lasts on average 6-12 hours. The second stage of lab*— I screamed. Yelped, rather. All the times you've heard women talk about this pain it's remained a mystery. Then one day it comes to you. Your version. The only version that matters. I thought of my Aunt Vera telling my mother about the thirty-hour labour she had for my cousin Andy: *They kept telling me to pant like a dog, but it didn't make a damn bit of difference. I told that dumb-ass doctor why didn't he try meowing like a cat...* In Westerns it was men pacing up and down outside and trying to get in and being shooed away by a plain old housemaid suddenly filled with occult authority, or a sour grandmother everyone thought hated the girl but it turns out loves her and delivers her baby. There was this mental blur and flutter, images of people ripping up bedsheets and putting water on to boil, female screams and the sweaty big-thighed woman in the Sex Ed video, Lauren whispering, *If your kid's too big your pussy tears open and they have to stitch you up.* It rewrites the contract, I'd read somewhere. Your self's no longer central. This thing comes out of you and drags half your soul along after it like a blanket.

Another pain went through me, an effect like the sudden splintering thunder of a fighter jet overhead. *They kept telling me to pant like a dog.* Like a dog. Ha ha—

A moment of blindness, the world swung up. I found I'd fallen to my knees and bent forward, elbow-deep in the snow. My head was giant and wayward, too much for my neck. I crawled into the moonlight expecting its balm, but there was nothing. Just another contraction that doubled me, lips curled, fists clenched. I thought of the care Poulsom had taken of me in the white jail, the Harrods towels and beaming bathroom. In his own way he'd contributed, if this child survived. I wanted my mother. Her ghost, her voice in my head, anything of her so I wouldn't be going through this alone and she could tell me it would be all right and because it was her I'd believe it.

But there was nothing. Of course there was nothing.

I got to my feet and lurched, wet-thighed towards the drive.

Cloquet knew immediately something was wrong, and almost simultaneously *what* was wrong. He let go of Kaitlyn (who collapsed) and came towards me, but I waved him back. (Waving, gesturing, miming. Not many worse times to lose the power of speech.) He stopped, suffered a moment of paralysis, mouth open, arms held slightly away from his sides, then turned, grabbed Kaitlyn's hand, yanked her to her feet and all but dragged her back into the house. By the time I crawled across the threshold he'd cuffed her, semi-conscious, to the cistern pipe in the downstairs bathroom.

'*Merde... merde... merde...*' he said, neutrally, as if the emotions under the word were missing. His face was pale and not just clammy but *wet*. '*Oh, mon ange, mon ange...*' still without discernible feeling. 'Jesus. Fuck. *Merde.*'

I had enough strength to get to the couch, but I knew that would be the last of my legs for a while. Cloquet, now that we'd come to it, froze. Through the pain I could see that confronted with the central fact – you have to deliver a werewolf's baby – he was capable of all sorts: fainting; taking a Ski-Doo and riding away; cutting my head-off; going for medical help; sitting down and smoking a cigarette.

He needn't have worried. I didn't want him there. Not just because in the absence of any real knowledge (despite his bedside *Essentials of Obstetrics and Gynaecology*) there was nothing he could do, but because I couldn't spare the consciousness his presence would demand. What was happening to me would require all the consciousness, all the being, all the anything I had. Which still wouldn't be enough.

48

A contraction came, and a last defiant surge of hunger met it head-on. One moment of balance – a salt whiff of groggy Kaitlyn; even Cloquet briefly risked a clawed swipe – then appetite went, seared away in the solar flare of another contraction, and I was left with the one priority, the womb's screaming monomania: *Get this fucking thing out of me.*

7

I ended up under the dining table, though I couldn't tell you how I got there. *Your bitch will seek a covered over or tucked-away place to litter. She may ignore the whelping box, however comfortable you've made it, but this is normal. Let her follow her inclinations.* A great hoot for *wulf* was doing away with any delusions of dignity your human half might have. Somewhere between hotel reruns of *Friends* and surreally perused *Elles* I'd gone to canine-health.com, the tone of which alternated between pseudo-clinical and gratingly down-home. *Mom will NOT thank you for bright lights and crowds on her big day, however much the kids (and adults!) might want to watch. Give the little lady some PRIVACY.* I'd visited the website in a moment of self-ridicule, and couldn't have spent more than two minutes scanning its content, but it had gone in. Lycanthrope hard-wiring or a subconscious concession to my one-in-thirty chance of needing it. And now here I was, needing it.

Push. Don't push. Breathe. Pant. Push. Breathe. Don't push. According to *Essentials* there was a technique, a method. I might have had it memorised once but I didn't have it now. What I had now was the feeling of slowly splitting – starting between my legs – in half. (Plus irritation that there even *was* a method. What about the millions of women who'd had their babies without being told when to push and breathe and pant? *This is all bullshit,*

Lauren had whispered in Sex Ed. *Women in the Amazon just go off into the jungle and give birth on their own. They dig a hole and fill it with leaves and squat over it. They don't have stirrups and enemas and fucking doctors talking about golf.*) No position was bearable for long. I had to keep moving: all-fours; side; back; squatting. The contractions emptied my mind of everything, the way God must have felt before creation, when it was just Him on His own, without the angels or even Time going by. Between contractions was the terrible fact of my finiteness, the exact shape and size of the body that somehow had to accommodate all this. *Mom will NOT thank you for bright lights.* This turned out to be true. The lodge ceiling had angled spots on its exposed beams and for some reason Cloquet (more miming had got him out of the house, from where he could have continued to Disneyland for all I cared) had left all of them on. In the moments when I wasn't God I was aware of them giving me a headache. My claws scored the oak floor. Blood gossiped and thumped in my skull. Random details came and went with pointless vividness: the little brass logo on the range door; Cloquet's yellow road atlas of the USA & Canada; a small carved wooden bear on the mantle; my The North Face jacket on a chair, one red thermal glove hanging out of its pocket. The room was like something stupidly smiling in the face of horror. Was it the Vietnamese who smiled when terrified? Some movie. *Platoon* or *Full Metal Jacket*. I was aware of my own crammed silence. At one point I heard something like metal grinding rhythmically in the bathroom where Kaitlyn was tied-up, then it went quiet again.

I don't know how long it lasted. I pushed when my body demanded it. Once or twice tried not pushing. Couldn't tell what effect it had, other than making me feel I was at the limit of what I could stand. I remember putting my hand between my legs to try to feel how much I was dilated (vaguely thinking:

four inches for humans – double it?) but I couldn't tell and my fingers came away wet with blood and in any case what was the point since I'd already started pushing? I thought: Okay, this is it. You die. *She died in childbirth*. Fittingly Victorian, for Jake. Then the reality of death struck me – death right here, right now, *actual* death – and all I had besides pain was fear. Vestigial fear of the Devil and hell quickly torn through into the bigger, up-to-date fear, of falling through cold black silent nothingness like an empty lift shaft between two universes – for ever.

But you didn't die. That was the treachery of suffering. It took you to the point from which you thought death must follow, then let you know it could hold you there indefinitely. That was when you stopped fearing death and started wanting it, praying for it, begging for it. I knew how that worked. Serves you right. Monster. Murderer. Mother-to-be.

I lay on my side, jaws clamped around one of the table legs. My thighs were sticky with blood. *During the final stages of labour the uterine contractions are very strong and usually painful. The baby's head presses on the pelvic floor, which causes the mother to have an overwhelming urge to push down.* In the gap before the final contraction I heard Kaitlyn thrashing around in the bathroom. Then it *was* the last contraction, and with a sharp scalloping sensation and a sound like a rubber glove being pulled off, the baby, in a knot of satiny gore, slithered out of me.

At that moment Cloquet crashed through the window and went flying across the floor.

8

They were here.

All the calculations and evasions and disguises and double-checks and now it was for nothing and there was no time and no strength. I started wondering how they'd found me – but it didn't matter how. Only *that*. I was turning to see the child when the first vampire leaped in through the broken window. I glimpsed close-cropped grey hair and a small neat face before he turned to take Cloquet's four shots in the shoulder with barely a twitch. There was an inexplicable suffocating pressure on my arms and chest, though my legs felt weightless. The front door opened. Cold air that should have been knife-fresh rushed in packed instead with the pigshit-and-rotten-meat stink of the Undead.

In spite of which the imperative was simply to see the baby, verify its existence, establish it was breathing. With immense dull elephantine effort I reached down and lifted him towards me.

It was a boy. His eyes were closed and he was covered in mucus and blood. I licked his muzzle, quickly, cleared the tender nose. He coughed and wriggled closer. I knew this was only a moment but it was pathetically intact, like a petal in a paperweight, my astonishment at the miniature hybrid hands and feet, the little penis and the soft covering of gold and black hair. He opened his eyes. They were dark, like mine, like Jake's. I thought: You walk around with it inside you and nothing prepares you for the absurd concreteness of the fact: a new creature suddenly here, disturbing its share of atoms. I put my hand under his head and sensed flickery consciousness inside. He blinked up at me, once, twice.

I want – you've no idea how much – to be able to say I loved him, instantly. I want to be able to say the miracle happened just as it was supposed to, that his life took immediate priority over everything. I want to tell you that as soon as I saw him the paradigm shifted, that the rubbishy clutter of my self fell away, that the contract was rewritten, that he'd come out of me dragging half my soul behind him like a blanket, that I was now – with molecular certainty and before I was anything else – a Mother.

The truth is I felt neutral. A living creature had come out of my body, but that was merely a bizarre fact, just another thing that happened to be the case. If I wanted to I could snap his newborn neck or rip out his newborn heart. There he was, warm flesh and banging blood, arms and legs and head, teeth and tongue – but in those first pure moments he was simply a live alien object in my hands, nothing to do with me. He was like a word you repeat so many times it loses its meaning and becomes raw sound.

Delilah Snow's legacy.

Everything since I'd met her had been leading up to this moment.

The table lifted and spun away through the air to crash against the range. Two vampires stood over me. A Henry Mooreish perspective, their heads remote. One was a petite young (looking) male with dark brown curly hair and a smug long-eyelashed face like the early Bob Dylan's. The other was a slim, attractive, green-eyed woman in her (nominal) late thirties with coppery red hair cut like Hitler's. Both wore black jeans and zip-up leather jackets with a red leather emblem – something like a cuneiform character, I thought – embossed on the left lapel. Both had a stripe of thick white paste beneath their nostrils – an olfactory block, though from the look on their faces not completely effective. *Their* smell made me gag. The redhead was terrifically excited, at a pitch that gave her a steady gleam. I could hear a helicopter. The sound brought a feeling of exposure. I didn't know why I could barely move. My legs were pillowcase light. An invisible weight lay across my abdomen. I tried to turn so I could shield the baby (if a reflex then a lumbering one, something I dimly knew I was *supposed* to do) but the woman kicked me hard in the side of the head, and in the time it took me to absorb the blow the youth rammed something big and sharp-pointed straight through my throat into the floor, pinning me. The pain rolled me up to the edge of blacking out, then back again in a sickening blur. I raised my left sandbag arm but found it grabbed and held by the grey-haired vampire. With no hint of effort in the natty, civilised face he forced it down, produced a second spike (not silver; someone wanted me alive through this) and impaled my helpless hand. I began to choke.

COME TO ME. NOW.

The three of them stared down at me. The young Bob Dylan smiled. The helicopter was close with its sound of monotonous urgency. Whisks of snow-cold air played over me. My legs were negligible, two scraps of chiffon. I tried to turn my head to see if Cloquet was alive, but it was impossible. The only two certainties were my helplessness and the weight of the child's gory head in my hand. My heart still didn't move. It was like a racehorse that just stands in the stall after all the others have gone: I didn't feel anything about him (apart from curiosity) though he'd looked at me with such mesmerising nude wideawakeness. Maybe his heart was suspended too? There was that between us, the intuition that as yet there was nothing at stake. No love lost, as they said. There was leisure to consider all this. The emotional universe found room in a split-second for elaborate expansions.

FASTER.

With a glance at the redhead for permission, the young vampire jammed a third steel skewer through the upper part of my right arm, the hand of which was still holding my child's head. The metal went through the long hairy bicep at an angle, missed the humerus, dragged at a knot of nerves. Pain jangled like a stumbled-into wind chime. Blood and oxygen frothed around the wound in my throat. It reminded me of a school biology experiment we'd done with bicarbonate of soda. Which in turn reminded me of a line from Jake's journal: *I have lost, I thought, mental appropriateness*. My legs were afloat. I was a cripple tied to a post in a fast-flowing river. The redhead pulled a military knife from her boot and cut the umbilical cord. She was beautiful. Her lipsticked mouth worked slightly with concentration.

THAT'S IT. FASTER.

'Grab it, Noah,' she said.

The Bob Dylan youth, Noah, reached down for the child – and the child bit him.

Noah snatched his hand back, bloodied. 'Ow!' he said, half-laughing. 'That fucking *hurt*.'

'We're wasting time,' the grey-haired vampire said. 'Give me the things.'

The woman had a leather satchel. 'Here,' she said. 'Do it.'

There was a separate frail rage that I'd done all that exhausting work of getting this child out safely into the world and now here they were, erasing it. Separate, that is, from the over-whelming desire to close my eyes, turn my head away, let them take him. What did it matter? Why should I care? Did women getting raped suffer this profane indifference? Were some abuses so extreme it was easier to surrender the self than sustain it?

'Watch that mouth,' the redhead said. 'Careful...'

'The things' were a cattle prod, a ketch-pole and a woven steel-fibre sack. They worked as a team and I got it all in dreamy detail, the prod's dry zaps, my fingers one-by-one prised back, the child's jerks and flinches, his high-pitched yelps and snarls showing white canines and a shrimp-pink tongue, the two-tone shimmer of the woven steel bag that reminded me of zoot suits or the iridescence of street oil, the redhead's delighted absorp-tion and pearly skin and pounding stink. She had no malice towards me. This was something valuable to her, that was all, a necessary object. Despite the cold coming in I felt as hot as a new-baked loaf. I watched my offspring lifted, throttled, jabbed, bagged, tied. The darkness closing over his head tore something between us.

For a moment all sound and movement ceased, as if someone had pressed a pause button on reality.

Then the helicopter's whine and chop ripped through – and everything rushed back into motion. The aircraft was right outside, whisking-up snow and shooing-in freezing air.

KILL THEM! KILL THEM NOW!

There was a burst of automatic weapons fire, barely audible over the racket of the propellor blades, then the first of the wolves – last night's black – was through the door.

The animal's bite and slash tore a third of Noah's face off. He went down onto his knees with a falsetto shriek and a violent shudder as if he was revolted. Simultaneously the grey-haired vampire, holding the sack with my child in it, shot straight up through the air and came to rest with his back against the ceiling and the wriggling bundle pressed tight to his chest. A second grey wolf sprang at the redhead. She got her left arm up and the creature's jaws locked around it, its momentum knocking her backwards into the range. For a moment she looked like a woman at a bar resisting an insistent bad-breathed drunk. Then I saw the detail of her little round nostrils flaring as in complete silence and with a kind of delight she stabbed the animal repeatedly in its belly with the knife she was still holding from cutting the cord, until at the sixth or seventh puncture the big body slid from her to the floor, as if not dead but triumphantly passed out. Three more wolves ran in the door and a fourth appeared at the broken window. The warmth of them reached through the freezing air and went into me. I could feel my will in their shoulders and hind-quarters and necks. A kind of frantic joy raced back and forth between us. The black tore at flailing Noah's throat. Shots fired. The wolf in the window fell with a yelp. My womb contracted. The grey-haired vampire was inching backwards on the ceiling to get his feet against a beam. Two grey wolves leaped and snapped under him, though it was obvious he was out of their reach. As he stared down at them, blinking, a big bullet-wound opened silently in his left temple without visible effect. I tracked the shot back: Cloquet, one arm useless, the other holding the Cobra, clearly without the strength to squeeze off another round. For a moment Cloquet frowned, struggling to haul himself into full consciousness, then with a confused scowling look of having been betrayed by something, collapsed. One of the greys had sprung onto the redhead in an exact replication of its brother's move, except this time the jaws had locked around the knife hand. The vampire's free hand – diamond-ringed, French-manicured – fumbled at her belt. A wolf the colour of burnt toast joined the attack on Noah, and after a queer, intense, concentrated moment, as if the animals were having difficulty holding still for a photo, the vampire's head came off his shoulders with a wet crunch. Immediately the corpse's capillary system began to darken, as if death had only a small window to stake its claim.

Outside, the chopper dipped and a cloud of snow shot in and swirled. I thought of TV feather-pillow fights. It was what TV girls did, in nightshirts, in panties, in men's dreams. I'd never had a pillow fight in my life. The wolf on the redhead contorted as a spray of bullets struck its flank, then slid to the floor, tongue lolling. Two tall young vampire males with machine guns stood in the doorway, one facing in, the other out, laying down covering fire. I could feel wolves getting hit in numbers, a faint gunshot tattoo in my bones. The redhead, splashed and smeared with blood, ran to her friends at the door. Wolves were howling and yelping, jack-knifing, taking bullets. Three leaped in through the broken window and stood guard over me. Their good rich odour blotted out the vampires' smell. I looked back up at the ceiling. The grey-haired one, crouched against a beam, stared down at me for a moment, the sack clutched tight against his chest, then sprang and swooped for the door, where the other three, as if choreographed, ducked down to let him, with his bagged captive, out over their heads.

'*Au revoir*, Talulla,' the redhead said. Then all of them ran for the chopper.

9

Clouds had come up from the south and covered the moon. Outside the darkness and the snow had a yellow tint. Cold air meandered through the wide-open door and broken window, ruffled the pages of *Moll Flanders* on the dining table. (Keep reading, Lu, Jake had advised. Literature is humanity's broad-minded alter-ego, with room in its heart even for monsters, even for you. It's humanity without the judgement. Trust me, it'll help.) On the back of the dust jacket, I remembered, was a quote: 'Moll is immoral, shallow, hypocritical, heartless, a bad woman: yet Moll is marvellous.' That was the sort of character I was supposed to have become. That was the sort of character I'd failed to become. No, I thought, as two of my guard wolves struggled to get a grip with their teeth on the steel skewering my right hand, Talulla is not marvellous. Talulla is *fucking useless*. I kept seeing them prising my fingers back one by one. I kept feeling the distinctive weight of the child lifted from me. I kept groping in the void where my horror or rage should have been. I remembered reading a story about a woman whose ten-year-old daughter goes missing and is eventually found dead, having been raped and murdered. There's this moment when the police come to the mother's house to tell her they've found the body, and even as she's hearing the words and understanding what's happened she's staring at the living-room floor where there's a TV guide with Monica and Chandler from *Friends* on the cover and along with *I'm very sorry to have to tell you, we've found the body of a girl matching the description* is the thing about Matthew Perry being in a sex-addiction clinic and the two things are both in her head at the same time and it's a disgusting equalisation and it must mean she's evil or insane.

That was me. I was like that. Always had been. When I was nine I had a pet mouse and neglected it and it died. My dad had just said, very quietly, I'm so *sad* about this, Lulu. And my heart had filled up with panicky self-hatred to hear him say that and to see that he really was sad, but also there was a sensual thrill that I'd done this to him – me! My face had felt warm and soft, just as it had when I'd turned and seen Aunt Theresa standing there in the basement and my pants were round my ankles and she'd said, Talulla Demetriou, you are a dirty, *filthy* little girl.

I'd expected emptiness in my womb, like the space left by a scooped out avocado stone, but it felt undelivered. The pains (I would have said contractions if the baby wasn't already out) meant something was wrong. Something other than the blank where instant love should have been, something other than my dead heart, my failed motherhood, my third recurring daydream.

It was filtering through to the animals that they couldn't grasp the spikes. I watched their long teeth slip and slash. Distress began to gather in them, my distress. I turned my head. Cloquet was still unconscious, for all I knew dead.

The only way to free my hand was to slide it up the shaft of the spike and off the other end, like a chunk of meat off a shish kebab. Three feet, give or take. It made me think how time must have crawled for Christ on the cross, a horse's tail swishing, a centurion easing his leather cap, a boy drawing with a stick in the dust. That was the world: innocent vivid continuity, regardless.

My wolves lay down around me. There were a dozen of them in the room now, and others arriving. I wanted more than anything just to be able to turn on my side and curl up in a ball. I clamped my jaws together and began to force my hand up the spike, slowly at first, then when the scale of the pain registered, quickly, to get it over with. Three seconds with a white-hot circle in my palm – then it was free. The first moments of welling blood were worse than the impalement, but with a sudden disgust at the figure I cut – helpless, legs spread, choking – I willed myself through it, gripped the skewer in my throat and yanked it out. My left arm was still pinned, but I had the joy of being able to turn onto my left side and draw my knees up a little, as far as my still-big belly would allow. Blood pooled from my neck like a cartoon speech bubble. Cloquet coughed and groaned, then fell silent again.

I passed out.

When I woke the door was closed and there were at least twenty wolves lying in a circle around me. Their warmth quilted me but was spoiled here and there by the air from the broken window. I pulled out the last skewer and fresh blood oozed from the wound. Then another contraction came – and with it the realisation that the reason I felt as if I was still in labour was that I was still in labour.

10

My son, whom I'd lost the right to name, was born into violence and death. His twin sister, whom I named Zoë, was born surrounded by the warmth of wolves.

I fell asleep after delivering her. In spite of the conviction the vampires would return I dropped down into darkness and darkness closed over me. It was wonderful to surrender. The last thing I remember was licking her snout clean, turning on my side and holding her close to my chest. That and three of the wolves dragging the vampire's body and head out into the snow.

•

Hard to tell how long I was out. It could've been minutes or hours. At any rate it was dim daylight when I woke. In human form.

With a human baby in my arms.

I'd slept through transformation.

I thought of how exhausted I would have to have been for that, how vulnerable I would have been if—

Wait. Her too: she'd changed back. No sign of trauma. She was awake, quiet, blinking dark-eyed out of her bloodstained face.

Then immediately there it was.

What they'd done.

Like a careful rape.

And I'd just let them.

I'd seen a news report a few years ago. A group of project-housing mothers in New Jersey who'd been charged with assaulting a neighbour when they found out he was on the child sex-offenders register. One of them had kept repeating: If you gotta kill to protect your kids then you kill. You got no right to call yourself a mother if you wouldn't kill to protect your kids. You got no right to even *have* kids if you wouldn't kill to protect them. The mob of women around her were ravished and pouchy-faced with righteousness. You *ain't* no kinda mother if you wouldn't kill for your kids.

I lay still. Molecular renewal tickled my wounds. My jacket partly covered me and the child. A grey wolf lay pressed up warm and soft against my back. Another lay close to my front, keeping the baby snug. The room throbbed with the pack's consciousness and the heat of their bodies and the not-silence of falling snow. All the animal corpses had been removed and the lodge's front door pushed shut. Peace had returned to my womb, which for a moment made me feel small and sorry for myself and grateful.

But there it was again like a reflex. What they'd done. And I'd just let them.

Animal documentaries loved to linger over the horror of mothers who rejected their offspring. The robotically grazing ewe deaf to the shivering lamb's cries. Now I'd joined the club. As with all appalling self-discovery it brought a thrill – and a feeling of déjà vu. And as with all appalling self-discovery there was nothing to do but accept it, like the first time a hairdresser holds up a mirror and shows you the back of your head.

When I moved to ease the pins and needles in my left leg I felt something wet and pulpy between my thighs. *The placenta is pushed out 5 to 15 minutes after delivery of the foetus.* Two placentas, in this case. Zoë's umbilical cord still attached her to hers – panic again – until I remembered reading that it didn't matter: left alone the cord detached naturally. It was doctors who were in a hurry to get everything snipped off and tied up, with racquet-ball and call-girls waiting. *There are no nerve endings in the umbilicus, therefore neither mother nor baby feels the cut.* Still, the thought of cutting it myself gave me a twinge. Me, who ripped people apart and ate them. Serves you righ—

Cloquet coughed, and I realised that was the sound that had woken me. I turned to see him sitting on the floor with his back against the couch, holding an improvised dressing against a wound in his left shoulder. He was pale and haggard and piebald with blood. His hands and face were badly cut from the crash through the window. One deep gash along the line of his brow needed stitches. His hair was greasy. Along with his body's other woes, I knew, his scalp would be aching. There were these thoughts, but they were little details against the continuous pounding consciousness of what they'd done and I'd just let them.

'How badly are you hurt?' I asked.

'The bullet went through. You?' He was avoiding looking at me because despite the jacket a lot of me was on show and he was still weirdly delicate about all that.

'I'm okay,' I said. 'They took him.'

'I know. I'm sorry.'

They took him. Having language back made it precise and ugly and real. Suddenly there *was* the scalloped space in me, the hole left by the scooped-out avocado stone, shocking, raw, basic. The room held a pungent memory of what had happened in it, like the smell of cordite after a gunshot. I saw them sticking the skewers in me and prising my fingers from his warm body and stuffing him in the bag. I saw myself pinned and felt the helicopter's dark mass lifting, higher, further, quieter, silence, gone. The mental re-run filled me with anti-energy, a self-perpetuating mass of weakness. The scalloped space wasn't empty after all. It was full of failure.

I imagined myself saying to Cloquet: *I'm going to get him back.* I saw the future saying it would commit me to, all the things I'd have to do, Jake's loathed rubbish heap of *if*s and *then*s, the certainty that I wouldn't get him back but would die trying and leave my daughter an orphan. I mustn't think about her. Her brother had left her behind so I'd never forget what I'd let them do to him – and why I'd let them do it. Again I imagined saying to Cloquet: *I'm going to get him back.* I knew that's what I should say. *This calf*, the animal documentary voiceover said, *has been rejected by its mother. Weak and unprotected, it offers an easy target to predators on the lookout for a quick kill.* I thought how long it would be before I'd be able to take pleasure in buying a beautiful pair of shoes, or walk on a beach in the evening, or sit at a café with a cup of coffee and a cigarette watching total strangers go by. Probably never. Amongst other things I hated him for having *been* taken. I could have laughed at that. A different hilarity, not dark, but the colour of nothingness.

A wolf got up, stretched, yawned. A third time I imagined myself saying to Cloquet: *I'm going to get him back.* It made the nerves in my mouth wilt.

'It was her,' Cloquet croaked.

'What?'

'The woman. The vampire. It was Jacqueline Delon.'

Au revoir, Talulla. It had registered, that she'd known my name. Well, now I knew hers. Jacqueline Delon. Jake had fucked her, of course (and according to the diary *got her off, orally*, as I recalled), for which my obsolete self resented him, unfairly, since I knew all too well how it was on the Curse. The last he'd seen of her she was being used as a human shield by – ah, the little grey-haired vampire with the neat demeanour. But she'd survived. And somehow become his superior, if I'd read their dynamic right.

'I thought she was dead,' I said.

'*Moi aussi.*' He'd been in love with her. The ramifications of which were obvious. I was amazed he'd been able to deceive me. I could have laughed again.

'*Calme toi,*' he said, reading me. 'It wasn't me. I don't know how they found us. You think I betray you? Ask your wolves!' He said it with mad fracture, but he was right. The animals would have known if he was false. I could feel it in the current that moved between them and me. Power over canines Jake had used to get their young lady owners into bed. I missed him, his voice saying my name, his arms around me. The stupidest part of me *still* expected to see him soon. All this while being aware of what had happened like a gaping hole in the room, in the wall, in the fabric of things, knowing that if I looked into it I would see pure black nothingness, going on for ever in total silence.

'Ahhh,' Cloquet said. '*Dieu est miséricordieux.*' He'd found yesterday's not-quite-empty bottle of Jack Daniels by the side of the couch. He took a swig, closed his eyes, sighed. His shoulders relaxed.

'I'm sorry,' I said. 'I know you loved her.' Gentleness. Out of the extremity of my failure. Out of the peace of having no further to fall. These amoral relations were available everywhere. He took another swig.

'I have a feeling,' he said. 'Like when your body tells you you've hurt it with too much booze or coke or whatever poison. You understand?'

'Yes.'

'It's like that — but my soul. I feel sorry for what I let her do to my soul. I was nothing. I was *un drogué*, a fucking useless junkie.'

'Okay.'

'*Je suis libre.*'

'I understand.' I did understand. He'd replaced Jacqueline with me. Not a beaten addiction, just a different drug. And I wasn't even sleeping with him. Maybe I *should* sleep with him, haul his sexual self back to the land of the living to seal the allegiance, fuck his brains out and to hell with the werewolf protocols. Either that or kill him. I'd have to if I couldn't trust him. Meanwhile distance unravelled in the helicopter's wake. Miles already. Hundreds. I thought of all the things the vampires knew that I didn't, all the preparations they would have made, all the powers they had at their disposal. Their advantage was laughable. It was a joke. *Couldn't* I just forget him? Take my chances with my daughter and run? I conjured the first recurring daydream, the two of us a few years from now in the white Los Angeles villa — Brentwood or Marina del Rey or the West Hollywood Hills — with bougainvillea and the cactus garden and the turquoise pool, quietly going on with our life. We'd get tennis lessons and take trips to the mall and have occasional parties and somehow manage to kill and feed once a month without anything going wrong or anyone finding out what we were. I'd love her tan legs and arms and good balance and shyly-worn jewellery and her plucking up courage to ask me difficult things.

But the first recurring daydream only brought the second, of the little werewolf boy in a shredded school uniform, covered in blood.

And the second brought the third. With compliments of Delilah Snow.

Cloquet closed his drained eyes. Right up until I opened my mouth I didn't know what I was going to say.

'I'm going to get him back,' I said.

As soon as I'd said it I knew it was hopeless. Knowing it was hopeless was a relief. The relief of discovering after all your rushing and madness to get to the departure gate you've missed your flight, and now there's just the weight and heat of your own body and time stretching ahead.

'Yes,' Cloquet said, opening his eyes. 'Of course.'

'If you don't want to help me against her, I understand.'

He stared at the floor for a few moments, as if receiving something from the underworld. Eventually blinked, took the bottle's last mouthful, smiled – then abruptly stopped smiling. Looked at me. 'She's dead to me,' he said. '*C'est tout.*'

With a struggle I managed to get the jacket on and myself into a sitting position, the baby cradled in the crook of my left arm. The placentas slid to the floor. They looked like a pair of revolting purses. (I had wondered if I'd want to eat them. Animals did. Some humans too, I'd read. I didn't.) My wounds ached, but had stopped bleeding. In an hour or two there would be barely a sign of them. *Twenty thousand years, you think you've seen it all.* Blood in the eardrums. Aural hallucination. *Wulf* fucking with me. One of my victims talking in his sleep. Whatever it was it shrank next to what lay ahead. I dismissed it.

'I know you're hurt,' I said to Cloquet, 'but do you think you could boil the kettle and sterilise a knife? I need to cut this. If you open the door the wolves will go out. It's okay, they won't do anything to you.' The animals stood en masse as I spoke. Cloquet wobbled to his feet and let them outside. The majority would stay close to the house. A few would patrol. The black stayed inside with me. My will was still loose in him a little, like last wriggles of electricity after a giant shock. Cloquet

69

worked gingerly but efficiently, and took a moment while the kettle was boiling to hand me a throw from the couch. He also dug out the lodge's First Aid kit I didn't even know existed. Latex gloves, hydrogen peroxide, iodine, dressings, band-aids, sutures.

'I'll hold her,' I told him, 'you cut.'

A moment of silence. His bleeding hands shook. His breath was raw with whisky. I had a vivid image of him plunging the scissors into her tiny chest.

'*Aie*,' he said, very quietly. But the job was done.

'Thank you,' I said. 'You're good to help me.'

He did a shy, ducking movement with his head and looked away, embarrassed, and suddenly I knew if I let myself I could cry.

I never saw a wild thing sorry for itself.

So I swallowed, swallowed, swallowed.

11

At least half a dozen of Cloquet's injuries – most obviously the bullet's exit and entry points and the long deep gash on his forehead – needed stitches. All I knew was you had to get the wound as clean as possible, sew the two halves together, then keep it covered and sterile until it healed. I gave him five milligrams of morphine. The effect was rapid.

'Does that hurt?'

'No. Go ahead.'

Two hours later I'd done what I could. After washing the baby, wrapping her in a blanket and improvising a cot from a laundry basket packed with clean towels, I took a shower (locked her in the en suite with me), cursorily inspected my own whispering injuries and changed into fresh clothes. The post-partum weight-drop was disorientating. Fourteen, maybe sixteen pounds. My womb pulsed astonishment. Curse dregs snagged the blood in my shoulders, haunches and wrists, tingled where my teeth met my gums. The wolves' collective awareness ran through and around the lodge like a live circuit. I could go into and out of it. Going into it offered the solace of scattered consciousness: the misery was distributed, my self's edges blurred. Pointless postponement. Sooner or later I'd have to come back to my own lousy dimensions.

I began packing, mechanically, listing the facts, trying and failing to come up with a first move, to turn this into a problem that I could *take steps* to solve: The vampires wanted him for the Helios Project, yes. Jacqueline Delon was one of them, yes. I had power over wolves, yes. Cloquet could be trusted, yes. There was my daughter to consider, yes, yes, yes – So what? *I didn't know where to start looking for him.* That was the big ignorance.

There was also the big obscenity.

I'd felt nothing.

A younger version of myself, the girl in her early twenties (I saw her: me with more make-up and less understanding and something that made me think of the old-fashioned word 'ardour'), was somewhere near me, breaking her heart because she'd failed, because her future self – me – had turned out to be a dead-hearted bitch who didn't love her babies. The mother and child from the diapers ad broke their trance of love to turn and look out of the screen at me. Serene condemnation. Between them and the moms from the projects was a quivering righteousness that wiped out their social differences. You got no right. You got no right *having* kids if you wouldn't kill for them.

Cloquet knocked on the open bedroom door.

'I know where we can start looking,' he said.

'What?'

'There's a guy in London, Vincent Merryn. Antiquities. He handles the European merchandise for Housani Mubarak. Jacqueline used him. He knows vampires. He's like *un honoraire*. He might know where they've taken him.'

Housani Mubarak? I'd seen the name... Jake's diary. *Egyptian dealer in stolen antiquities. Not to be confused with* Hosni *Mubarak, though he's probably got as much clout....* Someone broke into his warehouse and stole a crate full of junk. Not junk. Quinn's Book. *The Men Who Became Wolves.* The origin of the species. Allegedly.

Vincent Merryn I'd never heard of. *Jacqueline used him.* Harley had told Jake it was an inside job.

'You know this guy?'

'I met him a few times. I know where he lives. His London house, anyway.' He could feel it petering out. Lowered his head. 'Fuck,' he said. 'It's not much.'

Too many things jostled: images of London from my last time there, the kill just before I met Jake; the vampire helicopter unravelling the miles; the hot sack closing over the small head; *got her off, orally*; immediate practicalities – passports, identities, airlines, tickets; and in spite of myself a faint rush at the thought of Quinn's Book, *The Men Who Became Wolves*, the possibility of answers. *Don't bother looking for the meaning of it all*, Jake told me. *There isn't one.*

'Do you have a number for Merryn?' I asked.

'*Oui.*'

'Why would he tell us anything?'

'Because we make him. You'll have to call him. He might recognise my voice.'

'Call him and say what?'

'We'll think of something. You'll have something to sell.'

Feeble. Both of us knew it. My skin was a settled swarm of flies. The hole in the fabric of everything was in this room, now, the window into pure nothingness I daren't look through. It would be in every room I was in from now on, until I got him back. (You? Aunt Theresa's voice in me said. Get him back? A dirty, *filthy* little girl like you, who just lay there, who just lay there and let them take him? And we know why, don't we? Yes, we—)

'I'll go and get the stuff loaded,' Cloquet said.

'I'll do it. You're still woozy. Go lie down.'

He nodded, headed for the stairs – but he was back a few moments later. As soon as I saw his face I knew what he'd realised: we'd forgotten, both of us, Kaitlyn.

'She's gone,' he said.

'How?'

'The pipe was loose. There's water all over the floor. It's my fault.'

She'd seen both of us.

'I'll go and look for her,' Cloquet said. 'Maybe she never made it to the highway.'

I put the last of the journals in the bag and zipped it up. It had stopped snowing. 'Forget it,' I said. 'We don't have time.' It wasn't that I believed she'd reached the highway safely, it was that if we found her we'd have to kill her, and for better or worse I couldn't face it. Just couldn't. I should never have pictured her feral bedroom and sad acceptance of the lousy demands guys made on her. 'Go and lie down for a minute,' I said. 'I need to feed the baby before we leave.'

Which I did not want to do. I hadn't fully admitted her existence. Even through the appalling intimacy of washing her I'd kept her in peripheral consciousness only, a trick of self-misdirection that had given me the emotional equivalent of eye strain. It hadn't worked, either. There she was, small and clean and absurd in her plastic laundry basket, radiating power to recreate the world. *Every humble atom glorified*, Jake had written of Heathrow's vivification when we'd met. Now here was the soft grey sky and the pink curtain and the oak floorboards and room's smell of dust and mothballs and old linen all wondering why I wasn't accepting their beatification.

I undid my shirt, tried to feel nothing, then raised her carefully to my breast.

The physical sensation was shockingly literal, once the tough little anemone mouth had found my nipple and latched-on: a living creature *sucking nourishment out of my body*. (*Essentials* said milk proper might take three days to come in; meantime colostrum,

74

the pre-lacteal secretion rammed with antibodies and who knew what lycanthropic extras.) I went in and out of bearable horror, as if a six-pound parasite had attached itself to me, but also in and out of the feeling of having come bloodily into an inheritance. All those Madonnas with Child; my dad's *Compendium of Greek Mythology* showing Hera's breast-milk spurting out to create the Milky Way; connection to every female animal I'd seen with an offspring tugging at its teat (the dismal *word* 'teat'); Richard coming back from a visit to his sister who'd just had a baby and me saying So how was she? And him saying 'fucking bovine'; the Polaroid of my mother breastfeeding me under the maple tree and you could feel my dad's thrill and pride and fear of her through the photograph back into his hands holding the camera and his man's beating heart that still held the awed and jealous little boy in it.

Meanwhile the baby stared at me like an emotionless deity. *That* was the Divine trace, if we carried one, a fragment chipped-off from God's infinite capacity for neutral observation. Or so it seemed, as long as she stared at me – then she'd blink, long-eyelashed, or her face would twitch, and God would vanish, leaving a blank human infant, barely more than the instinct to suckle made flesh and blood. There was the seduction I'd read about, the rhythm of succor that lulled the glands, but there was revulsion too, and a riffle of pornographic breasts and silicone implants gone wrong, and the time in biology class when Mr Shaeffer said feeding babies was what breasts were *for* and Lauren said, Listen, mister, these are *my* boobs, which means *I* get to choose what they're for, and Jennifer Snow's pale breasts splashed with blood and a detached sadness at what a crucifixion by contraries the story of the human female had been so far. Followed by a little cheap self-pity, because I – of course – wasn't even a real human female any more.

75

12

'What do we do about the vampire's body?' I asked Cloquet. The baby, in her laundry basket, had been transferred to the couch. She was gurgling, quietly, pouring out the godlike recreative energy I had to keep ignoring. I had an image of Jacqueline Delon slowly inserting a wire into my son's eye. There were dozens of similar images queuing up, bristling with detail.

'*Rien*,' Cloquet said. 'Go and see for yourself.'

I opened the front door and looked out. At least a dozen wolves occupied the front yard. I knew there were more surrounding the house. Where the young Bob Dylan's corpse had been was a declivity in the snow covered with a greyish residue and a few blackened strands of what looked like intestinal tissue. In another hour there would be nothing. I closed the door. *Wulf* set off a dozen tiny remnant firecrackers in my spine.

Cloquet was in no condition to drive, so I took the wheel, with the baby in the laundry basket wedged between us and the wolf on the back seat. Even with snow-tyres it was a tense, nosing crawl through the woods, but we made it to the highway without incident. We had a back-up car (plus a bagful of wigs and glasses and false moustaches, standard precautions) in a parking garage in Fairbanks. The plan was to change vehicles and get the first available flight out of Alaska.

A plan with a big problem: the baby. We might be able to get her on domestic without ID, but not international. And even for domestic I guessed she'd need a birth certificate. Which was one of those ostensibly simple things that would turn out to be incredibly difficult. No doctor, no midwife, no pre-natal care… How, exactly, could I prove she was my child? DNA testing? How long would that take? (And on immediate second thoughts: DNA? Not an option.) I imagined the authorities' reasonable questions: if I knew I was having a baby what was I doing in the middle of the Alaskan wilderness? Was I crazy? On the run? Did I have a criminal record? Reasonable questions would become suspicion. Suspicion would become investigation. Investigation would become, eventually, horror.

So no bureaucracy. My forger was in New York. His had been the first name on Jake's list of people I could trust: *Rudy Kovatch – DOCUMENTS / IDENTITY.* I knew his number by heart and I'd been trying to get cellular reception since we'd left the lodge. So far, nothing.

Twenty-five miles down the highway I pulled over. The road was bordered on both sides by soft-snowed forest. An avenue of fleecy grey sky above. No other traffic. Cloquet looked at me for explanation.

'Edge of his territory,' I said. 'He has to go. Much as I'd like to keep him.' I opened the back door to let the wolf out. Again the animal and I barely exchanged a glance. It wasn't that there was no need for thanks, it was that thanks would be meaningless. I'd be thanking myself. As his being morphed back into separateness I felt it as a slight physical bereavement. He shook his coat, sniffed the ground, then made a low-shouldered dart into the shadows under the trees. Gone.

13

'I can't eat any more,' Cloquet said. We were at the Grand Hotel in Anchorage, in a third-floor room overlooking the lights of the rail depot. It was just after midnight. Prussian blue sky with dark patches of cloud over the big cold sentience of the nearby water, the Knik Arm, which as the light faded had gone blue-silver, then slate grey, then black. 'It's making me feel sick.'

Staying in Fairbanks would have been asking for trouble, but in any case the thought of sitting still and doing nothing (Jacqueline's scientists raring to go) was suffocating. So I'd driven three hundred and fifty miles to Anchorage, stopping only to feed the baby, while Cloquet, morphined, dozed on the back seat. I'd spent the journey in shock that made random mundane chunks vivid: a Texaco sign; red cattle in a field of snow; a crow taking four springy steps to get into the air; the giant wheel of a passing truck. I felt what a small detail my whole life was, how the planet had seen so much that now things like this didn't even register. Only wars and earthquakes were still drowsily noted. When something happened that was everything to you you realised it was nothing to everything else. Meanwhile I kept feeling the younger interior versions of myself full of fascinated disappointment at what they'd amounted to. Me. *The modern adult,* Jake had written, *has really only one thing to say to its inner child: I'm sorry. I'm so fucking sorry...* And the same thing to say to its biological child, too, I thought. I bought disposable diapers and Vaseline from a gas station. Money. Items. Change. Have a good one. You too. It all still went on. Of course it did. Kovatch called. He could get 'Zoë Demetriou' and her half-dozen aliases birth certificates in twenty-four hours and overnight them. Fax no good, they'd want the originals, or rather what they took to be the originals. In two days we could fly to London. The number Cloquet had for Vincent Merryn reached an answering machine at V. M. Antiques and Fine Art in Bloomsbury, one of a dozen European dealerships that formed Merryn's trading front. I rehearsed my message – My name was Lauren Miller; I had several items of significant value and would deal only with Mr Merryn directly – and left it. A plummy English woman, Althea Gordon, called back four hours later. All prospective vendors met with her in the first instance. Subject to her assessment (for which read assuming it could be established you weren't undercover or a crank) a meeting with Mr Merryn might then be arranged. Was Mr Merryn in London? I was going to be there for forty-eight hours only. Yes, Mr Merryn was in London, but she must repeat, any meeting would be subject to her etc.

'Drink the water at least,' I told Cloquet now. 'You need fluids.' I'd changed his dressings and ordered him up food (poached salmon, french fries, tomato soup) since he hadn't eaten in more than twenty-four hours, but he'd barely touched any of it. Bizarrely, I was beginning to feel hungry myself. Or maybe not bizarrely: I hadn't fed. Was this what happened? Miss a *wulf* meal and your human appetite returned in a day instead of a week? I tried the corner of a buttered roll from the tray. Not straightforward. For a moment after swallowing I thought I was going to throw up. But a deeper register said, No, keep eating, for the milk to come. I took another bite. The monster's ghost-teeth objected. Muted *wulf* outrage from the other dimension.

'How is she?'

'Sleeping. You should too.'

'Her wardrobe's improved.'

Earlier I'd been out with the baby – with Zoë; using the name gave me a feeling of sickening fraud – swaddled in blankets and my jacket, for essentials. Now she had clothes, more diapers, a bassinet and bedding, a carrier and, pointlessly, a small soft golden teddy bear. The department store had been hot and glittering and smelled of industrial carpet and I'd thought of the money at my disposal, all the things I could give her. And her brother. When I got him back. Except every cell in my body knew I wasn't going to get him back. I kept remembering him – then feeling my scalp shrink because to remember you must have forgotten, and how could you have forgotten? How could it not be searing your heart every second of every minute of every day?

Total self-disgust is a kind of peace, Jake wrote.

Total self-disgust was available, a sleep I could enter while still awake. Only the baby's presence in the room kept disturbing it.

'Did you book the flights?' Cloquet rasped.

'Yes.'

'I wish I could have a flying dream. I used to have them all the time when I was a kid.'

'Me too.'

'Did you ever have a dream you were dreaming?'

'What?'

'You know. In your dream... In your dream you're having a dream. Dreams are the nearest *univers parallèle*. Like the universe next door. So when you dream, you're really entering the universe next door. But if you dream you're dreaming, that's the universe *next* to the universe next door...'

He fell asleep. His flesh heaved out its odours: stale tobacco, old sweat, greasy hair. A residue of his body's recent efforts surrounded him like a subsonic hum. I fixed myself a cup of instant coffee and went, feeling slightly nauseated at the first sip, to look at the baby.

She was asleep with her warm face turned to the left and her hands closed. Her cheek was as soft and downy as the skin of a peach. *Until you have one of your own, you just can't understand it.* Naturally I'd rolled my eyes at new parents' fascination with their infants. I'd loathed the helpless shrug, the fatuous surrender. Well, here I was, and here *was* one of my own, and here, too late and vetoed by my deformed motherhood, was the same appalled fascination. Look at the fingernails, the eyelashes, the nostrils, the mouth. Look at the dark shimmer and winking lights of her future. It was obscene, the love-fee a child could pull down just by existing, just by being there. A fee I couldn't pay now, late, having failed to pay it on time. Wouldn't. Mustn't. Daren't.

Because nothing compares to killing the thing you love.

Of course it wasn't Cloquet who'd sold us out to the vampires. It was me. They'd come because I'd obscurely called them. Wasn't that the tradition, that a vampire couldn't enter uninvited? The first steel skewer going through my throat was a consummation devoutly to be wished: better someone else killed my child than I killed it myself.

I was very close, just then, to total breakdown. It's amazing how close you can be, without realising you've been going that way. It's right there. You can see yourself as through a two-way mirror, broken down, liberated, not counting the cost because only the ego counts that and the ego's gone. You can see yourself in a room of warm soft harmless chaos where everyone's stopped expecting anything of you.

Everyone except your children.

I was on the floor, curled up on my side, though I didn't remember lying down. I wasn't crying, but I knew I couldn't move. Something like my own voice kept talking to me about what a complete disgusting failure I was, but I had silence — a share of the vast mathematical silence I'd discovered the night I met Delilah Snow — to blot it out. If I lay there long enough I'd be able to summon a share of the impenetrable darkness as well. Then I wouldn't be able to see or hear anything at all. Longer still and the other senses would go too.

PART TWO

THE THIRD RECURRING DAYDREAM

'And just then it crossed my mind that one might fire, or not fire – and it would come to absolutely the same thing.'

Albert Camus – *L'Etranger*

14

It happened in upstate New York, under a full August moon, when I was six months gone, making what I knew would be the last kill before pregnancy put me in need of Cloquet's hands-on help. The victim was George Snow, seventy-four-year-old retired attorney at law, widower, father of four, grandfather of six, *great*-grandfather of three, who lived alone with two cats, walked three miles every day, fished, kept up with Current Events, read the odd literary novel, ate a low-fat diet and listened to forties jazz for himself and Joni Mitchell in loving memory of his wife. The family house was a sprucely kept six-bedroomed property in its own four acres of meadow grass and woodland between Spencertown to the south and Red Rock to the north, just under two miles from Beebe Hill State Forest, and in about five years it was going to be too much for George to manage, which he tried not to think about, though if he noticed an oblong of sun on the oak floor in the hall or the dry timber smell of the back porch or the deep-carpeted calm of the upstairs landing it hurt his heart, because to leave here would be a second brutal bereavement, after the loss of Elaine.

The murder logistics had been simple. Country Road 22 ran straight through the forest and there was luxuriant cover virtually all the way to George's front door. Cloquet had dropped me close to the change site an hour before moonrise, and would pick me up at the arranged rendezvous on the east side of the forest three hours later, from whence we'd hit the highway. Three hours was a small window – and there'd be five hours of cooped-up *wulf* to deal with in transit afterwards – but increasingly my preference was for getting as far away from the crime scene as quickly as possible. (The long lunar nights had proved tricky. You had to weigh the difficulty of staying concealed till you were human again against the risk of being spotted – nine feet tall and covered in blood – getting into the back of a van. And while not sticking around for moonset let you put some miles between you and your victim's remains, it also left you exposed to the risks of the road: engine trouble; an accident; getting pulled over for a faulty brake light. Okay sir, I'm going to need to take a look in the back of the vehicle...) In any case that was the plan, and in accordance with it, just after nine p.m., high on hunger and the relished creep through the moonlit forest, I opened the back door, ducked my giant head for the lintel and entered the house.

It's a delight to sneak into a stranger's home, to feel its appalled paralysis, all its helpless historied objects made naked by your unauthorised eye. Here was a big clean kitchen that murmured in its atoms of sunlit family breakfasts, American plenty, manage-able dysfunction, love. But long ago now. The room knew its glory days were over. I crossed it and went silently down the hall to the study.

The door was open. Grey-haired George, in pale green flannel shirt and grey corduroys, was sitting in a leather swivel chair at a pine desk, illuminated by an angle-poise lamp, going through some envelope files. His back was to the doorway, to me, to death. Everyone's always is.

My hands were big and heavy and electric. I thought of how all his body's alarms would go off at once, the spectacular chemical chaos. He was just beginning to register the slight change in the light, the peripheral tremor of my shadow. The room stilled its details. He raised his head and removed his reading glasses.

I sprang across the floor and spun his chair around to face me.

You want them to see you. You want them to see you because horror fills the flesh with everything it's going to lose. Memories mass in the cells, rush to final coherence, as if they know that for death only maximal life will do.

George wasn't afraid of dying, but he enjoyed being alive. The seasons still spoke to him; his child self was still there when the leaves shivered or thunder broke. He loved his family, hopelessly, *hope*lessly, those little ones with the genes still being cashed-out, inexhaustibly. The smell of air and stone and grass on those kids when they came in from outdoors was the smell of life. He still allowed himself to get involved in HBO dramas. He still had friends in New York. Last year he'd had a six-month fling Philip Roth would've envied with divorced Chattham restaurateuse Amber Brouwer, a woman twenty-one years his junior. The first real sex since Elaine's death almost four years ago. (There had been, in the deranged early months of grieving, when everything ugly had seemed not only allowed but obligatory, half a dozen desolate nights with call girls in Manhattan hotels, but it was a firework of inversion that had soon burned out.) They'd both known, he and Amber, that it wasn't going anywhere, but known too that for a little while that wouldn't matter and so made the most of it. Sunday mornings in her bed (his moribund Episcopalian deep structure still issuing vague guilt for not going to church, though he hadn't been for practically his whole adult life) were slow and rich and astonishing. He'd forgotten how it could be. The mesmerising particularity of a lover's body, the thin skin over her clavicle, the lilac scribble of varicosis in her thigh, the surprising graceful taper of her hands. The world had shuddered wider awake for him in those first weeks. But eventually their window had closed. He hadn't realised how much he needed a woman, physically, until she'd said it had to stop. Now he felt sexually lonely all over again.

And how did I know any of this? Because after wrenching his head back and opening his throat (vocal cords, take the vocal cords) with my fingernails I threw him to the floor and sank my teeth into his shoulder, went in the first two ravenous bites through the carotid, subclavian and axillary arteries, mastoids and trapezius muscles, dozens of capillaries and a screaming multitude of nerves. His life, hurrying, grabbed all the above and countless other things on its way out (into me) but flashed between all of them was oh Jesus Jenny get out honey get—

I turned.

A skinny girl of around eighteen in pink sweatpants and a white bathrobe was backed against the flank of the staircase opposite the study's open door. Her dark hair was wet from the shower. The look on her face was the look you get used to, the look of strained revision, the human system trying to accommodate something that seems to invalidate the system itself – the way everyone thought computers were going to feel at the Y2K moment, midnight 1999.

For perhaps two seconds we looked at each other. I was thinking that no matter what you did to eliminate risk, risk found a way. Between us Cloquet and I had spent a week watching George, establishing his routine. Today there had only been an hour, two hours max, he hadn't been under surveillance. But risk doesn't need hours. Risk can work wonders with five seconds.

Jenny's eyes were full of me. Werewolf. Real. All this time. Horror movies.

A tardy *wulf* muscle popped in my shoulder, made me twitch. I packed my haunches for the leap. She turned and ran.

She didn't get far, but that's not the point. The point is that along with her own blood-delivered montage of kindergarten's disinfectant smell and her mother letting her lick the spoon's granular sweetness and the upside-down green world that time she fell out of the tree and Chris's face when he came and how the vision she'd had of her future had come apart into uncertain pieces she couldn't pull together the moment the peed-on indicator went unequivocally blue – in with all this like a repeated explosion was THE BABY THE BABY THE BABY and I realised (blood from her neck in rhythmic spurts like a magician pulling out silk hankies) that she hadn't, as I'd thought, been going for the front door. She'd been going for the stairs.

For the baby.

My teeth had just met in her midriff. For a little while I kept them there while her pulse dimmed into mine and I saw it all, the unplanned pregnancy, the suspended college degree, the family shaking its collective head, Grandpa George taking her side (*any time you need to get away, honey, you come and stay as long as you like*) and the pain of labour like nothing else and the nurse saying you've got a baby girl and holding it up all covered in blood and gunk and despite months of not having the faintest idea of what she'd call it the name Delilah had sprung right out and she'd known straight away, under the hot lights, as if the baby itself had told her: Delilah Jane Snow.

But now, she thought, as her heartbeat eased into mine and her blood waved feebly and the darkness closed like warm black water over her head, *a monster... a monster... that's all my blood oh God it's like sleep the way... sleep... steals... you...*

Her heart gave its last soft shrug – and stopped. The house was in shock from the blood on its carpets and walls, my obscenely basic graffiti. I tore the flesh I had in my jaws (external and internal obliques, *transversus* and *rectus abdominis*) and felt her spirit slip not quite secretly into me. There's always an obscure interim when the taken-in life struggles to find its place in the new prison. I chewed, stalling, thrilled in my palms, soles, anus, snout. A flicker of intuition in my clit.

One option (there was no denying it was a matter of options, of choice, of free will) would be to feed on Jennifer and/or George until I was full, until I literally couldn't manage another bite. Then what? Leave the baby alone in the house? Take her with me and get Cloquet to deposit her on the local church steps? Call 911? Obviously I couldn't speak, but if the line stayed open long enough they'd send a car. By which time I'd be gone. Or the nearest neighbour, half a mile down the road. There was cover. I could leave her on the porch, as in the movies.

Another bite of Jennifer. My fingernails had pierced her left breast. Blood and the close-packed odour of mother's milk. The bulk of *wulf* strained and bucked, outraged at being held back from full plunge into the feast. But the slyest sliver of its being smiled, an effect like the pleasure of letting your pee out in a swimming pool, because it knew, it knew, it knew: these were only options because of the *other* option, the one that saw me going with thumping pulse and teased appetite up the stairs, to the pale pink room that had once been Jennifer's mother's, and had become – whenever she *needed to get away* – Jennifer's.

And Delilah's.

•

My third recurring daydream was of a werewolf turning to see its reflection in an unfamiliar mirror, a dead werewolf baby hanging from its jaws.

●

Wolves are not known to eat their young, Google told me, every time I asked.

Not known to eat their young. Not *known* to eat their young.
Wolves are not known for killing the things they love.
That's *were*wolves, honey.

●

I'd been waiting for this moment ever since I'd found out I was pregnant. And now here it was, God's last chance. My last chance. There must be some things I couldn't do. There must be some things a mother couldn't do. A spacesuit of heat surrounded me. My head was a lump of soft fire. *Wulf* smiled in me, the deep reassurance that all manner of thing should be well. I moved as if choreographed, mesmerised by the sight of my long-muscled hairy thighs going up and down for each ascended step in time with the throb of the new life up there. My human self was in deep adrenal enchantment, repeating its mantra like a dazed priest: I won't actually do this... I won't actually *do* this... while my legs climbed and framed Snow family photos went by, one by one bearing witness to this thing that I wasn't, actually, going to do, because if I could resist this then surely, surely with my own... and then the bathroom's whiff of steam and damp towels and coconut body butter and Jennifer's young wet skin as it used to be only minutes ago, and then the pale pink room with its smell of diapers and talc and laundered clothes and the thing that I wasn't, actually, going to do.

Delilah Jane Snow. Two months old, quiet and awake in her cot. Jennifer's dark hair (as dark as mine, as dark as my baby's would surely be) and a neat, round, cleanly detailed face that made me think of God using a very fine sculpting tool. She was absurdly unique, involved in her own schemes, which required occasional punches, swipes and kicks, as if an invisible bluebottle was testing her patience.

I wasn't, actually, going to do this, as I slipped one hand under her and lifted her out. I wasn't, actually, going to do this, when I turned her to the window, where the delighted full moon made a silhouette of her downy head. I wasn't, actually, going to do this, because there must be some things I couldn't do. There must be some things I couldn't do.

For a moment it was fascinating, this thought, as small and vivid as a lone swimmer in a tidal wave's thousand-foot wall of water. Everything depended on it. There must be some things I couldn't do.

•

You want to not know what you're doing. You want the swoon, the fall into darkness, the obliteration of all that isn't the beast. *I was drugged and an obscene act was performed on me*. No such luck. Nor are you helplessly looking on while the monster runs amok. The Curse insists on full fusion. You and the wolf won't do. Only the werewolf, single and indivisible. And who is the werewolf if not you?

•

She'd be dead in five seconds. I'd feel her sternum go and my biggest canine puncture her heart while its opposite neighbour

94

went through one of her lungs with a poignantly audible gasp. Something would break in me, too, a tiny bone in the soul that when it snapped let the whole godless universe in. Her blood would be warm and sweet-sour and empty and would go into me with innocence, too young to understand it was being shed. In the old human life meaninglessness was an idea, a hunch, a philosophy. Here, now, looking through the vision of Delilah's five-second death, it was a fact. No one was watching. No one was keeping score. There was nothing. Just a vast mathematical silence. There was nothing and so there was nothing I couldn't do. Even the worst thing. Especially the worst thing.

And we knew, Delilah, my unborn child and me, that soon there would only be one thing the worst thing could possibly be.

I held her up at the level of my snout, my big hands a dark cradle. She didn't object. Just gurgled slightly, kicked her right leg, the fat little foot like a lump of Turkish delight. Jennifer screamed in me, the faintest neural tickle.

At which moment a car pulled into the drive and tipped the balance (the only perfect balance I'd ever achieved) and saved Delilah Snow's life.

PART THREE

LOVE BITES

'In this city a woman needs two cunts, one for business and one for pleasure.'

Jerzy Kosinski – *The Devil Tree*

15

The night before our bogus meeting with plummy Althea Gordon was scheduled to take place I sat with Cloquet in a hired Corolla parked around the corner from Vincent Merryn's large detached house in Royal Oak, West London. It was raining. The city's first leaves had fallen.

•

Vast mathematical silence and impenetrable darkness. Yes. For a while. But some perverse gravity had forced me back, to the hotel room's details, to the rolling boil of full awareness. Returning to myself that night in the Anchorage Grand had felt like being born into a death sentence. I'd opened my eyes with a feeling of surrender. Cloquet was still asleep. Zoë was still awake. For a long time I sat looking at her in the bassinet. I was scared to touch her.

(The car that had saved Delilah Snow and condemned me belonged, subsequent news reports revealed, to Amber Brouwer, George's former lover. She'd come by because her dog had died and she'd got a little drunk and weepy and suddenly realised she missed George. A dead dog. Sentimentality. A drive. Headlights swimming over a bedroom ceiling. A life not taken.)

Only when my daughter closed her eyes did I rest my hand

lightly on her body, felt the tiny ribs, the solidity and heat, the heartbeat and the sleeping wolf inside her. That, and how unentitled to any of it I was.

I had an imaginary conversation with my mother.

Ma, what do you do if you're capable of anything?

Just because you're capable of anything doesn't mean you have to do everything. It's not a death sentence, Lulu. It's a life sentence. Sorry, angel. You're going to have to either walk away or give it a try.

•

'This is insane,' Cloquet said. The rain accelerated for a few seconds, then slowed again.

Without Zoë I might have been able to walk away. Without her I might have been able to swallow the loss, cauterise it, grow a new deformed version of myself to accommodate it: The Unfit Mother. But there she was. Her brother's insurance policy.

They have your son. Thinking of him as a person made me feel sick. There was a vertigo of the heart. I had to think of him as an object. Like a lost suitcase I had to get back. It was a relief, suddenly, to be reduced to a single purpose. Nothing else matters, we say, when we fall in love. I knew it was hopeless. I knew all I was doing was choosing a route to my own death. It didn't matter. It was as much of a liberation as walking away would have been.

Zoë's brother wasn't 'he' or 'him' any more. As Cloquet pointed out, we might have to travel far and fast if and when we found him; it wouldn't do to have to wait on papers again. He was right, but it didn't lessen the peculiar agony of naming him. It felt like taking something that didn't belong to me. My mother had a miscarriage two years after I was born. It was a boy. She told me later they were going to call him Lorcan. So I named my son that, with clinical perversity, since it already had death attached to it. I'd phoned Kovatch before we left Anchorage, and the birth certificate (plus aliases to match his sister's) had arrived this morning. The name in print unhinged me for a moment, as if I hadn't known until then that the God who wasn't there took these dares seriously. I put the documents away and told myself I wouldn't use the name, even in my own head. But of course that was already impossible. It was entailed in the idea of him, and now every time I thought of him I thought of the name, *Lorcan*, and it was like an invitation to Death to come and claim his property.

I'd made a will, leaving my dad more than he'd know what to do with, enough for Cloquet to keep him for the rest of his days, one of the restaurants to Ambidextrous Alison, a million dollars to Lauren, who'd made a mess of her life, *one* dollar to Richard – and all the rest to the twins, in a trust to be administered by my dad or his nominees until they were of age. It helped to have done this, to know that materially at least I wasn't leaving any loose ends. In a small way it made me less afraid of dying.

A black Land Rover sat across the road from us. In it, wearing police uniforms, were Draper and Khan, the two guys supplied by Charlie Proctor at Aegis Private Security. Charlie's name was on Jake's list of People I Could Trust. Draper was a fair-haired soft-voiced Scot with a way of moving that never looked hurried and a core of gentleness it seemed his life's violence hadn't touched. Khan was a third-generation British Pakistani with liquid black eyes and a thin, clever mouth, shallower than his colleague, and happier giving orders than taking them. They'd spent yesterday scoping the place out. (Two CCTV cameras at the front of the house, three at the back. Two goons. A housekeeper. A Siamese cat.) It was their job to get Cloquet in and secure Merryn for questioning. They didn't know what I was. As far as they were concerned I was just another client who could afford their company's services. The first moment of eye contact with them had said sex, yes – then their professional override had shut it down. It was a source of pride for both of them that this system worked, that they could be soldiers first. I envied them: my libido still slept, but I'd known since the second child left my body that it wouldn't sleep much longer. The thought galled me, the accommodations I'd have to make. Her kid's being tortured and here *she* is – screwing! Christ!

'This is insane,' Cloquet repeated. 'I hope you realise that?'

'I'm sorry. I have to be here.'

I wasn't supposed to be there. I was supposed to be at the hotel in Kensington with the baby. The baby was asleep in her carrier strapped to my chest. Since the kidnapping I'd found it disturbing to be alone with her. Alone with her, love threatened. Alone with her love came to me like the Devil, rich with temptation. I daren't look, had to somehow keep myself turned away. I kept thinking of the line from the Old Testament *But God hardened Pharaoh's heart*. It was something you could do, I believed, harden your heart.

'It's com*pletely* fucking unnecessary.'

'Look, shut up. I know. I'm sorry.'

'When I go in you *stay here*.'

'I know.'

'I mean it. In the car.'

'Yes. I know.'

Cloquet's eyes were raw. We were both jet-lagged. He was weaning himself off morphine and it was making him irritable. Draper, a unit medic, had checked the shoulder wound, pronounced it well sutured and free of infection and given him a week's course of antibiotics.

Khan's voice came over the headset. 'You reading me?'

'Yes.'

'Okay, we're going in. You sit tight. Don't use the com. *We* contact *you*, okay?'

We watched them until they disappeared around the corner. Five minutes passed. Ten. Fifteen. The Corolla's little atmosphere filled up with our waiting. I was mentally busy with the question that had first occurred to me the morning we left Anchorage and that had since become monolithic: why *had* the vampires taken my son? The reflex answer – that they wanted him for the Helios Project – didn't stand scrutiny. Assuming Jake had it right, for at least the last hundred and seventy years werewolves had been carrying a virus that had stopped them passing on the Curse. Instead of Turning, bitten victims died within twelve hours. *Vampires* bitten by infected werewolves, however, not only survived, but showed an increased tolerance for sunlight. Hence werewolves' sudden relevance to Helios.

But I wasn't infected. WOCOP's serum killed the virus in newly bitten victims (they'd never established whether it cured *existing* werewolves, although I vaguely remembered Ellis telling Jake they'd been slipping it to him in drinks from time to time) and I was living proof of its efficacy. But there was no reason to suppose the vampires knew that. To them I was just a werewolf. Werewolves had the virus. The virus conferred sunlight resistance. Ergo, I was a valuable research commodity.

Except they hadn't taken me. They'd taken my child. Again: why?

Obviously they'd known there was going to *be* a child, otherwise why the bag, the cattle prod, the ketch-pole? No doubt they had a WOCOP agent or two in their pockets, which would explain how they knew I was pregnant (if not how they knew just when I was going into labour), but if that was true then surely they'd know that I – famously – *wasn't* carrying the virus? And if I wasn't carrying the virus, chances were my offspring wouldn't be, either.

So what did they want with him?

I'd put it all to Cloquet on the flight out of Alaska, but he couldn't come up with anything. Or so he said. He'd seemed a little distracted. At the time I put it down to him being in a lot of pain (no prescription for the morphine so he was downgraded to Advil on board) but wondered since if there was more to it.

There was something else bothering me. Since arriving in London I'd several times had a feeling of... not quite being watched, but of invisible things passing near. *Someone walked over my grave.* In the street outside the hotel I'd stopped and turned, expecting to see someone I knew behind me – but there was no one. I'd said nothing about it to Cloquet. But it had kept happening – and now I couldn't stop thinking about it.

A click-scratch in my headset.

'You reading?' Khan asked.

'Yes,' we said in unison.

A pause.

'They're all dead.'

'What?'

'We've got five bodies. The two guards, the housekeeper and your man Merryn...'

For a moment I thought somehow Draper and Khan had completely misunderstood the mission and were telling us they'd accomplished it by killing everyone in the house.

'... Plus... I don't know. I guess it's a body. It's basically black slime with bits. Looks like it's gone through an acid bath.'

Cloquet and I looked at each other. Vampire corpse.

'How are the others killed?' Cloquet asked.

'The two gorillas took one each in the head at close range. The housekeeper and Merryn... I don't know. Big neck and thigh wounds. Massive haemorrhaging. And the geezer in the acid bath, I haven't a fucking clue. Looks like something from outer space. We need to, ah, get the fuck out of here. CCTV discs are all gone and the system's off, so if we're very lucky we *might* not be suspects in a multiple murder investigation.'

'Wait,' I said – then to Cloquet: 'You have to go and take a look.'

'Forget it.'

'That's a vampire's body.'

'So what?'

'Don't be idiotic. We have to take a look. We *have* to.'

Cloquet closed his eyes and let his head fall back against the seat. He looked like he needed to sleep for a week.

'Khan?' he said into the headset mic.

'Here.'

'I need to get in there. I need to take a look.'

I discerned Khan covering his own mic. To confer with Draper.

'Five minutes. Then we're out. You got gloves?'

'No,' Cloquet and I said together.

'No worries, we've got spare. Just don't touch anything on your way in. Are you...' Something off-mic to Draper...'Are you both coming in?'

'Yes,' I said.

'No,' Cloquet said.

'Roger that,' Khan said. 'Front door's open. Don't step in the blood.'

16

Cloquet raced through a cigarette as we walked. Skirls of wind whisked the rain around us, blew it into our jet-lagged faces. A tracksuited jogger with a Collie on a lead ran past, looking like he was in a foul mood. Zoë, shocked by sudden emergence from the Corolla's warmth, woke up silently. Black onyxy baby eyes in the dark. This was her first rain. One of the countless first things the world had to offer. Her brother would be experiencing first things too, if he wasn't already dead. The image of Jacqueline inserting a wire into his eye was right there. Don't think of it. But you can't not think of it. Thinking of it's entailed in saying don't think of it. I saw him tied spread-eagled to a brushed-steel table, head strapped and muzzled, eyelids clamped open, fur hot and damp. Jacqueline made an unanaesthetised incision. He screamed, unable to move. Vampires in lab coats made notes. I had these visions all the time now. I told myself it didn't make any difference: the project was still to get him back. I told myself it was lucky I hadn't felt anything for him, otherwise imagine how these visions would make me feel. Imagine.

Zoë sneezed against me, minutely. The night smelled of wet leaves and tarmac. Rain cross-hatched the street lamps' haloes. We moved quickly.

The front of Merryn's property was bounded by a high stone

wall but the iron gates off the pavement were open. A short, brick driveway went from these in a single curve between small shrub-planted lawns to the front of the large white house. Georgian? Edwardian? I was ignorant of such things. It looked like it dated back to powdered wigs and horse-drawn carriages, but for all I knew could've been built last year. One big glistening horse chestnut overhung the pillared porch. Behind the closed curtains the downstairs lights were on. Upstairs was in darkness. The wet lawn exhaled its heavy peaceful odour.

Draper met us at the front door, closed it behind us, issued us with latex gloves. 'I don't know what you're looking for in here,' he said, 'but whatever it is you've got five minutes. That baby starts, we're out of here immediately, no argument. Understood?'

'Got it.'

'You sure you want to see this?'

'We have to.'

'You're not going to throw up or anything?'

'No,' I said, moving past him, 'we're not.'

The housekeeper's body was at the foot of the stairs in a lake of congealed blood. She was face-down, one leg bent, the other leg turned completely the wrong way in its socket. Her throat didn't look like it had been bitten, it looked like it had been wildly machined. The veins were out: jugulars, pharyngeal, thyroid. Oesophagus and trachea severed. (Learn anatomy, Jake told me. It helps. Why do you think doctors can live with being such assholes?) She was in her early fifties, grey roots under a honey-blonde dye. A tortoiseshell barrette hung from her bangs. Cream woollen sweater, navy blue skirt. The wrenched around leg evoked all the dolls Lauren and I had ever abused. One shoe was missing, baring her surprisingly well-kept foot, toenails painted peach. I imagined single parenthood, a guy who hadn't appreciated her, a life with a hole in it now the kids had left for college, a touch of unexpected late glamour working for Merryn.

Draper's surprise at my *sang-froid* was palpable. 'The others are in here,' he said, eyebrows raised.

We followed him into a large study, floor-to-ceiling books, a green leather Chesterfield, a colossal desk of dark red wood, a gold Persian rug, a fireplace with the fire long since gone out. The room was chandelier lit, filled with spangly light. Khan, silencered pistol in hand, stood by the window's closed curtains keeping a lookout. From his double take when we entered it was clear that between the car and now he'd forgotten the baby's existence. 'Christ,' he said. 'This is surreal.'

The two guards had been shot in the head and lay unspectacularly side by side on their fronts. Merryn – I assumed it was Merryn given his prominent placing – had been extravagantly ripped at the throat and groin, feasted-on, then propped in an open-armed sitting position on the Chesterfield. I put him in his early sixties. He was long-limbed and long-faced, with a hooked nose and a big intellectual forehead from which the grey hair had receded. His mouth was open and his eyes were closed. He looked as if he was waiting to receive the Holy Communion wafer.

The vampire remains were on the floor by the window. The head was missing, as far as I could tell. The bulk of the body was far into its reduction: the abdominal area was a black viscous puddle; the ribs were stubs of charcoal; one thigh remained recognisable, as did the left foot, long and delicate and showing in black every minute detail of its dead capillary system. Toenails of polished glass. Beyond that what wasn't gone was going fast.

'D'you want to tell us what the story is?' Khan said.

'We can't,' Cloquet said. 'We don't know.'

'I take it you know what you're looking for?' Draper said.

'See if his phone's on him,' I told Cloquet, indicating Merryn, while I poked around in the boochie's leftovers for the same. 'An address book... anything.'

Nothing. All six of the desk's drawers were out on the floor and all six of them were empty. I checked the fireplace. In the movies you found just enough of a charred map or diary, but there was nothing like that. 'Look for a computer,' I said. 'A laptop, cellphones. We need to search the house prop—' then Zoë coughed, and started to cry.

'We go,' Draper said. 'Now.'

'Wait—'

'No argument, remember?'

'She just needs feeding,' I said. But they were already heading to the hall. 'Wait!' I hissed. 'Khan! Stop!' Incredibly, he did. 'I'm *paying* for this,' I said.

'No one said women and kids. No one said *crying babies*, okay? That wasn't the job. You want to stay, fine. But you're sitting here with four stiffs and an alien and a bawling kid and fuck knows who turning up any minute, so I'd advise against it. Be smart, come out with us now.'

'I'm not leaving till we've searched this place properly,' I said.

I thought Draper might have stayed. All that quiet masculinity. But he gave me an apologetic smile that said he was getting out of this game soon, had another identity almost ready (I saw a mousey woman he loved, a small house in the middle of nowhere, pleasure in ordinary things), and in a matter of seconds he and Khan were gone. So much for Aegis. So much for Charlie Proctor and People I Could Trust. I wondered who else wouldn't pan out.

'I'm going to feed her,' I told Cloquet. 'You keep looking.'

'Keep looking? Keep looking for what? Secret vampire addresses stuck on the fridge?'

'Listen,' I said, settling Zoë at my breast, 'Jacqueline knew that you knew Merryn. Merryn knew where they were taking my son. Jacqueline killed Merryn to stop him from talking to you. That's it. Now, please, will you just see if you can find anything that might be a clue?'

'That's it? What about *that*?'

The dead vampire, he meant.

'I don't know. Maybe Merryn managed to stake one of them. Maybe there was another guard who got away. Just keep looking!'

There would once have been a long hypothetical list of things I didn't imagine ever doing. Somewhere on it would have been: breastfeeding a baby in a house kept company by five corpses, one of them a vampire's. As it was I sat in the desk's ergonomic leather swivel chair with Zoë drinking from me and found nothing strange. The milk came from some other dimension through me into her, like an electric current. A microclimate of physical peace formed around us, though my brain continued labouring, frantically. I'd blurted out my explanation of Merryn's death readily enough, but did I believe it? Was it really likely Merryn had known anything? According to Cloquet his big interest (aside from trading stolen relics) was vampire *literature*. He was as close as humanly possible to being an expert on vampire languages. I glanced at the nearest bookshelf. Mesopotamian history, archaeology, antiquities, rare coins, hallmarks. Nothing unusual. I imagined my son somehow seeing all this, his mother following the wrong leads, blind alleys, red herrings, squandering time and energy while he... while he—

Stop it. It won't help. You have to think of him as an object. Like you did when he was born.

Zoë's hand was tangled in my hair. I looked down at her. She had Jake's long eyelashes. Lucky girl. At the Los Angeles villa she'd wear a coral ankle bracelet one summer and be surprised when I didn't care if she got a tattoo, though I'd have to warn her she'd be stuck with it for four hundred years. She'd start off reading trash but one day I'd notice a volume of Emily Dickinson or a copy of *The Catcher in the Rye* on her nightstand. When she got out of the pool the sun would gleam on her wet shoulder blades. There'd be no grieving for the time before the Curse because for her there would be no time before the Curse. I'd bring her up unashamed, elite, triumphal, loved for what she was, a natural born werewolf. Then boys. And no Jake to play the scary dad. She'd be embarrassed by Cloquet. Hey, Zoë, that French dude's a fag, right? Or some kinda eunuch, or what? She'd ask me to tell her about her father and I wouldn't be able to stop myself. I'd lose some of her to him, to the glamour of the dead. She'd start looking for him in guys, and then all the trouble would start.

But God hardened Pharaoh's—

'We should go,' Cloquet said. He'd been upstairs, searching the bedrooms. 'I'm sorry. It may be right what you say, that there's something here, but we need a week to look. Maybe we should go and see the assistant tomorrow after all? She could know something.'

It was remote. But with Merryn dead what else did we have? My search-the-house plan was desperation, and in any case to do it properly would take hours. Still, the thought of walking away no closer to finding my son was intolerable. We had to have information.

'I'm going to look,' I said. Zoë had stopped feeding. I put her over my shoulder and stood up, feeling suddenly dizzy. The residual stink of the Undead had been sickening me since we'd entered. 'We're not going to get the chance again. There has to be something, an invoice to one of their companies, an email…

Fuck, I don't *know*.' Moving out from behind the desk I banged my knee on its edge and shut my eyes for a moment to absorb the pain.

I still had them closed when an American male voice said: 'Don't move, please.'

17

I opened my eyes. A good-looking boyish guy with tangled brown and blond hair stood in the study doorway holding a gun pointed directly at Cloquet. Two-handed grip. No shake. Professional. Glamorous blue-green eyes and a mouth that wanted to smile. Levis, red plaid shirt, pale green combat jacket. An odour of damp clothes and tired skin. He looked twenty-five but something told you he was ten years older. *Charmer*, the female consensus would be.

'Hey, there,' he said, and the mouth did smile, with what looked like delight at being alive. 'Any weapons, very slowly, out and down on the floor.' The accent was East Coast, maybe even New York. I wondered if I'd ever passed him in the street or sat next to him on the subway. I could see him in Veselka with a rapt East Village hipster girl who wouldn't know he was unmaliciously and comprehensively screwing her roommate as well. 'Cloquet, you first. Miss D, please, no acrobatics with the kid.'

'Who are you?' Cloquet said.

'Weapons first, then introductions. Do it now, please. Slowly.'

Cloquet reached in and removed a Beretta from his left shoulder holster. He had a Luger in the right but didn't touch it. I had a Smith and Wesson M&P (all supplied by Aegis) in a rear holster under my jacket. Going for it was out of the question.

'Okay, slide it over to me. That's it. Couldn't have done it better myself. Now, Monsieur Cloquet, face-down on the floor, hands on your head. Think toupée, think gale.'

A second guy appeared at the gunman's side, also armed. Taller, older, dark hair flecked with grey. Black eyes polished by exhaustion. Midnight-blue jeans and a donkey jacket. He gave the younger one a single nod: upstairs clear.

'Okay. Fabulous. Miss D, are you armed?'

'Yes.'

'You know the drill. Can you manage?'

I tightened my hold on Zoë (who'd been negligibly sick on my shoulder) and reached around slowly for the gun in the rear holster. I bent and put it on the floor. The older guy frisked Cloquet – whereupon the Luger was discovered and removed, without comment, for all of us to see. New York came over to me. 'In the light of which,' he said, 'my apologies, but...' He frisked me, efficiently, without indecency, despite my blouse being still half unbuttoned from feeding Zoë. He had an outrageous gentle glittering confidence about him. Closer up, I could see he hadn't slept in a while. I could also see a small white scar just below his left eye.

'Okay, that's the guns,' I said. 'Now can I get dressed and put my daughter in her carrier?'

'Sure, sure, go ahead. Again, my apologies.'

'What is this?' Cloquet said. 'Who are you?'

New York indicated the captured weapons with another big smile. 'We ask the questions,' he said. 'You didn't kill these people, I'm guessing, but did you see what happened?'

'No,' Cloquet said. 'Let me get up off the fucking floor.'

'Easy, tiger, *easy*. Foot off the gas. You can get up, very slowly, very calmly. Calm as Carradine. There you go. Beautiful. Couldn't've done it better myself.'

I'd buttoned my blouse and resettled Zoë in the carrier, snug against me. I kept imagining the sensation of a bullet hitting her while I held her. The older guy was down on his haunches, examining the vampire remains. He poked at the foot with a pencil.

'How do you know who we are?' I asked New York.

'In our organisation everyone knows who *you* are. Colleague of mine's got you as his desktop wallpaper. And with the greatest respect, the picture does not do you justice.'

'What organisation?'

'Ex-organisation. We don't think of ourselves as WOCOP any more. Not since they started trying to kill us.'

'WOCOP?'

'Let's go,' the older guy said. The *L* of 'Let's' indicated Eastern Europe, Russia maybe. He'd snapped out of whatever fugue he'd been in.

'Go where?' I said.

'If you harm her,' Cloquet said. 'If you do anything—'

'Easy, easy, *easy*,' New York said. 'With the *drama*, this guy, always. You must be hell to share a kitchen with, Slim. We're just talking about going somewhere that's not quite so much of a murder scene. Have you seen the lady in the hall? I don't know about you but I'm not—'

'Let's go,' the Russian repeated. 'Now.'

18

New York, smiling, held us just behind the gates. My skin tingled. Adrenaline forced its way through exhaustion. Cloquet buzzed with pointless action calculations. Less than a minute and the Russian pulled-up in a mirror-windowed BMW 4x4. The only available blindfold was Cloquet's vast handkerchief. Could I be trusted to keep my eyes closed? Or was I going to have to have a jacket over my head? The Russian drove. New York turned in his seat to make sure I wasn't peeking. He should have been a surfer. His face was full of masculine prettiness and immensely likeable. Which, by horror's law of inverted aesthetics, made me sure we were being taken to our death.

We travelled for less than ten minutes, then were hustled stumbling from the car into the lobby of what I assumed was a projects block. A shuddering graffiti'd lift that stank of urine and hash took us up to the twentieth floor. The Russian checked the landing before we crossed to the unnumbered door of a flat. From a floor below someone was singing with a karaoke machine, Paul McCartney's 'Simply Having a Wonderful Christmas Time', completely out of tune. 'Beyond doubt the worst Christmas song ever written,' New York said to me, quietly. 'Like a request to God to end the universe. Watch your step there.'

Inside was dismal second-hand furniture, threadbare carpet,

a spartan bathroom with exposed pipes and the side of the tub missing, and a tiny but surprisingly clean blue and white kitchen off the living room. Smells of Chinese take-out and empty beer bottles and stale cigarette smoke. A dartboard broken almost completely in two leaned in a corner. The living room's one large window gave a view over night-time London: St Paul's; Canary Wharf; the Eye; the Gherkin. A sprawl of lights under the low soft cloud. The beauty of it hurt my heart for a moment, the way the Christmas tree in the diner used to when my dad turned the fairy lights on for the first time. To the left of the window a glass door opened onto a narrow balcony occupied by a rusty bike frame and a broken clothes rack. It was just after two a.m. The rain had stopped. I thought, This is the way of it: a place turns out to be the place you die.

They shut us in the living room and went into murmuring confab in the hall. Mainly New York, by the sound of it. Cloquet had turned how terrified he was into simmering fury. He tried the door to the balcony, which wasn't locked, and did us no good, unless we wanted to jump twenty storeys. Jumping twenty storeys wouldn't kill me – or Zoë – but even with *wulf*'s recuperative powers it would be a while before we got up from the concrete. I walked back and forth with Zoë, rocking her. In a minute or two she was asleep. I was thinking about what she meant in this situation. In this situation she meant they could make me do whatever they wanted. There was no end to the things they could make me do. (How come? Hadn't I hardened my heart to her?) I started thinking about these things. I thought about how slowly time would pass once they began. I thought about how familiar the drab room would become, the broken dartboard, the faux leather couch with the stuffing coming out, the oil stain on the green carpet. I thought how familiar *they* would become, the two men, the feel of their hands and mouths and cocks, the sound of their voices, the unique smell of their violence. I thought how if they were WOCOP – even ex-WOCOP – they'd have silver ammunition or the means to cut my head off. That meant they'd do whatever they wanted to do knowing that when they'd had enough, when they were sick of me, they could kill me, and that would be that. I imagined Jacqueline showing the footage to my son. I'm sure you must have been thinking *maman* will be coming for you. Well, as you can see, she won't be, now.

I hadn't realised but while all this was going through my head I'd been scouring the place for any kind of weapon. There was a bread knife in one of the kitchen drawers. A sharp little fruit knife in another. I filled the electric kettle and put it on. That would be boiling water, if I could get to it. There was nothing else. I gave Cloquet the bread knife. He tore the lining of his jacket and slid it in. I tried the fruit knife in my jeans back pocket but it cut into me if I sat down. In the end I put it in my jacket pocket and told myself I'd have to make whatever move before they made me take it off.

All with a baby strapped to me.

The kettle switched itself off just as they came back in.

'Okay,' New York said, taking a seat at the battered dining table and giving us another delighted smile. 'Who wants to start?'

The Russian, who'd been poking around in the kitchen, emerged carrying an almost full bottle of Stolichnya and four (odd) glasses. He set them down on the dining table, poured us each a large measure and handed them round. Which he surely wouldn't do, I thought, if the two of them were going to kill Cloquet then rape, torture and murder me? (Not necessarily. One thing didn't always mean another. Reality could be serving drinks first. The world was free with its extraordinary juxtapositions. Even the movies had cottoned on. These days you rarely met an on-screen psycho who didn't hum Bartok or reel off chunks of *Paradise Lost*.) I knew I was supposed to avoid alcohol when breastfeeding (or rather I knew humans were) but since we were going to die here anyway what difference did it make? I took a big gulp. Instant benevolent fire in my chest. The first liquor since the road to California with Jake. It reminded me of him, brought the raw space where his ghost should've been. I thought of meeting him in the afterlife I didn't believe in. Our dead children wouldn't be there. They'd be somewhere else. We'd never see them again. He'd say: It wasn't your fault, Lu. I don't blame you. But he'd seem strange to me, a version of himself I didn't know. The version that lied.

'Hey,' New York said, glass raised. 'You didn't give me a chance to say *stin iya sas*!'

'It's *stin iya* mas,' I said. 'Unless you're excluding yourself from the toast.'

'Damn. I always screw that up.'

'What?' Cloquet said. 'What does he say?'

'Nothing. He's saying cheers in Greek.'

'*Stin iya* mas,' New York said, and downed his shot in one.

'Do you work for WOCOP or not?' Cloquet said.

New York sighed, closed his eyes, opened them. Which meant: I'm trying to be civilised about this, but this person is fucking it up. Or it was a pretence of that, part of a satirically polite persona he adopted for this kind of thing for his or the Russian's amusement, although the Russian looked as if his amusement circuits had been burned out – along with his capacity to sleep – decades ago. 'How about this,' New York said. 'A radical suggestion: I tell you our story, you tell us yours.' He looked from Cloquet to me, smiling, always smiling. To Cloquet the smile said: you need to dial it down, motherfucker, because I'm losing patience. To me it said: this schmuck's going to get you killed – and yes, I'm attracted to you, yes I want you, in that way, but only if it's mutual. (And since life loves impropriety, *wulf*'s libido twitched in its sleep, sent the first signal that waking up was on the cards. Of course *now*. Of course when it was least wanted. Of course when death might already be in the room. I looked away.) 'I promise you,' New York said, 'you're in zero danger from us. I'd give you the weapons back right now to prove it, but the problem is – " looking at Cloquet – 'there's a good chance you'd shoot us out of Gallic indignation.'

'You don't need the knives,' the Russian said. Soft voice the colour of his starved eyes. 'But keep them if it makes you feel better.'

'Knives?' New York said, but the Russian just shook his head. We weren't going to be any trouble with our knives.

'Oh, right, the kitchen. And the boiling water. I get it. You won't need any of that. But I understand. No offence taken.'

Cloquet, standing by the window, had his jacket's hem in his hands, a tic of his I hadn't seen for a while. I sat down on the end of the couch. Zoë's head smelled the way babies' heads smell, which was one of those things that without warning refreshed or reloaded the fact that she was mine. *One* of mine. I felt, suddenly, the gulf of time that had passed since the vampires had taken Lorcan. If these two really were ex-WOCOP maybe they'd know something. If they had information and weren't interested in killing us I'd give them money for it. A lot of money. I'd fuck them, if that would help. A surprisingly easy decision to make, but pointless, since I couldn't let myself believe they *weren't* going to kill us, whether either of them wanted to fuck me or not.

'Will you tell us who you are?' I said.

New York refilled his glass and the Russian's, then held the bottle out for Cloquet, who let go of his jacket hem but shook his head, no.

'I'm Walker. He's Mikhail Konstantinov. We used to work for WOCOP. Now we don't. Now we're freelance.'

'What do you want us for?' Cloquet growled.

'Jeez Louise,' Walker said. 'It's lucky we *are* friendly because otherwise I'd've shot you in the nuts by now. Is he always this uptight?'

This playful shtick of his would have started as a defence against something, his conscience maybe, memories, whatever had happened to him. Now it was part of him, like a hat he never took off. To the people who knew him it would be alarming if he ever did take it off. I groped for a sense of what the relationship between him and Konstantinov was, but there was too much else going on. The Russian was simultaneously intense and remote, like a star seen through a telescope.

'To answer your question,' Walker said to Cloquet, 'we don't want you *for* anything. We were as surprised to see you at Merryn's as you were to see us.' Then when Cloquet visibly didn't soften: 'Okay, listen. I get it. You're suspicious. I'll go first.'

I tried to keep hold of the belief that the friendliness was a sadistic ruse, designed to heighten our horror (and so their pleasure) when the moment came for us to realise we'd fallen for it. But the longer Walker talked, the harder it was not to be disarmed. WOCOP, he told us, had split. Ellis's plot to kill Grainer and key upper-echelon players had provoked a backlash. A programme of 'identifying and eliminating' members of the rebel faction had been launched, initially based on intelligence, soon spiralling out into Stalinesque paranoia. Agents who'd had nothing to do with Ellis were 'exposed', court-martialled, executed. 'You know the way it goes,' he said. 'People getting arrested for wearing suspicious glasses, for having suspicious haircuts. The organisation's killed more than two hundred of its own in the last four months.'

'So you were with the rebels?' I asked. I'd remembered

– astonished at my own slowness – that the renegades' agenda was to avoid redundancy by letting werewolf numbers go up. World Organisation for the *Creation* of Occult Phenomena. In which case, obviously...

'No,' Walker said. 'I mean I got it – Ellis's logic was sound: the organisation was making itself obsolete – but I was ready to get out anyway. I'd had enough. Plus I couldn't stand Ellis. He was too white and too wacko. I always imagined him having alien genitals. Like maybe a ball with stalks coming out of it. Or something like an artichoke. Anyway he gave me the royal heebie-jeebies.'

I was getting an idea of Walker. I couldn't help it. Some early loss or violence had made the particular form of how he made a living irrelevant to him. He'd been shoved by shock too young into the truth that nothing meant anything. The smile, the delight, the slacker clothes, it all derived from that. *That* was what the shtick defended against. He could sense me reading this from him. It excited him, but it unnerved him too, took him back to whatever it was that had broken his contract with life in the first place, the thing around which this sad bright pearl of his identity had been wrought. Love. Or death. Or both. Meanwhile a part of me stood off, arms folded, lips pursed, shaking her head at the rest of me, the shambles. Really? This? *Now?*

'So if you weren't with the rebels,' I asked, 'why's the organ-isation after you?'

Pause. A glance exchanged between him and Konstantinov.

'The guy who took over from Grainer is John Murdoch,' Walker said. 'He runs ground operations now. He's not a fan of mine.'

Pause.

'It's purely personal.'

'He slept with Murdoch's wife,' Konstantinov said, neutrally.

'Yes, I did,' Walker said, with a serious face he couldn't take seriously. 'And I testify to you here and now that it was a good and honest and beautiful event between two people in a chaotic world. Angela's a good person. Getting away from that psychopath was the best thing she ever did, and if I helped her do it I'm glad as butter. She's a beautiful smart complicated spirit and he... isn't.' The smile flashed on and off as he was speaking. Here was more information, whether I liked it or not: he'd always had women. Women gravitated to him in spite of themselves. Even when he was a kid at school the little girls would have found themselves exempting him from their exasperation with *boys*. At fourteen or fifteen there would have been a divorced aunt or local widow, horrified at herself, but nonetheless... Since then he'd accepted it as a gift, like a photographic memory or perfect pitch, compensation for the broken contract with life. There was no cruelty in him. He was a child of Eros. I pictured Murdoch's wife as an unstable brunette with strappy high heels and confused energies and a quota of crazy things she had to do to get away at last from the toxic marriage. I couldn't help thinking it probably *had* been a good thing in the world. For the first time since Merryn's, I relaxed a little.

Meanwhile Cloquet was all but levitating with suspicion.

'Anyway,' Walker continued, 'Murdoch didn't appreciate it. He worked a simple frame-up: faked email traffic between us and the rebels. His guys were all set to arrest us but we got a tip-off and got out. Since then Murdoch's got crazier, and it's not like he wasn't gaga to start with. With any luck the suits'll shut him down, but until they do he'll keep coming after us and the Purge will continue.'

'What about you?' I asked Konstantinov. 'Whose wife did you sleep with?'

Konstantinov looked at me and I realised I'd said the wrong thing. The room was instantly crammed with my misjudgement. His black eyes spoke of inhuman endurance.

'Go have a smoke, Mike,' Walker said. 'I'll do this.'

Konstantinov sat still and unblinking for a long moment in which I could feel the room's wretched furniture and stained walls holding their breath. Then he got up, moved past me – his aura brushed mine – and out through the door onto the balcony, closing it behind him.

'Bad choice of words,' Walker said. 'Mike's got a wife of his own. Married six months ago. Now the vampires have her. Revenge for one of their crew he took out. They're feeding on her just enough so she stays alive. They've been sending him video footage.'

'Oh,' I said. 'That's awful. I'm sorry.' I pictured Konstantinov's wife as a pale, dark-haired woman, ballerina skinny with eyes as black as his, someone most men would think plain. You could see in his drained face that for him the sun rose and set with her. And now she was a vending machine for vampires. Video footage. I could picture that, too, along with all the other footage I could picture, of my son on the brushed-steel table, the wire going into his eye, the coven of doctors, Jacqueline's smile of happy concentration.

'I'm sorry,' I said again.

'You weren't to know,' Walker said. 'He won't hold it against you.'

Feeding on her just enough so she stays alive. Naturally the language of feeding had brought *my* nature into the room. Walker had to keep reminding himself what I was. The bright sexual man in him came towards me, smiling the dazzling smile, then got yanked back by the human: She's a *werewolf,* for Christ's sake. Are you insane? To which the bright sexual man, turning towards me again with the smile that wouldn't be suppressed, said, Yeah, maybe. It was hard to look him in the eye. A little Manhattan holy spirit of inevitability hovered above us. All the sex I'd had since Jake had been bad-tempered and bleak. This was an invitation to something else. *Wulf* stirred, yes, but so did the long-neglected human female, the stupid *girl* who hadn't been honestly loved-up in what felt like an age. There was no end to my inappropriateness, apparently.

'Which vampires have her?' Cloquet said.

'What's that?'

'Which vampires have his wife?'

'Jacqueline Delon's crew. The Disciples of Remshi.'

'The what?'

Cloquet moved to refill his glass – then remembered we were still technically under guard.

'Go ahead,' Walker said. 'Just don't do anything athletic, will you? I'm exhausted. Here, take a look at this.' He pulled out his iPhone, tapped, scrolled, swiped, handed it to Cloquet. 'Ever seen that before?'

Cloquet stared at the image on the screen, then passed it to me. A red cuneiform-style symbol on a black background. The emblem Jacqueline and her friends had on their jackets.

'They were wearing it,' I said.

'Who were?'

'The vampires who took my son. Jacqueline Delon's vampires.'

'Your son?'

I told him what had happened. All of it, without hesitation. Partly out of jet-lag, partly out of attraction, partly out of shared geography. Mostly because I'd had all I could take of not being able to trust anyone. 'It's what we were doing at Merryn's,' I said. 'We thought he'd know where they'd taken him. But by the time we got there Merryn was dead. The vampires got there first.'

'I can tell you what Merryn *would* have told you,' Walker said. 'He would have told you Jacqueline's vampires were at a former winery in Provence. But that doesn't help you. They cleared out. They found out Merryn was leaking intelligence.'

'Merryn was a double agent?'

'He worked for WOCOP for years, until this latest thing with the rebels. He favoured the breakaway group, naturally. The twilight zone was his life.'

Cloquet lit a cigarette. Something was wrong with him. The muscles of his face had lost some coherence. For a moment I thought it was jealousy – the attraction between Walker and me was a supple little cat in the room with us – but it wasn't that. Or rather it wasn't just that.

'But how do you know the vampires moved?' he asked. 'How do you know they left the winery?'

'Because we just got back from Provence,' Walker told him. 'They're not there. They knew we were coming. The only way they could've known we were coming is if they discovered Merryn was a mole. Which is why they killed him.'

'But they were in Alaska,' I pointed out.

'Jacqueline's got more than three hundred in her posse,' Walker said. 'They weren't all in Alaska. There was *no one* at the place in Provence. It had been completely abandoned. They found out Merryn was a leak, cleared out and killed him. They could be anywhere by now. Along with Mike's wife, if she's still alive. And your son.'

They could be anywhere. A montage of places: airports; fields; city streets. The last six months' travelling had shrunk the world. *They could be anywhere* made it vast again.

Cloquet's discomfort was growing. I was remembering him saying: You think I betray you? Ask your wolves! And the wolves, out of their meaty breath and loose shoulders and the thousands of miles in the pads of their paws said he was telling the truth. What was it then?

'What did you call Jacqueline's vampires?' I asked Walker.

'The Disciples of Remshi.' He looked at Cloquet. 'You know what I'm talking about, right?'

Cloquet didn't answer. And couldn't look at me.

Suddenly I understood: the kidnapping was nothing to do with the Helios Project.

It was to do with this. The Disciples of Remshi.

The sound of it made me feel hopeless. The sound of the disciples of anything made me feel hopeless. Cloquet had known, and hadn't told me. Now he felt sick. So did I.

'Mike thinks the dead boochie back there was one of their priests. They have a tattoo on the foot.'

Cloquet still wouldn't meet my eye.

'Look at me,' I said to him. 'What is it you're not telling me?'

A moment of suspension, his feelings jammed like typewriter keys. Then he mashed the cigarette in the table's foil ashtray, exhaling his last lungful with a look as if it tasted foul. 'Remshi is a...' He stopped. Rolled his head in a rapid tension-easing movement. Started again. 'According to vampire mythology Remshi is the oldest of their kind. He's been there from the beginning. There's no point telling you this, because he doesn't exist. Jacqueline said that to the vampires themselves he was like *le Pére Noël* or *La Petite Souris*, a fairy tale. But she believed in him. She was obsessed. He was supposed to have extraordinary powers. He could change his shape to look like animals or people. He could become invisible. He could make fire out of thin air. It's why she wanted to become a vampire. Because she believed—' He stopped, made a vague dismissive gesture. 'It doesn't matter. She's insane. All of this is because her father died. You know he was fucking her from the time she was eight years old?'

Because she believed—

I should be careful. Maybe he couldn't afford to say what he'd been going to say in front of Walker.

'He's right,' Walker said. 'To the vast majority of vampires Jacqueline's just started the boochie equivalent of the Flat Earth

Society. There's always been a handful of vamp astrologers who've taken the Remshi myth seriously, but *they* haven't been taken seriously for a century or more. Our girl's started this revival either as a bid to grow a new political power or because she genuinely believes the prophecy.'

'What prophecy?'

'Prophe*cies*,' Walker said. 'There are a bunch of them. Problem is that *The Book of Remshi*, which is where they're collected, is unreliably translated and massively bowdlerized. It's also tedious beyond belief. But the big prophecy is that Remshi's due for a return – although it's never been clear to me where he's supposed to be returning *from*, exactly. Suspended animation or whatever. Astrological consensus says it's now, this year. In fact he's supposed to already be awake, as yet unrevealed...' Then to Cloquet: 'Right?'

My helplessness felt external, as if the space around me was solidifying. Eventually it would hold me like a fly in a lump of amber. I thought how much better it would be if I knew Lorcan was dead. Then I could turn away from all this. Then there'd be just the slag-heap of guilt to clamber over into a new version of myself and a fractured life with my daughter.

'This Remshi thing,' I said to Walker, 'you believe in it?' I wondered, briefly, what a conversation with the oldest living vampire would reveal. Briefly because almost immediately I knew the answer: nothing conclusive. Maybe not even anything new. Another creature, another set of hungers and fears and delusions and unanswered questions.

'Who knows?' Walker said. 'This job keeps your mind open. My guess is if he exists he'll be one more character running around wondering where his next meal's coming from and trying to get laid. Or maybe not trying to get laid, if he's really a vampire. Although allegedly his sex equipment still works.

Anyway, if it's a religion then what we need to worry about is who does believe in it and what they're likely to do in its name.'

Konstantinov came back in.

'I'm sorry,' I said to him. 'Stupid of me.'

'Not your fault,' he said. 'Forget it.'

Jet-lag had let time misbehave. There was a fizzing edge to consciousness. I was aware through the blur that Walker had paraphrased my own thoughts. A small satisfaction in the jumble. I had images: the bag closing over the little wolf head; Jake's dark head moving like a mechanical toy between Jacqueline's legs; my dad's look when he'd said, I'm so *sad* about this, Lulu. Delilah in my hands. Rockabye baby.

'So according to the prophecy,' Walker continued, again looking at Cloquet for corroboration, 'Remshi wakes, establishes himself king of the boochies, inaugurates the era of vampire world domination, and while he's at it, takes himself a bride, the new vampire queen, with whom he shares all his extraordinary powers. According to believers he can even father children. You've got hand it to Jacqui: she doesn't think small.'

At some point the radiators had come on, and now the room was wadded with copper-flavoured heat. My face was flushed. I knew if I closed my eyes and lay down I'd go straight to sleep. Her son's kidnapped and tortured and here *she* is – sleeping!

Zoë woke up and gurgled. A sound of absurd innocence. I was very aware that the thing to do was get us out of there so Cloquet could speak freely. To press him now was a risk.

'I want you to tell me everything you know about this,' I said to him. 'Right now.'

19

The last of his tensile apparatus, visible in the shoulders and knees and the left foot up on its toes, collapsed. As with all defeats it was also a liberation. He closed his eyes for a few moments, then opened them. 'I only kept this from you to protect you, *chérie*. You must believe me.'

'Just tell me.'

He sighed. Poured himself more vodka. When he spoke his voice was ragged.

'Jacqueline was obsessed with the story of Remshi and the prophecy of his return. She found the vampire scholars who took it seriously and gave them whatever they asked for in exchange for information. It was disgusting, the things... Anyway. Of course she saw herself becoming his queen, his *amant royale*. The prophecies were very clear on the point of him choosing a bride. You have to understand: her father... It's just a kind of extension of—'

'I don't care about her fucking childhood traumas,' I said. Walker and Konstantinov were rich with listening. The same quality the pine forest had in the snow. (There were these pointless correspondences. I thought: that's what art's for, to chase them down, to reveal them. The nightmare was when you couldn't switch it off, when you didn't *want* art.) 'Just tell me what they want with my son,' I said. I don't know why I said that, since I already knew the answer.

Cloquet ran a hand through his exhausted hair. 'There's a ritual,' he said.

Of course there was. I'd known that since Walker had said 'the Disciples of Remshi'. I imagined Jake shaking his head the way one did at those morons who dressed up to recreate Middle Earth or the American Civil War every weekend. Jake not being with me for this was like cold air coming up against my back from a chasm right behind me. For a moment I hated him. He'd left me too much to do on my own – and no one to go to for comfort when I failed to do it.

'The prophecy says Remshi doesn't achieve full power until he's... until he drinks the blood of *gammou-jhi*.' Cloquet said. '*Gammou-jhi* is an ancient vampire word for werewolf.'

And there it was.

I saw a B-movie underground cave, *papier-mâché* boulders, a long-bearded vampire lifting a ceremonial dagger (a thing like a multicoloured stalactite) over my son's hyperventilating chest while Jacqueline and her king watched, her lipsticked mouth slightly open, her short red hair slicked down and glistening in the torchlight.

'He's dead then,' I said, trying out the words, wondering what I'd tell Zoë about the brother she never knew. Whom I never knew. Whom I never loved. Whom I let them take.

'No,' Cloquet said, leaning forward. 'The ritual can only be performed *au milieu d'hiver*, on midwinter's day – but Lulu, it's not *real*. This thing doesn't *exist*. There isn't going to be a sacrifice because there is no one to sacrifice *to*. Jacqueline, this vision she has, this believing in Remshi, *c'est une fantasie.*'

'He'll die anyway,' I said. 'Or spend the rest of his life in a cage. If he's no use to Jacqueline she'll sell him to WOCOP or the Helios Project.' I could see it ahead again like a loveless marriage, all the things I'd have to think of and plan and attempt, the pointlessness of it, failure guaranteed. And no matter how pointless it was I knew I wouldn't be strong or brave enough to turn my back and walk away. I was a bad mother, but not bad enough to be any good to myself. My limbs ached. Cloquet sat with his head bowed. He was running around inside himself trying to find a door into this not having happened. I understood why he hadn't told me. I'd still have done everything I'd done so far, but maybe with a desperation that would've made me careless. The wolves hadn't misjudged him. He'd had my interests at heart. My face and hands were full of stalled anger.

'How long do I have?' I asked.

'Till December twenty-first,' Walker said. 'Winter solstice. This year coincident with a full-moon lunar eclipse. But listen, we need to discuss—'

'I only did it to protect you,' Cloquet said. 'I didn't want you to have to carry it around in your head.'

'It wasn't your decision.'

'I just—'

'It wasn't your fucking decision. Shut up about it now.'

My heart laboured. All this new information my exhausted strategist could only frantically manhandle, to no purpose. Konstantinov and Walker sat still, Konstantinov with one bony dark-haired hand around the tiny glass of vodka, Walker with his arms folded and his legs stretched out in front of him, ankles crossed. The exchange between me and Cloquet had ravished them a little, Walker especially, seeing me shift up a gear, the flare of passion. I pictured the B-movie cave again, the multi-coloured stalactite dagger. Was that the sort of thing my son was going to die for? Hocus pocus? Mumbo jumbo? *Magic*? But of course, we were magic ourselves. Zoë. Konstantinov. Cloquet. Walker. My own cursed carcass – what was that if not magic? It didn't feel like it. It felt heavy with ordinariness. The vodka was an unwanted seduction in my fingertips, yet another indication of what a useless mother I was.

Zoë needed changing. There were two disposable diapers in the pocket of her carrier. I didn't want to do it in front of everyone, with trembling hands: Look, kids, the Werewolf mommy. Just like a human mommy, except she doesn't love her babies and she kills people and eats them.

I pulled out one of the diapers. 'Is there somewhere I could see to this?'

Walker got to his feet and nodded for me to follow him. We'd passed three small bedrooms on the way from the front door to the living room, one of which clearly wasn't in use. A single bed with a bare mattress, a bedside table, a falling-apart white Ikea wardrobe. I unhitched Zoë's carrier, took her out and laid her on the bed. Walker stood in the doorway. His consciousness touched me at my hips and collar bone and breasts and thighs. There were these moments when the universe insisted it was purely perverse, had no other aspect or trick: *Now she knows they're going to kill her son, her libido wakes up*. It meant nothing. Or it meant what it always means, that we're strange creatures, that there are internal weather systems we're not answerable for. Less than three hours after I'd found out about Richard's affair I'd masturbated, furiously, thinking about the two of them together in our bed, and had a huge climax. It didn't mean I didn't despise him. It was just something else that was going on. I remembered the Sontag quote from Jake's journal: *Whatever is happening, something else is always going on.*

'I'll tell you what I think,' Walker said.

'What?'

'I think you want us to help you get your son back.'

'I'll pay you.'

'I know. Money'll come in handy for Mike and Natasha.'

135

'Not for you?'

'Sure, for me. I'm not noble.'

'So you'll help me?'

'Well, it's either that or kill you.'

I said nothing. The room smelled of damp carpet and radiators. I wondered who had lived here before it became the place these guys used. I pictured a tired woman, three children, welfare, the television never off.

'You're going to try'n get your kid back anyway,' Walker said. 'Same vamps have Mike's wife. We don't help you, there's a good chance we'll get in each other's way.'

So why not kill us now? I didn't need to say it. We looked at each other. The attraction was a stubborn softness between us. It was also the first sexual honesty I'd felt in months. It didn't mean he wouldn't kill me or I wouldn't kill him. I thought: all men and women should start from that understanding.

'What about Konstantinov?' I asked. 'He doesn't want me dead?' Cynic's advocate, just in case. Maybe they wanted to trade me for Konstantinov's wife? But Jacqueline had the wife, and if Jacqueline wanted me she could have taken me in Alaska. Okay, but there were other vampires. Jacqueline might not care about the Helios Project but the eggheads among the Fifty Families did. If they didn't know I was virus-free they'd want me. Maybe enough to force the Disciples to give up a prisoner. I'd have to tread carefully.

'Mike doesn't want to kill anyone he doesn't have to,' Walker said. 'That might sound crazy to you, but it's all I've got.' Then after a pause: 'Look at me.'

The command startled me, the sudden masculine shift of tone that registers in a girl's heart. And cunt, if she's the wrong type of girl. I looked at him. I had disturbed him, brought him unexpectedly awake. It had been a long time since anything had. But he was disturbing me too. I could imagine all his sweet golden boyhood still there in his shoulders. *Nothing compares to killing the thing you love.* But that was okay because this wouldn't be love.

'I'm not lying to you,' he said. 'You know I'm not.'

Implicit was *how* I knew. Because I was like him. A killer. Killing's a club. No secret handshakes. Just a look. *You've done it too.* Yes.

I conceded, silently, then looked away, ran my index finger down the side of Zoë's cheek. She kicked her legs, made wordless shapes with her mouth. As Delilah had. The thought of the Disciples was a mental loop that made me frantic and exhausted, though I kept telling myself Lorcan was better off with them: They wouldn't need him until midwinter. They'd have to keep him alive till then. Whereas the Helios scientists would have started work straight away. I kept telling myself this but I couldn't shake the nausea, knowing religion was involved, priests, prophecies, rituals. Mumbo fucking jumbo. It meant all bets were off. It meant anything that didn't make sense was possible. Probable, in fact.

'How many of you are there?' I asked.

'Nowhere near enough for what we need. You forget we weren't with the rebels, and most of them have gone underground anyway. I doubt we'll see them again. The ones Murdoch misses will get new faces, new IDs.'

'So I get what, a force of two?'

'Hey, it's two very good guys. But no, you get more than two. There are twenty or so in the same boat as me and Mike, wrongly accused and on the run, plus a few people on the inside who are helping us keep a step ahead. And don't forget you've got Clouseau.'

'He's not ridiculous,' I said. 'I know you think he is, but I'd be dead by now if not for him.'

'I'll take your word for that. But he better understand: no catwalk tantrums.'

'Don't worry about it. He'll be fine.' I was thinking: Twenty or so. Jacqueline's got three hundred vampires. Hollywood odds. Like it or not I was going to have to call Charlie at Aegis again. This wasn't the time to mention it to Walker, however.

'What's in it for you?' I asked. 'Or rather what *was* in it for you, before the chance to make some money presented itself?'

The smile reflex fired, started to allude to our sexual potential – but he couldn't carry it through. He lowered his eyes. 'I owe Mike,' he said. 'You know how it is.'

Not now, whatever the story. Masculine honour, presumably. Fine. It made no difference to me. I was tired. My back ached from the baby carrier. I knew how wonderful it would be to lie down on the bed and curl up with Zoë next to me and let sleep close over me like black water.

'Tell me something,' I said, unfastening the diaper. 'Doesn't it bother you that I've killed your kind?'

The ugly question asked uglily not just out of annoyance with libido's timing but out of the knowledge that if I slept with him it would be good – and however good it was it wouldn't be good enough. For what I was there was only one thing that would ever be good enough. Only one thing and no one to share it with.

'Why?' he answered. 'Does it bother you that I've killed yours?'

20

Back at our hotel in Kensington I settled Zoë in her bassinet and sat Cloquet down opposite me. 'Okay,' I said. 'Tell me the vampire fairy tale.'

The rooms – one bedroom with en suite and a separate lounge/dining area – were luxury corporate, done in shades of beige with occasional planes of dark brown. London's tense damp evening was like a listening intelligence pressed up against the window.

'You think I should have told you,' he said. 'Maybe I should.' He looked tired, and a little crazy.

'Just tell me everything you know,' I said. 'And no bullshit, please, whether you think it's in my interest or not.'

He sank back into the leather armchair, which received him with a sigh. His face was unshaven, bloodshot, pouchy. If I thought of getting rid of him I found I couldn't imagine him living any other kind of life. It was his default to dissolve himself into the will of a monstrous woman. My human occasionally hefted the idea of getting him help, but she couldn't hold it up for long, not with *wulf* sneering and telling her she was wasting her time. *He'll be worse without you, now. That's the nature of the familiar's disease: he can't live with the cure.*

'I told you everything already,' he said. 'Truly.'

'Then tell me again. I want to know what we're dealing with.'

I knew what we were dealing with: the desperation for meaning, for answers, for an invisible scheme of things underpinning the absurd concrete here-and-now. We were dealing with vampires terrified of the vast mathematical silence. Every time I saw Muslim masses bowed in prayer or the Catholic faithful gathered all I saw was fear. Moronically nodding Hasidim, paint-throwing Hindus, shimmying and jabbering Evangelicals, they were all scared shitless this was all there was. Even the Buddhists (whose crinkled tee-heeing lamas always made me want to slap them) were terrified of their own flesh and blood, needed some disembodied desire-free fairyland to shoot for. The Disciples were no different. The belief in a messiah was their collective confession that they couldn't hack it alone. My own darling Jake had spent forty years of his life obsessed with the closest thing werewolves had to a sacred text, Quinn's Book, the story of *The Men Who Became Wolves*. According to Cloquet the book (and the stone tablet that belonged with it) actually existed, though thanks to Mme Delon it was now in the hands of the Undead. Cloquet claimed he'd seen it with his own eyes (though never read it) and there was no reason to disbelieve him, but my feeling was the one Jake ended up with: that even if the book was real it didn't follow that the story it contained was true. And since there was no way of verifying the truth of the story, what difference could it possibly make? Furthermore (since there was no denying the two things had wearily connected, whether I liked it or not), even if the oldest living vampire was old enough to have been alive at the time of the events the story described, there was no reason he'd know anything about them. Certainly no reason he'd know if they were true.

I emerged from my reverie to find Cloquet repeating what, between them, he and Walker had come out with earlier: that according to legend Remshi was the oldest living vampire, that he'd existed, as the useless phrase had it 'from the beginning', that he had extraordinary powers, that periodically he returned to reclaim his kingship.

'Where does he return from?'

'Sleep. He sleeps for long periods, decades, maybe centuries. He comes back when the vampire race needs... needs a kind of renewal. It's vague.'

'So there must be records. They write their history, don't they?'

'There was a fire that destroyed the big vampire library at Pasargadae in 2500 BC,' Cloquet said. 'That was where almost all the authorised histories were kept. There were copies, but not many. Over the years they were scattered, lost. *Some* records since then say Remshi appeared again for a short period in China, around 400 BC. But after that, nothing, and even by then there were many vampires who didn't accept him. Now the world has moved on. Vampires are *pragmatique*. The idea of a messiah has lost... credibility.'

'But if Remshi existed there must have been *living* vampires who remembered him.'

'It's possible. But they don't live that long.'

'What do you mean? They're not immortal?'

He got up and poured himself a Jack Daniels from the minibar. Went into his pocket for cigarettes – remembered Zoë, checked. Old habits. 'They are immortal,' he said. 'But that doesn't mean they can stand living for ever. Most of them give up. They walk out in the daylight or throw themselves on a wooden stake. Not many make it past a thousand years.'

'How do you know all this?'

'Jacqueline.'

Vampire burn-out. (Literally.) It was feasible. The thought of a mere four hundred years gave me vertigo if I dwelt on it, and that was four hundred years *without* losing the ability to have sex and eat normal food and move around in daylight. *Boochies are depressives*, I recalled from one of the journals. *Centuries of no sunlight. Seasonal Affective Disorder on a massive scale. What do you expect?*

Cloquet remained by the minibar, leaning against the wall, visibly in pain. It was high time I found someone to check his shoulder wound. 'The idea of Remshi survived,' he said, 'through Greece and Rome, but always with fewer and fewer believers. There was a revival among the Vikings, but it didn't last. By the time of the Renaissance it was barely a cult. Before Jacqueline came along it was a handful of zealots gathered around two or three priests. The Fifty Families thought of them as a few harmless fools.'

'But not any more.'

'No. Now they are starting to be concerned. The fools are no longer harmless. Or few.'

'What about this *Book of Remshi*?' I asked, hating even having to say the words. 'What about these prophecies?'

'Jacqueline believed they were authentic, but to me it was the weakest part of the story. There are different versions of the book. No one knows where they originated, who wrote them. The earliest copy was from second-century Athens, but claimed to be a translation of something much older. I don't know.'

'But you've seen it?'

'Of course. She had copies.'

'And?'

He shook his head, slowly. 'I didn't understand it. It was all… *devinettes*… riddles. Also mathematics and astronomy. Supposed to give somehow the dates and places of his returns.'

'And Jacqueline knew the where and the when, now, this time?'

'The date is no secret. A full-moon eclipse *au solstice d'hiver* hasn't happened since 1638. But he surfaces before that. Where, only the priests were supposed to know. The priests were supposed to keep it secret until the last moment, in case anyone… in case someone tries something. But she found a way.' He laughed, sans humour. 'She finds a way, always.'

Images again: Lorcan on the altar, Jacqueline naked, mouth open, Jake on his knees, licking her cunt. I realised that right up until this moment I'd felt nothing about her. She'd been an obstacle to be overcome, not a person to be liked or disliked. Now, in the wake of *she finds a way, always*, I knew I wanted to kill her. I wanted to look into her face, let her know I was savouring the moment, then kill her. It would give me a deep, structural satisfaction. It was a small, distinct pleasure to know this, as if a thorn in my foot I'd been blindly putting up with had suddenly been removed.

'I'm sorry I don't know more,' Cloquet said. 'But at the time the whole thing was ridiculous to me.'

It was ridiculous to me now, but that didn't mean my son wouldn't be slaughtered. *Until he drinks the blood of gammou-jhi.* The phrase left me furious and exhausted. Furious because it was hokey and arbitrary and dumb, exhausted because it was no more hokey and arbitrary and dumb than turning into a nine-foot monster every full moon and ripping someone to pieces and eating them. Who was I to dismiss it? Two years ago I would've dismissed the reality I was living right now.

In spite of which I dismissed it. I couldn't help it. When I asked myself if I believed that a several-thousand-years-old vampire had passed-on predictions for his regular reappearance through the coming millennia, and that those predictions had been accurate and successfully preserved, the answer was No, I did not. When I asked myself if Jacqueline and her Disciples believed it, the answer was Yes, they did. And as Walker had pointed out, as far as my son's life was concerned, that was all that mattered.

Walker.

I knew two things. One was that sleeping with him would be a profoundly bad idea. The other was that I was going to sleep with him.

'I'm going to take a bath,' I said to Cloquet. 'You should get some rest.'

He remained where he was for a moment, staring down into the whiskey's flamy gold. Then he lifted the glass, drank what was left, put it on the bar and crossed to the door. Stopped. Didn't turn.

'Maybe you're right,' he said. 'It wasn't my decision to make.'

I didn't reply immediately. My human knew how little it would cost to give him a word of comfort. *Wulf* remained affronted that its familiar had taken the law into its own hands. For a few moments the Curse's grammar insisted a dose of suffering here would be salutary. I balanced. Tiredness had given a flicker to my peripheral vision. Then I remembered Jake telling me a story about Harley storming out of a lover's boudoir once in such a rage he didn't realise until he was in the street he'd put his shoes on wrongly, left shoe on right foot and vice-versa. Jake had laughed, with genuine warm delight. Then, when he'd subsided, he'd said My God, I wish I'd been kinder to Harley.

'It was wrong of you,' I said to Cloquet, quietly. 'But it was wrong for the right reasons. Now for God's sake go and get some sleep.'

21

The next afternoon I phoned Walker with what I thought was bad news: Charlie Proctor, Jake's (and subsequently my) man at Aegis, was gone. When I'd called the number a woman with a very slight Irish accent told me Mr Proctor was no longer with the company. No, there was no new number. No, she couldn't pass on a message. No, there was no further information she could give me. She *could* put me through to Mr *Hurst*, Mr Proctor's replacement – but I knew by then these were all the wrong noises. I told her I'd call back. Initially I wasn't going to say anything about it to Walker. What would be the point? We couldn't use Aegis now anyway. But something made me call him.

There was a silence his end, then he said: 'Don't say anything else. Hang up. I'll leave you a message at reception. Don't use this number and don't bring your cell. Tell Cloquet not to use his phone either.' Then *he* hung up.

Four hours later he picked me up in the parking lot under the Hammersmith mall. The BMW 4x4 had been replaced with a Ford mini-van that said EMMERSON ENGINEERING on the side. Seeing Zoë strapped to me in her carrier he said: 'You know it's going to be tough getting camouflage gear to fit her, right?'

'What's the matter?' I asked him.

'Did you leave your cellphone behind?'

'Yes. What is it?'

'Guess who Murdoch worked for between leaving Special Forces and joining WOCOP?'

A moment for it to sink in. Aegis. I felt stupid – and incapable of calculating what damage I might already have done. Leaving aside the warning klaxon of Proctor's disappearance (was he dead? For refusing to rat me out? Had he been a Person I Could Trust after all?) it was obviously possible Murdoch knew about the aborted mission at Merryn's. But if he did, why was I still alive? Maybe, like Grainer before him, he was old school, killed werewolves only in their full-moon form? In which case I had twenty-four days before I could expect an attempt on my life. And what if Draper and Khan had stuck around and seen Walker and Konstantinov arrive? Murdoch could be following us right now.

'It's probably okay,' Walker said. 'It's ten years since Murdoch worked for Aegis, so I doubt many of his buddies are still there, but we don't want to take unnecessary risks. Sure it's possible he heard about Merryn's, but there's no reason to assume the Aegis grunts knew who you were. Besides, supernatural targets aren't much on Murdoch's mind right now. All he cares about is the Purge. You're probably safe. It's me who's about to get shot in the head. Maybe you should drive?'

It was raining, heavily, and almost dark. We were headed west out of the city, towards the M4.

'I should've told you I was thinking of using Aegis,' I said. 'I'm sorry.'

'Forget it. But from now on...?'

'Okay.'

It was, of course, pressing on us that we were alone together. After last night's mutual blatancy we enjoyed a rich awkwardness.

Whether I liked it or not the Whore of Babylon's vacation was over. There was no denying what was going on, to employ Aunt Theresa's euphemism, 'down there'. In the morning's snatched sleep I'd had surreal sex dreams: faceless glistening male and female bodies fucking in groggy desperation to a soundtrack like an abattoir. Sometimes I was one of them, in human form. Other times not. One very clear repeated image of dragging my monster snout across a guy's come-lathered belly, leaving a trail of dark blood. I'd woken face hot, hands unequivocally at it between my legs. I'd hesitated – *you see this through, Missy, and the genie'll be well and truly out of the bottle* – then yielded, and come, giantly, with a delicious feeling of comprehensive unravelling. *Now you've done it*. Well, yes, I had. *Come what may*, dark hilarity said, pun intended.

'Anyway,' Walker continued, 'in the bag by your feet are two clean phones, one for you, one for the Frenchman. It's unlikely yours were tagged, but since Proctor's disappeared we'd be dumb to take chances. Use only these as of now. You'll have to switch hotels too.'

The masturbation memory had made me risibly wet. *Wulf* was properly awake now, curling her lips and licking her teeth. It wasn't supposed to be this way. As the mother of a missing child my existence was supposed to be unrelieved agony. There wasn't supposed to be room for anything else, especially not this. Still, here it was. Whatever is happening, something else is always going on. It's only bad art and gutter journalism that insist otherwise.

'How long before we hear anything?' I asked him.

'Can't say,' he said. 'Jacqui'll split her people up. It's not like you can move three hundred vampires in somewhere without somebody noticing. She'll disperse the bulk of them but keep her favourites close. She'll keep your kid with her, for sure, but Natasha? I don't know. You understand that's our priority, right?

I mean, no offence, but the only thing Mike gives a fuck about is his wife.'

'I know,' I said.

'And look – ' the smile again, the slip back into sparkling defence – 'if we get her out and I'm still alive, I'm guessing that'll be about where I quit while I'm ahead. Unless of course you and I have fallen in love by then.'

'We never discussed fees,' I said.

'No, but you were going to fork out for Aegis, and I know *they* don't come cheap.'

'That's true. I should've kept my mouth shut. I'm not very good at this.'

'Let's talk about it later. It's ruining the atmosphere. That's one quiet kid you got there. You know, if you need to breastfeed her, I won't be embarrassed.'

'I'll bear it in mind, but I just fed her.'

'Does she never cry?'

'Hardly. I think maybe four times since birth. She's like the little Lord Jesus. Or maybe she'll be a mute.' It was true Zoë was an extraordinarily quiet child. She slept, she woke up, she fed, she peed and threw up and negligibly pooped – but she rarely shed a tear.

Silently judging you on her brother's behalf.

'What *are* you going to do with her?' Walker asked. 'If and when we're good to go?'

Well, yes, that was the question. Leave her with Cloquet? Stay home with her and trust someone *else* to rescue her brother? Take her along? The first two options were hard to swallow. The third was farcical. So far I'd dealt with the problem by hoping something would come along to magically solve it. 'Ask me when we're good to go,' I said. 'In the meantime, what's the story with – Fuck!'

'What's wrong?'

Someone walked over my grave.

Or rather ran over it, dragging a rake. Zoë's body against mine registered it, as if we'd shared an electric shock or an explosion of pins and needles. I felt her tighten, then relax. Two seconds and it was over.

'What is it?'

'I don't know. Some weird... Since I've been here I've had these little episodes of...'

'Of what?'

'Of something being close. Something passing close to me.'

'Something bad?'

'I don't know.'

'Do you want me to stop the car?'

'No, it's okay. Actually, wait, can we not go on the freeway? I mean, can we just stay in the city?' Whatever it was it was here, I was certain. No matter how much I wanted it to be Jake's ghost hurling itself at the barrier between us, I knew it wasn't.

'No problem,' Walker said. 'You sure you're okay?'

'I'm fine. Sorry.'

It was a reminder to him of what I was, what he was in the car with. I could feel sanity working in him against the attraction. Last night's adrenaline had said anything was possible. Now he was marvelling at himself. He wanted to say something, make a joke about it, but the moment had left him adrift. The road lights slid over his pretty profile. *His pretty profile.* See what you've done now? See what you've let loose?

'I'll ask you what I was going to ask you,' I said. 'What's the story with Konstantinov?'

I wasn't intending to listen, whatever the story was; it was just to give him something to do while I continued groping after what I'd felt a moment ago (fear? déjà vu? a kind of abstract

149

arousal?), but once he started talking I got drawn in in spite of myself...

Konstantinov, he told me, grew up on a State Farm in Morshansk and at fourteen fell in love with the director's daughter, Daria Petrov, who was his age, and had his depth, and was in love with him.

'And when I say in love,' Walker said, 'I mean *unholy intensity*. These two could've sat down with Romeo and Juliet and held their heads up. You can't talk to Mike about it, or at least you couldn't, for years. Even now you've got to pick your moment and watch your tone.'

The young lovers were in the habit of sneaking out late at night for erotic trysts in a nearby woods. One such night, in the summer of 1980, they were joined by an uninvited guest. A vampire.

'It was one of those lousy synchronicities,' Walker said. 'Up until then they'd fooled around, but they'd never actually fucked. That night, for the first time, under a big oak tree, they went all the way. It changed Mike for ever.' Walker shook his head, as in sad amazement. 'I guess there are only a handful of first times like that per millennium,' he said. 'Everyone else's seems to be a horror story. Or a comedy.' He gave me a quick look.

'Horror-comedy,' I said, thinking in spite of the lingering disturbance of my first time, when I was sixteen, with Luke Peters in the dunes at a Rehoboth beach party. Everything was going okay until a breeze blew a torn garbage bag onto his bare ass and he got the fright of his life, and I couldn't stop laughing, then had to crawl away and throw up because the evening's booze and weed had caught up with me.

'You were lucky,' Walker said. 'Mine was straight horror. Anyway, as far as Mike was concerned that was it: this was the girl he was going to spend the rest of his life with. It's a Russian thing, that epic certainty. Americans aren't built for it.'

Blissfully razed, sensually reinvented, the young Konstantinov had walked a few paces off to empty his bladder. When he came back, he saw a strange sight. Daria seemed to be asleep, but with her back arched and her head several inches off the ground. Her arms were limp. It was as if an invisible magician was halfway through levitating her. For a moment Konstantinov stood, uncomprehending. Then he perceived the large white hand at the base of her neck, and cried out – at which the vampire looked up, and the visual puzzle solved itself. The creature – a mature male, dark-haired, long-bodied – was hanging upside down from the lowest bough, one hand under Daria's back, the other under her neck. It must have been in the tree the whole time, watching them. It stared at Konstantinov for a few moments, then raised Daria further off the ground and returned its teeth to her throat.

'He could've run,' Walker said. 'She was dead anyway. Anyone else would've run. *I* would have.'

Konstantinov didn't. He bent, searched the ground, picked up in his left hand what he knew was an inadequate bit of dead wood, and advanced on the creature.

'He had a pencil in the other hand,' Walker said. 'In his jacket pocket, hidden. That's Mikhail. A *pencil*. He's going to feint with the deadwood in his left and punch this pencil in as hard as he can with his right. I asked him why he didn't run. You know what he said?'

'What?'

'He said: "Have you ever been in love?"'

We passed Kew Bridge station, and in a moment were crossing the bridge itself. Londoners were under umbrellas, or hurrying, shoulders hunched, faces crimped, or steaming in shop doorways, talking on cellphones. The human world I wasn't entitled to any more but couldn't ditch. *Have you ever been in love?* The words had softly alarmed both of us, in the van's little fan-heated space.

I had a piercing feeling of love moving through history like a thin glimmering waterway. Suddenly in the middle of things you suffered these poignancies, found yourself blinking or swallowing or having to look the other way.

'According to Mike,' Walker said, 'the vampire was surprised, maybe even a little moved. He put the girl's body down and dropped to the ground. Mike was five feet away. He could smell Daria's blood. He said that was the first time he realised blood had a smell, you know?'

Walker had forgotten what I was again. I didn't answer. Then he remembered. Yes, she knows about the smell of blood. Still, there was part of him that didn't care, that had gone on ahead and was waiting for the rest of him to catch up. If it ever did there was no telling what shape his life might take. I imagined my mother saying: Have him, Lulu. Do you know how few men there are *worth* having? I imagined the feel of his hard waist between my hands, the sweet shameless sensation of wrapping my legs around him, around all the delicious complications...

Konstantinov never got to find out if his pencil plan would've worked. Something disturbed the air very close to his head. Simultaneously, he saw the vampire jerk, as if someone had jabbed him with a cattle prod. At that moment the moon slipped clear of the clouds and he saw the wooden shaft – thicker than an archer's arrow – stuck in the monster's chest. A man's voice said, in Moscow Russian: 'For Christ's sake, kid, I nearly took your fucking head off. Why didn't you run?'

'And the rest,' Walker said, 'is history.' The vampire's killer was a member of the Hunt's Soviet division. He and his partner had been trailing the booch for a week. Mikhail would've left with them there and then, but they wouldn't let him. It took him two years to track the organisation down and get in, but once he's set his mind on something...'

Since then, *for thirty years*, Walker stressed, Konstantinov had refused to get close to a woman – until twelve months ago, when he'd met Natasha. 'Who knows?' Walker said. 'Maybe there was a specific enormous amount of not loving anyone he'd set himself to do, a penance he had to complete. I think he didn't even know himself until he met her. But when he did meet her he reacted as if she'd been sent to him by God.'

And since God was never satisfied, Konstantinov had lost *her* to the Undead, too.

'It's my fault,' Walker said, as the Thames reappeared on our left. 'He was only two verified kills away from a serious bonus, and the money would've been a big help to him and Natasha. They were going to buy a little bar in Croatia or Turkey or Greece. He wanted to get out as soon as he met her, but I talked him into holding out for the bonus.'

Which was my cue to tell him it wasn't his fault, but my mind had gone back to *someone walked over my grave*. I still couldn't pin it down, not even whether I'd been afraid. The only thing I knew for sure was that Zoë had felt it too.

'The vampire body back at Merryn's,' I said. 'You said it was one of Jacqueline's priests. What's the story there? You think one of Merryn's goons killed it?'

'Well, it was decapitated, so I'm guessing not. There wasn't anything there it could've been decapitated *with*, as far as I could see.'

'So... ?'

'I don't know. Maybe there was someone else there we don't know about. I'm waiting for a call from my WOCOP guys. They'll have discovered it by now. They're slow, but they get there eventually.'

We drove back to the parking lot under the Hammersmith mall. The place smelled of freezing concrete and aluminum ducts and exhaust fumes. Now it had come to getting out of the car I didn't want to. The thought of the journey back to the hotel made me feel exposed. The city's spaces would be full of abrasive surveillance. I wondered what Walker would do if I kissed him. Amongst other things he'd think of all the human flesh and blood my other mouth had chewed-up and swallowed.

'You okay?' he said.

No, I'm not. I'm lonely and exhausted and no kind of mother and on top of all that migrained with fucking idiotic desire.

'I'm fine,' I said, and opened the passenger door.

At which moment a silencered bullet went with an unmistakable *tch* clean through its window and just past the side of my head.

22

Walker yanked me towards him and slammed the vehicle into gear. 'Stay low,' he said, very calmly. A second bullet – daintily audible despite the gunned engine and screeching tyres – pierced the windshield and buried itself in the back seat. Silver? Zoë's head had just missed the stick-shift. I swivelled quickly to get myself between her and the dashboard as the van lurched and swerved out of its bay, passenger door still open.

'Watch her head,' Walker said. There were other tyres squealing somewhere behind us. The passenger door smacked a concrete pillar and slammed shut. Its window shattered – as if it had just remembered what, being glass, it was supposed to do. My face was in Walker's lap. Khakis with a washed smell that reminded me of the laundry room in the basement of the 11th Street brownstone – this and the connotation of fellatio, since even in these moments the connections are the connections, the brain says Don't ask me I just work here. Zoë, startled by the slam and crash and live to my shot-up heart rate, started crying. Which added the precise minor torture of not being able to comfort her properly.

'Hold on,' Walker said.

I lost all sense of direction. There was a pattern – accelerate, brake, sharp turn, accelerate – and I knew we were climbing the ramps to street level, but I was no better oriented than I would've been in a tumble drier.

Suddenly a longer, straighter run, Walker's abdominals tense, what felt like a moment of pure silence – then the windshield shattering as we crashed through the exit barrier, and the smell and sounds of London's wet evening rushed in.

'Are they still following?' I asked.

'Can't be sure. Stay down. We're in the goddamned high street here.'

'Who is it?'

'Can't see. Murdoch's guys, probably. Her ladyship okay?'

The change in air and sound had shocked Zoë quiet again. 'She's fine,' I said. 'What are we going to do?'

'Got to ditch this van. It's made, obviously. I think the best thing is… Wait. Hang on. Bump coming—' How high Zoë and I came up off the seat told me we were still travelling fast. Car horns detonated around us. A pedestrian right outside my absent window said, 'Fuck *me.*' The air flowing in was cold, tasted of wet pavements and exhaust fumes and fried food.

'Can you run?' Walker said.

'Yes.'

'Fast?'

'Yes.'

'Okay, in a minute I'm going to stop. We're going to be right outside the Tube mall. We get out, we run through. There are cabs on the other side.'

'Are you fucking crazy?'

'Tougher to follow a car that's got twenty-thousand doubles. Trust me. This shit-heap's no good to us now. You got the clean phones?'

'Yes.'

'Okay, when I tell you. Only when I tell you. Got it?'

'Got it.'

It happened fast but was filled with detail: the smell of Walker's leather jacket; a pink and white ice cream van going by; Zoë's moist hand like a little sea creature momentarily pressed to my lips.

'Big bump then we go,' Walker said. 'Ready—' We mounted a kerb violently. Pedestrians scattered with a weird collective sound, part fear, part outrage, part delight that something unexpected was happening.

'Go!'

People's faces went by not, as the convention has it, in a blur, but in vivid snapshots. I had a brief awareness of London's cold darkness and the softness and heat of the crowd, then we were through the entrance and racing down the central concourse, Walker with the gun tokenly concealed under his jacket, me clutching Zoë like a football, thinking any second now... any second now... you feel the bullet just that awful fraction before you hear the shot... Shop fronts were distinct and urgent and inane – WH Smith; Superdrug; Tesco Express; lousy soulless things to be the last things you see – then we were past the escalators and back out in the street.

I looked behind us. If there was pursuit it was concealed by the trawling shoppers.

'In here!'

Walker was already opening the door of the first cab in a line of three. The lit interior was a thing of beauty. Holding Zoë close, I got in.

23

I t took half an hour and a lot of side streets before Walker
was satisfied we weren't being followed, and even then he
advised against going back to the Kensington hotel.

'Were they shooting at you or me?'

'Who knows?' he said. 'It wasn't Murdoch, though.'

'How come?'

'He wouldn't have missed. I'm just surprised he's opened it
up to the rank and file. I thought he'd want the pleasure himself.'

'Maybe they were shooting at both of us,' I said. 'I mean it's
still WOCOP, right? It's not like there's been a werewolf
amnesty.'

'Either way we've got to assume your hotel's made. My place
too. Mike and I are running out of safe houses.'

I was worried about Cloquet. I'd been gone hours. He'd be
chewing the wallpaper by now. But if his cell and the room phone
were bugged, how could I reach him and tell him to get out?

In the end I called the concierge. By the grace of the God who
wasn't there he remembered me (I'd run out of diapers for Zoë
the night we checked in and had to find the nearest twenty-four-
hour store) and though it took a little persuasion he agreed to
what I asked. He would call 'Mr Malraux' in Suite 472 and tell
him to come to reception for an urgent message from 'Ms
Atwood'. I would wait ten minutes, then call the concierge on

his own cellphone, which he would hand over to Cloquet. Even Walker's suspicion didn't extend to the concierge's personal phone being tapped.

Cloquet was predictably hopped-up. He didn't say it but it was obvious he thought I was planning to ditch him. He'd wrecked my trust and I'd absconded with my American beach boy. There would have to be reassurance, I knew – but not now. Now was practicalities. I gave him the clean cell number and told him what had happened. He had to get out of the hotel. We travelled light, so it shouldn't be hard for him to leave discreetly. The concierge would arrange for a car to pick him up at the kitchen exit. From there he could join me at the Dorchester, the first hotel that sprang to mind, probably from a James Bond movie. Walker advised me to get out of London altogether, but I couldn't face it. I wanted to be here when they got a lock on Jacqueline and the Disciples. Besides, my British geography was lousy. At least in London I could find my way around.

I checked in: Jane Dickinson. (Cloquet would be Pierre Rennard again for a while.) Walker came up with me to what turned out to be a warmly lit art deco suite. Pink, cream, pale green, walnut trims and deep carpet the colour of Caribbean sand. The snug solid feel of a luxury liner's cabin, a welcome shock after the raw evening and spent adrenaline. I closed the drapes. A fifty got the bellhop out to the nearest seven-eleven with a list of infant essentials, and twenty minutes later Zoë was back in Pampers and Sudocrem credit. I fed her (with my back to Walker; unembarrassed mutual understanding; and a nod to keeping the flesh's erotic powder dry) while he called Konstantinov and filled him in. No news on Jacqueline from their WOCOP insider. I put Zoë over my shoulder, did the rubbing, the patting, the humming, the pacing, while Walker fixed himself a Laphroaig from the bar. Five minutes and one unladylike burp later my girl was asleep. In the absence of her bassinet the only place for her was the vast bed. I put her down in it, stabilised by four of the hotel's monumental pillows. Then I rang reception with a message to be given to 'Monsieur Rennard' on his arrival: Check in. Go to your room. Wait for my call.

None of which was lost on Walker.

When I put the phone down there we were, looking at each other.

The gunshots and the chase had rushed us here, but now that we *were* here postponement – which is all it would ever have been – was pointless. We stood facing each other, ten feet apart. I wondered if I was still too close to childbirth for him. Or, less vaguely, still too fat. The post-partum weight had dropped at (how not?) freakish speed, but I was a way off my regular hundred and fifteen pounds. I've been a hundred and fifteen pounds since I turned eighteen, and the Curse had made no difference. (No difference to the human weight, that is. I'd only weighed myself transformed once, after my ninth kill: a widower in a high-ceilinged spidery house on the edge of the *Parc National des Cèvennes*, who for some reason had an archaic set of pharmacist's scales in his kitchen. Blood-groggy and meat-slow, I'd clambered gorily on. The scale read 185.5. That seemed impossible – until I realised it was in kilograms. I had to wait till I was human again to work it out. Four hundred and nine pounds. *Hey, Lauren, it's Lu. I know we haven't seen each other in years, but I just thought you'd get a kick out of this…*) I never bothered weighing myself when I was pregnant, but I must've been one-forty at least. Now I guessed I was around one-twenty-seven. Thirteen pounds shed in six days. A human record, if only I'd been human. I still had a cheeky little pot belly, and my breasts remained double their former size (although 32B doesn't double-up to much), but the rest of me was almost back to pre-pregnancy dimensions.

So here we were, Walker and I, looking at each other the way you look at each other when there you are, looking at each other. I knew the longer we waited the more I'd start to think that no matter how good it was it wouldn't be good enough, so I crossed the room to stand in front of him, sufficiently close for our bodies' heat to touch. Deep gravity brought his hands to my waist. *Wulf* was making silent fiesta in my skin, yes, but it was humanly good to be touched too, to be alone with someone at the secret feast that went all the way back to Adam and Eve. You looked at each other and felt just how old the contract was, the warm-faced commitment to the adventure, the stepping together out of the light into the rewarding darkness.

There were forces aswirl in him. Desire was one. Fear was another. The knowledge that if he did this he'd be leaving himself behind. The admission that leaving himself behind was what he had to keep doing. *I was getting out anyway*, he'd said of WOCOP. It was the pattern of his life all the way back to whatever it was that had first derailed him; he went into things for a while, let them give him a new skin, but always, sooner or later, shed it and moved on. Only the smile and the brightness were constant. That and the benign desirability, the infallible charm.

I kissed him. His mouth was Laphroaig-flavoured, but that was fine, that was grist to my mill. His hips pressed against mine, hands tightened on my waist. The heat between us blurred and a little net of electricity settled on my cunt.

Something still restrained him.

'What?' I asked, leaning back to get his face into focus.

He kept his hands on me. 'Are you okay?' he asked. 'To do this?'

Anatomically, he meant. He was the sort of guy who'd know

how long after having a baby a woman's parts would be out of action. He'd know because he was the sort of guy who would've been in this situation before.

But not with a woman like me.

'I heal fast,' I said. 'Very fast.'

'Really?'

'Yes. Kiss me.'

It was hard not to hurry. If Zoë woke up or Cloquet ignored his instructions and knocked we knew we probably wouldn't recover. I took down the spare comforter from the wardrobe and spread it on the floor. No chairs, no tables, no up against the wall, no bent over the escritoire or swinging from the ceiling light. Nothing that might increase our chances of fucking it up. This was the other reason it was tough not to hurry: I was *in* a hurry. The morning's self-help excluded I hadn't had sex in over three months. Now, with *wulf* back at full libidinal tilt, dalliance was the last thing on my mind. *I only have sex with women I dislike,* Jake had written. To avoid falling in love and killing the beloved. Yes. But this was all right because it wouldn't *be* love.

Still standing, I unbuttoned his shirt and pushed it and the jacket off his shoulders. They fell to the floor with a sound that settled us deeper into not needing to say anything. His upper body was understatedly muscled – honest function rather than the confections of the gym – and flecked with little scars like ciphers. Our eyes met, risked lingering, but looked away before the smile that might have sounded a fatal note of mere friendliness. He tugged my blouse out from my jeans and began with the buttons. Got all four undone without time too loudly simmering. The bra, too, hallelujah.

In a great flash of awkward practicality I realised milk might come if he sucked my breasts – but again, he'd know that, and know that I knew. It would either happen or not, and if it did

162

it wouldn't bother him. He was a creature of easy physical promiscuity, Dionysian without fuss: once his desire was established everything of the body was sacred.

Guilt was available to me, of course, but my human was bigger than it and *wulf* simply didn't give a shit. Superficial aesthetics said what I was doing – having sex while my child was in danger – was ugly, but the deeper being dismissed them. There were these necessary dark segues, unarguable with. Even dumb movies these days knew Eros found its way to the borders of grief, loss, longing, boredom, anger, shame – and was given entry. The real danger here wasn't guilt but sadness. Not just mine (and not just for my son or my failed heart, but for my amputation from *normality*) but Walker's too, for whatever long-ago damage he'd wrapped his mix of levity and glitter and sex around.

This was my human, by the way, busy, humanly, with him, Walker, the person. There was the forlorn flame at his centre, the lost boy around which the smiling hidden man had grown that my vestigial romantic was sniffing after, while a later self (with Lauren's voice) said, No, leave it, it's nothing to do with you and in any case it'll ruin him sexually for you just like the little old guy behind the curtain ruins Oz for everyone the first time they see it. So I kissed him, dirtily, and felt through his mouth and his chest under my hands the last threads of his resistance sweetly snapping. He was going to do this, oh yes, surrender to the devious drug. The big taboo – *another species* – broke negligibly in the end, and let him into warmth, my warmth, me. I could feel his imagination making room for the atrocities, since there was no denying them, since they were there in my skin and in my mouth and in the sly heat of my cunt that he wanted now, oh yes, he wanted, no matter what, no matter what, no matter what.

By telepathic agreement we separated to get our jeans and

underwear off, then reconvened, side by side, face to face. I pushed him onto his back and slid on top of him. A little milk *had* crept out. He neither avoided nor made a fetish of it. To him it was part of the body's casually sanctified continuum. If he desired you, physically, he desired all of you. It was what the girls in the schoolyard had animally sensed in him as a kid. It was why they'd exempted him. I reached over to my purse, extracted a condom, tore the foil and slithered down his torso. His cock, modest in size but with a lovely lewd optimistic arch, visibly throbbed. *Packed with blood,* the monster reminded me, with a nudge and a wink and a lick of her teeth – but I was far enough from full moon to shush her. He got up on his elbows. His face was full of life focused on me, the blue-green eyes glimmering, the mouth edging into a less innocent version of its smile. I breathed, open-mouthed on the head of his cock, watched its rhythmic obedience, suffered a mental image of trying to bite clean through it, a mess of flailing blood, Walker screaming. One more cunning look up at him – *yes, I know exactly how good this is going to feel* – then I took him into my mouth. I felt him swallow, sensed his head tip back – then forward again for another greedy look.

Later. More of this later. For now I was desperate, unequivocal, righteously selfish. I got the condom on without disaster, slid back up his body, took him in one hand, looked down at his wholly seduced and radiantly hungry face, and lowered myself onto his cock.

24

I t wasn't perfect, but it was more than enough for a start. His instincts were good, hands and mouth read the signals, moved more or less to where they were wanted. It was understood between us that the first big expenditure was for me, me, me, all for dreadful me, and he held back and worked with a mixture of gallantry and artisanal concentration to make me come. Not that that – in my state – was any great achievement. It took about three minutes. Then another three, then five, then ten. Then I settled down and could be reasoned with. When *he* came (we were approximately in the spoons position) all his strength gathered in his hips and chest and his arms wrapped around me and his breath jabbed soft and hot at my ear and a note of tenderness was there at the end like a lovely curlicue and I liked him because there was no disguising the honest male gladness that went from his body out to mine.

'Holy moly,' he said, afterwards.

'That's my phrase,' I said.

'Is it?'

'Yes.'

'I'll never use it again.'

'The way to handle this, by the way, is to not talk about it.'

'This?'

'What we've just done.'

'My lips are sealed.'

'I don't mean other people. I mean each other.'

'Got it.'

'Are you always this biddable?'

'Well, you know, you're like a horse whisperer.'

I was thinking of the diaries. (I would often be thinking of the diaries. Perennial bloodless infidelity would be part of my package, for decades. Maybe for ever.) *Modern humans talk their love affairs into an early grave*, Jake had written. *Eros hasn't got a fucking chance with people yammering at each other about everything the whole time.* I think we should talk. *No, believe me, we shouldn't. You want to give love a chance? Find someone you can't communicate with.*

Walker's cellphone rang. It was his WOCOP insider, Hoyle, with an update. The attempted hit on us in the Hammersmith parking lot was from a couple of loose cannons from the organisation's Spanish division – get this – *on vacation*. Murdoch had risked an international meltdown by beating them half to death when he found out. The dead vampire was definitely one of the priests, almost certainly six-hundred-year-old Raphael Cavalcanti, since he'd been logged in London only one week before, but until the remaining (known) priests were accounted for it was impossible to be sure. Meanwhile still no news on Jacqueline and the Disciples. Therefore no news on Lorcan. Which shrivelled me back to my dreary dimensions.

Walker felt the mood shift. Loudly didn't ask what the problem was. Part of me was thankful he didn't, part of me wished he would. I hadn't told anyone, not even Cloquet, the filthy truth of the kidnapping: that my heart had remained grotesquely neutral, though I'd held him in my arms still warm and wet from birth. *You can't live if you can't accept what you are,* it said in Jake's last journal, *and you can't accept what you are if you can't say what you do. The power of naming, as old as Adam.*

If I stopped to think about it too long the moment would go.

'There's something you should know about me,' I said. 'Something *else*, I mean.'

'What?'

'I'm defective.'

'Defective?'

'Yes.'

He didn't say anything. Zoë whimpered for a moment in her sleep, then fell silent again. We were still lying on the comforter on the floor, on our backs now, not touching.

'When my son was born,' I said, to the ceiling, 'I didn't feel anything for him. There was just a blank space where love should've been. Then he was gone.'

He didn't reply for a while. Nor, thank God, did he try taking my hand or giving me a hug.

'A lacuna,' he said, eventually.

'What?'

'A lacuna. You know the word?'

In spite of everything a slight irritation because I couldn't, immediately, remember what it meant. Then I did. A lacuna was a gap or a blank or a blind spot. In manuscripts a missing word or section of text.

'Yeah,' I said. 'I know the word.'

Again he fell silent. Then he said: 'There's no comfort.' Not a question. A diagnosis.

'There's no comfort,' I agreed.

'Even though you know it was nothing.'

'Was it nothing?'

'It was just bad luck that they took him in a lacuna. Sixty seconds later the love might have come flooding in. It's there for her ladyship.'

It's there for her ladyship.

Was it? The Devil's subtlest temptations are the ones you yield to without even knowing you've given in. There was footage, which, though I'd shut the bulk of myself off from it while it was happening, made itself available now: me kissing her head and smelling her scalp and talking to her and calling her Sugar or Missy or Toots, which were all names my mother had called me. I'd done all this obliquely, in terrible secret from my hardened Pharaonic heart, all without really looking at my daughter, who was like a little murderer, who, if I did look at her, met all my hidden love with all my exposed failure. Her eyes held all the rights I'd forfeited. She was like God: said nothing, reflected everything I'd done, everything I'd failed to do, everything I was and everything I wasn't. If I came in from the dreamy periphery of talking and kissing and not looking, if I came, honestly and fully to her, she could look at me so that my love felt like an obscene thing, a greed, a vice, and I got a feeling of falling away from her, thinning, into nothingness. Love turned me to her and turning to her exposed the too-lateness of the love.

'It wasn't a lacuna,' I said. 'I felt nothing for him because I thought if I did I might kill him. That would've been the worst thing. And that's what we do, our kind. We do the worst thing. Just so you know.'

Our auras lay against each other, allowed the passage of unspoken information. What I'd just told him wouldn't stop him wanting me. He was drawn to monstrosity greater than his own. He'd long ago stopped looking for anything more than temporarily diverting sex among the normal women of the world. He believed his only chance for depth was with someone more lost or mutant than himself.

'What about now?' he asked. 'Do you think you're a danger to your children now?'

In the pale pink bedroom with Delilah Snow the wardrobe

door had mysteriously opened, and when I'd looked up at the sound I'd been introduced to my reflection in its mirror. A monster with a human baby in its hands. Like the third recurring daydream. Except of course in the third recurring daydream the baby was a werewolf, and it was hanging from the mother monster's jaws.

'I don't know,' I said.

I lay still, existing with what I was, with what people would think of me. There was a superficial or movie-ish impulse to get up and get dressed, disgusted afresh at my talent for carnality where there should just have been visible torment, but I ignored it, let it burn out, leaving only the level of reality that wasn't interested in the movies, the alleged consensus, the bad script. It wasn't defiance or self-forgiveness. It was my soul's weird expansion to accommodate itself, all its opposites and approximations. I thought of how exhausted the God who wasn't there must be, who'd been doing this from the Beginning, with no end in sight.

We didn't speak for a while. He didn't say: Don't cry. He just waited it out. The hotel hummed gently under our backs. *Never underestimate the solace of a quality hotel*, Jake had written. *It's like you. Full of ghosts. For the werewolf, natural sympathy of structure.*

'I forgot to tell you,' Walker said. 'According to Hoyle, Merryn was working on a new translation of *The Book of Remshi*.'

Let the other stuff go, for now. Good. I'd said all I was going to say about it. I liked him, bitterly, for sensing it.

'For Jacqueline?' I asked.

'We don't know. It may have had nothing to do with her. Merryn was a genuine scholar.'

'Seems a bit of a coincidence, though, doesn't it?'

'I know. But even if he was working on it for her, if she found out he was a mole the commission would've been revoked. Terminally.'

'Where is it, anyway?

'The translation? God knows. Jacqueline's crew were pretty thorough. WOCOP have been over Merryn's place since we were there. According to Hoyle they didn't find so much as a note for the milkman.'

'Can you get me a copy? I mean not Merryn's, obviously, just the most widely used one? I feel like I'm flying blind.'

'From what I remember it's pretty impenetrable. Mike might have a copy somewhere... Or maybe on disk. I'll see what I can do.'

Zoë woke up. Reintroduced herself to the world in a short series of burbles, then fell silent, as if waiting for its reply.

I got to my feet. I was the reply. I was the reply she was stuck with.

25

The days that followed were a static ordeal of waiting for the phone to ring, relieved by increasingly good therefore increasingly bad sex with Walker. Around the fourth or fifth time we did it I stopped kidding myself I wasn't playing with fire. Our understanding was immediate and shocking, mutual intuition that skipped chunks of language without surprise and said, loud and clear: Danger. Ten years ago we would have congratulated ourselves. Now we kept our mouths shut and our eyes averted. Not just because we were older and sufficiently mangled, but because we knew that in our case cause for congratulation was cause for retreat. There was no avoiding it during sex, however, when our eyes met in moments of letting it be what it was: something far more than was good for us. This isn't safe, is it? No, it isn't. Don't stop. Oh God don't stop.

Post-coitally the Hollywood every American carries insinuated its norms, repeatedly suggested the afterglow scene where I doodled on his chest and asked the history of each of his scars, or told him some endearingly embarrassing story from my girl-hood. We ignored it. Silence stopped us slipping into the lousy script, but exposed us to the ominous thrill of how little we needed to say. And despite our efforts prosaic epiphanies ambushed us. Once, getting back into my jeans, I got my foot caught and lost my balance. I didn't fall over, but went through a Chaplinesque sideways hopping routine which he watched, smiling and saying: Easy there, tiger... *easy*, which made me laugh for the first time since before Alaska, and which opened another terrible flower of sympathy between us. At some point I'd realised he was shy of saying my name. He called me Miss D, if he had to call me anything. Then once, without thinking, he said, quietly, 'Talulla?' when I was lying on him and the room was dark and he wasn't sure if I'd fallen asleep. The smart thing would have been for me to pretend I *was* asleep — but instead I found myself up on one elbow, kissing his mouth, all femalely tender and lit-up by him unguardedly saying my name, unguardedly, that was the thing, it was such a frail brave thing to be unguarded with someone... telling myself the whole time, don't do this... don't do this... for God's sake don't do this you *idiot*... and feeling the gap between him and his previous self widening, as if it were a planet he was drifting away from into vast and utterly unknown space. Me.

We carried on not-talking about any of it. Talking about it could only lead to how stupid we'd been to start and how stupid we'd be not to stop. I imagined my mother watching the delicious mess I was making of things. She would have approved, since she was always for life and life was at its best a delicious mess; she would have approved but cut short the honeymoon period of shirking the facts: He's not a werewolf, Talulla. Which means either make him one or dump him. Otherwise the delicious mess becomes a car-wreck. The question of whether I *could* Turn a person was, naturally, refreshed, but no less bedevilled by common sense: who in his right mind would thank me for doing it? You couldn't start a love affair with a more selfish act. A love affair? Hardly, by the measure of mine and Jake's — but there was potential around us like a massing storm. Superficially we had the strangers-in-a-strange-land myth to draw on, bodies that fit together in expert cooperation, the aphrodisiacal near-ness of death and the mesmerising profane turn-on of *not being the same species*, but beneath all that was my liberating moral bankruptcy and his fall towards someone who (he thought, wrongly) could cut him off from his past once and for all by turning him into Something Else. *That* was the potential: part of him *wanted* to be Turned.

There were moments when I knew he was on the verge of telling me what had happened to him. He rolled right to the edge of it... then back, every time. Until at last one night in the small hours (he was never at the hotel for longer than two or three hours at a time) when we were lying side by side after sex we'd forced on fractionally too long, and I was thinking there couldn't be more than ten minutes before Zoë woke up for a feed, something shifted or broke in the immediate atmosphere between us, and I knew before he spoke what was coming.

'It's quite something,' he said – then stalled.

Hollywood wouldn't give up. On offer was the scene where the woman maternally cradled the man and silently absorbed his horror story and afterwards told him it was all right. I always found such scenes aesthetically sickly. I always ended up thinking less of the guy after he'd unburdened himself. I was very close to saying: Don't bother. Whatever it is I don't give a shit.

'It's quite something,' he repeated, 'that it can't be anything other than minor to you.'

The thing that had happened to him, he meant. The thing he'd wrought himself around.

'Why don't you just give me the facts?' I said.

Pause. Both of us were momentarily aware of the hotel's sad essence as a thing always passed through, always left. Then the tension fell out of his shoulders, fell out of all of him, as suddenly as if it had dropped though a trapdoor.

'I killed my father when I was seven,' he said. 'He was a cop. I shot him with his own gun. He was smashing my mother's face into the television. Those are the facts.'

If you'd asked me what I'd thought he was going to say I couldn't have predicted it, precisely, but every word and image had the quality of a dream I was remembering now in a rush, vivid and inevitable: the little boy struggling to lift the weapon; the low-ceilinged room; the woman's forlorn knees and the man's mouth down-curled like the tragedy mask's, like DeNiro's, in fact, which was who I pictured his dad looking like. I could see the moment fixing the boy like a pin in a butterfly. I could see the assassin and the smile and the levity and the sex and the skin-shedding like speeded-up film of something growing out of it. There was a weariness in being able to see this, a deflation that came with understanding. I thought: All insight makes us sad. It reminds us of the perfection we used to think was our original state.

'Did you mean to kill him?' I asked.

'I'm not sure. I meant to make him stop. Anyway, he died. My mother dialled 911 but he was dead before they got there. I'd shot him in the heart, it turned out.'

'What happened to your mother afterwards?'

'She went off the rails. We had two years of moving from place to place. I'd thought now he was gone she'd be okay, but she wasn't. She'd never been okay. She died of an overdose three weeks before my tenth birthday.'

I could imagine the story that followed. Child Protection Services. Foster care. Institutions. Too much experience, accelerated exposure, all the wrong shapes. At first I didn't feel anything. Then when I thought of him saying, Easy there, tiger… *easy*, and how pure a relief it had been to me to laugh for a moment, I felt sorry for him. But almost immediately and seemingly involuntarily jerked myself out of it.

'It's minor to you,' he said. 'It can't not be.'

'Minor' was hardly the word, but I knew what he meant. He was used to being the biggest deformity in the room. Now he wasn't. It was a relief and a loss. Part of him resented it. Again the visibility of all this made me feel tired. Trying to find something to say was trying to escape from of a chamber with lots of open doors, each one of which slammed shut the second I got to it.

'You know how it is for me,' I said, eventually. I'd surprised myself. The way out was simply to state the truth, neutrally. He did know how it was for me. Me, the woman whose high-point to date was getting fucked by her werewolf lover snout-deep in their victim's guts and whose low was watching indifferently as strangers kidnapped her son. The woman with a dozen-plus murders under her belt and ghosts yammering in her blood. You shot your dad in the heart? Impressive. My last beau killed and ate his wife and child. You know, I run with a tough crowd. Ask Delilah Snow.

'Yeah,' he said, quietly, as if I'd said it aloud. 'I know.'

That was all. The exchange had left us both sad, as both of us had known it would. Someone with an early flight pulled a wheelie case down the carpeted hall. A belated surge of pity for Walker rose in me, so that for a few seconds I was balanced between the desire to turn to him and touch him in animal sympathy, and the knowledge that it wouldn't, in the long run, help.

At which point an odd thing happened. I thought of how my dad used to sometimes take my mom's hand and make her press it on his face because he loved the feel and smell of her palm and because he was one of those men who was always ultimately looking to dissolve himself into a woman. And how my mom just accepted it. Why wouldn't her palm on his face make him feel better? That image, of my mom carrying on a conversation with me while my dad took her hand and placed it over his face, tipped the balance (and reminded me with a sudden inner temperature drop of the other balance that tipped); I turned to Walker and kissed him.

●

I dreamed of Lorcan nightly now, with all dreaming's shifts and superimpositions of identity, but always the same structure: desperation, obstacles, loss. In a recurring nightmare I was back in the house at Park Slope. I could hear him in one of the upstairs rooms. The place was busy with relatives preparing a meal, my dad drunkenly superintending, my mom talking on the phone. The atmosphere was warm and lazy, and it took a while for me to shift from calm curiosity (where is he, exactly?) to edgy self-ridicule (don't be silly, he's right there upstairs!) to slightly unhinged irritation (where *is* he, God dammit?) to full panic (oh, God, please...) as I went from room to room without finding him, until in the last room I opened the closet door to find not a closet but a sheer drop into black, roiling water that stretched away as far as the eye could see.

●

I wasn't supposed to leave the hotel (aside from Walker's injunction to lay low there was Cloquet's default paranoia) but by the sixth day I couldn't stand it any more. The rooms were suffocating me. A strangling pressure came up out of the carpets.

At least that's what I told Cloquet. The truth was *someone walked over my grave* wouldn't leave me alone. Hadn't left me alone since Hammersmith. It was with me now like a continuous sound. It grew in the suite's deeper silences, crept into what little sleep I got, whispered and sometimes blared out when I climaxed. *Wulf*, normally entering her quietest time of the month

176

(ten days since her last appearance, eighteen till her next), remained raw-eyed and awake, ghost ears pricked, ghost snout baffled. It was no good. There would be no peace. Whatever it was it was out there and I was sick of not knowing. I said nothing about it to Walker, who would have tried to stop me.

Cloquet looked in on me just as I was pulling on the white-blonde wig. The suite's windows, overlooking Hyde Park, showed high bright clouds and the trees with their remaining leaves shivering. Cold, softly threshing air I wanted to feel on my hands and face and neck.

'You're going out,' he said. He was annoyed by the liaison with Walker, yes, but more because he thought he'd done irreparable damage to my trust in him. I hadn't told him about *someone walked over my grave,* either. It wouldn't have helped. He was tightly enough wound as it was. 'I just came to see... I just came to see if you needed anything.'

He just came for a little company, he meant. The last few days had pared our relationship down to its functional bones. It suddenly occurred to me how gentle he was with Zoë whenever he had to handle her, and I felt a great tenderness towards him.

'Come here,' I said. I was sitting on a pink velvet stool at the maple dresser. He crossed the room and quite naturally knelt and put his head on my knees. I ran my fingers through his hair and received, in his muscular surrender, how much he'd been starved of physical contact. There was an ache around his body. Unloved, uncaressed, the flesh developed a wrong microclimate that made it more unlovable, more uncaressable. I let myself imagine there would come a time when, my son restored to me and God in His heaven and all right with the world, I could *order* Cloquet to take some comfort in the arms of a woman, whether his libido was dead or not.

'You're exhausted,' I said. 'Do you know that?'

177

He didn't answer. The medic Walker had brought to check Cloquet's shoulder had pronounced it infection-free and healing, but it was still a visible drain, a force that gnawed his energy and made him clumsy.

'I'm going to go for a walk with the baby,' I told him. 'Why don't you take a nap?'

'I can't sleep.'

'Just try. Have a brandy and put a movie on and take your shoes off and lie down on the bed. Just do that. Just rest.' I spoke calmly, running my fingers through his hair, thinking of the scar on his foot from where his mother had burned him with the poker. Again I felt the unjustifiable nature of our relationship. And again the obscure entitlement. *Wulf* knows its dues, and will have them. 'Listen to me,' I said. 'I know you wanted to protect me. You think I don't trust you? You're the *only* person I trust. Don't you know that?'

He couldn't answer. Tenderness upset him, having been so long absent from his life. When it appeared now it was like the return of a glamorous unreliable parent who'd abandoned him umpteen times before. He knew it wouldn't last.

And it didn't. With gentle insinuation from my knees and hands I let him know it was time for him to get up. His shoulder pained him when he did.

'How long will you be gone?' he asked, quietly.

'I don't know. No more than a couple of hours. I'll call you if it's going to be more.'

I added Zoë's last layers, hatted and mittened her, stuffed a couple of diapers in the pocket of her carrier, then snapped her into place against my breasts. 'This is what Dolly Parton must feel like the whole time,' I said, straightening my spine against the weight. 'I'm going to end up a hunchback lugging this critter around.'

26

God knows what I was hoping for. For whatever it was that was stalking me to be sufficiently provoked, I suppose, to stop all the sneaky stuff and walk right up to me and do whatever it was going to do. Not that I was sure I was being stalked. The feeling was more like the one I got close to transformation, that call of the wild that went from innocent to sly to vulgar to raging, the need for moonlight and the ground rolling under me and air streaming over my snout and the sudden exploded stink of a victim...

Whatever I was hoping for, I didn't get it. Hyde Park was green and wet and littered with red and gold leaves, but empty of supernatural signals. I bought a hot chocolate from the Serpentine Gallery and turned back on myself, northeast, towards Marble Arch. Zoë rested snug against me, stupefied by the world's soft tumult and shifting odours. The temptation wasn't a temptation now but a frail revolt, a forlorn rebellion against the hardened heart. Don't. Don't. Don't. But there whether I wanted it or not was my daughter's lethal particularity, that uniqueness that called up the too-late love that must fall away, atomising into nothingness, the same nothingness my mom saw between morphine doses, the same nothingness that was where I wanted Jake's ghost to be, the same nothingness everyone glimpsed now and then, and denied. I pulled her hat down to cover her ears, inside still falling away, falling away. Serves you right, Aunt Theresa's voice said. You had your chance.

I took a cab to Leicester Square. Maybe whatever-the-fuck-it-was hid in crowds. Here *were* the crowds. Humans, woollen-hatted and scarved, raw-nostriled, frowning, jabbering into cellphones, wrapped in their own details. Christmas had already started to show in window displays, glitzy and merciless as Lucifer. The capital's nerves were shot from the financial melt-down, and Londoners everywhere had the look of trying not to think about how bad things were going to get. I moved among them, struggling to block out regular perception and open myself to its twilight-zone counterpart.

With zero success.

I got nothing. Spent two hours getting nothing. If anything the signal dimmed. What had been a continuous nagging inter-ference faded, sometimes disappeared altogether.

Charing Cross Road. Soho. Piccadilly. Regent Street. Oxford Circus.

Nothing.

My back ached. My left eye watered in the cold. Zoë wanted feeding. She fed every two and a half hours, like clockwork, with a four-hour sleep between one and five a.m. My choice was find a mother-and-baby room in a store or hail a cab and go back to the hotel.

I hailed a cab.

Traffic was slow going west on Oxford Street. I took out the cell to let Cloquet know I was on my way home — then thought better of it: I didn't want to tie it up and miss a call from Walker. Zoë wriggled and kicked her legs against me — then suddenly went still.

I'd felt it too.

One second of... of *what*? Something like forced intimacy. A lecher's breath on the neck. Furious tingling in my legs and breasts and scalp. Then it was gone.

'Please stop here.'

'You don't want to go to the Dorchester?'

'No. Here, please. Stop.'

Back on the sidewalk I turned slowly through 360 degrees. The street was tagged with globalised brands: McDonald's; Nokia; Subway; the Gap. Light bounced off the flanks of cars. An open-topped bus went by with an enormous diesel yawn, tourists on the exposed top deck, freezing, taking photographs.

Nothing.

All but on tiptoe I walked back the dozen yards it had taken the cabbie to find a space to pull in.

Cold. Colder.

I turned again and walked slowly west. Zoë had her eyes closed against the flaring and subsiding light. She looked like a tiny ancient trying to recall something from long ago.

A little warmer... Warmer...

I stopped opposite Selfridges.

Warmer.

I crossed the road.

Warmer.

Moved towards the one of the doors – GO IN – and went in.

Perfume counters. Prismic, noisy, jammed with scents in migrainy concentration. Bottles like science fiction *objects d'art*. Precisely made-up sales girls with glittering eyes and *chignons* you could see the effort it cost them to keep intact all day. Women and men bent, sniffed, frowned, debated as if the fate of the world was at stake. It made you wonder – the way a gridlocked freeway or heaving Burger King did – why we lived this way. Why humans lived this way, I mean.

The store was hot and lit by too many halogens. I took off Zoë's cap and mittens. She was quiet and alert. There was nothing to do but keep moving.

Bags. Sunglasses. Jewellery. Menswear: a wall of ties like a paint colour chart. Odours of new leather and serge and talc. Very faintly… *very* faintly, a pull up the escalator.

I was sweating by the time we reached the second floor. Womenswear. The familiar vibe or subsonic murmur of female concentration. Self-assessment, self-doubt, self-loathing, self-cruelty, self-love. The endless argument with shape and size. Some women stood in front of mirrors holding things up in front of themselves and evaluating the result the way a pathologist might a corpse. Others visibly willed themselves different – hips, thighs, belly, breasts – working through the finite range of minute adjustments to posture and facial expression that ought to but never did make any difference.

I moved into the designer section.

Warmer.

Versace. Karen Millen. Armani.

Much warmer.

Dolce & Gabbana. Diesel.

Hot.

Prada—

I stopped. Zoë tensed against me.

It was in the changing room.

And I knew without doubt, as the full impossible scent hit me, exactly what it was.

My skin was wet and heavy, my head full of blood. I looked down at Zoë's face. Her black eyes were wide open. Questions massed. I had to ignore them, ignore them and think – think!

'Madam?' a woman's voice said. 'Madam? Are you all right?'

I was leaning on the edge of the doorway to the dressing

room. A young sales assistant with corkscrewy brown hair and hazel eyes too close together had her hands out towards me.

'Are you not feeling well?'

'I'm okay,' I said, my face fat with heat.

'Let me get you a chair. I'll be two seconds.'

'Really, it's—'

'I'll be right back.'

I stood, concussed, skin tingling. Zoë's scalp was piping hot, her soft hair aloft with static. My legs felt empty. It's not possible. It's not possible.

Then the door to one of the cubicles opened – and the were-wolf stepped out.

27

I t was a girl in her mid-twenties, blonde hair scraped back in a ponytail, lime-green eyes in a catty little face and a small body without an ounce of fat. She wore no make-up but you could see she'd be pop-kitten glamorous if she did. Men, without exception, would go: Yes. Absolutely yes. It was a huge part of her life, men looking at her. It was her aura, that was both a power and an irritant. She was dressed in a white roll-neck sweater, black leggings, oxblood leather knee-boots and matching satchel. She had a black frock coat over her left arm.

For what felt like a long time we stood staring at each other. The air between us pounded with Jake's first words to me at Heathrow: I know what you are and you know what I am.

'Here you are, madam, have a sit down for a minute. Can I get you a glass of water?' The sales assistant had returned with a plastic chair. 'Any luck?' she said to the blonde girl.

Neither of us was capable of responding. Now that I knew what *someone walked over my grave* was it seemed it could never have been anything else.

'Well,' the sales assistant said (thinking Okay, fuck you both), 'the seat's there if you need it. I'll be back in a moment.'

And even when she'd gone, and the girl and I were alone face to face, time and silence solidified around us. Meanwhile the world quietly rearranged itself like a CGI effect on a planetary scale. Alarming sorority flowed between and through and around us. (*How do we really know there aren't any others?* I'd asked Jake. He'd said Harley would have known. But Harley was nine months late finding out *I* existed.) Somewhere in the store I'd passed the ad slogan for the latest iPhone: *This changes everything. Again.*

At last I made my mouth move. 'Who are you?' I said.

She swallowed. Opened her mouth, closed it. Started again. 'Who are *you*?' she said. Her voice surprised me: working-class London, East End I supposed. From the horsey get-up I'd been expecting public-school posh.

'It's not "who", is it?' I said. 'It's *what*.'

'Fucking hell,' she said. 'Fucking *hell*.'

Someone tutted in one of the other cubicles.

'You're American,' she said.

'Yes.'

'Who did it to you?'

'Maybe we should—'

A cubicle door opened and a heavy woman in a quilted over-coat stepped out between us, arms laden with items. Her face was flushed. She wasn't the tutter. She was deep in her own schemes and anxieties. I had to stand aside to let her by. When she'd gone I half-expected the girl to have disappeared. Except the ether remained dense with her scent. So different from Jake's. Breathing it caused a pile-up of feelings: excitement, familiarity, claustrophobia, arousal, a dash of shame. I could see the same in her face, the stunned compulsion, the forced imme-diate intimacy. It was as if someone had grabbed us and shoved us against each other.

'Let's go somewhere we can talk,' I said. She stood motionless, face still struggling to accept. 'It'll be fine,' I said. 'Don't worry.'

'I can't believe you've got a baby,' she said.

Zoë had assimilated her. The small body had relaxed. Now

my daughter was just a hungry infant again. If I didn't feed her in the next few minutes she *would* start crying.

'How is this possible?' I said. 'I mean how did this happen?'

'Was that you on the Great West Road?'

'What?'

'Were you in Hammersmith the other day?'

'Yes.'

'I knew it.'

'Were you there?'

'I've been...' She couldn't complete it. Too many thoughts. Too much.

'Ever since I got here,' I said, 'I've had this feeling, in different parts of the city. I thought it was... I don't know what I thought it was.' Relief – joy, almost – was like a physical presence nearby, because whatever else it meant it meant I wasn't – *we* weren't, me, my daughter, my son – alone. Not alone! The dressing room, the cubicle, her hands and face and voice and her tight-packed *wulf* stink – all of it formed the point from which the world shifted again to let me back in. It was like a broken love affair against all the odds getting a second chance. I could have lain down on the floor and slept with relief.

'Do you know about it?' she said. 'I mean do you know anything?'

Again I could feel my Heathrow questions leaping up in her: What does it mean? How did it start? Is there a cure? I remembered the sudden conviction as soon as I met Jake that since it wasn't just me, since it wasn't just a freak occurrence, then someone, somewhere, must have the answers. I felt sorry for her, since I could only tell her what Jake had told me: *Don't bother looking for the meaning of it all. There isn't one.* Unless of course Quinn's Book turned out to be more than a bagatelle.

'Let's just go and sit down somewhere,' I said. 'There's got to be a cafeteria in here, right?' Zoë let out the first plaintive note. 'Fuck,' I said. 'Listen, I've just got to – oh, to hell with it, I'll do it in here.' I went into the dressing room and sat down in the cubicle she'd just come out of. The dress she'd been trying on was still hanging there, pale green Twenties-style in silk with a tasselled hem. There was an olive green chiffon scarf to go with it. 'I've got to feed her,' I said, making the necessary adjustments to the carrier and my clothes. 'Look away if it grosses you out.' In a Wendy's with Lauren once a woman had breastfed her baby in full view. Lauren had said: I think I'm going to puke my goddamned nuggets.

'What? Oh, right, no, I don't care. Jesus fucking Christ I can't believe this.'

'*Lang*uage,' the tutter said, half under her breath.

'Fuck *off*, you stupid cow,' the girl called out. She stood in the cubicle doorway, tense, both arms folded under the black coat. There was a lot of quick nervy life in her white hands and throat. I just sat there, incapable of picking a place to start. Milk came from the universe and bounded through me into Zoë – but the universe had changed. I thought: What if we don't like each other?

'How long have you...?' she whispered. 'How long have you been one?'

'A year and a half,' I whispered back. 'How long have you?'

'Nine months.'

Which brought the number of moons, the number of kills. What we were flared suddenly around us in the confined space. I got a mental flash of a teenage boy's face with eyes wide and mouth full of blood. It's only the best for us if it's the worst for them. Incredibly, she blushed. Not so incredibly: I was blushing myself.

'What about him?' she said, nodding at the baby.

'Her,' I said.

'What about her?'

'She's like us.'

'Holy fucking shit.'

A cubicle door opened and closed. I couldn't see who it was but I knew it was the anti-swearing woman. 'Yeah?' the girl said to her.

No reply.

'Walk away,' the girl ordered. I felt the woman obey. 'God, it's so weird,' the girl said, turning back to me. 'We knew there was someone. We've been saying for days.'

Stop.

We.

Plural.

An effect like an enormous fleeting change of light. A split-second eclipse.

'Who's "we"?'

'Me and the others.'

'What others?'

'You know. Like us.'

'There are others, like us, here?'

'Aren't there any in America?'

The milk and blood beat, steadily. My face was hot. In spite of everything I was still negotiating the effect of her scent. It was like the time in Lauren's bathroom when Lauren had left the clothes she'd changed out of in a heap on the floor and because curiosity always won with me I'd picked out her underwear and smelled it. A cramped, profane little thrill with a fleck of disgust and delighted secrecy, but also a sprouting of species sympathy, a feeling of accommodating something you never imagined you'd have room for. At the time I'd thought: that's what God wants us to do, find room for each other the way He finds room for Everything.

'Are any of the other cubicles occupied?' I asked.

She took a quick look. 'No.'

'Okay, one thing at a time. You're telling me there are others, like us, here, in London, right?'

'Yeah.'

'How many?'

'There's four of us. I did it for Trish. Then Lucy was an accident. Then Trish fucked it up with this guy Fergus and now there's him, too. He says he's kept it to himself, but I dunno if he's lying. Lucy, too, for that matter. I mean I don't really know her, not as a person.'

You take a moment to establish you're not dreaming. I had an image of them together in an unloved little meeting room. Like a support group.

'We've all been feeling it,' she went on. 'You, I mean. We've been like: Something's happening. Someone's here. Trish said the other day she nearly fainted in South Ken. It's like a whatsit, compulsion. She didn't even know what she was doing there. It's like me, now, in here. I'm not shopping, really. I just... You know?'

'I was in South Kensington,' I said. 'I felt it too. This is... Wait. What do you mean you did it for Trish?'

'She asked me to.'

'Asked you to what?'

'What d'you think?'

'*Turn* her?'

'Yeah.'

'*Why*?'

'Well, it's a long story. You've got to know the background. She's had *way* more than her share of shit to put up with. Then she saw what I did to that arsehole... There was this tosser, Alistair. What he was getting away with, you know? It's complicated.'

A calm detached incredulous part of me was filling in the narrative gaps anyway. Trish enslaved by tosser Alistair, the blonde girl paying him a visit one full moon, Trish seeing the short-cut to a life of never getting pushed around... I thought: Jake, you should have been here to see this. The New Feminism.

At which thought the most obvious question – the one that should have been first in the crowd – suddenly pushed its way to the front.

'Who did it to you?' I asked her.

She rolled her eyes, as if recalling a minor absurdity. 'This guy I was seeing. He's disappeared. So really that's four others apart from me.'

'What was his name?'

Zoë had stopped suckling but I couldn't move for a moment. The air in the cubicle ached with our mutual intuitions. Her odour intensified, suddenly.

'Jake,' she said. 'I never knew his second name.'

The world-sized CGI effect was almost complete. Beyond the feeling of inevitability, I was hurt: Why didn't he tell me? And how did he do it? Didn't he have the virus? Wasn't he incapable of passing on the Curse? Wait. No. Ellis had told him WOCOP had been slipping him the anti-virus when they could. Drinks at the Zetter. The hotel in Caernarfon. Had it *worked*?

This guy I was seeing.

The Zetter. Caernarfon.

The last detail of the giant CGI metamorphosis resolved. We had our new shape.

'You're Madeline,' I said.

'Yeah,' she replied. 'How d'you know?'

28

It was foolish to go with her openly back to the Dorchester but I was in no state for nice judgements. I'd told her we couldn't speak in the cab, so by the time we were behind closed doors in my suite the questions were at a rolling boil. I explained what I knew as quickly (and simply) as I could: Jake; the near-extinction of the species; WOCOP; the vampires; the virus. She knew nothing about the Hunt, had never, to her knowledge, been pursued, and had never met a vampire, though she took the discovery of their existence without question. I left out any mention of the journals. She'd want to read them and Jake hadn't been flattering. That we had him in common thickened the intimacy, of course, forced me to picture things, her neat little face's concealments when he pushed his cock into her anus, the two of them drinking champagne, standing up, naked, her rolling over on his cellphone in the Caernarfon bed. It should have meant enmity, or at least jealousy, but it didn't. *Wulf* trumped everything: we were mutually fascinated, like newly introduced sisters. There were the surface differences, nationality, education, taste (her human had me pegged as smart, maybe a bit stuck-up, crucially and gratifyingly not as pretty as her), but they burned away in the heat of the monster we shared, who sat with us now like a delighted paedophile uncle with his two corrupt nieces. In any case, for all Jake's scorn of her faculties she'd registered the businesswoman in both of us, the smudge of commerce, the no-nonsense relationship with money. That and the commitment to self-preservation, to life at all moral costs. *You love life because life's all there is. There's no God and that's His only Commandment.* Jake wouldn't have needed to tell her that.

She'd Turned the night after their last encounter at the Castle Hotel in Caernarfon. She went back afterwards looking for him, but of course by then he was already in France.

'He used to tell me about it,' she said. 'How he was two hundred years old, how he killed people every full moon.' She was sitting in one of the suite's cream leather chairs drinking a gin and tonic, one slim booted leg crossed over the other. Zoë, milk-stunned and with a perceptibly increased feeling of safety, was asleep in her bassinet. Cloquet was in his room. I'd rung him to say I was back but didn't want to be disturbed. I needed Madeline to myself first; he would have complicated it. 'Clients are always telling you things,' Madeline continued. 'Half the time that's what they're coughing-up for. Normally you take it with a major pinch *of*, right? But he was different. I mean when he told you stuff it was like he was reading from a book or some-thing.' 'He', Jake, kept flaring and subsiding between us like pleasurably shaming sunlight. It was as if she and I were seeing each other naked. 'And then that poor bloke's head in the bag,' she continued. 'Christ. And the other guy goes, "He's a werewolf, honey, didn't you know?" and I'm like: Fucking *hell*. I mean he tried to pass it off afterwards, make a joke of it, but I knew by then there was something seriously weird going on.'

'I still don't understand how he did it to you,' I said.

She shook her head, shrugged. 'At the time I just assumed...' She made a face to indicate sex. 'You know?'

'But it's not spread like that,' I said. 'As far as I know it's got nothing to do with sexual contact.'

'Look, you might be right, but what can I tell you? He didn't bite me, that's for sure. He didn't *change*. All I know is it definitely happened after that last night we were in Caernarfon.'

We both fell silent – *hit* silence, actually, because what she'd just said had brought her kill from that first time – the teenage boy – into the room with us. We looked at each other – one moment of absolute transparency (yes, we knew what we'd done; yes, we really had done it) – then away, not embarrassed but shocked at the dirty thrill of mutual admission. I could imagine the first incestuous touch between siblings being like this. I also thought – had *been* thinking, practically from the first moment of recognising what she was: Should I let this be my first sex with a woman? What would fuckkilleat be like with her? Would she even want to?

'Something's wrong with you,' Madeline said.

'What?'

'Something's happened to you. What is it?'

Superficially I'd held back from telling her about the kidnapping to put *wulf* intuition to the test, to see if she'd pick it up. *Not* superficially because telling her would bring the totality of my failure back. Failure as a woman, as a mother, as a *She*. My own disgust had been bad enough. Now there'd be species disgust to contend with as well.

Heat swelled between us. The moment stretched. Our eyes kept meeting then looking away because neither of us was sure we were ready for the rough telepathy on offer. I was thinking of the Alaskan wolves, the way my will had gone into their shoulders and haunches and jaws and feet –

'Stop it!'

She'd tensed in the chair. I thought the glass was going to break in her hand.

'I'm sorry, I didn't real—' But there *she* was, in the back of my neck and forearms, a shocking counter-intrusion.

'Wait,' I said. 'I'm sorry. I didn't know that would happen. Take it easy.'

We stared at each other. The panic and revulsion was human. Meanwhile *wulf* eased into delight. We balanced like that for what seemed a long time. Then both of us – out of a mix of embarrassment and sudden reciprocal trust – laughed. We withdrew simultaneously, a sensation like the thin dissolving edge of a wave receding over the sand. *Shshsh*.

'Is it like that with the others?' I asked her.

'Yeah, it is.'

'It takes getting used to.'

'Tell me about it.'

'I want to meet them.'

'What, now?'

'Well... No, wait. We've got to think about this. We've got to be careful.'

'How d'you mean?'

'What you said before, about there being something wrong, about something having happened to me? You were right.'

'What is it?'

Zoë made a little staccato noise in her sleep, kicked her legs a couple of times, went quiet again. It started raining. I hated the words. Each one was like a big live insect in my mouth.

'My son's been taken,' I said, sitting down on the edge of the bed. 'I've no idea where he is. They're going to kill him.'

29

I told her everything and she told me everything. Dusk deepened. The room became a secret place, with our voices speaking quietly. Our kills burgeoned through our blushes in silence around us while we talked. I knew she'd made the shift, recognised guilt as pointless since here she still was, in spite of what she'd done, what she'd kept doing, what she knew she'd go on doing. Here she still was in good clothes and Dior Addict, with money in her purse and people in her life. You tore into terrified human flesh, saw the satiny heart and rubbery liver, all the body's hidden things it turned out obeyed the laws of your violence. You broke the bones and guzzled the blood. You took a life and the theft went unpunished. God didn't strike you down. The sky didn't fall. The morning after, you turned on the faucet and water still came out. Ad jingles still stuck in your head. It was still good when you raised your arm for a cab and one came towards you out of the flow like magic. You did things that were supposed to end you and found they were only things that changed you. It was a disappointment and a revelation and a bereavement and a new thrilling nudity. It was the basic prosaic obscenity: you kept going.

Impossible to know if she'd ever been the one-dimensional dolly Jake had portrayed her as, but either way the Curse – to state the obvious – had altered her. According to Jake her entire personality had been driven by insecurity: the vanity, the materialism, the tabloid clichés, the celebrity fixations and cosmetics lore. The whole thing was a nebula that had to be kept swirling protectively around a core of fear. Not any more. The vanity was still there, as was the impoverished vocabulary and complete absence of reading. But *wulf*, if it didn't make you mad, made you smarter. Whether you liked it or not every victim forced you to absorb a stranger's life. Your vision broadened. Strange perspectives became available. New sympathies surprised you. You deepened. The victims *were* the reading. She had an appetite for it now, this expansion she never knew existed.

Lucy, 'the accident', was a thirty-eight-year-old recently divorced ophthalmologist at Moorfields Eye Hospital who'd come out of the settlement with, amongst other things, a detached cottage in Wiltshire, where she'd gone for a solitary weekend three months ago. Madeline, with nous enough not to kill on her own doorstep, had been in the area, had watched the house, had got in through an upstairs window. Then been interrupted. 'I heard a car and people getting out right outside,' she told me. 'I panicked.'

And fled, leaving would-be victim Lucy with a nasty bite, a horror story and a brand new constitution. 'That's how I found out how it worked,' Madeline said. 'Lucy tracked me down six weeks later.'

Yes, assuming no virus, that *was* how it worked. You got bitten, you survived, you Turned. But here was Madeline, positive she *hadn't* been bitten. How could that be?

Trish was a friend of hers since elementary school who'd ended-up in thrall to tosser Alistair. Alistair had a very simple system. He got teenage girls hooked on heroin then forced them into increasingly extreme porn to pay for it. He'd put Trish in hospital a dozen times, most recently with four broken ribs and a miscarriage. When Madeline went to see her, Trish asked Madeline to lend her the money to have Alistair killed. Madeline made a her an offer: She'd get someone to put an end to Alistair if Trish promised to get off the drug.

Arrangements weren't difficult to make. Alistair had been trying to get into Madeline's pants for years.

'You know what the weird thing was?' Madeline said. 'I told Trish the whole story, what I was, what I was going to do to him – and she believed me. Just believed me straight off like that. She said she wanted to watch. So I let her.'

The trouble was, even after Alistair had met his end, Trish couldn't get the monkey off her back. 'She'd been through too much,' Madeline said. 'You seriously don't know. Stuff he did to her? Unbelievable.' She shook her head, disgusted. 'And after all that she goes and tries topping herself. Twice! Honestly, the woman was a wreck. In the end she just asked me flat out if I'd... You know. She said she'd seen what it had done for me. I mean I'm different to how I used to be. I used to be... Well. Anyway. You know. I mean you *do* know.' I thought I did. Whatever else the Curse had done to me it had removed physical fear. You don't know how much physical fear you've been carrying around until it's gone. Imagine every time you find yourself alone with a man you don't know. Walking on a street. At a gas station in the middle of the night. Imagine knowing he can't kill you. Imagine knowing you can pull just enough *wulf* to the surface to let him know pissing you off will be a really, *really* bad idea. Madeline sipped her gin and tonic and continued: 'So I thought: You leave her to herself, Mads, and she'll be in a coffin in a month. And then what was it all for? Sounds barmy, I know, but I didn't really see what she had to lose. So I did it.'

A maid pushed a tinkling trolley past the door. The world had receded from us. The room was dark. Getting up and turning on a light would've been brutal.

'She's off the shit now,' Madeline said. 'She's gone completely the other way. You should see her. She's like bloody Lara Croft.'

Lara Croft or not, Trish botched her kill last month, and now they had Fergus, a three-times-divorced fifty-three-year-old alcoholic sales rep, to add to the family. Like Lucy, he'd tracked his maker down. 'That's what's different with you,' Madeline said. 'Lucy and Fergus, they could find us. I mean we've all got a feeling for where we are. Instinct or whatever. If I go out of here and start walking, pretty soon I'll know which direction to go for any one of them. It's not like that with you. It's more confused.'

She wasn't sentimental. When I told her about the birth and my dead heart, the empty space where love should have been, she didn't say I mustn't blame myself, or that it wasn't my fault, or that there was nothing I could have done. She just sat, intrigued, hooked on the *story*. A couple of times I paused too long in the narrative. *Then* what happened? she demanded. I found myself liking her. She couldn't disguise her satisfaction at the thought of never aging. She wanted confirmation of the four-hundred-year lifespan and immunity to disease. I told her that was what Jake had told me – and if anyone knew, he did.

It was a bitterish fascination to her that Jake had loved me. Not because she cared about Jake, but because she was compelled to find out what merits or skills other women had. I could feel her trying to imagine what it had been like between him and me. I could feel her getting it, reluctantly, that it was the other thing, the mysterious thing, the thing of which even fabulous sex was only a part. She'd never been in love. Not as an adult. She was unformed in that department. I'd felt it in the slim, tight shoulders. It was there in the appetite for *things*. It was there in the prostitution. There was a weird moment when I asked her if she was still working as an escort and she told me she was. Weird because obviously it brought Jake again, the images, the speculation (with you, did he like to... ?) and weird again because in spite of everything she thought I might disapprove (she put on a bright little pretence of pragmatic shamelessness at first); but weird chiefly because it raised like a hot flush in both of us the other, gentler atrocity of our condition: *wulf* libido. Suddenly the fact of Curse nymphomania was there, unignorable, and for a moment we didn't know whether to acknowledge it. There was a brief silence. Then, as before, we found ourselves laughing. 'I got three months off when I was expecting,' I told her. 'Now it's on again.'

She was on her fourth Hendricks. 'Way I look at it,' she said, 'why pack the job in now? At least there's more to it than just the money.'

It was after eight o'clock when Cloquet knocked to see what I wanted for dinner. By which time I'd done what I could to drum into Madeline the need for extreme caution in all our movements and communications from now on. She'd also managed to reach two of the three others (Trish and Fergus) and arrange a meeting for nine tomorrow night, location (I insisted) to be called-in by me not more than two hours beforehand. She gave me her number, and didn't make a fuss when I told her I couldn't give her mine on the clean cell. I told her I'd sort another phone out tomorrow and thereafter we'd use that. I introduced her to Cloquet as a friend and said nothing about what she was. Partly to see if he'd be able to tell (it was one of the things I was never sure of, whether we didn't – through some vibe or pheromone – give ourselves away to humans) but mainly because I couldn't face going through the whole explanation again with Madeline there.

'Did you notice anything odd about her?' I asked him, when she'd gone. We were alone in my suite, him in the window seat, me on the edge of the bed. It was fully dark out, and raining. The TV was on, with the sound down. CNN, which Walker and I had been half-watching on his last visit, like two people looking back through time and space to the world they'd lost, long ago.

'Odd? No. Why? What's odd?'

He'd reacted oddly himself when I'd introduced them, said barely a word, seemed unsure whether to shake hands with her. Now he was reacting oddly to the question.

'You seemed a little strange with her.'

'Strange? *Pas de tout*. I know nothing about her.'

'Oh my God,' I said, with belated intuition. 'You liked her.'

'Don't be absurd.'

His sexual self had been dormant for so long I was astonished at my certainty that that's what it was. But no less certain, astonished or not. 'Of course,' I said. 'She's beautiful.'

'She looks like someone I worked with once, that's all.'

'It's nothing to be ashamed of.'

'*Merde alors*. She looks like a fucking *model* I worked with, years ago.'

'She's a werewolf.'

'What?'

'That's right. Still want her number?'

He listened in frowning silence, then asked question after question, most of which I didn't have answers for. It was unhinging him, all this sudden change, first Walker and Konstantinov, then me and Walker, now *four more werewolves*.

'They're a pack,' he said.

'So what?'

'Maybe nothing. But I don't like it that they can find you so easily.'

'Not so easily, apparently.'

'That they can find you at all then.'

'I can trust her. I know. Don't ask me how. It's a species thing.'

'She's one of four.'

'Yeah, well, beggars can't be choosers. They're going to help us.'

He opened his mouth to say something – then stopped.

'*Mon Dieu*,' he said. 'Look.'

The TV, he meant. On screen was a large dark building in the middle of nowhere up to its ground-floor windows in snow. I didn't recognise it at first. Then did. It was the Alaskan lodge. The next shot was inside the lounge kitchen. A team of guys in thermal gear conducting what looked like a forensic sweep. Cloquet found the remote and unmuted.

'… very early stages,' one of the team said to an off-camera interviewer. 'But we *have* found what at first sight appear to be genetically anomalous materials. We're not jumping to any conclusions, you know, but this business teaches you to keep an open mind.'

'An open mind?' the reporter's voiceover asked us, rhetorically. 'One person whose mind is already made up is the young lady whose incredible story started this investigation.'

And there she was: Kaitlyn. She looked harried and greasy in the lights' glare. She was wearing an enormous Parka and big boots. 'Look, I never believed in any of this stuff,' she said. 'But what happened here was real, and these guys with the scientific… these guys with the equipment and all, they've already found particles, right? I mean that's biological evidence, that's hard evidence. This thing was as real as you standing right there and for all those people who say I'm crazy they can just talk to these science guys, they can just… you know? This thing was real. It was absolutely real.'

Cloquet and I watched the rest of the report. The story would have started as a tiny item on a Fairbanks radio phone-in or low-rent TV talk show and someone's interest would have been piqued. A paranormal nut with money. Now science. Now the police. There were county badges among the forensic team.

'Fuck,' Cloquet said. 'Great.'

'There's nothing we can do about it now,' I said. 'We didn't fly on the IDs we rented the place on anyway. They won't be looking for us. They won't even know we left the country.'

'She'll have given a description,' Cloquet said. 'If they look at the Anchorage airport CCTV—'

'Look, forget it. It's out of our control.'

The phone rang.

The Walker phone. My scalp went hot.

'Hello?'

The silence just before his voice was like deep space. I knew what was coming.

'We've found them,' he said. 'They've got your boy and Natasha together. But we have to move fast.'

30

According to Hoyle they were in a derelict farmhouse fifteen miles outside Macerata in the *Le Marche* district in Italy. Jacqueline Delon, five other vampires, four familiars, Natasha Konstantinov and one baby werewolf boy, two and a half weeks old.

I told myself to stay cold. Don't let the heart in. Let the heart in and you fuck it up. But I sat on the bed sick with adrenalin and hope and fear.

'We fly to Rome,' Walker told me, 'then on to Falconara, where there'll be transportation. The big problem is weapons.'

'Because?'

'Because there might not be any.'

I tried to visualise it. I had an image of myself, Walker and Konstantinov moving through a field of long dry grass under an aquamarine sky. I had a very clear sense of what being completely unarmed would feel like, the air passing over my empty hands.

'How can we do this without weapons?'

'Well, we go in in daylight, so that eliminates the vamps. Then you're only looking at four familiars.'

'Four *armed* familiars.'

'I know, I know. But there'll be six of us.'

'Six? What happened to twenty?'

'Well, Murdoch's killed four of them. The rest are either

underground or flat-out not interested. It's not like *all* of them give a shit about Mike's wife. And *none* of them gives a shit about you or your son. I told them you're paying, but money's not what they care about right now. What they care about right now is staying alive. I'm sorry. You're just going to have to trust that we can get this done. Also, don't mention to the team that there might not be guns. If there aren't, we'll deal with it when the time comes. Now, give me your passport details.'

'We're going on a regular flight?'

'As opposed to?'

'I don't know. Something under the radar.'

'Those were the good old days. We're outside the organisation now. Helicopters, big hardware, ghost flights, carte blanche mobility – that's all gone.'

Then why am I hiring you? I didn't need to say.

Because it's us or you on your own, he didn't need to reply.

A little silence in which we both felt over the connection how much more complicated we'd made this by sleeping together.

'What are we going to do with her ladyship?' he said.

Ask me when we're good to go, I'd told him.

Well, we were good to go now – or rather had to go, good or not.

•

Cloquet sat there on the edge of the bed and took it. I'd just run through the instructions for formula milk, which, having known this moment would come, I'd bought and hidden in my room.

'There's no other way,' I said.

'I know.'

'You're going to be okay.'

'What if you don't come back?'

'I'll come back, I promise.'

'You can't promise.'

'No. I can't. I'm sorry.'

It was two a.m., raining heavily, audibly. The first flight Walker could get us on left in three and a half hours. I was meeting him at Heathrow. I'd wire-transferred extra funds to Cloquet's account and written a letter to my dad Cloquet would have to hand deliver if I was killed. The will was with the Manhattan lawyer who'd handled my divorce. I'd thought of writing a letter to Zoë (to both of them, since it was theoretically possible Lorcan would survive even if I didn't) but I couldn't do it. It felt bogus, something for me disguised as something for them. Better to be a clean mystery. Better to leave them free to imagine the mother they would have wanted. As they'd have to imagine their father.

I gave Cloquet Madeline's number.

'You're not serious?' he said.

'If they survive they're going to need their own kind. I know you'll look after them, but you'll need help. Madeline's not a bad person. Trust me, I know. Plus, you know… who knows, right? She could be good for you.'

'This is—'

'This is necessary. Don't argue. Now you're sure you know what you're doing with the formula?'

I'd packed, if you could call it that. IDs, cash, cards, Lorcan's birth certificate, a toothbrush, three changes of underwear. Jake's last journal. I wanted not to be ready until the car came. I wanted to have to leave in a hurry and not have to think of anything to say. I wanted not to be able to hold Zoë for more than a moment.

To kill time I went into the en suite and put on some

make-up. Flossed. Rinsed my mouth with toothpaste. Sat on the toilet for what seemed a long time after I'd peed. Found myself taking in the bathroom's details they way you would if it was your last few seconds before being executed. The vast mathematical silence was here, in the white porcelain and delighted halogens. Again I imagined moving through the field of long dry grass with no weapons in my hands – and my hands in reality felt as if half their mass had gone. I bent over the toilet, convinced I was going to throw up. Nothing happened. I straightened, trembling.

The room phone rang.

'Car's here,' Cloquet called.

He had Zoë in his arms when I came out of the bathroom. I took her, quickly, held her, looked at her. Felt everything I wasn't entitled to like a contained quivering tidal wave. Her face was hot from a nap, lined on one cheek where a crease had pressed. She went cross-eyed focusing on me. Quick, before the falling away into nothingness, quick, quick. I kissed her, smelled her head, held my face against hers for a moment, began inwardly *I'm sorry, angel, sorry for everything* – then stopped. It rolled darkness down over the winking lights of her future. It softened Pharaoh's heart and I thought I can't leave her which immediately sent me into the sickening fall away from her because who was I? Who was *I*? When I put her back in the bassinet the transfer of her weight from me pulled at my insides, a gentle evisceration. Turn away right now or you'll never be able to leave. Right now. Right *now*.

Cloquet was suddenly full of realities, all his denial and postponement mechanisms failing. His face was frank with fear. I hugged him, quickly, mumbled 'Don't say anything.' His arms came up around me. I knew if I let him establish a proper embrace it would be a long labour to extricate myself. 'I have to go,' I said, pulling away. I grabbed my backpack, crossed the suite and opened the door. I imagined my mother standing behind me like a talisman saying, quietly: Don't look back. Don't look back. Don't look back.

So I didn't.

31

At Falconara we picked up a Land Rover and a Mercedes saloon. To Walker's visible relief there were weapons in the trunk of the SUV: four pistols with a clip each and two Lancaster Tactical AK-47s with one thirty-round magazine apiece. Which still left one person unarmed. With Walker and Konstantinov were three other ex-WOCOP agents – Hudd, Carney and Pavlov (all on Murdoch's death-list) – none of whom would countenance going in without hardware. 'I guess that means I get the prize,' Walker said. 'Presumably no one will object if I bring up the rear, with my lethal kung-fu skills?'

Hudd was in his early thirties, squat, demonic, muscled, with a shaven head and a black goatee. Carney was younger, tall and thin, with a blond crew-cut and a gentle blue-eyed face. Put him in half-mast jeans and a check shirt and a straw hat and he'd be the likeable village idiot. The third renegade, Pavlov, was mid-forties, with straight, shoulder-length greying red hair and a placid, broad-cheekboned face. Narrow hazel eyes full of such amused nihilism that he couldn't possibly be here for anything other than money. Don't get ahead of yourself, I kept telling myself, but I had love for them, such a wealth of warmth for them piling up, ready, in case they were the men who helped me get my son back.

We left the airport just after noon local time and headed

southwest, Walker, Konstantinov (driving) and me in the Mercedes, the others in the Land-Rover. It was cold. Blue sky and shreds of white cloud. Konstantinov had a calmness and precision of movement that spoke of terrible potential.

'It's not far,' Walker said to me. 'You should have another look at the visuals.'

These were a half-dozen satellite images from Google maps showing the ruined house and grounds, an enormous square stone building with a castellated roof and broken turret in seven untended acres backed by a low hill and edged at its southern boundary by a narrow belt of deciduous woodland. There were three outbuildings in various states of collapse, and a small overgrown orchard maybe twenty metres from the eastern side of the main house. That was as close as we'd be able get before breaking cover. 'We've got no silencers,' Walker had said. 'So once we start shooting we better know what we're doing.' We did have, thank God, communications kit. Believe it or not you're allowed to take walkie-talkies or transceivers on commercial airlines as long as you don't use them on board, so each of us was equipped with a mic'd headset. The plan was that Walker and Hudd would go ahead to scope the place and make sure we weren't facing more goons than we'd been warned of. Although the fact is, Walker had confided to me, it isn't going to make any difference to Mike. One way or another he's going in. (Which means *I'm* going in, he didn't have to add.) After that it was simply a case of eliminating the familiars, locating the captives and bringing them out. *Simply* a case of, Walker had repeated. That's my idiom of choice for these things. No point being negative. An hour into the flight I'd wanted to make love to him. *Wulf*, naturally, kept up its come-rain-or-come-shine demand, mouth open, tongue lolling, eyes glinting with honest filth, but the big aching pressure came from my human, from my girl, who'd only just woken up to the nearness of death and felt a great tenderness for herself and her body and all the rich finiteness that would be lost. She wanted, one last time, to get as close to another human being as it was possible to get. But contrary to what the movies say, it's not so easy to have sex on a plane. For one thing the plane was tiny. The cabin crew's work station was practically *in* the bathroom. For another there was a permanent line of people waiting to use it. I sat there next to him not saying anything about it and feeling increasingly absurd and desperate and ultimately, since it was obvious it wasn't going to happen, crushed. The flight's other reality slap was that I'd given no thought to having suddenly stopped breastfeeding. By the time what would've been Zoë's third consecutive feed had come and gone the unsuckled milk had started a knifey protest. *Look, I know we're on a mission — but would you mind if we tried to find somewhere that sells breast-pumps when we land?* I did what I could to express a little manually in the bathroom, dropped a couple of ibuprofen and told myself it wouldn't be long before I'd need the milk for Lorcan.

Along with the satellite images of the house was a Xeroxed portrait of Konstantinov's wife, Natasha. All the guys have a copy, Walker said, so no one shoots her by mistake. The picture showed her looking straight into camera, not smiling, a slim-faced woman with dark hair pulled back and tied. No glamour, but black eyes there would be no deceiving. *She sees right through you*, people would say. She looked at least fifteen years younger than Konstantinov, yet I could imagine the two of them together. Same intensity. No fear of death — especially now they had love. If she was in a room with Madeline nine out of ten men would ignore her. Konstantinov was the one out of ten for whom there would *be* no one else in the room.

'Okay,' Walker said. 'This is it.'

We'd pulled over on a narrow, chalky road that ran along the side of a steep hill. Trees going up the hill on our right, open farmland going down on our left. Around a bend some seventy-five yards ahead, according to the map, the road ran past the entrance to Casa del Campanile. We'd follow Walker and Carney to the south side of the orchard and wait for their signal to proceed.

'Obviously the vamps will be below ground,' Walker said, once we'd grouped a little way under the trees. 'So will the prisoners. They'll have someone watching the kid, so however many familiars we make above ground we should assume *at least* one more and probably two in the basement. Everyone good?' Silent tense collective affirmation, a diluted version of what I'd shared with the Alaskan wolves. Carney gave a slow thumbs-up, and for no reason, while I watched him make the gesture, everything caught up with me and gathered in my body: the lack of sleep, the flight, the foreign country, the nearness of my son, the realisation that this place – smelling of fallen leaves and cold stone and dead wood and drying grass – was where I might die. Exhaustion was there but *wulf* dismissed it. Not because its child was near, but because there was something to be stalked and killed. Transformation was eighteen days away, but the human in hunt mode had dragged the ghost animal hot and shivering to the surface. I could feel her in my fingernails and feet, backbone and scalp. I could feel her frustration at what she had to work with. But thanks to her all five senses had been violently upgraded. Gladness went through my limbs like fast-acting booze. Plus, the pain in my breasts subsided.

Walker looked at Konstantinov. 'Not long now, Mike.'

Konstantinov said nothing.

32

We waited, me, Konstantinov, Carney and Pavlov, for what felt like a very long time at the broken fence where the wood met the orchard. Then Walker's voice came through, quietly. 'You guys reading?'

'Roger,' Konstantinov said. 'Go ahead.'

'Okay, we've got two goons, repeat, two goons visible, both armed with machine guns. First goon just inside the front entrance wearing a navy blue soccer shirt and black leather jacket. Second goon doing slow circuits of the roof, green sweat-shirt, dark glasses, black woollen cap. Acknowledge.'

'Got it.'

'On my Go, come ahead slowly through the orchard. Keep low and move fast and you'll get here before the roof watch is back on this side.'

'Roger that. On your signal.'

It took us less than two minutes, and when we joined Walker and Hudd the roof goon still hadn't reappeared. 'We've got to get a closer look,' Walker said. 'This is a big house. There could be fifty guys in there.'

'Intelligence says four,' Konstantinov said, without emotion.

'Mike, you know we only get one shot at this.'

'We need to get closer,' Hudd said. His bald head and bulging eyes and black goatee made him look like a chaotic deity. All he needed was to stick his tongue out, Maori haka-style. 'Ninety percent of this place we can't see. There's three floors, for fuck's sake.'

I knew what Walker was thinking: even if they got closer and *discovered* fifty guys, it wasn't going to stop Konstantinov going in.

'Wait here,' Konstantinov said – and before anyone could argue he was out of the orchard, going at an extraordinary low sprint across the open ground to the side of the house.

'Jesus Christ,' Carney said, quietly.

After so much stealth Konstantinov looked appallingly visible. For the few seconds he was exposed it was as if the sun had turned up its dial, desperate for him to be seen. But he made it to the end of the building and got his back against the wall.

'It's not so bad,' Pavlov whispered, covering his mic. 'The front door guy can't see him from this angle, and the roof guy won't see him unless he comes to the very edge and looks straight down.'

There was a window space – no glass – six feet from the Russian. He edged towards it. Got upright. In tiny increments stole a look inside. Signalled back. Empty. He moved quickly past the window to the building's rear corner. Paused. Slipped around it.

A minute passed. Two. Four. Five. Heat came off Walker's flank next to mine. The Dorchester seemed weeks ago. For the first time since the kidnapping I had a sense of what pure relief it would be to have my son back – but *wulf* scotched it: it got in her way. She was impatient. The scents of the four bodies close to her tugged, prematurely, at the hunger.

Konstantinov reappeared at the edge of the rear corner. He held up three fingers. Walker said: 'Pavlov, guy on the roof, now.'

Pavlov stood, raised the AK-47, fired a short burst that seemed to splinter the sky. The man on the roof fell backwards. We heard his weapon clatter. 'Go!' Walker said — and everyone, including me, moved. Konstantinov swung himself up through the window into the house. The long grass was a maddening soft impediment. Carney tripped, swore, got up, felt a spray of bullets go past him and hit the turf. He looked at me with a face of mild surprise, as if being shot at was the last thing he'd expected. The three-second dash stretched, distended, took a dreamy hour. Pistol shots sounded from inside the house. Walker leaped through the window. Carney and Pavlov went around the back of the building, Hudd took position at the opposite corner for a moment, then he too disappeared. Another two shots fired. Then silence. Suddenly there was the Italian countryside in complete peace again. *Wulf* chafed and writhed in its human traps, the inadequate arms and legs, the laughably labouring muscles. I hauled myself onto the window-ledge and dropped into the big empty room on the other side.

33

Thirty feet across from me a doorway opened into the next room. Walker appeared in it, beckoned me to come ahead. The second room was bigger than the first. Daylight pencilled through several large holes in the brickwork. A precarious stone staircase ran along one wall to the upper floors. Konstantinov, Hudd and Carney were up there, going room by room. The soccer-shirted goon lay dead in the open front doorway. A second body lay by the stairs, and a third was visible, lying face-down in the adjoining chamber.

'Through here,' Walker said.

I followed him into what might once have been the house's kitchen, where Pavlov stood guard at a doorway from which more stone stairs led down to a basement.

'We wait for the upstairs clearance,' Walker said.

It was a peculiar few minutes. There was nothing to say. The house, since it had no choice, started offering us its ruined details: a sunlit patch of yellowy green lichen; bits of rotten wood; gothic cobwebs; the smells of damp stone and cat piss and mould. As with strangers waiting for an elevator every second increased the absurdity. Then Konstantinov came through the doorway, followed by Carney and Hudd. The rooms upstairs were empty.

'Okay, so what I'm thinking here is—'

Konstantinov wasn't waiting. He went past Walker without a word and started down the stairs.

'Pav, take point here,' Walker said, then followed Konstantinov into the gloom. I went after him, with Hudd and Carney on my heels.

Cold air came up. The stairs were narrow, steep, mossed and damp, but the two men ahead and Hudd behind lit the way with torches. Fourteen steps. Buckling heat and an adrenal stink from the four human bodies. *Wulf* swelled and jabbed in the liminal zone under my skin. Memories of the kills popped and bloomed: the French widower's cock on the floor like a king prawn in a puddle of blood; the Mexican pimp's bare leg kicking, repeatedly, despite my arm rummaging elbow-deep under his ribs. Something was struggling to come forward in my mind, had been trying to form while we'd waited by the door at the top of the stairs.

'Mikhail!' Walker hissed. 'Jesus, slow down.'

Konstantinov had moved quickly away from the steps and was opening the darkness section by section with his torch. The space underground appeared to occupy half the house's footprint. Undressed stone walls and floor, what looked like the remnants of broken crates and bottles, rusted oil cans, shelves hanging, more fantastic cobwebs.

'Okay, check it,' Walker said. 'Easy does it, gentlemen. Miss D, stay close. Pavlov, you good up there?'

'Good,' Pavlov answered. 'Take your time.'

The team moved around the cellar's perimeter, guns and torches trained. Konstantinov's silent furious energies were palpable through the darkness. The rest of us had dropped away for him: he was alone in the inscrutable universe.

For as long as it took to cover the ground we kept up a token suspension of judgement, but no one was really in any doubt: there was nothing down here.

Konstantinov was on all-fours searching the floor – for a trapdoor or hidden way to a lower level. Out of awkwardness Carney and Hudd joined him. The thing that had been struggling to come forward in my mind got through, with a strange inner sensation of *wulf* suddenly falling, clawing space. I couldn't believe it had taken this long. 'Walker,' I said. 'If he was here I would have felt him by now.'

'What?'

'My son. And the vampires. They're not here. There's no smell.'

Konstantinov's method was unravelling. He got up off the floor and began running his hands over the nearest section of wall.

'Mike?' Walker said. 'Something's not right here.'

Konstantinov ignored him.

'Pavlov,' Walker said. 'Anything your end?'

No reply.

'Pavlov, are you reading me?'

Silence.

Carney and Hudd leaped to their feet, weapons readied. Konstantinov rested his head against the wall. The torch in his hand made a pointless fierce ellipse of light on the wet stone.

'Here,' I said to Walker, giving him the pistol. 'You might as well have this. You need it more than I do.'

At the top of the stairs we found Pavlov unconscious with a tiny dart in his neck. The land around the house was attentive again. *Wulf* in me was muddled and fiery, as if a burn had swollen its eyes shut. My human had to re-establish itself, haul control back to the inferior system.

'Fuck,' Walker said. 'We're in troub—'

I don't know what deployment reflex the four men were about to manifest, but I never got to find out, because at that moment a figure appeared in the doorway between the kitchen and the next room, paused for a moment, attempted a step forward, then collapsed.

34

It was a man and he was naked. He was also, courtesy of what had happened to him, barely recognisable *as* a man. It was hard to understand how he'd been on his feet. In the mess of his injuries – the facial swellings like a cluster of grotesque fruits, the bruises psychedelically curdling yellow and puce – two details registered: that the ulna of his left arm was sticking out of the skin just above the wrist, and that his penis was covered in what looked like venereal sores but which the context made clear were cigarette burns.

'Oh, no,' Walker said, quietly.

'Who is it?' I asked.

'It's Hoyle.'

He took a step towards the collapsed man. As he moved, the light altered slightly and everyone turned to the gap in the kitchen wall, where the goon in the blue soccer shirt and leather jacket stood, smiling. Walker, Carney and Hudd all fired – but the guy just stood there, *waving*, I thought, until I saw he was holding in his hand the torn remains of a small plastic pouch: formerly, it was now obvious, filled with blood. Animal blood. Stage blood. Either way not *his* blood.

'The beauty of you relying on us for guns,' a voice said, 'is that it leaves us at liberty to load them with blanks.'

We all turned again.

Standing above Hoyle was a tall man in his mid-forties dressed in black Hunt fatigues and carrying a machine gun. He had close-cropped grey hair and blue eyes that seemed to have an extra iris. A slight frown you knew was perpetual gave him a bald eagle's look of dignified madness. I felt Walker's energy dip like a plane in an air pocket.

At least two dozen fully-armed members of the WOCOP Hunt filed into the building, some through the gap in the wall, others in the bald eagle's wake as he stepped over the man on the floor and approached us. An odour of clean canvas and leather and medicinal soap preceded him. 'I thought I'd bring Hoyle along,' he said to Walker. 'So you could see what you'd got him into. It's been a long night for us all.' He turned to me. 'Miss Demetriou,' he said. 'You must be regretting getting mixed up with these men. Not that I blame you. Little one goes missing, a woman gets desperate. You take help where you can find it. That's understandable.'

Little one goes missing.

Did he know where the Disciples were?

I could feel what it was costing Walker to keep still, the ache for Hoyle; the heart that wanted to scream and the will that knew it would be a defeat if it did, useless to the man on the floor. Walker's logical working-out was all but audible to me: Hoyle had suffered because he was Walker's mole. But Walker hadn't forced Hoyle. Hoyle knew the risks. Any tenderness that passed between them now would be an exquisite satisfaction to their enemy. Hoyle would have agreed, if he hadn't been incapable of speech. Therefore Walker slapped his heart down and instead turned to me and said: 'If you saw his wife you'd be amazed. She's really pretty. Not to mention a *sorceress* with her index finger.'

Murdoch (Walker's jibe explained) looked at him for a

moment, smiling. Said nothing. Then to one of his team: 'Mr Tunner, let's get these people secured and on their way.'

Several Hunters equipped with hand- and leg-cuffs moved forward. Hudd leaped at one of them and was immediately shot in the hip. Carney dropped his redundant pistol and allowed himself to be secured. Three hunters approached Konstantinov. 'Easy way or hard way, Mike?' one of them said. 'Up to you.' Then before Konstantinov answered shot him in the leg with a tranquiliser dart. Konstantinov slumped to his knees, dropped his pistol. His dark face was slack. With an enormous mesmerising effort he got back onto one knee, got his right foot underneath him, pawed the air once, looking for a hold... then keeled over.

Murdoch returned to Hoyle. I could feel in Walker a kind of exhaustion because he knew how far away from certain things Murdoch had travelled, how pointless it was to hope for compassion.

I wanted Hoyle to be unconscious, but he wasn't. He couldn't move, but he was aware of the man standing over him. Feelings I wasn't entitled to flickered.

Murdoch was at a familiar dead-end of irritation. It was always irritating, eventually, that you could find out exactly how much violence a body could absorb before it died. Every body was initially fascinating and unique. Every body was initially the body of a person. As in pornography. But like pornography's rituals violence wore through the uniqueness so quickly. Soon the person was gone and all that was left was dumb finite flesh. And the dumbness and finiteness was a dead-end, because your will was infinite and impossible to satisfy. Your will needed the person to last for ever.

(Whereas for the werewolf... What? The person did last for ever? Certainly my victims never stopped being people. Certainly they lived on in me. Certainly the person was never separable from the flesh. Here was a new room in the house of many absurd mansions: I read the books, Murdoch burned them. I was erotica, he was porn. Jake would have been proud of me.)

Murdoch lifted his boot and stomped as hard as he could on Hoyle's head. Hoyle's eyelids fluttered. Blood ran from his mouth, exactly as the juice from a can of cherries I once pointlessly punctured with Lauren's penknife. Murdoch swung his foot back and kicked Hoyle in the face. Hoyle's head snapped back and a tooth flew out. Murdoch stood for a moment with his thin mouth closed, breathing through his nose. Then he unslung the machine gun and took hold of it by the barrel. He positioned himself carefully, swung the weapon up over his shoulder, then brought it down with all his force on Hoyle's skull.

He did this repeatedly for perhaps a minute, fifteen or twenty blows, then stopped.

Hoyle was dead, of course. His left eye was on the floor and his brain was half out. A halo of dark blood had formed around what was left of his head. There was a Monty Python drawing it reminded me of, one of Terry Gilliam's surreally compelling animations. Murdoch poked at the eyeball with his toe. There was a mass of silent energy in the men around us. Murdoch looked at Walker, emptily, for a few moments. It seemed one of them must say something, but neither did. I had a profound sense of all the time and energy I'd spent telling myself not to believe but believing anyway that this was going to bring me to my son. All that time and energy and belief poured into nothing, like trust into a traitor, like billions into a scam.

Then I felt a stinging sensation in my shoulder, and within five seconds everything went black.

35

I woke to the stink of vampires.

And disinfectant. Joined immediately by the memory of Murdoch's bored face and Hoyle's eye out on its optic nerve and Zoë's hot fragile sleep-scented head when I kissed her goodbye.

I rolled over and vomited.

I was alone on the floor of a prison cell. Ten by twelve, bare concrete on all sides except one, which was a row of four-inch-diameter steel bars even *wulf* in all her glory wouldn't be able to budge. A yellow bucket. A large plastic bottle of water. The hum of air-conditioning and the soundproofed feeling of being deep underground. A tired fluorescent buzzed, gave the light an irritating tremor.

Assume Walker's dead.

The thought was there like a standing stone with me in the cell. I admitted it was there, but that was all. The thought was there and that was all. That was all I had to concede.

For a while I could do nothing but lie curled on my side with my arms wrapped around myself, breathing, humbled. It was like my time on the floor of the safe-deposit cubicle at Coralton-Verne. Every time I told myself, Right, get up, stupid, I found I couldn't. If it hadn't been for the smell tormenting me I might have dropped back into sleep.

Eventually, by degrees, I sat up. Dehydration banged in my head. Unsuckled milk stabbed my breasts. *Blocked ducts, abscesses, cancer.* Hardly mattered now. My neck was numb from where the tranquiliser had gone in. I crawled with what felt like audibly tearing muscles to the water bottle, found I *just* had the strength to unscrew the cap, then drank, all the while thinking, *don't drink a lot, you don't know when you'll get more,* but too thirsty to take my own advice. When I lowered the bottle it was half empty.

I got, via a series of wobbling false starts and failures, to my feet. Let the blood in my limbs loosen. My backpack was gone. I stepped up to the bars and looked out.

There were six cells, three either side of a short corridor which was sealed by a bank vault door at each end. Card-swipe entry. A line of CCTV cameras along the corridor ceiling, one trained on each cell. My cell was the middle of the three. I couldn't see if the ones on my left and right were occupied, but in the cell opposite me was a boy of maybe eleven or twelve, skeletally thin, lying in the foetal position on the floor with his arms wrapped around himself, staring at me. He had a skullish face, large green eyes and tangled white-blond hair. All he had on was a pair of dirty white Adidas sweatpants. His circulatory system showed through his skin. He looked like a thing of porcelain webbed with fractures.

The stink was coming from him.

'Hey,' I said.

'Hey,' he replied. He was wet with what looked like pale pink sweat, jellyish in places.

'Is it just me and you down here?'

He nodded.

'Where are we?'

He swallowed. Closed his eyes. Swallowing hurt. Existence

hurt. 'Don't know,' he said. An English accent I couldn't place. Or an English accent interfered with by lots of places.

'Where were you when they caught you?'

'Scotland.'

'How long have you been here?'

'Twenty-one days.'

'Are there other vampires here?'

With bizarre fluttery speed he got up onto his elbows and retched, shuddering. A single pinkish strand of what looked like mucus hung from his bottom lip. He spat it out. There was a small puddle of the stuff next to him on the floor.

'Is that me?' I asked.

He couldn't answer. I realised he had his arms around himself to contain what looked like muscular spasms. Each time one came his capillary system darkened, then faded again when it passed. I thought: Twenty-one days. Jake said vampires needed to feed every three or four. They were starving him.

'You... a werewolf?'

'Fraid so.'

'They told me you lot stank. I mean—' Pain hit him again. He brought his knees tighter to his chest, clamped his jaws. Breathed through it. 'That didn't come out right.'

'Yeah, well, if it's any consolation, you stink too.'

He didn't smile, but his eyes said he would have if he'd had the strength. 'You don't have to... talk to me... like I'm ten,' he said, shivering.

'I didn't realise I was.'

'It's the tone. I'm seventeen.'

Now that he said it I realised I'd been pitching as if to a child. Old habits. For all I'd known he could've pre-dated Moses.

'Sorry,' I said. 'Stupid of me.' It was an effort not to react to

225

how bad he looked. An effort not to be so obviously thinking: you're dying, kiddo.

'How old are you?' he asked.

'Thirty-four,' I told him. 'I'm new. Listen – oh, fuck.' *I* had to vomit again. This time I made it to the bucket. The disinfectant's ammonia was a brutal palliative against his stench. I kept my head over it. 'I guess they think this is hilarious,' I said, once I'd recovered and crawled back to the bars. I'd brought the bucket with me, held under my nose.

He nodded, but I could see the effort talking was costing him.

'Do you know how long I've been here?' I asked. 'Was there anyone with me when they brought me in?'

'Don't know,' he said. 'I was asleep. Woke up... a couple of hours ago. You were here.'

Assume Walker's dead.

More was required now. Just admitting the thought wasn't enough. So here was the feeling, as if something vital had been surgically removed from me while I was unconscious. Assume he's dead. The different quality of reality without him in it. Fresh loneliness, fresh failure, the world like a big brashly-lit room, a huge empty space for me to feel sorry for myself in. *Serves you right*. Assume he's dead. Assume Konstantinov's dead. Assume you're alone in here and you'll never get out and your daughter will never know you and your son will die. Make all the worst assumptions.

'How'd they... catch you?' he asked.

'We got set-up,' I said. 'It's a long story. Look, I'll tell you the whole thing but can you just tell me what you know about this place first? What's your name, by the way?'

'Caleb.'

'I'm Talulla.'

He made a slight movement with his head. Official hello. The pink sweat had darkened.

'Are you up to talking?' I asked.

He swallowed. As if forcing down powdered glass. 'Tired,' he said.

'I understand. I'm sorry.' I was sorry. Species revulsion was no joke – *wulf* wanted as much distance between us as possible – but the shared predicament did a lot of the sympathetic work. 'It's okay,' I said. 'Just rest a while. We'll talk when you feel better.'

'I won't feel… better. I'll feel worse. They'll… be coming soon. I'm going… to die in this fucking place.'

Another spasm took him. The veins blackened. It was an ugly thing to watch but solidarity demanded it.

'They'll regret it,' he said, when he'd got his breath. 'When Remshi… comes… they'll wish they'd never… been born.'

36

Before I could pounce on that the vault door at the right-hand end of the corridor emitted a string of electronic blips, followed by a hydraulic sigh and the sound of a heavy lock opening. I looked at Caleb. His eyes were closed. Whatever it was he was familiar with it. Whatever it was it was bad.

The door swung open and Murdoch entered, followed by a younger, smaller, musclebound Hunter with too much energy dressed in black combat pants and vest, carrying a set of restraints and what looked like a cattle prod. He had a skinhead and sticking-out ears, round blue eyes and mouth like a chimp's. The overall effect was of a bouncy, steroidal little ape. A crowd's murmur followed them in. Murdoch came directly to my cell while the chimp-thug fitted what looked like a radiator key (hung on a chain around his neck) into one of six sockets on a control panel next to the door. One turn anti-clockwise and a red indicator light turned green. Two seconds later the middle six bars of my cell slid upwards, precision engineered, friction-free, and disappeared into the roof.

'How are you feeling?' Murdoch asked.

'Where am I?'

'You're at a detention facility in the Royal County of Berkshire, England. It's Tuesday the sixth of November and the time is...'

He looked at his watch... 'Seven-thirty-six in the evening. You were brought here by air under sedation, along with Walker and his team, who are alive, you'll be glad to hear, housed variously and elsewhere in the building. Now it might seem unwarranted but I'm... ' The chimp-thug entered my cell with the set of wrists-to-ankles restraints... 'going to have to ask that you wear these for now, so we can give our full attention to the business in hand.'

I hesitated.

'Please,' he said, reading me. 'No antics. You won't be able to get my gun, and even if you did there are twenty men in the room next door. Not to mention Mr Tunner here. Absolutely no harm will come to you if you cooperate. It's just a bit of peace of mind for your uncle John.'

'You don't need to cuff me,' I said. 'I'm not going to—'

He punched me, hard, in the stomach, faster than I would have thought possible. The universe sucked all the air out of my lungs and I dropped, first to my knees then onto all-fours. The pain absorbed me, immediately and completely. There was nowhere to go to get away from it because it was every-thing. I could see how far away being able to take a breath was, like a light on a distant shore. I'd be dead long before I reached it.

'The way it works with me,' Murdoch said, 'is that I ask you to come into line with my will voluntarily. If you don't come voluntarily you're brought by force. I should have told you I only ask once. That was an oversight. I apologise.'

'Getting sloppy, Nuncle,' Tunner said, as he began fitting the now-redundant restraints.

'She's going to vomit,' Murdoch said.

Tunner grabbed the bucket and got it under me just in time. I threw up in three abrasive installments then collapsed onto my side. As far as I could tell I still hadn't breathed in. There was an anvil of blood where my lungs used to be.

'Bring her in when she's herself again. Here, give me that.'

Murdoch, now armed with the cattle prod, returned to the control panel, inserted his own key, turned, got the green light, then moved to Caleb's cell, where the bars were already rising.

I couldn't see Caleb, but I would have heard if anything passed between him and Murdoch. It didn't. Murdoch just stood there for a few moments with the cattle prod in his hand. Caleb, evidently, was too weak to move.

Murdoch went back to the vault door. 'Sobel,' he called. 'Give me a bag.'

Someone handed Murdoch a clear plastic pouch about the size of a man's wallet.

It was full of blood.

37

The room next door was big and windowless, with the echoey feel of a school gymnasium. It contained nothing but a very large cage (maybe twenty by twenty feet with walls twice an average person's height) that had clearly been constructed from other cages, doctored and bolted together. Razor wire had been bound along two of its opposite sides. Two dozen or so Hunters stood around it, most relaxed (one or two smoking, another drinking a Coke) but a few doing warm-up stretches. Two doors, one closed, the other showing a brightly-lit corridor. A whiteboard on the wall displayed a list of names and numbers in different colours.

Caleb was in the cage. The blood had given him enough strength to drag himself there, goaded by Murdoch with the prod. Now he'd collapsed again. Tunner, having fastened my restraints to a bar on the vault door, had removed his black vest and was limbering up by the cage, deltoids twitching, abdominals like a pack of *boules*.

Murdoch raised his hand. The men's murmur died. 'All right,' he said. 'Mr Tunner. Time selection, please.'

Tunner rolled his head a couple of times as if to ease neck-tension, pursed his lips, took one deep breath, then said: 'Two minutes forty-five seconds, Nuncle, if it please.'

Murdoch took out a stopwatch from his pocket. 'Two minutes

231

forty-five on the clock for Mr Tunner. Number of bags, Mr Tunner?'

'Two more bags, Nuncle.'

'Two more bags, Mr Sobel. Time starts on completion of second bag. Ink-up and get yourself in there.'

One of the Hunters handed Tunner a police nightstick and a fat red felt marker pen. Sobel, meanwhile, reached into a bag and produced two more plastic pouches of blood. Tunner entered the cage and the door was locked behind him. Sobel tossed the blood-bags to where Caleb lay. Caleb stared at them. I wondered how many times he'd been through this battle with his thirst. However many, he'd lost every time. Would lose every time. It was in his face. The only way out was not to drink. But the vampire always drank. Always.

I watched everything that followed. Partly because again the forced solidarity of imprisonment demanded it, but mostly because I was no longer (in fact, never had been) the sort for whom not watching was an option. Whatever horror it was, if it was put in front of me, I'd look. (My mother was the same. I'd caught the tail-end of an argument she'd had with my dad. You haven't got a heart, he'd barked. You've got a fucking *eyeball*. With no eyelids, just permanently open, obliged to *see* everything. Yes, my mother had replied, with terrible calm sweetness, like God.) What followed was that Caleb bit into the bags and drank the blood. The livid circulatory map faded a little. He got first to his knees then to his feet, though it was obvious he was still weak, and, now that he'd had a taste, desperate for more blood.

Tunner approached, brazenly relaxed.

'He's not up for it,' one of the spectators called.

'He bloody is,' another replied. 'Come on, son, bar's open.'

'Let's go, Casper.'

'Teach him a lesson, son.'

But Caleb stood still. I could see in his jaw what it cost him, his rider simultaneously digging in the spurs and hauling on the reins.

'Look at the will on my boy. Look at the *will*.'

'He's going... He's going... '

'He's not. He's a fucking Zen master. You keep it down, my son. Good lad.'

'Come on, Tunner, for fuck's sake.'

Tunner was almost within reach. Caleb stared at the floor. His bare white feet were beautiful, fine-boned things.

'*Goo*-orn, son, you show him.'

'He doesn't want to look soft in front of his new girlfriend.'

Which remark had two effects. One was that Caleb's head snapped around to see who'd said it. The other was that it inspired Tunner. He leaped forward and yanked down the elastic waistband of Caleb's sweats. Suddenly the boy's small genitals were exposed – to a cheer from the crowd. It was only a second before he'd snatched his pants back up – but that was the end of his resistance. He flew at Tunner, mouth open, fangs exposed – with a speed Tunner manifestly hadn't expected, since his evasive leap took him straight into the razor wire. Caleb spun back on him and suddenly the room's atmosphere was tight. Tunner, now bleeding in several places, got away from the boy again, but only just. The crowd focused. The human heat and smell thickened.

'Forty seconds gone!' Murdoch shouted.

Caleb took two steps forward and went down on one knee – but got up again immediately. The blood-ration was still taking effect. Tunner came close, hesitated, came closer. They circled each other. 'I don't know what you're getting so embarrassed about,' Tunner said to him. 'It's not as if it's any use to you, is

233

it? I mean it's just as well it's *not* a whopper, really, because what a waste that'd be.'

The boy staggered forward. Tunner dummied him left – then came in from the right and cracked the nightstick hard and fast on his kneecap. I heard the bone shatter. When Caleb went down Tunner marked him on the back and shoulder – once, twice, three times with the felt pen – to another cheer and a smattering of applause.

'Sobel!' Tunner called. 'Give him another bag. He's slower than my fucking *nan.*'

Sobel looked at Murdoch. Murdoch held up two fingers. *Two* more. Sobel grinned. Tossed the pouches in.

This time Caleb caught them, both, with astonishing hand-speed, tore into one and sucked.

'Nuncle, that's not fair!' Tunner said.

Murdoch ignored him.

Tunner kicked at Caleb's hand – and the unopened pouch flew to a corner of the cage. Caleb turned to go after it and Tunner pounced on him, actually landed on the boy's back and began whacking his head with the nightstick. Caleb took three or four steps – an eleven-year-old giving a one-hundred-and-seventy-pound man a piggy-back – then went down on both knees. Tunner had marked him ten or twelve times with the felt-tip pen.

'One-minute-thirty gone,' Murdoch called.

Tunner dropped the pen behind him and with the now-free hand grabbed Caleb by the hair and yanked his head back. Caleb was six inches from the blood pouch, straining to reach it. The circulatory webbing was fainter now. Tunner smashed the night-stick across the boy's trachea. Caleb, gagging, shoved himself to his feet – then launched himself backwards, jamming Tunner against the razor wire. Tunner screamed and twisted, ripping the flesh on his back and speckling the nearest Hunters with blood. Several of them were looking at Murdoch. Murdoch, lips pursed, kept his attention on the watch.

Caleb was weakening again. It took both his hands to tie up Tunner's nightstick arm, which left the Hunter's other arm free. With a strange precision he reached around, got a grip on the side of Caleb's head, then dug his thumb into the boy's eye.

'I shouldn't worry too much,' Murdoch said to me, when the eye – or rather half of it – was out, 'he'll have another by tomorrow morning. You know how it works.' Then to Tunner: 'Two minutes gone. Aesthetically very poor, Mr Tunner. Aesthetically *very* poor.'

The rest of the contest was leaden and repulsive. Tunner gouged Caleb's other eye enough so that the boy could barely see, after which the Hunter could strike virtually at will. After kicking the unopened pouch out of the cage he had leisure to retrieve his felt-tip pen, and by the time Murdoch stopped the clock the boy lay curled semi-conscious on the floor covered in dashes of red ink, face a mess of black blood. As a final insult Tunner yanked the sweats down again and made a big red tick on one bare buttock. It took Caleb, sightless, limbs hot and confused, three attempts to pull his pants back up.

'Cheers, fuckhead,' one of the warming-up Hunters said, as Tunner exited the cage. 'He's not much use to the rest of us *blind*, is he?'

38

What felt like several hours later Murdoch came to see me. I'd been put back in my cell and given half a loaf of bread and some cold chicken, which, after a clash and wrestle of hungers, I'd eaten. I'd spent the time trying to express milk and pinballing off the same few thoughts: I was going to die in here. The vampires would kill Lorcan. Cloquet would abandon Zoë. The Hunt would find her. I'd never see my dad's face again. I had to get out. I was going to die in here...

My rhythms were scrambled. *Wulf* surged, came with confused violence right to the edge – the sudden deep strength in the chest and haunches, the iron in the eye-teeth, the shriek in finger- and toe-sockets – then exploded, left its ghost like a mist on the human machine. I kept wondering if, changed, I'd be able to bend the bars. I kept knowing the answer: No. The steel told my human hands exactly how far short *wulf*'s power would fall: not much, but enough. And anyway I'd be dead by then, or a vegetable on a gurney.

They'd brought Caleb back in a couple of hours after me. He was unconscious – or perhaps, if it was daylight outside, merely sleeping the sleep of his kind. His stink was dense and boiling. If I hadn't already vomited myself empty I'd have been at it again. I'd watched the damaged tissue of his eyes blacken, shrivel, drop off. Murdoch was right, I did know how it was: the silent jazz of cellular regeneration. When he woke up he'd blink and look at me out of his big green eyes, good as new.

'You'll be wondering if you're going to get raped,' Murdoch said. His odour of leather and clean canvas had been joined by the smell of spruce male toiletries. He'd showered and shaved since the cage. 'The answer is No. Science is coming tomorrow to begin a complete exam and analysis and my men are under orders you're not to be touched. In any case, it's not something I allow.'

I almost said, That's a shame, I could do with the action. I would've said it just to provoke him, but having thought it, there, like an embarrassing odour, was its truth. Desire was, whether I liked it or not, writhing around in me like an insomniac snake. Now, along with the struggle not to loathe myself for my *fucking uselessness*, plus the effort not to think about Lorcan and Zoë, plus despair like a soft white bed waiting for me to get in, plus the reality of death hitting me at random moments like blasts from a furnace – along with all this was the grinning idiot reliability of *wulf* lust. *Yes, well, say what you like about the Curse*, Jake had written, *but don't say it doesn't have a sense of humour. Sadistic or slapstick or absurd, but humour nonetheless.* In Poulsom's white jail I'd had a room with a door and a light that could be turned out, and though deep down I'd suspected infra-red surveillance there was at least the illusion of privacy. Not here. The lights in the cells stayed on 24/7 and the CCTV never slept.

'Sex is a force for chaos,' Murdoch explained. He had a lovely mellow-toned voice. 'I let it into this arena, pretty soon I've got distraction, conflict, insubordination. It's a rogue energy. This is an insight I have.'

I had a vivid re-run of him smashing Hoyle's skull in. He'd done it with a peaceful face. The face he'd wear sitting alone in a café staring out the window at the rain. It made me wonder what state Walker was in, wherever he was.

'What's going to happen to me?' I asked.

'Up to Science,' he said. 'Research on lycanthropes was shut down a couple of years ago, but recent events have opened it up again. Poulsom's work, mainly, the anti-virus. The eggheads'll put you through your paces and take a decision on it. If it were up to me, obviously, I'd cut your head off. Whatever happens, you won't be seeing the outside world again.'

Sometime in the past women (via *a* woman) had failed to live up to what he thought they promised. I imagined unappreciated passions, an intensity first awkward, then desperate, then disastrous. He was all wrong for women in just the mysterious way Walker was all right. Which it turned out didn't prohibit getting married or working alongside female agents. A woman was only a problem if she impinged, fundamentally. The wife, Angela, who'd seemed negligible enough, had in fact turned out to be an impinger. Analysing him and fucking other men. I might be an impinger. He hadn't made his mind up yet.

'Do you know where the vampires are holding Konstantinov's wife?' I asked him.

'And your son? You don't mention him in case we don't know about him. But of course we do know about him.'

Heat filled my scalp. A sudden fury and sickness and disgust at always being the patsy, at being every minute further behind the information. This was a version of hell: the closer to my son I thought I was getting, the further I was moving away. I imagined Jacqueline watching it, the *Talulla Show*, wincing with quiet delight at my fuck-ups. I imagined Jake, staring at the footage, unblinking, silent, burning.

'Your little girl too, obviously,' Murdoch said. 'Thanks to Hoyle. Thanks to Walker. Why did Walker think it necessary to give all that information to Hoyle? The answer is he didn't think it was necessary. He just didn't think. He's got a loose mouth.'

Which choice of words he regretted, a tiny shift in the hawk eyes conceded. *Walker's mouth*. On his wife's mouth. On her breasts, between her legs, all over her. Not that that was the root of the enmity. The root of the enmity was that both of them, he and Walker, had the same boredom, the same aloneness, the same certainty that what you did didn't matter – and yet Walker had a kind of virtue, if only the virtue of being likeable. For Murdoch that was the annoyance that had bloomed into monomania, that Walker casually proved there was another response to the vast mathematical silence. And fucked Murdoch's wife.

'Also,' Murdoch said, 'his birth certificate was in your backpack. Along with...' He pulled the journal out of his jacket pocket... 'Jake Marlowe's diary. I hadn't known killing and eating people was sexually arousing for you.'

I wanted to say something flip – but I wanted the book back more.

'I know the answer to this is probably no,' I said, 'but could I have that back? I mean you've made copies or scanned it for the files or whatever, right?'

'Yes.'

'Well, could I have it?'

The question brought us to a curious silence. There was no reason for him to comply. Except the pleasure it would give him to confound my expectation that he wouldn't comply. Which he knew I expected. So he'd do the opposite. Which he also knew I expected – therefore the inclination was to confound *that* expectation... And so on, potentially ad infinitum. It was as if we were having this hypnotic conversation out loud – yet I knew if I actually said anything out loud – *Please, just to keep me company while the kid's asleep* — he'd simply stare at me with the calm unhinged dignity... then turn and walk away without a word.

He handed the journal to me through the bars. The mind-reading made the gesture intimate. It was as if he was testing his own hatred. These were the curiosity margins he operated at.

'To answer your other question,' he said, 'no, I don't know where the vampires are holding your son, or for that matter Konstantinov's wife. Once we've dealt with Walker et al, and the lab-coats have decided your fate, I'll give this Remshi business a proper look.'

'You know the legend then?'

'We all know the legend. Everyone goes through a *Book of Remshi* phase at one time or another. "Phase" being the operative word. It's an appealing idea, the oldest living vampire — think of the stories he could tell! — but the book's boring. No one actually reads it.' Jake would have added (or I would have, or Grainer or possibly even Ellis): It's WOCOP's *Finnegans Wake*. But Murdoch didn't read. Like women books had failed of what they'd once seemed to promise him. Like women books were sly and false and in the end no kind of antidote to the emptiness he'd been falling through screaming all these years. Like women, books couldn't stop him.

'But do you believe he exists?'

His headset clicked. He held a finger to the earpiece. 'Go ahead.'

Pause.

'All right, I'm on my way.' Then to me: 'Duty calls.' He crossed the corridor. 'If he does exist,' he said, 'he won't make any difference. He won't know where he came from or where he's going. He'll have stories... He will have the stories. But that's all they'll be. Ultimately he'll be one more freak living off human beings, which means, in the end, it'll be my job to find him and kill him.'

He swiped the card, got the sequence of blips and the hydraulic sigh. The door closed behind him with the subdued sounds of precision technology. I rested my head against the bars. Realised, amongst other things, that I was getting used to Caleb's smell.

39

I read Jake for a while. Self-lacerating escape: Heathrow, the Plaza, the long drive west to Big Sur; love, love, love – but some of the Madeline material too. I couldn't help it now that I'd met her. Not a good idea in my state. The love hurt my heart and the sex (mine and Jake's, but if I'm truthful his and hers as well) got me pitifully turned-on. Walker wove in and out of all of it. I wanted to see his face and hear his voice. I contemplated – with an inner smile for how much Jake would've sympathised – just biting the bullet, lying down in the corner and having a hand-job. I didn't, however. I couldn't stand the thought of Murdoch watching. With the same look on his face as when he beat Hoyle to death. For what felt like a long time I lay on my back trying to think of anything – the formula for quadratic equations, the novels of Graham Greene, the sequence of US presidents – other than sex. Eventually, because even the werewolf body is an honourable machine, I fell asleep.

When I woke, Caleb was lying on *his* back, staring at the ceiling with his brand new eyes.

'Hey,' I said.

He didn't turn to look at me. Of course: The pants pulled down, the exposed genitals, the humiliation by a human male, the impotence and girlfriend taunts. A seventeen-year-old boy in a pre-pubescent body. The more I thought about it the more I saw it couldn't have been much worse for him. And he'd been here twenty-one days. How many times had he been in the cage?

My first instinct was to not say anything about what had happened. Give his ego time and room. But the more I thought about it the more I knew that wouldn't do. He'd see it for what it was, was already seeing it, in the silence while I figured it out. It would patronise him. It would inflate the misery it was supposed to diminish. I had to keep reminding myself he wasn't a child.

'I'm sorry that happened to you,' I said. I couldn't think of anything less blunt. 'If it's any consolation, I'm pretty sure it's going to be me next. We've got to get out of here.'

He didn't answer for a while. He was working out whether he could get past the shame. An alternative would be turning his back and never speaking to me again. I forced myself not to cajole him. Let it be his decision.

After a couple of minutes, still not looking at me, he said: 'How?'

'I don't know, yet. But they're going to move me tomorrow. Scientists are coming. Maybe it'll give me a chance to get a look at the layout of this place.'

'They'll give you diseases,' he said. 'To see how your immune system works. They make you eat stuff to see what happens when you reject it.'

'I *can* eat stuff,' I said. 'Just not all the time.'

'They cut bits off you.'

'Oh.'

'Will that hurt you?'

'Yes.'

'But you'll regenerate?'

'Seems that way. Everything except the head, apparently.'

'It's another thing they bet on. How long different parts of you take to grow back.'

'Don't tell me any more,' I said. 'I'd rather not know. Did you get a look at any of the rest of this place when they moved you?'

'No, they took me when I was asleep. It won't make any difference. We're going to die in here.'

'Suppose Remshi comes?' I said. 'Wouldn't he know where you were and come get you?'

A pause. He'd forgotten he'd mentioned Remshi. I watched him mentally retrace his steps.

'It's not Jesus and the lost sheep,' he said. 'It's not about *love*. I'd be no one to him.'

'I thought you said this lot would be in for it when he comes.'

'They will, but that's nothing to do with me. Humans aren't going to know what hit them. He can walk in the daylight. We'll all be able to walk in the daylight again.'

'Who told you that?'

'Jacqueline. But it's in the book.'

'Did Jacqueline... Was she your maker?'

Silence.

'Is it bad etiquette to ask?'

He still didn't answer.

'Well, it's up to you,' I said. 'I just need something to take my mind off what's coming to me.'

For a few minutes we remained like that, me sitting with my back to the wall, him lying staring up at the ceiling of his cell. When he spoke, it was obvious he was choked. 'We're not supposed to just tell anyone,' he said. 'But if I'm going to die anyway I suppose it doesn't make any difference.' The green eyes were filling with what in a healthy vampire I guessed would be blood; in his case thin pinkish-grey fluid. 'And if you get out of here,' he added, 'you can tell her I was sorry for being such a fucking idiot.'

'Jacqueline?'

'No. The one who made me.'

He'd been in Trinity Hospice in Clapham, dying of cancer. Gastric cancer in the first instance, which took doctors so long to diagnose (it's rare in children) that by the time they did he had tumors in his lungs, pancreas and lower bowel. He had eighteen months of radio- and chemotherapy, to no avail. His mother, a single parent (father a long since vanished one-night stand), had died in a car accident when he was four, and he'd been raised since then by his aunt and uncle in Wimbledon – not badly, it sounded like, but not with much love, either. 'I wasn't their kid. Jeff was my auntie Rochelle's second husband, and he didn't want me around. He worked in the City and she was training to be a psychotherapist. I spent my time with a string of au pairs and nannies. It wasn't bad. Jeff and Rochelle had a lot of money and felt guilty about not loving me, so by the time I was eight I was drowning in fucking toys and gadgets. I'm pretty sure if I'd asked them for a coke dealer and Kylie on a retainer they'd have sorted it, somehow. Then I got sick.'

The weird thing was, he told me, he never really believed he was going to die.

'I could see it in the other kids, the way they looked out of the windows at the grounds and the sky, I could see they were slowly grasping it, that they were going, that this world and all the things they'd taken completely for granted was going to be gone, and they'd be wherever, heaven or hell or whatever the fuck. They all thought they'd be somewhere, even if it was just floating around like a mist in space or walking the earth as miserable ghosts. There was only one girl, Hannah, who didn't think she was going anywhere. *Dead and burned up to ashes*, she said. *Finished. No fucking fairy stories.'*

There had been young feelings between him and Hannah, the little pause here said.

'I went back,' he continued. 'Afterwards, when I was a vampire. I was going to Turn her, if she wanted it. But by then she was dead.'

I wondered – but resisted asking – how many child vampires there were. It was obvious from Caleb's core of oddity there weren't many.

'But that's jumping ahead,' he said. 'Before all that my mother began visiting me in the middle of the night.'

'Your mother?'

'My maker,' he said. 'Mia Tourisheva.'

Mia. I knew the name. The beautiful blonde vampire Jake had flamethrowered at Harley's. Too much to hope – the name being uncommon, God being dead, irony still etc. – that this was a different Mia.

'I'd wake up and she'd be there,' Caleb said. 'Standing by the window or sitting by my bed. Her hair was the same colour as mine.'

She visited him every night for a week.

'It was like déjà vu that went on for days,' he said. 'Everything she said, everything we talked about, the sound of her voice, the hospice smell, her white skin and her hand like ice on my forehead – it was as if all of it had happened before. She knew everything about me. She knew about my mother, and Jeff and Rochelle, and the cancer. She said if I wanted her to, she could cure it, and that I could go and live with her.' He paused. Talking, and perhaps what he was talking *about*, was taking it out of him. The circulatory net had darkened in his skin. He was wet with the pink-grey sweat. He swallowed, an effort like clambering over something. 'She wasn't lying,' he said. 'In a film she'd be lying. In a film an eleven-year-old boy wouldn't really understand what he was being offered. In a film she'd be sly, evil, mugging at the fucking camera or something. She wasn't any of that. She said – ' another powdered glass swallow – 'she said she couldn't have children like a normal woman. I understood. You tell yourself later you didn't really understand, but you did. She never used the word "vampire", but it was in everything she said. I could live with her and never get sick again. I knew it was true. I can't explain...' He had to stop for a moment. The last of the blood's benefit was going. A convulsion took him for a couple of seconds. His odour sharpened, started to get to me again. 'I can't explain how I knew. It just seemed like the most obvious thing in the world. I asked her if it would hurt. She didn't – ' a spasm that lifted him almost into a sitting position – 'she didn't lie about that, either. She said it would hurt at first, but only for a few seconds. Then it would feel like drifting off to sleep.'

I wanted to hear the rest, of course, but I wanted to flick back to the Mia sections in the journal too. She'd made this child. Jake had set fire to her. I'd been Jake's lover. Now here I was in jail with her child. Connections. Life with the plot again. *Which will prove harder for humanity?* Jake had written. *The shift from a meaningful universe to a meaningless one – or the shift back? There are only these two modes, endlessly passing us back and forth like Tweedle fucking Dum and Tweedle fucking Dee...*

'It did hurt,' Caleb said. 'A *lot*. But like she said, only for a few seconds. Then it was like sinking into darkness and warmth. She told me to imagine a rope fastened around my wrist, so that no matter how far down I sank I was still connected to the surface. When I felt a tug on the rope, no matter how... No matter how tired I was... I must start to climb.'

Which, when the first drops of her blood touched his lips, is what he did.

'It's really hard at first. As if all your bones and muscles have gone. Then it gets easier. Then really easy. Then happiness. It's not... climbing then. It's like... being pushed up by a force... from underneath...'

He couldn't continue for a while. Again I thought of the twenty-one or probably now twenty-two days he'd been here at this level of suffering, all alone underground. Like my son, wherever he was – though as soon as I thought it I told myself the idea of them torturing him made no sense. They couldn't risk something going wrong with him. They'd want him healthy for the sacrifice. I told myself this while my facetious self said, Yeah, you tell yourself whatever you need to hear, hon.

'She'd told me she'd need my help afterwards,' Caleb went on. 'Said I'd be strong and she'd be weak. I saw it all like a film, what she was saying, how she was telling me it would be. I took her to the room next to mine. There was a boy... I remember thinking... at school – oh, fuck—'

'It's okay,' I said. 'Rest. We can talk later.' But he wanted this. I remembered the relief, telling Jake about the night I was attacked in the desert, about my first kill in Vermont. *You can't live if you can't accept what you are, and you can't accept what you are if you can't say what you do. The power of naming, as old as Adam.*

'At school,' Caleb said, 'before I got sick, people had started giving each other lovebites. It was a... craze. You were... cool... if you had a... lovebite.'

'Oh my God,' I said.

'What?'

I could have laughed. I almost hadn't asked Murdoch for the journal back.

But I had. And he'd given it to me. *Keep reading, Lula,* Jake had said. Well, I had kept reading. I thought of Lauren's face when Mrs Maguire in English class had said that if a book wasn't worth reading twice it wasn't worth reading once. Lauren had waited till her back was turned then said, Yeah, ditto guys and fucking, but unfortunately there's only one way to find out.

'Never mind,' I said. 'I'll tell you later.'

'Tell me now. What is it?'

How many days since they'd brought me in? No more than two. That meant at most fifteen or sixteen days to full moon. Two weeks. Maybe just over two weeks. With a lot of work to do. God being dead, irony still rollickingly alive.

'I think I know how to get us out of here,' I said.

40

'Science' was three lab-coated unapproachables, all male, two (in obedience to the god of stereotypes) in their sixties, bespectacled and bald, but a third who looked like a young Clint Eastwood – or rather, given his polished skin, a waxwork of the young Clint Eastwood. No good. He had a bright, steady, impenetrable obsession with his discipline, impenetrable being the key word. The baldies' age and aesthetic low-scores ruled them out. Even leaving my preferences aside there was an obvious credibility gap: they'd have to be narcissists or unfeasibly stupid not to realise something was afoot. If what I had in mind was going to work it wouldn't be thanks to the men in white.

Fortunately, there were guards.

'I don't see any cameras in the corridor. Is that right?'

It was day three since my transfer to laboratory quarters. No amputations (yet) but I'd had swine flu, hepatitis C, HIV and TB, all of which my immune system had dismissed with a languid swat. Endless blood and urine tests; no stool (thank God) courtesy of *wulf* throwing up everything they force-fed her, although they bagged the vomit and carried it away with religious reverence. The great relief was that they gave me a battery-operated breast pump. Not out of compassion, but because they wanted the milk for analysis. I was drying up. By the third day I was down to a couple of spoonfuls. Not humanly normal, but then we all knew what the response to that was. I hadn't looked in a mirror since leaving the Dorchester, but I could tell the last of the post-partum weight was almost gone. A world record, presumably, another random and redundant boon from the Curse – and a condition that (vanity or obtuseness) I hadn't realised the plan depended on.

My new room wasn't quite the minimalist luxury bedsit of Poulsom's white jail (no TV, no en suite, no Harrods toiletries, no bath robe), but it was an improvement on Murdoch's hospitality. The same concrete windowless walls, but a floor of blue gym mats that evoked, comfortingly, high school; a pillow, a woollen blanket, and a nifty little camping toilet that smelled of brand new plastic and bleach. My clothes were confiscated (though I was allowed to keep the book) and replaced with a stiff white hospital smock. Restraints depended on the guards. There was a single leg-cuff on a steel cable bolted to the wall that allowed me to pace-out my little square, or there was the wrists-to-ankles contraption, or, for the ultra cautious, both. All sealed behind a steel door with a food hatch and a viewing plate an observer should've been able to slide open or shut but which was in fact jammed permanently open. Beyond my cell door was a corridor – cameraless, it appeared – containing three more (empty) cells and at the end a tiled recessed shower cubicle, where I was allowed to wash (and brush my teeth – joy!) when my stint in the lab was done. From the corridor another door led to a small white-walled antechamber, where one of three rostered guards sat with laptop and com-unit at a fold-out table and chair.

Three guards.

Three men.

'No, there aren't any cameras in there. Why, what did you have in mind?'

This was Devaz. Of Goan descent, in his late twenties, not much taller than me, with a schoolboy's side-parting, a roundish face, bright brown eyes and a fruity little gap between his upper front teeth. He wasn't good-looking, but there was nothing insurmountably wrong with him. He'd sneaked me the tooth-brush and toothpaste, so I couldn't hate him. Crucially, he was so plainly susceptible to sex (which was probably behind the toothbrush and toothpaste) that whoever was responsible for putting him on duty here would be in epic trouble with Murdoch if my plan worked – and if Murdoch survived it.

'I see, sir, that you derive an ungentlemanly pleasure from making a lady ask.'

'Madam, not at all. Not at *all*.'

This was the established nonsense. He knew what I had in mind (though not *why*) because I'd told him on my first day under his guard. He'd overseen me showering, drying off, dressing, by the end of which I knew all I needed to know. Later, through my open door-plate, I'd spoken to him very quietly and reasonably, exactly in the manner of an intelligent woman mastering enormous self-disgust because she had to. The levity and decorum, I made it obvious, were in inverse proportion to the hateful lowness of my desire. Colonial memsahib in houseboy's power. He loved it.

'Did you talk to Wilson?' I asked him, the next day, when he started his shift.

'Yes.'

'And?'

'It would be lovely, I'm sure, if it weren't for these notions I have about keeping my job.'

Rhetoric. His having talked to Wilson told me it was a *fait accompli*. I could of course have talked to Wilson myself, but of the two of them Devaz called the shots. Plus the Goan's ego was precious enough to have been miffed if I'd gone to Wilson first.

He'd been adored by his mother and sisters. It was there in his eyes' twinkle and the uncorrected tooth gap.

'Well,' I said. 'You know where I am.'

It was a two-part seduction. Part One was simple. It addressed, through or beneath or cunningly alongside the established nonsense, the pornographied man exclusively. All it required was me looking at him in a way that said I knew the things he wanted and would do most of them willingly and the remaining few with either arousingly obvious resentment or hot-faced surprise at myself. Part Two addressed the sceptic and the lousy WOCOP employee. It required persuasion, reasoning, argument. Didn't he know what happened to *my kind* the closer we got to full moon? On top of everything else I was suffering – imprisonment, the loss of my children, the indignities of the lab, the certainty of death – was the non-stop assault by *you know what.* I told him, again very calmly, that in the world outside I wouldn't look twice at him, but that these were extraordinary circumstances. In these circumstances, believe it or not (again calmly) he'd be doing me a favour. I'd even keep the restraints on, if it made it easier for him. The pornographied man had already said yes, yes, Jesus *Christ,* yes. The sceptic and the lousy WOCOP employee had a period of denial to work through.

'How can you expect me to have relations with you when you've told me you don't find me in the least attractive?'

'Because I know that's just the thing to pique a gentleman's ardour.'

'My God, what a thing to say!'

'Not at all. We modern ladies know how things work.'

'I'm shocked and stunned. I'm *saddened.*'

'Oh, I can help you with that. I really can.'

I had to remain playful and calm, a combination of convincing sexual readiness and resigned realism. Not easy, given the loudly ticking clock. If the amputations started I'd be in trouble. Bloody or bandaged or visibly regenerating stumps wouldn't help. There were of course men who liked that sort of thing (Lauren's brother had a stash of warped porn: one picture of a woman with amputated legs and two bearded men rubbing their cocks against the big satiny stumps) but Devaz didn't strike me as one of them.

'Really, sir, I do think Wilson's agreement in this matter removes the last obstacle to our happiness.'

Naturally, Wilson, a tall, wiry twenty-six-year-old with red hair and an Adam's apple that bent his gullet like a little elbow (but who was nonetheless the unit's arm-wrestling champion) and who'd have to keep lookout while Devaz was with me, had wanted to know what was in it for him. What does he *think* is in it for him? I'd said to Devaz, having momentarily lost patience with the established nonsense. He's not gay, is he? It's not as if you and I are getting engaged. The fact was I needed Wilson. Devaz on his own might not be enough. The third guard, Harris, was the best-looking of the bunch, with angelic dark eyes and cruel cheekbones, but he was also, according to Devaz, Wilson and my own intuition, a stickler for protocol and a WOCOP idealogue in the making. It was a shame. I really needed three. Three was the number I'd had in my head from the moment I'd decided what I was going to do.

'I don't feel you fully appreciate the risk involved, madam. The *atrocious* risk to my reputation.'

Shower time was the window. The eggheads quit the lab and some fifteen or twenty minutes could pass before I'd be expected to appear, scrubbed, fresh-breathed, wet-haired and smocked, on my cell's CCTV. Fifteen or twenty minutes of alone time in the camera-free corridor with my armed *voyeur*. Wilson would man the antechamber and send Devaz word if anyone showed up. All I had to do was not lose my temper with Devaz.

Harris the stickler wouldn't speak to me at all. When he was on duty there was nothing to do but sit or lie in my cell, running through The Plan (which was really just a single idea, an all-or-nothing bet) or fretting about my children or mulling over everything that had happened. Caleb had gone quiet when I told him which *gammou-jhi* it was they were going to sacrifice. After a while, he'd said: If I knew where they were holding him I wouldn't be able to tell you. Then after a further pause: So I'm glad I don't know. Sorry.

Mia, his 'mother', wasn't a believer. As far as she was concerned the Disciples were fanatical idiots and Remshi was in the same bracket as Cinderella or the man in the moon. Like all cults Jacqueline's at first gently discouraged, then frowned upon, then outrightly forbade contact with non-members. A crisis had come. Caleb had broken from Mia. And broken her heart, I read between the lines. Their last fight had been toxic. He'd railed at her for trapping him for ever in the body of an eleven-year-old, for turning him into a murdering monster, for making him hate himself, for robbing him of the chance to die with a clean soul. His last words to her before leaving were that he despised her, that he wished she were dead. *Really* dead. Three days later WOCOP had caught him.

'Better than nothing,' Devaz said, when, on the fifth day, without warning, he dropped the established nonsense and dragged one of the blue gym mats out of my cell into the corridor.

I thought of all the times I'd been so close to screaming *Will you just* fuck *me already, for Christ's sake?* – and thanked the God who wasn't there for giving me patience.

'Put your hands out. We don't have much time.'

The shift into plain speaking unnerved us. I wondered, briefly, if he'd be violent, then realised he couldn't afford to be: violence would leave marks. Science would know. Science would investigate. Murdoch would find out.

'I have to leave the com on,' Devaz said, which conjured Wilson next door, listening. 'No,' he added, reading me, 'just the headphones.'

We were ambushed, somewhat, when it came down to it, Devaz, unlocking the wrists-to-ankles restraints, by my body's hot aura, by my particular femaleness and personhood, me by lust's sheer drop and drowning vision: this close to *having* sex, how much I needed it was no joke. The word 'yearning' presented itself, fresh and legitimate and surprised. My clit was fiendishly awake and calling the shots, the no-nonsense rep for all the intoxicated flesh and blood, for the whole dumb chorus of desire. Holding on to the plan would be like holding on to a talisman on a peyote'd visit to the underworld. I realised (*as* Devaz was removing the restraints) that we mustn't lose momentum. Pausing or saying the wrong thing would spook him. Off the back of which thought I worried, suddenly (as I had with Walker; assume Walker's dead, assume Walker's – but please God let him not be) that milk would come if he sucked my nipples. The morning's breast-pump had scored zero but who knew what a human mouth would do? No point mentioning it now. It'd be just the sort of thing to freak him out. Or maybe he'd like it? There wasn't anything out there a guy might not like. If he did it wouldn't be Walker's Dionysian ease but a dreary kink, a secret kept in his psyche like a big rat in a too-small box.

'Kiss me,' I said, since it was obvious when we stood face to face that he didn't know whether some occult prostitutional code prohibited it. 'Kiss me.'

Kissing surprised him. He'd forgotten its intricate powers. He was unerect when our lips met, but I knew what I was doing, and he was hard by the time we took the first breather. He'd become very quickly intense, his concentrated sexual self, and was balanced now between pornography and all pornography

256

wasn't. *Wulf* was awake, greedily grabbing through my blood's blur, wanting the moment for itself. My woozy strategist laboured as if against a powerful drug: *Keep him on the pornography side of the line. If you let it be anything else to him he won't want to share you and you need Wilson. You need* at least *Wilson.*

So I kissed him differently, with scorn for tenderness, and felt him shut something down in himself in response, felt *his* scorn, in fact, for the soft-hearted putz in him that had nearly wasted a tremendous pornographic opportunity. His odour was cinnamonish and his face had a tropical little force field. I got down on my knees, unzipped him, freed his cock. He'd washed, thank God. My *wulf*-sharpened nose at his fly got first canvas and a mild salt dash of urine then a burst of coconut-scented shower gel and melanin and clean pubic hair. He was the sort for shower-gel brand preferences and quality underpants, living in perpetual optimistic readiness for sex, for which the doting mother and sisters had prepared him. His cock was large, uncircumcised and had a downward instead of an upward bend. My look must've been too nakedly evaluative, however, because he softened slightly under my gaze. Remedially, therefore, I turned corrupted school-girl eyes up to him – *yes, I really am going to, in full, dirty knowledge* – and in steady, sly increments slid him into my mouth.

'Uh,' he said.

Uh indeed, but don't get too comfy there, hot-shot. It was a fine calculation (as far as calculation was possible through my blood's giggling urgency) how long to keep sucking him. Long enough so that he didn't feel short-changed when I stopped, but not so long that he ejaculated – and foiled the plan. And if I kept up *this* performance – oh, I *am* a dirty little girl, aren't I? – he'd be off in the next half-dozen strokes.

'No,' he croaked, when I did stop. 'Turn around.' I'd pulled him down onto the mat with me and he'd torn off the condom's wrapper with his gappy teeth. His face was moist and had new lights on. 'Turn around.'

Hoist by my own petard: I'd been so convincing in my omniscient slut act that he expected to proceed directly *au derrière*. *Wulf* was ready to give him an affronted slap, not because the area was off-limits, or because going straight there spoke so clearly of sexual selfishness (even if a girl's got the mental twist that makes it fun there's *always* so much more in it for the guy) – but because *in that position I wouldn't be able to execute The Plan*.

'In a minute,' I whispered. 'In here first. Please, just for a minute. Then anywhere you like.'

Nervous calculation in the Devaz eyes. I *was* a modern girl; I knew the modern male math: if a woman was willing to let you fuck her in the ass you didn't want to blow your load in her cunt. It was depressing how pornography had so emphatically demoted the vagina. The poor old vagina! No wonder the *Monologues* were such a success. 'Don't worry,' I said, licking his earlobe while he fit the rubber with trembling hands, 'you'll get what you want. Just don't come yet.'

He looked like a man not confident of his control (mouth open, eyes showing too much white) but with a little manoeuvring I got myself under him and eased him in. Thoughts and questions shot up like gun-startled birds. Would Zoë have got used to my absence? Caleb would have been back in the cage. Full moon nine days away. My children would change, crave flesh and blood, young as they were. Cloquet would have to call Madeline. What would the vampires do for Lorcan? Nothing? Add starvation to his sufferings? What was his reality? A world not warm enough, no scent of his kind but presences over him like cold cloud shadows. Like a careful rape. And I'd just let them. Fuck me, fuck me, oh God Jesus yes that's it...

Meanwhile, as *wulf* laid shameless grinning claim to my loins, my poor blood-blinded strategist staggered onwards in accordance with The Plan. I'd given Devaz a few preparatory nips mixed with kisses on his chest and shoulders, which he didn't seem to mind, but I had to be absolutely sure he wouldn't pull away at the crucial moment. And the only way to guarantee that was to render him incapable of volition. And the only way to guarantee *that*... I worked my left hand around his buttocks and down to his furiously puckered scrotum. A little fluttery stroking with the fingertips.

'Like that?' I asked him.

'Too much.'

I was wet enough to provide my own lubricant. Nimble manoeuvring with my right hand...

'Are you going to stick your cock in my asshole?' I whispered in his spicy ear.

'Oh Jesus,' he said.

'You are, aren't you? You're going to fuck my nasty little hole—'

'Please... don't...'

I slid my moistened middle finger up against *his* nasty little hole.

'You know I want it, don't you?' Faster fluttery ball-stimulation with left hand.

'Wait—'

'Deep in my dirty, sweet, tight little—'

'You've got to sto—'

'Oh, angel, come for me, come for your little whore—'

His universe stopped. He said: 'Oh, my God,' with metallic neutrality – and in I went with the prepped finger, all the way up his thank-God empty anus to the hapless prostate. Simultaneously I locked my mouth onto his neck.

'Ahhgggh,' he said. 'Fuck... fuck... fuck... '

I sucked and bit. As hard as I dared, but not so hard it would be taken for anything more than crazy bitch passion. 'Ummm,' I said, still biting, still sucking. 'Ummmm.'

'Holy mother of Christ,' he said, seemingly on the edge of tears.

Then, as his universe reassembled and flowed again and the squandered anal opportunity took fresh hold: 'God dammit.'

'Shshsh,' I consoled. 'Never mind... never mind. We can do it again tomorrow.'

'God *damm*it.'

Holding the condom on, he withdrew. He was dazed, not ready for the world. He'd lost his chirrup. His face looked pouchy. 'You didn't...?' he said.

No, I didn't. And though my strategist was sobbing with relief, the Whore of Babylon was frowning and breathing exasperatedly through her nostrils. This was the downside of The Plan: if it didn't scratch the *wulf* itch it would only make it worse. At the very last second I stopped myself from saying: Just fuck off and send Wilson in, will you?

'It's fine,' I lied. 'It's okay.'

'No, it's not. Lie down.'

Good Lord, the man had completely forgotten where he was! Christ knows how many selves I had in play just then, but one of them was struggling not to laugh out loud. However many selves it was, *wulf* was the biggest and loudest of the lot, and delighted to find Devaz sufficiently a creature of the absurd to feel it his masculine duty not to leave a woman unfulfilled. Not that I was capable – once he was down there sucking and licking my clit with touching enthusiasm and surprising efficacy – of anything other than grabbing his head and enjoying the ride (I considered trying to get the finger that had been up his ass into his mouth, for the Sisterhood, for revenge, but didn't trust myself to do it subtly) but in any case what, other than composure, had

I got to lose? If my theory was correct then so far everything had gone according to plan.

And in any case, fuck it, I deserved it.

He did, after perhaps ten minutes, make me come, though I nearly took his teeth out with my pubis in the throes. I felt a little giddy afterwards, and, *moron* that I was, better disposed towards him.

'Hurry up,' he said. 'That's twenty minutes. You should be back in your cell.'

'Wait,' I said.

'What?'

'The shower. I need to wet my hair so they'll think—'

'Okay, do it – but hurry up.'

He disappeared. A moment later, Wilson entered. He stood, half-blushing and half-smirking as I fastened my smock. Sexually he was less secure than Devaz, needed clear parameters and someone else to be unambiguously in charge. So for him I'd been clipped and schoolmistressy, annoyed by my needs, manifestly the sort of will he could surrender to for twenty minutes. His mother *hadn't* doted on him. I doubted he'd had sisters. There was – of course – a pornographied man in him too, but unlike Devaz he wasn't at ease with it. I could probably have made him fall in love with me, given a little more time.

'Let the camera see you put me back in the cell,' I said. 'And don't forget the leg-cuff.'

'Right.'

'You're coming to see me tomorrow, yes?'

He didn't answer, but the heat around him was palpable. His hands shook as he locked the cuff.

'Good,' I said, not quite looking at him. 'I'll see you then. And make sure you wash, will you?'

41

Two days later, after I'd fucked Wilson once (and Devaz a second time) the scientists cut my right hand off.

42

I wish I could say the time that followed was a blur, but it wasn't. It was dense with detail. I learnt two things. One was that no amount of violence you've done to others prepares you for violence done to yourself. The other was that you can't escape the marriage with your body. Divorce isn't an option. Even when you want to stop caring about it you can't. Even when the solution to knowing they're going to cut off your left breast is to disown it, you can't. It's yours. It's a friend you never realised you loved so tenderly and completely – until they separate it from you. It screams in silence. It retains, for a while at least, its life, its bond with you. But then, when it understands you're never coming to reclaim it, that the contract has been utterly broken, it dies, alone and betrayed, and becomes an inert, pathetic object, indecent and forlorn.

The new totalitarian regime was pain. Pain was exhausting in its inane imperviousness to everything. There was nothing, no persuasion or bribe you could bring to it. It was a monolithic idiot, the dumbest thing in the universe given complete power over the smartest, a heartbreaking inversion. I got used to the sensation of my screams locked in by a gag, having to back-up and cash themselves out in my skull. I discovered pity for my body. It was endlessly renewable, this well of pity. Every mutilation drew its unique portion. Every amputation subtracted, poignantly, took away – literally – some of who I was. I cried. Not in front of them. Later, strapped to my bed, surrounded in the dark by the Christmassy lights of lab technology I cried first for my losses and second because who deserved them if not me? The scientists were indifferent to my suffering – but at least they didn't relish it. *It's only the best for us if it's the worst for them.* Those were my words to Jake, in bed. *It's only the best for us if it's the worst for them.* Unlike the men in white we, *monsters*, wanted the person we were killing to know – through the blood-blur and the din of their own screams – not only that we knew what we were doing but that we loved doing it. We wanted our victims to see that our pleasure increased with their horror, that their horror was *required*, that their situation was hopeless. That was the dirty truth, the obscene heart of fuckkilleat: their hopelessness serviced our joy. In the court of human appeal the scientists were better off. At least they weren't doing it for fun. At least it didn't turn them on.

Not that that made any difference to me when they cut my breast off or gouged out my eye or wrenched the teeth from my jaws. The flesh in pain isn't interested in Old Testament justice or ironic justice or any other kind of justice. It isn't interested in anything except the cessation of pain. I hated them and wept for my poor body and my lonely self in the winking darkness, even as *wulf* rushed the butchered cells into regenerative action, a sensation in bone and nerves and tissue like a mass of insects racing towards something. No matter what atrocities you've committed you rage at those committing them on you.

They performed a hysterectomy.

I slept, on and off, dropped into and struggled out of fire-buckled dreams: one (not surprisingly) of being eaten by ants; another of Jacqueline's French-manicured fingers peeling back the skin from Lorcan's skull; another of the diner on Tenth Street, with the Coors neon and the pink leatherette booths and the faux shellacked counter where Clay would let me sit with my vanilla shake and talk to me about the hell his girl was giving him as if I were an adult; another of the lab mixed with the night at Big Sur, Jake dipping his cock into the raw pulp where the torn-open scientist's heart used to be.

Then the fluorescents would vibrate and flutter into life and the white coats would appear and another session would begin. I'd never known fear before. You don't know fear – not the fundamental kind – until you experience knowing what they're going to do to you and being utterly powerless to stop it. Invariably I wet myself when the lights stuttered on. The scientists didn't mind. The scientists expected it. I saw my distorted reflection in a stainless steel kidney dish. The young Clint Eastwood leaned over me and I smelled garlic and an aniseed breath mint. They punctured my lungs and broke two of my ribs. One of the bald men was named Hugh. He had large deep-printed fingertips that smelled of latex. He lit an acetylene torch and held it against me, shins, abdomen, back. First degree. Second. Third. The main surgical lamp was like a *War of the Worlds* flying saucer. They pulled out my fingernails. A blue and white cardboard box on a gurney said ZENIUM X-ray detectable abdominal sponge. Sometimes a radio played a couple of rooms away. The Black-Eyed Peas; Kylie; Lady Gaga. The scientists' shoes squeaked on the rubberised floor. It sounded like a language. Hugh lifted my severed hand as if it had broken off a holy statue. They were interested in everything. Primarily regeneration speeds (my breast took twenty-four hours, eye six, hand and foot forty-eight, skin two, internal organs a matter of minutes), but everything else too, from T-cells to C-fibres, from lymph nodes to hormones. Sometimes they used anaesthetic, sometimes not. I healed thirty per cent faster without it, they established. A particularly rigorous session with the acetylene torch and pliers revealed that up to a point – up to a *point* – rate of regeneration increased according to the increase in pain. They called that point the UPH: the Useful Pain Horizon. Sex with Devaz and Wilson receded, became years ago. All the life before the first amputation was distant and sealed. Cauterised. Eventually, even the first amputation seemed remote. My mind was a terminal any old rubbish could enter: advertising jingles; pop songs; scenes from obscure TV movies; the laminated alphabet chart from kindergarten.

Meanwhile, through the haze, I knew days were passing: the hunger first stirred, confused, then woke, then despite the pain began to beat and scratch its distinctive demands. *Wulf*'s nose asserted itself, insisted on the scientists as *living meat*. Deodorants and the lab's chemical fug were flashed through by stinks of their sweat and blood, an occasional whiff of stale piss or recent shit. Clint's breath spoke now not just of a noon tuna sandwich or yesterday's scotch but of his own deep and vital secretions. The moon was fattening and drawing the monster up through my human knit. I felt her in the join of my jaws, my femurs, my spine. I wondered what they had planned for transformation. Whatever it was it wasn't the same as what I had planned. I spent my entire time secured in the lab now, and hadn't seen any of the guards for days – but Devaz and Wilson were still around, not far away. I could tell.

I tried not to think of my children. Failed. Would Cloquet have contacted Madeline? Had I been stupid to suggest it? There was no betrayal in her, but wasn't she reckless? Would she take the necessary precautions? Cloquet procuring a victim for my little girl was risky enough, but at least he was careful. Of course Zoë wouldn't be able to make the kill herself, not unless the victim was an infant. Cloquet would have to get his hands dirtier than ever. Was he up to it? Picking up Kaitlyn in a bar and bringing her to his mistress to be murdered was one thing. Beginning the murder himself was quite another. Maybe that on its own would drive him to the London pack. And Lorcan? In a way he'd be better off. If the prophecy's specification of sacrifice at midwinter was correct he had more than a month left to live. Since the vampires knew he'd have to feed I didn't doubt they'd provide for him. (A perverse vision – God being dead, irony etc. – of them feeding him Konstantinov's wife with a collective chuckle, but I ignored it.) *If* the prophecy was correct. Every now and then the size of that *if* made itself real. *Unreliably translated and massively bowdlerised*, Walker had said. Suppose the version of *The Book of Remshi* used by the faithful differed from the one WOCOP had acquired? Suppose it read not 'midwinter's day' but 'six weeks before midwinter's day'? Suppose it said nothing at all about midwinter? Suppose Remshi could take his victim's blood whenever he felt like it? My son could be dead already.

Then, abruptly, the mutilations stopped. I had a long stretch of morphine-edged stasis. It was as if they'd removed a hot suit of armour and put me in a bath of chilled aloe. Delicious protracted shock. Everything they'd cut off or broken or burned renewed itself, via molecular bacchanal, seamlessly. Actually not seamlessly. For a while there was a debilitating sensation where new cellular matter met old, an effect like the blood's shudder and buzz when you bang your funny bone. Clint & co. looked annoyed – not by the results, but by having to stop. I got the impression they'd been interrupted with plenty of science still to do. Once or twice through the drug's soundproofing I caught reference to 'they' or 'them' in a tone that said a decision they didn't support had come down from on-high.

One morning (or rather the time when the lights came on)

I woke to find Hugh preparing a hypodermic. I was still strapped down, but they'd removed the restraint that normally held my head still. Fear, it turned out, hadn't really gone away. It was right there, immense and immediately available. He must have felt it coming off me, because I remember him saying: 'Don't worry, it's just a relaxant' – before all the lights went out again.

43

The hunger dragged me awake. Even before I opened my eyes I knew full moonrise was less than twenty-four hours away. *Wulf*, impatient to fill her lungs, was all but crushing mine. Transformation's preamble crunched and popped in my muscles and bones. My spine wanted out, craved its full lupine length. Nerves shivered in the sockets of my fingers and toes and there, like a heavy helmet, was the ghost of the monster's skull around my own. I had one hand in the pocket of my smock, where, perhaps as a joke, perhaps as a no-hard-feelings gesture, Clint & co. had shoved Jake's journal.

No mistaking where I was: Caleb's freshly repulsive odour and the bucket's mean spirit of piss, vomit and bleach, yes, home sweet home – but with a new olfactory twist: the suggestively pressing smell of human flesh and blood. I opened my eyes.

I was, of course, back in my old cell – but I wasn't alone. Walker, thin, bruised, unshaven and stinking not just of living meat but stale excrement, urine and sweat, lay curled up in wrists-to-ankles restraints looped by a steel cable around the bars. He was so clearly incapable of doing anything the cuffs were an act of satire. Of the clothes he'd had on when they caught us only his pants remained, now filthy. His face was drained. The blue-green eyes were big and bright and fractured. One of them – the left – had a badly infected sty. It was the sort of irritant I knew he'd stopped noticing, the sort not big enough to register above the constant noise of the other injuries.

'Oh God,' I said.

'Don't touch me.'

Small words that said a big piece had shifted. Or died. It would've been less awful if his voice had changed, but it hadn't. It was still him, deeply altered.

'They brought him in today,' Caleb whispered, not out of delicacy but because he could barely speak. I looked over at him. He was still in nothing but the white Adidas sweatpants. The pinkish sweat had dried. His skin was tight and translucent, veins livid. How many times in the cage since I'd been gone? A detached part of me was surprised to find him still alive. A not-so-detached part relieved. *Don't get soft, idiot. You need him alive, that's all.*

I turned back to Walker. 'Hey,' I said.

He didn't respond. He didn't want me. I was sending signals to everything in him he thought he'd let die. If he'd had a silver loaded gun at that moment he might have shot me just to stop the appeal to his dead self. He was terrified it might not be entirely dead, might start placing horrifying demands on him, or rather just the one horrifying demand: that he find room for what had happened to him without becoming someone completely different.

I wondered what he thought had been happening to me. Here I was, good as new, no scars to prove anything *had* happened to me. There he was, utterly changed. It was a betrayal, to have your own body erase the evidence of the abuse it had suffered. It made the evidence on the inside harder to bear. The evidence on the inside was like getting raped in broad daylight in a crowded street without a single witness.

Getting raped. Telepathy like the shadow of a bird passing over us. Our eyes met. He looked away. I thought of a news story from years back, a Haitian prisoner sodomised with nightsticks and a fire hose in NYPD custody. Then a tumble of other images. The pictures of stripped and hooded detainees at Abu Ghraib. The peculiar glazed mirth of the MPs looking on. I wondered if Walker had it in him to recover from that kind of violation. If you were a woman a portion of your fear was given over, in installments that began when you were still a little girl, to rape. How not? Women got raped all over the world, every day. It was a structural latency. But not if you were a man. If you were a man you didn't start worrying about rape until you were on your way to jail. Did that make it harder to absorb it when it happened? Men would think so.

The uselessness of saying anything was with us in the cell like a grinning genie. Walker ran his tongue over his cracked lips. His aura was meagre and wrongly concentrated, an effect like the bad breath of very ill person. All the charm and the glimmering history of the women who'd desired him was gone. It was as if someone had found the last hidden gold of his boyhood and ripped it out of him. I thought of him saying my name that night in the dark, unguardedly – Talulla? – the tenderness and delight that had ambushed me. I wanted to put my arms around him and I knew it was the last thing he wanted me to do. He didn't want to be touched by anyone ever again, except perhaps brutally, to honour the vicious god who had visited him.

'You're going to kill me,' he said, still not looking at me. 'Tomorrow. That's why I'm here.'

I didn't bother saying, *What do you mean?* I knew what he meant. I'd known while he was still saying it. Live victim. Premium entertainment. Maximally sweet for Murdoch, who'd watch, maybe bring his wife in and make her watch. Here's your lover. Take a good look. Science would wait till I was back in

271

my human shape then roll me in for another session. So far they'd had the chance to study the empty-bellied werewolf. Now they could learn all about her when she was full. They'd electrode me up to see what was going on in my brain while I watched the footage of myself killing Walker.

'No,' I said. 'I'm not.'

'You won't have a choice. And anyway I—'

'It's not going to happen. You're not going to give them the satisfaction.'

Satisfaction. Bad word-choice. So many words now would lead him straight back to what had been done to him. He closed his eyes and drew his knees in to his chest. 'You won't have a choice,' he repeated.

'There's always a choice,' I said, quietly, gently. (Yes, there was. But it was always the werewolf who got to make it. Ask the victims. Ask Delilah Snow.) I wanted to wrap him in quietness and gentleness, let him sleep for a long dark season next to me. Except of course tenderness was cruelty to him now, anything that reminded him of the personhood that had been broken and defiled. He didn't want to be invited back into caring whether he lived or died. If you care, then what they do to you – what they've done to you – counts double. I got an image of Murdoch's face, a look of rage so resigned and extreme it appeared as mild boredom. Because destroying a person wasn't enough. No matter what you did it wasn't enough. You were still there after the last of the person's dignity was gone. You were still there, unsatisfied, like God.

Caleb retched, shuddered, jammed his jaws together, subsided. 'Kill me while... you're... at it,' he said. 'I can't... stand this... any more.'

'I'm not killing either of you.'

'Oh, yeah,' Caleb gasped, 'I forgot. You're getting us... out.'

Walker's eyes opened, but only to stare at the floor.

'She can't tell you *how*,' Caleb said. 'Because they're... listening.'

I'd had to assume they were listening. It was why I hadn't risked telling Caleb what I had in mind before Science carted me off. There was no point saying anything now. If my plan worked they'd find out soon enough. If it didn't then I'd spared them having their hopes butchered.

'Mike got out,' Walker said, still staring at the floor.

'He did? How do you know?'

'Overheard them...' He paused, seemed to drift off. The word 'them'. Certain pronouns had been reinvented. 'They', 'them', 'he', 'him'. They stalled him, these words, reminded him he wasn't himself any more. 'Overheard,' he said. '"The Russian got out."'

I pictured Konstantinov drinking from a forest stream like an animal, his flesh white in the green gloom.

'When?' I asked.

Walker's eyes closed again. It was an incalculable weight for him to lift, this talking as if nothing had changed.

'Walker?'

'A week, maybe more.'

'What about the others?'

'Dead.'

The vault door opened. Murdoch and Tunner entered, bow-legged Tunner with his trademark ape-grin and delighted muscles, Murdoch placidly winding up an alarm clock with his large headmasterly hands. The clock was the old-fashioned kind, with twin half-bells on top. I used to have one just like it in my bedroom when I was a kid. Walker, haemorrhaging adrenaline, curled tighter in the restraints, face shut, trying to find a place to hide deep within himself. I pictured him naked, cuffed hands to feet, held by two Hunters in black while Tunner jammed a bloody nightstick in and out of his ass and Murdoch took a cellphone call and continued observing.

'It's nine minutes past three in the morning,' Murdoch said, quietly. 'Full moonrise will be in fourteen hours and two minutes.' He put the clock on the floor, facing us, then stood over it, hands in his pockets. 'At that time, of course, Ms Demetriou will change into a monster.'

'A ravenous monster, Nuncle,' Tunner said.

'Ravenous, as you say, Mr Tunner.'

'Bereft of morality.'

'Bereft of—'

'Here's a thought,' I said. 'Why don't you skip the vaudeville and fuck off?'

Caleb laughed, wheezily. It was the first time I'd heard him laugh. I got a small detonation of pleasure from it, and from the effect of the interruption on Murdoch, whose mouth stalled for a sweet second or two. Then he said: 'That was very well done. Like getting a slap. I'm slightly embarrassed.'

For a few not-so-sweet moments no one spoke. Murdoch had a power over silence, like mine over the wolves. He could summon it and make it an extension of himself. In it we saw the smallness of the point I'd scored against the size of what was coming to us.

'Anyway,' he said, when he knew long enough had passed, 'I'll be back in time to see everything. So until then I'll say cheerio. Mr Tunner?'

When they'd gone, Caleb said: 'Can you reach the clock?'

'No,' I said. 'Why?'

He swallowed. Another throatful of crushed glass. 'That ticking... ' he said. 'Going to drive me... fucking mad.'

44

Walker slept. Eventually, at a quarter after seven (sunrise in the world outside, presumably), so did Caleb. Then it was just me and the clock and the hunger – and the two new questions.

The first new question was: what would Konstantinov do if he really had escaped? It was thrilling to imagine him gathering a team to come and get us – thrilling and unrealistic. He didn't owe Walker. Walker owed him. All Konstantinov cared about was getting his wife back. Besides, there was no team to gather. Walker had already tried that for the Italian trip: only three takers – and they were all dead now. Any way I looked at it Konstantinov free was no more use to us than Konstantinov locked up. Which didn't stop me looking at it all the ways, repeatedly.

The second new question was: what would happen to Walker if my plan didn't work, if the theory it was based on turned out to be wrong, if I lost the big bet?

The answer was: I'd kill him and eat him. If not this month then next. If Murdoch was bent on Walker's death-by-werewolf then sooner or later the hunger would give it to him.

There was of course a drastic way out for Walker, if my theory was right. But if my theory was right The Plan would work. And if The Plan worked he wouldn't need the drastic way out. If I offered him the drastic way out now and he took it (which he would, the state he was in) *and* The Plan worked, the drastic way out wouldn't seem like a way out at all...

Meanwhile the hunger went comprehensively about its business. *Wulf* paced its human cage, sometimes flung itself at the bars. The bars got the bruises. My blood packed. As always there was nothing to throw up. As always the dumb guts kept trying. As when I was in labour, no position was any good. The minute any part of my body realised I was lying on it it started to protest. I wanted a warm bath, painkillers, booze. Cloquet would have his hands full with Zoë. Assuming he hadn't dumped her somewhere. I pictured a garbage heap with her bare leg sticking out, flies swarming around her foot.

LISTEN TO ME. CAN YOU HEAR ME?

I let myself examine the thought of both my children being dead. *Wulf* didn't like it, slashed me from the inside. The monster bitch wasn't ready to admit maternal defeat even if the human bitch was.

DON'T FIGHT IT.

I saw myself with my fangs in Walker's shoulder and my fingers palm-deep in his thigh. *Wulf* pointed out the obvious: *You'd be doing him a favour. What time is it?*

Ten to three in the afternoon. The hungrier I got the slower the clock hands moved and the faster the monster paced her cage. Soon the nausea would pass and I'd be in the full-of-beans stage. Then *I'*d be on my feet, pacing with her. A cage with an animal in it that was a cage with an animal in it. An unsavoury version of a babushka doll.

YOU CAN FEEL ME. I KNOW YOU CAN.

Walker woke up for a while and didn't move anything except his eyelids. He stayed curled up on his side, watching me.

'Are your ribs broken?' I asked him.

He blinked, slowly. *He* wanted out. Of existence. Every waking-up now was a waking-up to disappointment that the dream he'd been having was just that, a dream.

'Listen to me,' I said. 'When the time comes, I won't be able to speak. You know that, right? You won't believe it's still me inside. You'll think I don't recognise you. But I will. When I change you have to remember I'll know it's you and I won't hurt you.'

When he spoke his throat was so dry nothing came out. I got up and gave him some water. Kindness was cruelty to someone who wanted to go out as much as he did. Quite go out, go out, go out beyond all doubt.

'You'll do what you do,' he said, quietly. The dirty brown and gold beard made him look like John the Baptist.

'Yes,' I said. 'I will, eventually. I'll be able to hold out for a few hours, but sooner or later, if nothing happens, I'll kill you.' I leaned close and whispered in his stinking ear. 'But something *is* going to happen. Trust me.'

YOU KNOW WHAT YOU HAVE TO DO.

He opened his mouth but I put my fingers on his split lips. 'Shshsh,' I said. 'Don't talk. Just rest.'

Which was all well and good, but the smell of his flesh and the heat of his blood wasn't doing *wulf* any favours. 'Just rest,' I repeated. 'It won't be long now.'

I got to my feet, arms wrapped around myself, and looked down at the clock.

Two hours and forty-five minutes to go.

45

I n the fuzzed and jiggling seconds before transformation Caleb woke, much worse. His skin was almost transparent. I wouldn't have been surprised to see the twitch or shiver of an internal organ. The circulatory system was black and throbbing, a look of non-negotiable outrage.

'You forgot to feed him, Mr Tunner,' Murdoch said. 'When we came in earlier and I got my verbal slap.'

I was on my hands and knees at the back of the cell. I'd thought there would be more spectators, but it was just these two, both in black combat pants and t-shirts, both with side-arms, Tunner with a nightstick.

'It drove it clean out of my head, sir,' Tunner said. 'Such was the shock of it.'

My fault, in other words. Without the inner chaos I might have cared. As it was even my strategist's flailing reminder that we needed Caleb alive was lost in the self-wrestling blood. Obscure instinct (to meet death standing?) had forced Walker to struggle to his feet against the bars. He couldn't straighten up properly. The ribs. 'Don't forget what I told you,' I said to him. 'Look at me. Don't forget. Trust me.'

He smiled, faintly, out of his wrecked face.

'Trust me,' I said again – then froze.

The alarm clock went off.

Oh.

Now.

The moon had found me, laid its ownership in the roof of my mouth and down the length of my spine and like a firm and expert hand between my legs. There was a little laughing admonishment in its touch, that I'd allowed myself to go down into the earth; a little mockery of the earth, too, that must know no matter how deep it swallowed me it would never break my lunar lover's hold. *Wulf* breathed deep, crushed my lungs. *Eventually, if nothing happens, I'll kill you.* Yes, the bitch reminded me, I will. She was the volatile adult, I was the child with the game it was mildly amusing to play along with for a while – until suddenly it wasn't. *I'll be able to hold out for a few hours.* That, she pointed out, was a foolish claim. She'd missed – had I forgotten? – her meal last month. She was already overdue. She was already *owed double*.

'I think, Sir... '

'Be quiet, please.'

The hospital smock was intolerable, suddenly (and in any case there was the thought like a sputtering torch that I'd need it if The Plan worked), so I pulled at the fastener and tore it off. Naked. Bizarrely, it felt empowering. Tunner's Murdoch-imperatives jammed: should he make a joke? Laugh? Pretend it hadn't happened? Gawp? As it was he remained still, mouth slightly open, odour gone zooish. Murdoch, on the other hand, absorbed the gesture with barely a twinge in his aura. Sex's money was no good there.

Blood hurried, backed, stopped, raced, broke its own laws to find non-existent room for what was coming. The first shock jerked my backbone. A precipitate canine shot through my upper gum and punctured my bottom lip. Hair sprang with a crisp sigh from the skin on my back, thighs, arms. Bone did what the Curse told it to. Imagine all those Plastisine figures you made then casually pulled and twisted until they were something else; imagine each one had a nervous system. Snapshots between spasms: the French widower shaking his head violently no, no, no, as his mouth filled up with blood; my mother fastening the strap on a pair of high-heeled shoes and then raising one eyebrow at me as if satirising her own glamour – then pulling a cross-eyed retarded face that made me laugh but at the same time slightly terrified me because the beauty momentarily disappeared; Jake's hand next to mine in Drew Hillyard's torn-open chest while *America's Next Top Model* sobbed and yammered on the blood-covered screen; Richard coming up the stairwell in our old apartment building the day I found out about his affair, the little nautilus whorl of his crown and me emptily knowing that whole part of my life was over; the Mexican pimp's face struggling to contain the horror of what he was seeing...

My skull stretched – stopped – stretched, a sudden fluid distention, the squeaks and snaps of which were tiny firecrackers in my head. All the claws came simultaneously, a feeling like ten big boils bursting at once, the only unequivocally pleasurable part of the whole routine. Lengthening thigh bones pushed me upright. There was space, at last, for my lungs. The hairs on the tips of my ears touched the ceiling. The final fang came up with a ludicrously intimate wet crunch.

'Jesus,' Tunner said, in spite of himself.

Walker stood, bent, looking up at me from under his brows, beat against by my new heat.

MOVE. DO IT. *DO IT.*

Caleb was watching me with a look that said he'd never seen this trick before. Even in his state there was room for wonder. *Don't die,* I sent him, though I knew he wouldn't get it. Hard to focus under appetite's total eclipse. Here, after all, were three human beings, warm and succulent and bursting with edible life, the nearest cuffed and bound and completely at the mercy I shouldn't have promised. I took a step towards him. I could feel the first bite coming all the way up from my soles, a movement like a tennis player's service action: the wind-up; the toss; the ball or my snout's frozen zenith – then the descent and jaws striking like the racquet's smash. Why had I thought I'd be able to hold back?

But *wulf*, it turned out, had her own divisions. My children were her children too – and she wanted them back.

THAT'S IT. HURRY.

Partly to discharge the piling-up energy and partly to hold the Hunters' attention, I threw my head back, opened my throat and howled. Good for me (the last trapped human bubbles burst), not good for them: the small space contained the sound terribly, mauled the human animals, roughed them up. Tunner's zoo-stink had changed again, some past-caring pheromone that said fear was flooding out. I leaped, snarling, at the bars. Tunner couldn't stop himself jumping backwards, though the gaps between the uprights were too narrow for me to get more than a hand through. Murdoch didn't flinch. I pictured myself on top of him, one hand pinning his throat, the other dangling his casually torn-off cock and balls just above his face. His flesh would hold all the flavours of his violence and the plaintive reek of his inverted life. *Wulf* wanted him, the furious energies crowding his blood, the occult childhood, the mysterious heart, lonely as the Devil's. She wanted it the way I (and my mother before me) always wanted to look, whatever the horror, if looking was possible.

Meanwhile Murdoch stood suspended. He'd been expecting me, I supposed, to start in on Walker the instant transformation was complete. Now the glazed blue eyes admitted slight confusion. I made a great show of snarling and gnashing and flailing about for a few seconds – then stopped, abruptly. Went completely silent and still. Stared at Murdoch. Yes, I have this under control. No, I won't be performing on cue.

He lifted his chin, slightly, a gesture to reinforce his position as overseer.

With pantomime exaggeration, I gave him the finger.

Caleb laughed, though it sounded as if the exertion might kill him. Tunner laughed – or started to, but was cut off by Murdoch whipping out a knife (it must have been behind the gun holster), springing forward and plunging it into Walker's shoulder.

Even by my monster standards it was a fast move, one jab, in, then out. Murdoch didn't say anything. He just stood with his hands on his hips and his hawk's look of unhinged concentration, waiting to see the effect of his action.

And, oh dear, there *was* the effect, the smell of fresh blood that hooked my nose like a cartoon potion. My nostrils opened and in went the scent of the body's precious red liqueur. Compelling detonations in the belly and the brain, a dirty loosening into animal joy. Everything reduced to one two-headed fact: I was starving, and I could eat. Walker had fallen to his knees again. Now, in geriatric increments, he lowered himself onto his side, laid his head on the floor and closed his eyes. Do it. I'm finished anyway.

I might have, too – if a very loud electronic alarm hadn't gone off.

Tunner covered his sticking-out ears. The sound was almost unbearable to me, with *my* hearing.

'Fire alarm, sir,' Tunner shouted, grimacing.

Murdoch's eyes closed for a moment in sublime irritation.

He opened them, took a deep breath, then gestured with a nod for Tunner to go check it out.

Tunner swiped his card. The door chirruped, gasped, unlocked – then flew open to the sound of screaming and the festival smell of slaughter.

46

T ime did what it does at these moments, expanded and slowed, created a space within which to observe the details – Tunner looking up, Murdoch turning and fumbling for his gun, Walker lifting his head as if from a nap he'd never intended to take, Devaz's arm – hairy, massive, blood-dipped and reeking of his new raw werewolf material – reaching in and wrapping its fingers around Tunner's throat –

NO. THE KEY. THE *KEY*.

Murdoch fired his weapon, hit Devaz in the shoulder. Devaz, muzzle dripping gore from the swath he'd cut to get here, swung Tunner up by his neck to catch Murdoch's next two rounds in the Hunter's back.

IT'S OKAY, THEY'RE NOT SILVER. GET THE *KEY*.

Which was still around Tunner's neck. Murdoch turned, ran to the opposite vault door and swiped the card. The blips' innocent tune, the lock's sigh and clunk. Devaz's new pure predatory instinct strained against me to go after him.

NO! FUCK HIM! GET US OUT OF HERE!

There were other Devaz instincts to work with. His cock was up, meatus pearled, dorsal artery pounding. Naturally: here was fresh prey and a female. A female who'd already fucked him in her human form. A current of mutual knowledge on top of the species imperative. It wasn't lost on me, either. The movie heroine would have seared focus: her child, therefore immediate escape, therefore no time for werewolf hanky-panky. Reality wasn't so accommodating. My clit throbbed and my cunt yearned. Not quite fuckkilleat (I wasn't in love with Devaz) but a cheaper, pornier alternative that was more than enough to drag at my will. In spite of myself I nearly went under.

But I wasn't, apparently, completely without control.

NOT NOW. THEY'LL KILL US. THEY HAVE SILVER.

Devaz's drowning human hated me for what I'd done to him (which didn't hurt his desire any, obviously) but the newly-made monster was under my will – just. It wouldn't last. This was pseudo-parental authority with a butterfly lifespan. Two or three lunations and he'd be telling me to go fuck myself – or rather trying to fuck me *him*self. But for now the newly-changed blood did as it was told. There was a flash of pleasure in it for him, the submissive's at his mistress's heel, a potential he never knew he had, though of course that fed back into his desire, so that doing as he was told made it harder to do as he was told. Absurdities bred and swarmed. Well, I imagined Jake saying, you go around dishing the Curse out willy-nilly, Lu – what do you expect?

The door closed behind Murdoch. Devaz ripped the key from Tunner's neck and moved over to the control panel. In the room next door the gunfire had stopped, though the screaming hadn't. Two or three different voices, I thought. I could smell Wilson out there, a thinner, meaner odour than Devaz's mardi gras funk. He was close to satiation, glutted and dazed from too many victims. If he carried on eating he'd regret it.

HURRY, PLEASE...

It was a dreamy agony to watch Devaz's hybrid fingers struggling for the precision needed to fit and turn the key. I wondered how many men the facility held, how many were still alive, how long before Murdoch got them regrouped. Someone, some-where, would be breaking out the silver ammunition. For all I knew containment doors for just this sort of contingency were right this second sealing the place shut.

One of the panel's red lights turned green. The bars slid up. Walker's steel cable dropped free. Devaz looked at me. He'd fed too, but not like Wilson. His hunger was still fiery, indiscriminate, up for anything – and here was Walker, barely able to get to his feet.

NOT HIM. AND WE'RE TAKING THE KID.

Devaz turned from me with a snarl and fell on Tunner, who was still alive, but barely conscious. One bite took half the Hunter's throat out. The jugular spat its blood like a well-pressurised drinking fountain for a few seconds, then subsided. Walker, still in his wrist- and ankle restraints, watched, while I switched the key into the socket for Caleb's cell.

The boy had passed out. Never to return, for all I knew. He was still breathing, at least. Either my tolerance for vamp odour had hit a new high or he was so close to death he'd lost his species stink. Whatever the explanation I gagged only once when I first picked him up. He was practically weightless. I might have been carrying a bag of polystyrene chips.

There was no shortage of blood. I dipped my fingers in the pool gathered around Tunner and touched them to Caleb's lips.

Two seconds. Three. Five. His tongue moved, tasted, registered. The soft mouth closed tight around my finger. I fed him a little more. His eyes opened. Fought back the reflex to get away. I opened Tunner's thigh with a claw and held Caleb next to it.

'Can't,' he said. 'He's dead. Can't drink... dead.'

Instead he lapped at the blood on the floor like a cat at a puddle of milk. Non-toxic, I supposed, because it had flowed while Tunner was still alive. I looked up at Walker, who stood holding his ribs, leaning against the remaining bars. Fear came off him, but weakly. This was quite something, what he was seeing, the situation he was in, but it didn't change what had happened to him. It irritated me, suddenly. *Stop being such a fucking baby. A woman is raped every minute in the US. You think they should all give up and die?*

I tore off Tunner's pockets until I found one that had a set of keys in it, then tossed the bunch to Walker. *You'll think I don't recognise you. But I will.* He knew I did, but he wasn't taking anything for granted. The confined space was hot and full of brutal possibilities. Since Tunner's thigh was open anyway I ripped a sliver of meat from it and crammed it into my mouth. Oh my God yes. More. More more *more*.

But there wasn't time for more. If we didn't get out now, we didn't get out. I ducked back into the cell, gathered up the gown and the journal and shoved them at Walker. Then I grabbed Caleb and hauled him to his feet. He hissed at me, but without conviction. He hadn't drunk a fraction of what he needed (he could barely stand) but it would have to be enough. Walker had got the restraints off. I stepped over Tunner's ravaged corpse, left a slipstream of will for Devaz, dizzy from the hit of fresh meat, to fall into. Walker, clutching his ribs and limping, brought up the rear.

The state of the next room — the site of Caleb's cage trials — testified to the soundproofing of the vault door, because even with lupine ears I hadn't heard any of the things that had evidently been going on in here. The cage itself was intact, though the door had been wrenched off and some bars bent. There was blood everywhere, grandly splashed, desperately smeared, clotting in puddles. The Tag Caleb scoreboard was face-down on the floor. One long spiral of razor wire had been yanked through the bars. A young dark-haired Hunter in a blood-soaked Metallica t-shirt and the regulation black combats was entangled in it, dead. Five other bodies, one of them, guts open, still being nauseatedly picked at by Wilson, who was flecked and winking with gore from head to foot.

Caleb's knees buckled and he fell. Wilson turned, saw us. He was going to spring. I felt it coiling in his legs and haunches.

NO! NOT THESE!

He knew me: I was the woman who'd fucked him and given him the mother of all lovebites; I was the werewolf voice in his head, the werewolf will in his limbs. The blood-glut weighed down the resentment he might have felt on an emptier stomach. *Wulf* had him, completely, from ears to claws. He stood upright and his cock arched up with him.

GET US OUT OF HERE.

Caleb had found potable blood and was sucking it up from the floor. I couldn't afford to let him take too much. Not just because we didn't have time. I reached down and grabbed his arm. He flailed at me. I hoisted him and slung him over my shoulder. Quicker this way, at least until we ran into trouble. Walker was on his knees over one of the dead Hunters. His hands were by his sides, his body completely relaxed. He might have been about to commence a meditation. There was a machine gun (Sobel's, throat bitten out, left arm off) within reach of my foot, so I kicked it across the floor to Walker. It struck the side of his leg.

Yes, pick it up. It didn't need telepathy. (The commands to Devaz and Wilson were in a medium that wasn't quite language nor quite pictures, available only in imperative chunks that had the feel, to those receiving them, of imposed instincts, forces that caught and moved them like an undertow.) Walker picked up the weapon, but made no move to get to his feet. In spite of everything else going on some part of me was considering the question of whether he was less of a man to me now. Yes, he was – too much of my human idea of masculinity was to do with power for it to be otherwise – but he was no less sexually interesting for it. This is how it goes, I realised. Once your own fundamentals start to morph and dissolve all the others matter less and less. Everyone should have a year as a werewolf. Like national service. Teach them not to be so hung-up on categories.

I have lost, I thought, mental appropriateness.

Wilson was already in the brightly-lit corridor accessed from the door across the hall, Devaz not far behind. A single leap took me with a feeling of deep joy clean over the cage (I remembered my dad lifting me up above his head when I was a kid, the ceiling's remote landscape suddenly shockingly close-up). There were three more Hunters with missing throats, blood spattered Pollock-style on the gleaming walls. We ran to the end and, following Wilson, turned right into another, broader corridor that led to a metal staircase. A section of fractured floor-to-ceiling glass on our left showed a room with a bank of TV monitors and three or four desks with laptops. An agent, gashed from navel to throat, lay shivering in a thickening puddle of his own blood. His visible guts looked like a curled-up alien creature in quivering sleep. His eyes were open and full of incredulous life. We ignored him and ran to the staircase. Five steps up I nearly fell, turning an ankle on a human head, the body of which remained on the first landing. Devaz stopped again, bent, bit a chunk from the midriff and all but swallowed it whole.

HURRY.

Wilson was two flights ahead, but slowing. The meat-glut was catching up with him, an effect like over-oxygenated blood: you went fat in the vessels and veins, hands and feet full to bursting. I joined him where the stairs ended – another corridor, with a reflective vinyl floor that smelled of disinfectant – just in time to see two WOCOP agents disappearing up a second stairway twenty yards away. I looked back past Devaz. Walker was struggling up the steps. He looked as if any minute he might stop, sit down, close his eyes. I couldn't wait for him.

A bullet hit me in the shoulder. Another struck Caleb in the thigh. A neatly muscled agent who looked about twenty, dressed only in red running shorts and blinding white sneakers and armed with a handgun, had sprung out of a door on our left, seen us and fired, though he would have known from basic training it was pointless without silver. Devaz caught him in three strides and spun him by his hair. The agent dropped to his knees, facing me. He got another round off – hitting a wall – before Devaz kicked the pistol from his grip. The young abdominals were beautiful things. Devaz yanked on the hair to get the head back, then claw-swiped the tautened throat, which waited a moment before splitting and sending out a thin arc of blood. It was too much for me. I leaped forward, dropped Caleb, slashed my lethal fingernails across the supple midriff, then fell to my knees and sank my teeth in just below the ribs.

A never-off-duty analyst in an alcove of my brain said: You'll have to watch it, there's a preference emerging for healthy young men. You can't afford to establish a type. Establish a type and you establish a pattern. Establish a pattern and you get caught... Oh, but it was good. It was good to feel his life thudding into me (it wasn't all mine; Devaz scored random chunks, having slammed his fist through the sternum and torn out the heart); the double hunger forced by last month's pass made each fragment bright: his fair-haired mother and a sun-smashed white yard with a red pedal car and the peachy diptych of a brunette's ass he couldn't believe had got straight into a sixty-nine with him that one time and the guy passed out in a pool of vomit at a White Stripes show and all the remote giant sensations of childhood like that time the clouds were racing and if you lay on your back in the street it looked like the buildings were falling and his dad carrying him upstairs when he was ill and suddenly through his fever he'd known in the warm strong arms the certainty of his father's love but somehow it spun away or diluted and so much of his head now was full of junk and TV and porn and he didn't even want to join these guys but Nog said he could get him in and it would be a laugh—

Stop. *Stop*.

But I didn't, immediately. Feeding cons you out of seconds, minutes, hours. The life-haemorrhaging flesh stretches time. Like a black hole. Just a few more seconds. Just another bite.

The corridor was qualitatively different when I raised my snout, as if someone had opened a sluice and all the noise and urgency had drained away. The fire alarm had stopped, but the silence had more to it than that. I turned and saw Caleb on his hands and knees lapping up the before-death blood. He was still weak, but there was a new tension in his bent elbows, new promise in his wrists. I got to my feet and grabbed him. He wasn't strong enough to offer anything but comedy resistance but I wondered what would happen to me if he bit me, which, when I slung him back over my shoulder, I felt sure he was going to do. He didn't, however.

Walker was at the top of the stairs, face rich with what he'd just seen: me, the woman who'd been fucking him with increasing nuance and dangerous warmth, down on all-fours eating an eviscerated human being. He was thinking of the times our eyes had met with profound recognition. Yes, that was me. And this was me. The woman was me and the monster was me. He hadn't grasped it before. He'd conceded it, intellectually, but he hadn't believed. Now here it was. Nine feet tall wearing blood evening gloves and winking gobbets of meat. The shock of it was a brutal refreshment. A possible paradigm shift into the future, since there was no route back to his past.

The lover wanted to comfort him. The monster was blood-buoyed and turned on and ready for more flesh. The mother was desperate, feeling time boiling away to nothing.

I turned and ran.

Two more flights of stairs brought us, I could smell, to ground level. Double doors stood open to a large, messy office, more desks and computers, papers scattered, no personnel. Identical double doors across the floor. Locked doors. Electronic. Card-swipe and access code required.

But these weren't vault thickness, and this time there were three of us. I put Caleb down. No need to even crudely instruct Wilson and Devaz. At the third yank the left door screeched and snapped free of its lock. Beyond, not the atrium or reception I was expecting, but a loading bay. Stacked metal crates, forklifts, a snub-nosed British truck with no trailer. The place was oil-stained and freezing and stank of rust. The roll-down door to the outside world was three feet off the ground. Devaz leaped the truck, grabbed the handle and flung it upwards.

Night air full of damp fields and moonlit cold. A large asphalt compound containing a few small trucks and vans, more ribbed cargo trailers, weeds coming up through the concrete. The whole space enclosed by aluminium fencing topped with razor wire. Thirty metres away the moist silence of close-packed trees. The smells and the moon-carved open-ness rushed my heart up to joy. It was like running into the arms of a lost love.

Devaz and Wilson, splashed with their first Curse moonlight, lifted their ravished heads to howl – which was when I saw the gunman.

He was protruding from the sun-roof of a 4x4 parked so that it was almost completely concealed between two trailers.

I flung *MOVE!* at Wilson with a violence that must have struck his head like a discus – then he was down, hit in the chest – and this time, I knew, the bullets would count.

There was no time to move and all the time in the world to feel myself not moving, the stalled synapses, the neurons' long-winded math that couldn't possibly be done before the bullet arrived. The moment expanded, big and slow and clear enough for me to think: this is my last moment, standing with a vampire child in my arms in a—

Then the blood-rush and cellular scintillation like a billion tiny stars coming on in the flesh as out of the darkness beyond the fence a werewolf dropped, the lethal end of her giant parabola, a jump that had begun twenty metres away, triggered by the silver exploding through Wilson's chest.

Madeline, transformed, hit the sniper like a meteor.

47

The 4x4's driver – Murdoch, I knew – reacted fast. Within a second of Madeline's impact on the roof he'd slammed the car into gear and motion. Madeline, having bitten through the shooter's throat, wrenched his head clean off and flung it towards us. Murdoch floored the gas. Tyres screamed. Side-arm shots cracked dry and small over the outraged engine. Madeline hung on. It took Murdoch sideswiping a cargo crate to dislodge her. A moment more and she would have had another head to pitch us.

Murdoch rammed the fence and burst through under the wire. He swung the car right and hit what must have been an access road. Automatic-weapons fire followed him, but he kept going.

Devaz was on all-fours over Wilson's corpse, head hanging, sniffing. I put Caleb down and ran to where Madeline had fallen.

KID OKAY. WITH LUCY.

She wasn't hurt, and was on her feet sending me this by the time I reached her. But she was starving. Her roiling scent and shimmering heat said hunger at the end of its leash. Her roused dead were there in misery on her breath; her livened cunt had its own prowling gravity. I could have put my arms around her. She felt that, had no room for it, was already moving past me, electric with appetite. Caleb's odour on me made her gag.

PLEASE WAIT. PLEASE.

She did, but it pulled her blood the wrong way. I could feel what she could feel: that the building was still manned, that *live prey* was scurrying around less than fifty metres away.

CAN'T WAIT. ASK THEM. LOOK.

Behind me. I turned. Konstantinov and Cloquet were approaching, armed. *Mike got out.* A metal gate swung on its hinges behind them.

'Zoë's safe,' Cloquet said. 'Thank God you're all right. Transport close by. Hurry.'

Konstantinov was packing an AK-47 but there was silver on him too. The holstered handguns, one on each hip. The blade in his boot. He wasn't taking any chances.

'Hurry,' Cloquet repeated.

Walker had collapsed a few feet away. Konstantinov ran to him and broke an ampoule of something under his nose. Caleb, pale as a root, had crawled to one of the trucks and now sat propped, semi-conscious, against one of its enormous wheels. I hesitated. Truth was I hadn't eaten nearly enough. The half-dozen mouthfuls from the youngster in the corridor had teased the hunger rather than satisfying it. If I didn't get more the humans would soon be at risk. A few hours from now even Cloquet wouldn't be safe. A cloud shifted from where it had been half-covering the moon and the light in the yard surged. It was too much for Madeline. She sprang towards the building's open maw.

At that moment several bursts of gunfire sounded from within. Screams. More shots – then three WOCOP agents came staggering and backpedalling from the loading bay.

Followed by two more werewolves.

TRISH, FERGUS, I got from Madeline. Both of them bleeding from a handful of not-silver bullet holes, manifestly not suffering for it. Konstantinov was the brains here. Attack from both ends.

295

Murdoch had slipped through somehow, another exit. Murdoch would always know another way out.

Devaz grabbed the first agent by the throat, lifted him off the ground, broke his wrist when he tore the machine gun from his hand. The other two agents were out of ammunition. There was nowhere for them to go.

48

T rish and Fergus were soon blissfully off-mission. In the time it took Konstantinov and Cloquet to get Walker in the van, they'd entered the state beyond reason, the state *beyond* – period. Trish was on all-fours, muzzle shoved under her victim's ribs, Fergus, throat up, snout blowing bouquet after bouquet of moonlit breath, was fucking her from behind. A nerve in their victim's leg made it jounce to their rhythm, as if he were enjoying the tune of his own death. I was wet from watching them, from the live flesh, from my share of the chaotic little pack consciousness, plus, obviously, haywire resurgence of the night with Jake at Big Sur. Not the same without love – no tenderness to sweeten the cruelty, no *refined* counterpoint to the beast – but still, a bacchanalian alternative, an exquisitely filthy feast for the Cursed.

Not that I'd spent all my time watching. I'd claimed *my* victim – mid-thirties red-haired Irishman failed swimmer with a long, sad, top-heavily muscled body – in a single leap and swipe and taken as much of him as I could in a furious and indiscriminate bolt: blood, meat, liver, kidneys, life; his life, his *life* – the drippy blonde babysitter he'd wanted to marry when he was six; shafts of orange gold sun like dividers in an evening forest; his mother's small, weaselly face and that time he'd come home and found her crying at the bottom of the stairs and a cobblestoned street with a car on cinderblocks and his face fat and hot when Sean Neagle hit him that icy morning in the playground at St Michael's in Ballyhist—

Madeline, meanwhile, was on all-fours next to me, *soixante-neuf*'d over her victim. She'd clawed through his pants and taken half the flesh from his left thigh. When her fangs had pierced the femoral artery warm blood had splashed me, mouth, breasts, belly. The air was musical with its odour. She was close enough, it occurred to me now, with a sly loosening of my sexual self. If I wanted to reach out and touch her, to inaugurate the new era of anything sexual goes...

But the time, the time, the *time*. Aside from the mother in me screaming at the rest that there were THE CHILDREN TO GET TO, my strategist knew the window we were in was tiny. We were only still in it because no one left inside liked the odds outside now. The facility's survivors weren't looking to get out, they were looking to stay in, find a set of blast doors to lock themselves behind and wait for the moon to set. But phones would be ringing at other WOCOP bases. If reinforcements turned up they'd be packing silver – and if they were airborne they could be here in minutes.

A giant hot hand touched my butt. Devaz, sporting a prodigious erection, had crept up and was now, with obvious pride, presenting himself to me. The meat in my guts and the blood on my tongue shot a blazing imperative down to my cunt. Oh, God. *Wasn't* there time? Surely there was time? Surely if we were—

The mother of my children was screaming and hopping about and pulling her hair and wringing her hands and forcing the pertinent images: I saw myself back on the scientists' table or lying dead and naked here on the asphalt when the sun came up and Lucy one day soon realising the novelty had worn off and feeding Zoë a silver earring or just leaving her in a hotel lobby

298

and Lorcan on the altar not knowing what was happening to him and never having known anything but aloneness and fear and looming alien presences...

It was enough – just. Even then I had to crawl out from under the seductive weight of the rest of me. Even then it took Cloquet blasting the van's horn to haul me at last into the right kind of action. I jumped to my feet and shoved Devaz out of the way. He snapped at me, missing by an inch, then immediately turned, dropped to his knees and prodded Madeline's thigh with his cock. Madeline stopped eating and looked at him.

Caleb had passed out a second time. He lay where he'd fallen by the truck's big wheel, which stood over him like a dumb guardian. I ran to him and picked him up.

WE HAVE TO GO.

Madeline turned to me. In her left hand she held her victim's bloodily torn-off cock, in her right Devaz's, still attached to Devaz. (I thought: That can't be much of an aphrodisiac for him, even in his state.) Like me she'd barely crossed the line into Enough, and like me she knew Enough was never enough for *wulf*. For *wulf* only more than Enough was enough. But also like me she was a businesswoman. Understood risk, gain, gamble, loss. They'd got me out, killed some of those who would otherwise have killed them, and fed. Not a bad night's takings. Quit while you're ahead. She dropped the severed cock, let go of the attached one and instead wrenched off what was left of her victim's leg – complete up to just past the knee, thereafter a lot of bare bone – to bring with her.

THE OTHERS.

But there was no shifting Fergus and Trish. There was barely any *reaching* Fergus and Trish. Even when – with that same creepy sense of mutual invasion we'd shared back at the Dorchester – Maddy and I opened to each other, plaited wills and mentally screamed at them in unison: *WE GO NOW!* we got nothing back. Or maybe something, like a drunk on the very edge of complete inarticulacy trying to say *Fuck you*, but it had too far to travel from where they were, out there in the wolf-constellated void. Trish's head was back now, soft-haired throat at full stretch. Fergus's hands roamed and squeezed as if madly searching for something concealed under her skin. The stink of their sex was concussively sweet, wrapped around the big olfactory mass of slaughter, which was even now, even *now* a profound temptation—

'Get in here now!' Konstantinov shouted. 'Or we go without you!'

I slung Caleb over my shoulder and ran towards the gate.

49

Ten hours later, human again, I sat washed and dressed in my own (Cloquet-provided) clothes at the breakfast table in Lucy's cottage, holding Zoë in my arms. Holding Zoë in my arms. Holding Zoë in my arms. Love still made me an obscenity. Love still forced the sickening fall away from her. That wouldn't change. Not for a long time. Not unless I got her brother back. This logic, like the idiot-proof logic of the Curse, was a comfort. Something to rely on. Something to help me through the cruelty I was going to have to inflict if I was ever *going* to get him back.

A wood-burning stove radiated narcotic warmth. All the curtains were closed but each window showed a lozenge of blue-grey light. The place was spotless, smelled (beyond the swirling perfumes of vestigial *wulf*) of fresh linen, frangipani incense, terracotta tiles and oiled oak – only occasionally muddied by the odour of the Undead: Caleb was in bed in an upstairs room, shivering, in and out of delirium, skin oozing the gelatinous pink sweat. I didn't know how long his system would take to burn the blood he'd had last night, but he didn't look like dying just yet. I'd tried to get a number for Mia out of him, but he was too far under.

A vampire boy, obviously, hadn't been expected. Lucy had almost thrown up when we carried him in. (Which, given *what* she would have thrown up, would have been a forensic disaster, despite the painter's plastic lining walls and floor.) I hadn't realised how used to Caleb's smell I'd got in prison. In the close confines of the van (yes, a Transit van with comedy contents: three humans up front, three werewolves, a vampire and half a human leg in the back) his stink had caused serious trouble: it left Madeline and Devaz too queasy to fuck. They couldn't eat, either. I ended up finishing most of the leg myself. (Who wants a leg? my dad used to ask, carving at Christmas or Thanksgiving.) They were disgusted and furious at the wasted opportunity. Devaz kept brattishly kicking the walls of the van, until Konstantinov turned in his seat with the silver-loaded Springfield and told him very calmly that if he didn't stop making such a fucking racket he'd shoot him there and then. We'd driven for maybe an hour – all minor roads, all unlit – to Lucy's divorce-settlement cottage, which appeared to be in the middle of nowhere, but which was in fact only a quarter of a mile from the nearest village – Yatesbury (which I'd never heard of, naturally) – but screened from the road at the front by a tree-lined garden and backed by sheep-dotted farmland. Unless anyone had been looking and listening for us they wouldn't have noted our arrival. Nor, if all the precautions had served their purpose, would they have any idea that inside the chocolate box cottage, with its limewash and thatch and honeysuckle and rose-bushes, a man had been killed and eaten by monsters. One of them less than a month old.

Even now, sitting in clean clothes and warmth and freedom with my daughter in my arms (and my obscene heart stuck in the loop of being forced near the love that forced it to fall away), I found it incredible that what had happened had in fact happened. After his escape Konstantinov had made it back to London and called Cloquet. Not because he had any regard for Cloquet's abilities, but because he needed money. Lots of it. To buy information and raise a team. I'd underestimated his friendship with Walker. He wasn't prepared to abandon him. 'The team' didn't materialise. Word of Hoyle's fate had spread. The WOCOP moles went silent and of the individuals on Murdoch's hit-list only three were still in the UK – and they emphatically weren't interested, at any price. Cloquet, meanwhile, having heard nothing from me for days, had contacted Madeline for help with Zoë. The dots were there to be joined: Madeline, Fergus, Lucy and Trish would come out of it loaded, Konstantinov would get four werewolves ready for human slaughter (or rather three werewolves, since one of them still had to babysit Zoë) and the monsters would get a free all-you-can-eat WOCOP buffet more or less without risk of legal reprisal. Konstantinov had guessed what sort of show Murdoch had in mind so he was confident Walker would be kept alive till full moon. They'd have to get in quick, as soon as the werewolf troops were transformed.

There remained – for Cloquet, for Lucy, for Zoë – the problem of feeding.

Cue Madeline – and the punter she didn't like.

'Wife beater,' she'd told me, earlier. 'He wanted to hire me to join in.'

'In beating-up his wife?'

'Yeah.'

'But not because she's a masochist?'

'You're not getting it. She's not a masochist – she's terrified of him. He wanted me to burn her with cigarettes then shit in her mouth. This is his *wife*, right?'

The expected moral reflex – checked. *It's only the best thing for us if it's the worst thing for someone else.* Moral judgement rights went that night in Big Sur. Before that, even. I kept my mouth shut.

'So I thought, Well, it's got to be *some*one, you know?'

She contacted him and told him she was considering his proposal (double her usual rate, to make the lie credible) but wanted see him on his own one more time before taking the plunge. This weekend she had the use of a friend's cottage in Wiltshire. Why didn't he come down so they could discuss it?

'And that was him fucked. I slipped him one in his drink and off he went to sleep. Luce said he didn't wake up till things started to happen.'

When he did wake up – when things started to happen – he was naked, gagged and hog-tied in Lucy's bathtub. With Lucy standing over him. Not looking like the Lucy any of her friends would have recognised.

'Serves him right,' Madeline had said. 'And I hope he was life insured up the arse too. Poor cow deserves a pay-out.'

I hadn't been able to discuss any of it with Lucy, how it had gone, how Zoë had been, whether she'd had any trouble feeding. Initially because we were all still in *wulf* mode and physically incapable of discussing anything, later because once the moon had set there were too many grim practicalities to deal with. Before it could be disposed of the wife-beater's body had to be prepped: decapitated, fingerprints burnt off, teeth knocked out, lungs punctured. I did most of it. It seemed appropriate. A lot of his face was gone. Not eaten, just rubbished. To erase the person, I knew. His St Christopher had survived, as if to prove its own uselessness. It went in the bleach along with his wedding ring and wristwatch, to be disposed of separately far from here. Separately from the rest of him. Lucy's ex had a tiny boat at a quiet mooring a few miles south of Weston-Super-Mare. As soon as she was back in human form she'd left with Cloquet (and a single portion of human remains) in the van. They were to take it out into the Bristol Channel and drop the weighted carnage overboard.

Konstantinov had gone with Walker in a separate car after dropping us here. Courtesy of my funding via Cloquet he had a crooked doctor on call and a place to hole-up. I hadn't been able (physically, again) to say anything to him about what had happened to Walker in custody. I wondered if he'd know. Masculine rape-radar. Thinking of Walker hurt my heart. I supposed it was over between us. Not just because of what had happened to him, but because of what he'd seen: me in all my filthy glory. Richard used to claim Linda Blair never got laid after *The Exorcist*; guys couldn't shake the footage. Nonsense, obviously – but maybe not when the footage was from real life. The goodbye between us had been a stare through the windshield. What else could it have been? An embrace? I was a nine-foot monster covered in blood. The woman in me was ashamed and the wolf around her was full of contempt. In any case, even if he wanted me (and hadn't been left terminally impotent) what future was there? What future had there ever been? *See you later, babe. Um-hm. Have a good kill.* And that was before we got to the other bitterly laughable truth: that the more I felt for him the more likely it was he'd end up *being* the good kill.

Unless of course I Turned him.

Why not? If I didn't get Lorcan back there'd be no end to the warped gestures I could make in the void. Well, I could imagine my mother saying, with arch reasonableness, *why* not? What's he got left to lose?

That wasn't the problem. The problem was that if I Turned him he'd end up hating me. Sooner or later he'd forget he'd wanted it. Sooner or later he'd start to wonder how I could have done it to him. Sooner or later every shitty thing that happened to him would be my fault. It was a structural certainty. I knew it, the monster knew it, even Walker knew it.

It was getting light out. Zoë was asleep in my arms. Bubbles of *wulf* were trapped in my veins and the ingested lives were standing around confused and weeping like children on their first day at school. Monster strands clung in my neck muscles, buttocks, calves. The virtues of victim blood and victim meat throbbed and glowed, a sensation like indoor warmth after freezing outside.

Devaz, who'd taken longer in the shower than any of us, was stretched out asleep on the couch in the lounge. *He* hadn't been expected, either, so there were no men's clothes for him. Instead he'd had to squeeze into a pair of Lucy's baggiest sweatpants. It was such an unappetising sight everyone was relieved when he conked out and we could throw a blanket over him.

'Shouldn't they be back by now?' I asked.

Madeline, also scrubbed, precisely made-up and in clean clothes (dark blue Levis, tight white t-shirt, black suede cowboy boots), had just come in and put the kettle on. There was a rich ambiguous atmosphere between us, *wulf*'s telepathy still volatile. I knew she was aware of me having turned over the sapphic possibility back in the WOCOP compound, though I couldn't tell how she would've reacted if I'd reached out and touched her. I supposed she 'did' girls, professionally, if only because it was economically dumb not to, but for all I knew it was strictly business. Besides, there were Devaz and Fergus now, if I was looking for a loveless version of fuckkilleat, no need to resort to lesbianism. I heard this phrase – no need to resort to lesbianism – in the voice of our neighbour in Park Slope, Mrs Spears, who was brisk and brusque and always absolutely knew her mind and yours too and always told you what not just you but everyone in the world should do. Good Lord, Talulla, there's no need to resort to lesbianism! At which I was forced to concede that I was more interested in Madeline than I was in either of the two males. Partly a little titillating masochistic jealousy. Partly an irritation with what suddenly felt like absurd (*super*-absurd, given my other activities) anachronistic bourgeois repression. Partly sexual curiosity that went all the way back to Lauren. Partly just the feeling that since it was going to happen sooner or later I might as well get on with it. Partly, of course, Jake between us. Jesus, he must be loving this. I imagined him settling down with a Macallan and a Camel and a big grin in front of his afterlife TV: and now, a little earlier than advertised, ultra-hot two-girl werewolf action. Fan fucking tastic. Where's the slow-motion on this thing? Where's the repeat?

'Don't worry,' Madeline said, opening a fresh carton of milk. 'Luce knows what she's doing. They'll be fine. Anyway, come on, you still haven't told me.'

How I'd ended up with Devaz and the late Wilson, she meant, werewolves conjured up from the WOCOP faithful. Jake's journal, incredibly, had survived the night, but she still hadn't seen it. It wasn't necessary. I knew the relevant lines by heart. I knew the lines and the scene: The Castle Hotel room, Caernarfon, night. Jake staring at the Harley phone in the wake of the Harley message. Madeline emerging from the en suite, post-coitally repaired, clipping up her hair:

'Look at that,*' she said, turning her cheek and showing me a tiny lovebite on her pliable young neck. 'That's a* mark, *isn't it?'*

I knew it well enough, having read and re-read it countless times once the penny – thanks to Caleb's story of his making – dropped.

'Jake gave you a lovebite,' I said. 'That night in Caernarfon.

The night Grainer and Ellis turned up with Harley's head in a bag.'

I watched her thinking back. It brought the images again, Jake fucking her, her face's worked-for look of professional collusion. Somewhere else in her the little girl (like Cloquet's little boy on the dock) was waiting for the reunion that would never come. And yet maybe it could come now. My own childhood self hadn't minded the monster much. It was the older versions that had freaked out. In fact it was like the little girl's revenge: See? I *told* you it was like this. All these terrible and wonderful things.

'He gave you a lovebite,' I said. 'It had to have broken the skin just enough. Meanwhile the anti-virus they'd been slipping him had worked. There's no other explanation. The next night, full moon, you changed, just like he did.'

A few moments while she took it in. 'How do you know all this?'

No avoiding the truth now. 'He kept a diary.'

'Did he?'

'Yes.'

More cogitation. Here were the versions of her face her customers never saw. She arrived at something. 'Don't suppose he had much good to say about me. Dumb blonde. Never read a book in her life.'

'He said he wished he'd kissed you more.'

Which caused a sudden psychic traffic jam in her. Embarrassment. Curiosity. Pride. It would be a while before she stopped being fascinated by the effects she had on people.

'You haven't given anyone any, have you?' I asked her. 'Any lovebites?'

She shook her head, still processing.

'No one with a fetish for them?'

'I don't think so.

'Because they come with a big price tag now. Just so you know.'

'Did *he* know?'

'Jake? No. He wouldn't have done it if he had.' Not to *you*, my mean-spirited realist could have added – which thought I hoped she was mentally occupied enough to miss. Jake hadn't known what he'd done, but he – or *wulf* – had known there was something that made him uneasy when he thought of Madeline in those last hours in the Castle Hotel.

Something nags when I think of Madeline here. This room's hauled it to the edge of memory but can't quite heave it over the border.

It was there in the journal, practically the last thing he wrote before Llewellyn arrived to take him to Beddgelert Forest, to me, to Grainer, to his death. Something smarter than his human knew: You bit her. She'll Turn. And if he hadn't bitten her, I'd be dead now.

Don't bother looking for the meaning of it all. There isn't one.

Maybe not, but life compulsively dangled the possibility. Life, the dramatist on speed. Life, that couldn't stop with its foreshadows and ironies and symbols and clues, its wretched jokes and false endings and twists. Life with its hopeless addiction to *plot*.

'Don't tell Fergus,' Madeline said.

'What?'

'Don't tell him you can Turn someone with a lovebite.'

'He'll start dishing them out?'

'I wouldn't put it past him. He's a loose cannon. In fact I wouldn't mention it to Trish, either. Don't get me wrong: I love Trish. But she's like a kid with a new toy with this, seriously. Can't blame her, mind, crap she's been through.'

Caleb coughed. Spat something out. His breathing was bad. I was going to have to find him blood. Would an animal's do? I could always give him some of mine, I supposed – but who knew what that would turn him into?

'So you just... bit them?' Madeline asked.

'Yes.'

'How'd you manage that?'

'How d'you think?'

A pause while she re-evaluated me. Now I was the sort of woman who could fuck strategically. I felt her realising she'd underestimated me – and felt her feeling that I felt it. These shivers and shadows of infinite-regress mind-reading. The forced mutual recognition was still fresh enough to tickle us – but we knew that wouldn't last: down the line we'd have to find a way of keeping private what was private. As it was, just then I read her wondering if there'd been any pleasure in it for me.

Not much.

She nodded. Men who were no good at sex. She knew all about it. Which rushed the ambiguity back so that my skin tingled and my face went hot and for a moment it was obvious we weren't looking at each other – but we were rescued by the sound of a car pulling up. A moment later Lucy and Cloquet came in, big-eyed and pale, smelling of residual *wulf* and mudflats and diesel and cold air.

'Everything okay?' I asked.

'Who knows,' Lucy said. 'We've done what we can.'

She was a tall skinny reddish brunette with warm, sad brown eyes, broad cheekbones and a wide but indistinct mouth. All her features slightly dissolved into her freckles. Her hairdo was a triangular shoulder-length bob with bangs. She'd look good in any shade of green, though right now she was wearing rust-coloured corduroys and a black roll-neck sweater. The majority of men would rank us in descending order: Madeline, me, Lucy, but for an alert minority Lucy would have more sex-appeal than Maddy and me put together. Updike would have rhapsodised about her oily skin and long fingers and freckled boobs.

'I never got the chance before to thank you,' I said. 'For looking after Zoë. For everything.'

'She was no trouble,' Lucy said. 'But before we go any further could you tell me what the hell that boy is doing upstairs in my spare room?'

In the febrile communication available to us when we'd arrived all I'd got through to her was PLEASE. EMERGENCY. PLEASE. Enough to secure Caleb a roof for the night, but very plainly with objections deferred. Now the deferral was over.

'He's a vampire,' I said. 'A very sick one.'

'That much I know,' Lucy said. From Cloquet, who'd heard what Walker had to tell up front in the van. 'Clearly you've got some investment in him, but would you mind sharing it?'

'It's obvious, isn't it?' Madeline said. 'They've got her son. They're going to kill him. Now she's got one of theirs. Bargaining power.' She looked at me. 'Right?'

'Right,' I said. 'Unfortunately, that's exactly right.'

It was a either a coincidence or a baroque touch by the drama-tist on speed that immediately the words left my mouth Caleb started screaming.

50

'Fuck, it's the sun,' I said, jumping up. 'Quick – a dark place.'

'Cellar,' Lucy said. 'But it's full of crap down—'

'He won't care. Where is it? Madeline, can you take her for a second?'

We'd closed the curtains in Caleb's room, but they weren't thick enough to keep out full daylight. When Cloquet and I got up there he was on the floor with the quilt around him trying to crawl under the bed.

'We're taking you underground,' I said, grabbing him. 'You'll be safe there, I promise.'

He couldn't answer. The quilt was leaking wisps of smoke.

Five minutes later he was in Lucy's cellar (which wasn't full of crap but was a small, clean orderly place stacked with airtight plastic boxes) wrapped in the comforter, curled up in the foetal position. His eyes were closed, his mouth was wide open and his breathing was terrible.

'He can't stay here,' Lucy said, when we were back in the kitchen.

'I know. I'll take him with me tonight. Don't worry.'

'Take him where?' Madeline asked.

I looked at Cloquet.

'South coast,' he said. The place Konstantinov and Walker were holed-up in. London was too risky for us now.

'Okay,' Lucy said. 'He stays till the sun goes down. Fine. But we need to talk.'

A surreal morning and afternoon. Lucy wanted answers. Superficially to questions of science – disease immunity, lifespan, genetics, drugs – underlyingly to the quivering metaphysical cry in the void: What the fuck does it all mean?

I had nothing to give her beyond what Jake had given me. We existed. No more nor less mysteriously than leopards or seahorses or whales. Lucy sat and frowned and took it all in. She was ragged, aggrieved, disgusted, afraid – but hadn't, I could tell, ever considered killing herself. She had an essence of stubborn entitlement. She'd thought the collapsed marriage (and apparent death-knell to child-bearing) would be her life's defining event. Now there was this. Along with the other feelings was a profane thrill that all the information wasn't, in fact, in, that for better or worse a new violent world was open to her. Grass still grew, birds still twittered, rain still fell. As long as you were prepared to stay in it life found room for you. Life was like that, helplessly promiscuous, a doorman who let everyone in.

'Why silver?' she wanted to know.

I shrugged.

'And if we abstain?'

'Death. I managed two moons on animals. I wouldn't recommend it. Jake told me he did four months and ended up ripping his own skin off.'

Madeline opened a bottle of Absolut and poured shots. Since transformation my breasts had milk again, but Zoë had shown no sign of needing to suckle. Adult werewolves didn't eat regular food for at least a week after the kill; intuition said it was the same for infants. Either way, one shot of vodka wasn't going to do any harm. We drank. No toast, but a silent acknowledgement of the absurdity and horror and ordinariness of our condition.

There was a profound temptation to laugh. Maddy's diamante earrings glittered when she tossed back her shot.

'It's not supposed to be like this,' I told them. 'We're not supposed to hang out together.'

'Why not?' Madeline asked.

'I don't mean it's not allowed, I mean according to Jake we're solitary, we avoid each other. He'd only ever met about half a dozen others, and he didn't seem interested. He said it was competition for food and sex. They were all males, mind you. Maybe if there had been females it would've been different.'

'Or he was just a loner,' Lucy said.

'He never mentioned *any*one to me,' Madeline said. 'Most clients, they'll mention a wife, or a girlfriend or a workmate or whatever, *some*one, at any rate. Not him. When those guys turned up at the hotel in Wales, I realised I'd never really imagined him knowing anyone.'

'There's something else. Jake said the number of females was tiny in comparison to the number of males. Something like one to a thousand. No one knew why. It can't have been that fewer women got bitten. It can only have been that fewer women survived the bite. But look at us.'

'Yeah, well, that's London water for you,' Maddy said, pouring refills. 'Chin-chin.'

Devaz woke up – lost. His face said he'd just had a terrifying dream. Then his face realised it wasn't a dream. For a few moments he looked from one to the other of us, reconstructing his history. His psyche wobbled, flirted with collapse. Then the picture of his recent past set hard, beyond denial or escape. He knew what had happened, what he was, what he'd done. He turned to me.

'You fucking *cunt*. You *did* this to me. I'll fucking *kill* you.'

314

Cloquet, still armed, drew the Luger. 'Silver,' he said, quietly. 'All silver rounds. The Russian insisted.'

I knew he was lying. Devaz didn't. His face was wet and his mouth was open, revealing the fruity gap between his upper front incisors. With a big moustache, I realised, he'd look like a low-rent Freddie Mercury impersonator.

'None of us asked for this,' Lucy said. 'We're all in the same boat.'

'She did this to me *on purpose.*'

'Yes, I did,' I said. 'Would you like to know what your colleagues did to *me* on purpose? You fucking dumb self-righteous prick.'

Cloquet had the gun to Devaz's head superfast. 'Don't think of it,' he said. 'Seriously. Don't give it a thought.'

'Everyone needs to calm down, please,' Lucy said. 'Right now.'

Fortunately, at that moment, Trish arrived. She was a small, gymnastic, twenty-seven-year-old with short chopped red hair and large jade-green eyes. The too-big black combat pants and jacket made it obvious where she'd picked up her wardrobe. The men's sneakers fit her like clown shoes. She couldn't keep a straight face when Madeline introduced us.

'Sorry about back there,' she said, grinning. 'Got a bit distracted. You know how it is.'

What was there to say? I did know how it was.

She and Fergus had left the detention facility maybe half an hour after we had (with a backpack full of Hunters' gear and about eighty pounds in cash – *thanks*, you lot, for leaving us completely bloody *stranded*, by the way), gone for a romp on the downs, dozed in an empty barn till moonset, washed in a water trough, then got dressed, strolled into the nearest village and taken a bus. Fergus had made his own way back to London by train. The place names involved – Wantage, Swindon,

Lambourne – meant nothing to me. She had clothes to change into after her shower, which freed-up the WOCOP gear for Devaz. As soon as he was dressed, he demanded to be let go.

'No one's keeping you prisoner,' I said. 'Fuck off.'

He didn't. Instead he sulked and prowled the cottage. I observed him shooting glances at Madeline. Observed her shake her head: No. As in, No, willingness to fuck you last night does not translate into willingness to fuck you now. Back off, dickhead.

I called Konstantinov. He and Walker were installed at the house on the coast. Walker had been treated by the doctor. Wounds cleaned, stitched, dressed, ribs strapped, antibiotics. He was sleeping. The doctor had left twenty minutes ago.

'Get him back,' I said.

'What?'

'Tell him to get hold of whatever kit he needs for a blood transfusion. We're bringing the boy with us. Listen.'

Konstantinov didn't interrupt. When I'd finished, he just said: 'Good. What time will you be here?'

I looked in on Caleb in the cellar. The vascular web was dark in his face and hands, but I'd seen it worse. In the confined space there was no escaping the ugliness of my intention. For weeks his life had been imprisonment and suffering. Now, thanks to me, it was going to continue. He'd thought I was his friend. I *had* been his friend. Some of his guilt and longing for his mother had been diverted my way, and I'd accepted it. Naturally: I had divertable guilt and longing of my own. He'd let his mother down, I'd failed my son. The surrogacy that dare not speak its name. Now, with the power to reunite vampire parent and child, I was going to keep them apart. The only Old Testament comfort was knowing that however things turned out Mia would come after me for revenge.

'You're going to need us,' Madeline said, when I was back upstairs. 'To get your boy back. You're going to need all of us.'

We were in the lounge. Trish was upstairs talking to someone on her cell. Lucy, Cloquet and, rather sheepishly now, Devaz were in the kitchen with the back door open to the bright morning, smoking and drinking vodka'd coffee. Outside was a high blue sky with static shreds of white cloud, cold fresh air shivering the leaves and grass.

'I already owe you my life,' I said.

'Bollocks,' she said. 'Had to be someone. Might as well be those fuckers. Anyway, point is, don't worry. We've got to look out for each other.'

I opened my mouth to say, I'll make it worth your while, meaning I'd pay, but I didn't say it. It would've been vulgar. It wasn't that Maddy wouldn't take money – of course she would – it was that this was something else. Without me realising it the feeling of being with (it was a warm shock in the blood now that I did realise it) *family* had crept in. The little collective consciousness, with its insights and occlusions, moved like a soft current between us. It was partly why Devaz was still here. Madeline – I got it, glimpsed the thing she'd been guarding in our peeled moments – was lonely. I saw her in a hotel bathroom touching up her make-up. At home in her flat, sitting on the loo and staring at the floor. In the back of a London cab, looking out at the liquid lights. Alone. Always alone. Now there was this, us, kin, the *pack*.

Lucy appeared in the doorway, hands wrapped around a red coffee mug, thin shoulders hunched. For a moment the three of us looked at each other. 'I suppose this is all actually happening,' Lucy said, shoulders going down. 'I keep thinking...' She shook her head, let it go. We knew what she meant. In spite of the hard evidence there was a certain amount of pointlessly asking yourself if it might not, even now, all turn out to be an illusion, a dream, a fabulous and revolting mistake.

'I was just telling her,' Madeline said. 'We'll help her get her little boy back. Fergus and Trish are up for it. Although — ' to me, with exaggerated disdain — 'Fergus *will* want to talk money. You'll help, won't you, Luce?'

Lucy's eyes met mine. I saw what she wanted me to see, that she didn't want anything taken for granted, that she hadn't accepted this yet, that she'd done what she'd done last night for the money because she needed to buy space and time, that she didn't have Madeline's desperation, that there was a connection but it would only take us so far.

'It's no one's responsibility but mine,' I said. (*Yes, I know. I understand.*) 'But I'll take whatever help I can get. I don't expect anything. You've all been so kind to me already.'

Zoë, on her back in my lap, opened her eyes. My love went to her again, with hopeless panic because it knew it would have to fall away. It occurred to me, *as* it fell away (like the disintegrating tail-end of a Fourth of July skyrocket), that I'd never seen her brother in human form. If you showed me his picture I wouldn't know who he was.

Trish came bounding down the stairs. She'd changed into tight black jeans and a mohair sweater almost exactly the green of her eyes. Bare white feet, toenails painted cerise. She looked like she'd slept for a week and woken completely renewed.

'You lot on the vodka already?' she said. 'Where's mine?'

51

L ymington is a Georgian market town and sailing resort on the Hampshire coast. Immediately south, the Solent strait separates England from the Isle of Wight. To the north is the New Forest, a hundred and forty-five square miles of ancient heath and woodland. Southampton and Portsmouth lie to the east, and to the west is Keyhaven Marsh, a four-mile nature reserve ending at a long shingle promontory known as Hurst Spit. The house Konstantinov had secured was at the very edge of the town, just where the saltgrassed marsh began, a detached, five-bedroomed property, high-ceilinged, wood-floored, draughty, chipped, scuffed and generally knocked about by decades of vacationing families.

The crooked doctor, Budarin, was a small Russian in his late forties, dark-haired but severely balding, with surprised pale blue eyes and a ridiculously cherubic little mouth. A functioning alcoholic. Konstantinov had known him for years. He didn't ask me a single question. In fact he barely spoke at all, and when he did it was in Russian. As requested he drew a pint of blood each from Konstantinov, Cloquet, Walker, me (kept marked and separate) and, when I threw another three hundred his way, himself, though some joyless joke about its quality passed between him and his countryman. He was staying at a hotel in nearby Keyhaven, and, courtesy of our retainer, would be 'on call' indefinitely. He could get us more blood, but it would take forty-eight hours and ten grand. I told him to do whatever was necessary.

Madeline and Lucy had come with us. Trish had gone back to London to take her motorcycle test. For her the rescue mission pay-day was going to finance a year's travelling: South East Asia through spring, then the US and South America in summer and fall. Fergus's plans were uncertain, but Madeline was confident we could get him at short notice. Devaz had gone AWOL.

'Give me Mia's number, hon, so I can tell her where you are.'

Caleb was on a camping cot in the cellar. I'd given him a quarter-pint of Cloquet's blood. Just enough to haul him into woozy consciousness. 'I have a phone right here. You can talk to her.' I moved his hot hair off his forehead, watched his eyes swim-up to focus. Lousy instinct told me he was sufficiently reduced to want his mother. Weeks of sickness and isolation and degradation and pain. He was seventeen. Seventeen was nothing. 'You just tell her you're okay,' I said. 'I'll tell her where we are and she can come get you.' His face dramatised a brief inner struggle. A dark pink tear crept out of his left eye. Then he gave me the number.

I let him talk to her for a minute – a slurred and confused narrative of our time incarcerated – then commandeered the phone and hurried back upstairs to the big lounge at the front of the house. The lights were off. It was dark out, but I could still see the long front lawn, the hedge, the fifty yards of saltgrass down to the water's edge, where Lucy had gone, warmly wrapped, frowning, for a walk. Yellow boat-lights twinkled on the Solent. I could hear Madeline talking softly to Zoë in the kitchen. Something spicy for the humans was simmering on the stove: Cloquet's handiwork. The phone was hot and heavy in my hand. Lucky I'd had all these months to get used to monstrosity.

'Mia?'

'Yes, who is this?' Very slight Russian accent. Calm as a frozen lake.

'My name is Talulla Demetriou. You need to listen very carefully.'

'Where's Caleb?'

'Shut up and listen to me or you'll never see your son again.'

Silence. Immediate recalibration. No hysterics. She was used to things not being the way they first appeared. I stared out of the window, aware of the room's normally shapeless sentience suddenly gathered tight. I gave her the instructions: She would find out where the Disciples were. She would join them. She would help us get in and get my son and Natasha out. Then her son would be returned to her. She listened without uttering a sound. Konstantinov appeared in the doorway.

'What makes you think I'll be able to find them?' she said, when I'd finished and, like an idiot, asked: *Are you still there?*

'Because your son's life is at stake.'

'Put Caleb back on.'

'No, that's all for now. You know he's alive. We have blood. He'll be comfortable and cared for, I promise you. I have absolutely no desire to harm him. But understand: there's nothing I won't do to get my child back. You fuck with me and I'll make it very bad for him. Is that clear?'

A pause. 'If you're going to talk like that,' she said, 'try not to make it sound like such hard work.'

I had a vivid image of her from Jake's journal: the fine-cut blonde woman dressed in black. White face, blood-covered mouth, blue eyes. *Legs that would've been at home in an ad for quality nylons.* Thank you, Jacob Marlowe.

'It doesn't help you to make me your enemy,' I said.

'You're holding my son prisoner. You're already my enemy.'

'I also saved his life. Anyway, this conversation's over. I'll call you again——'

'Wait.'

'What?'

'If you hurt him in any way, I'll kill your child myself. Do *you* understand?'

'Yes.'

'Now let me——'

Konstantinov took the phone from me and hit End. 'Don't let her talk,' he said. 'She's three hundred years old. She's smarter than you. You give her the instructions and hang up. That's all. No good for us will come of speaking with her. Next time I'll make the call.'

He handed me the phone. There was a moment between us in which I didn't say, Listen, it's thanks to me we've got a chance of finding your wife, and he didn't say, Listen, it's thanks to me you're not lying in a WOCOP freezer with a silver bullet in your head. We looked at each other, exchanged it all anyway, then mutually let each other off, without saying a word.

I went to the cellar door and unlocked it. The stairs descending into the gloom depressed me. I took a deep breath, felt ten thousand microscopic threads of *wulf* snap as I rolled my neck, then, still not knowing whether I was going to tell the truth or lie through my tingling teeth, I went down to speak to my prisoner.

52

I told the truth, and it was as bad as it could have been. It was a wretched thing to see so much misery and betrayal with so little physical strength to express itself. He tried to get up, couldn't, crashed from the fold-out onto the floor. I had to pick him up to put him back. He tried to hit and kick, but his limbs were like paper lanterns. He would have bitten me, so I held his head still by its nest of white-blond hair. He spat in my face.

'Do you remember when I told you it was my son they were planning to sacrifice?' I said, when what little energy he'd had was spent.

'Fuck you.'

'You said you didn't know where they were keeping him, but that even if you knew you couldn't tell me. I'll just repeat that for you: *Even if you knew you couldn't tell me.*'

'I never said that.'

'Yes, you did, and you remember saying it, so don't bother denying it.'

'It's not the same.'

'It is the same.'

His face crumpled again for a moment: fury, impotence, losing the argument, remembering his humiliations in the cage – but always, first and foremost, being trapped in an eleven-year-old's body. Always, first and foremost, looking like a child. It drove him to say the one thing that could hurt me.

'I trusted you.'

'I know you did.'

'I thought you were my friend.'

'I was. I am. I'm sorry. I wouldn't harm you.'

'What if my mother hadn't agreed?'

Yes, well, that was where the logic took us. *You fuck with me and I'll make it very bad for him.* Would I? Go to work on him like the WOCOP scientists and film it and send it to Mia Tourisheva? Cooperate and I'll make it stop.

'I don't know,' I said.

He hadn't expected honesty. It burned his heart all over again. But he forced himself to go cold. 'Well, you wouldn't have to get *your* hands dirty, would you? Not with all your werewolf cronies around. This place fucking STINKS.' The last word shouted, for the household's benefit.

'Is there anything I can get you?' I asked. I didn't like looking at him. It was so obvious how much this had hurt him, was still hurting him. It was so obvious how much he'd liked me.

'Yeah,' he said. 'Your daughter.'

I absorbed it. Exhaled. Turned to go.

'Cigarettes,' he said. 'Camels.' Then when he saw me smile: 'What?'

'I used to smoke those.'

'Congratulations. So fucking what?'

'Nothing. I'll get you some.' It was a good job I'd had so much practice hardening my heart. Even so I paused at the foot of the stairs, wondered for the umpteenth time if there wasn't another way. There wasn't.

'My mother's going to kill you,' he said, quietly, when I was three stairs up. The thought was ugly to him, amongst other things.

'I'm sure she'll try.'

'You don't understand. You can't do this sort of thing to her.'

'And yet here I am, doing it.'

He closed his eyes. Surrendered, broken, to the new predicament. The new version of the old predicament. He'd been exhausted for such a long time. Not many make it past a thousand years, Cloquet had said. I couldn't see Caleb getting through another ten.

53

Walker was sitting in the dark in a chair by his bedroom window, drinking a glass of scotch. The bottle – Glenmorangie – stood on the window sill, half empty. I sat down opposite him on the edge of the unmade bed. Our eyes met for a moment. The effect of all the times we'd looked at each other in shocked fascination was still there. But now a detached version of him stood over it, like a mortician over a corpse. I wanted to put my arms around him. He looked away.

'I know what you want from me,' I said, gently. 'I can't do it.'

He didn't answer. There was no comfort. Comfort by definition referred to what had happened to him. Comfort was logically self-defeating. In spite of which I wanted so *much* to put my arms around him. At these moments it was as if God said: 'See? There's a reason I put the soul in the body. The body is there for when the soul's money is no good.' But right now the body's money was no good, either. We'd had no physical contact – I literally hadn't touched him – since Murdoch's ambush in Italy. The loss was an ache, in my skin, in my heart. It had been so warm and collusive between us in the dark hotel hours. With a little practice we'd got the knack of coming, together, with him inside me. I remembered the first time it happened, the dark intuition, the sudden upgraded focus, the precarious rushing delight and at the end the second or two of astonishing unity that shears you both off into the void – then back, gratuitously enriched, stunned, deliciously finite.

'You don't have to say anything,' he said, quietly.

I imagined coming to his room in the small hours and starting to undress. I knew as clearly as if he'd said it aloud how cold and dead his *Don't* would sound, before I'd got past the second button of my shirt.

'You should eat something,' I said. These things you say that you know are useless and yet not completely because their use is to be there when not saying anything is unbearable.

'Did she go for it?' he asked.

Mia Tourisheva, he meant. This was an option. Discuss the objectives, the plans, the practicalities.

'She seems to have.'

'You know Natasha's probably dead.'

'Why do you say that?'

'When was the last time they sent Mike anything? The novelty's worn off.'

It hadn't occurred to me. But now that I thought of it there was an occasional wideness to Konstantinov's eye that said it had occurred to him. It had occurred to him, yes, but he was going to proceed as if it hadn't. I didn't see him surviving it if she was dead. He didn't have Walker's talent for staying alive on fascination with his own deformity. Maybe Walker didn't either, any more.

'It won't matter,' he said. 'He won't accept it until he's seen her with his own eyes. And that'll be the end of him.'

The bed was a third watchful presence with us. Is that good? Oh God, yes. Yes, it is. The memories of the two of us together were like children he'd been forced to disown. I got to my feet and moved towards him. He didn't object. I straddled him in his chair and put my arms around him, drew him close. He let me. As an experiment on himself. To see if anything was left, viable. I held him tighter, willing him back. Tiny, faint neural impulses... resulting in nothing. Which meant that in a matter of seconds my holding him was ugly. I got off him. The loss of his body heat was a peculiar distinct bereavement. Downstairs I could hear Cloquet setting plates and cutlery for himself and Konstantinov. Someone uncorked a bottle. Zoë made a single melodious noise of surprise, then went quiet. I wondered if Walker would stay, once he was well enough to travel, and if he left, where he would go. Nowhere would be right for him. He'd have to keep moving. Never stay long enough for anyone – especially himself – to start asking the questions that mattered.

'I'm sorry,' I said. He looked at me, but as if I was an image on a screen, something broadcast to him from light-years away. Remarkable what they could do with technology, nowadays. It disgusted me, the brokenness between us, that there was nothing I could do. Or rather that there was something I could do, but daren't. 'I'm sorry,' I repeated – at exactly the moment he reached for the bottle and his chair ticked, loudly, and the slight clash of the synchronicity snapped something and I turned and walked out of the room.

In the front hall I found Konstantinov and Budarin speaking together in Russian.

'Either way we're going to need personnel and weapons,' Konstantinov said to me, switching to English. 'Alexi might be able to help.'

'Either way' referred to the intractable logistics. If Mia located the Disciples there were two possible scenarios. One was that we went in immediately, as a squad of humans. The other was that we waited till the night of the ritual – full moon, winter solstice, lunar eclipse – and went in as werewolves. If we went in as humans we could go in in daylight, which, obviously, would eliminate the problem of dealing with the vamps. On the other hand we'd be laughable opposition to any half-decent guard of familiars. Only Konstantinov and Walker had combat skills, and Walker was fragile. But if we waited till full moon (making the nauseous assumption that Konstantinov and I *could* wait, could *bear* waiting once we knew where they were) to go in at full lupine strength, we'd have to go in after moonrise (ergo after sundown), which would mean God only knew how many vampires to deal with. And the window would be small. Moonrise was 21.03. Eclipse was maximal at 23.14. Two hours to gamble with my son's life. Madeline, I knew, had been picturing a re-run of the assault on Murdoch's place in Berkshire, a free-for-all pushover fuck-and-feed fest. All of them had, with the exception of Lucy, who in any case had subtly made it known she didn't consider herself committed to anything. Either way, as Konstantinov said, we were going to need help.

'Fine,' I said. 'Get whoever you can.'

'These are not good men, you understand?' Budarin said. 'These are not soldiers.'

'I don't care who they are or what they've done. If they'll fight for us they're hired.' I thought of Delilah Snow, for the first time in what felt like years, and heard myself laughing and saying, Who the fuck am *I* to care?, though I didn't, in fact, laugh or say that out loud.

'Very well,' Budarin said. 'I'll see what I can do.'

For the second time since Alaska I entered the hell of waiting.

Nothing helped. There sat the cellphone. There yawned around it the whole universe for me to reach out into looking for some way to make what I wanted to happen happen. You get up, walk from one room to another, sit down. Eight seconds have passed. Nothing's changed. You can't believe you have the reservoir to cope with thousands more seconds, hours, days. Every moment you enact the koan of bearing the unbearable.

On day five of this, Konstantinov said: You're going to have to raise the incentive.

I said: Not yet.

Things went on in the background. New papers for Lorcan arrived from Kovatch. Lucy returned to London and handed in her notice, then went missing for a few days, then turned up back at the Lymington house, then went again. Trish came down on her new motorcycle (with word from Fergus that he was 'professionally available' when needed) but took off for Cornwall after only a day. Madeline went back to her flat in West London. Libido made all of us claustrophobic, but between her and me it was acute. We both knew if she stayed there was a good chance something would happen – which, while it might have thrilled Walker in his old life, would've been a misery to him in his new one. He kept to his room, though sometimes he walked by the Solent at night. I missed him so much it made me angry with him. Then angry with myself because I should never have started it in the first place. I thought of reneging and Turning him. Sure it would make him hate me, eventually, but at least I'd have him *now*. I don't know what stopped me doing it. Possibly nothing more than the irrational conviction that in this brittle hiatus doing anything I didn't have to would be dangerous, a provocation to the God who wasn't there. Budarin kept the blood coming (no one knew from where and no one asked) and with it I kept Caleb weak but comfortable. He was allowed to talk with Mia Tourisheva just long enough to establish he was alive and unharmed. He stopped speaking to me when I went down to bring him the Camels (and eventually a TV/DVD, a stack of movies Cloquet picked up in town) until boredom drove him to start again. Konstantinov and Budarin were in and out. I met the guys they'd hired, ropey-looking men – three Russians, one Nigerian – with economic vocabularies and a physical self-containment that could have been instilled by an elite military training but intuition told me had been instilled by prison. I didn't care.

On day sixteen the BBC News ran a little lighthearted story on UK preparations for the full-moon winter solstice lunar eclipse. Bearded men and overweight women in robes and daisy-chains. Astronomers walked us through the math with graphics aimed at seven-year-olds.

'You have to understand,' Mia Tourisheva said to me on the phone. 'I'm doing everything I can. These people don't want—'

Konstantinov snatched the phone: 'Listen,' he said. 'Tonight my chemist friend is bringing me a gallon of HS_2O_4. Do you know what that is? It won't kill your child, but it will be excruciatingly painful for—'

'God *damn* you, Mikhail, stop it. *Stop it.*' I tried to get the phone back. Between us we dropped it. When I picked it up the line was dead. It rang immediately.

'Please,' Mia said. 'Don't. Don't. I swear to you I'm doing everything I can. The Fifty Families are looking for them and *they* don't know where they are.' She sounded exhausted. The pleading in the normally calm voice was horrible to hear. I left Konstantinov and took the phone upstairs with me. Locked myself in one of the bathrooms. I was ready to reassure her, but by the time I opened my mouth she'd recovered her composure. 'Do what you have to do,' she said. 'Just remember: I don't die. I have for ever to find you, and after you, your children, their children. It'll be a long time before I'm satisfied. Now, let me speak to my son.'

'Get some fucking results,' I said. 'Then I'll let you speak to your son. If he still has a tongue to speak with.' Then I hung up.

I slept with Zoë in her bassinet next to me, when I did sleep, when I wasn't staring at the ceiling or pacing the downstairs rooms or (naturally: *wulf* doesn't care) jerking-off. Ten days after her debut transformation my daughter had started taking milk from me again. I'd had nothing since drying-up in prison, but when she'd woken in the middle of the tenth night there it was, just as I'd known it would be in the dream I'd been having moments before. It was a unique grief, sitting with her at my breast, feeling the life and love there could have been. She stared at me with dispassionate comprehension, as if she knew my love was forced away from her but there was nothing she could do. Her primary hardwired connection was to her brother. Nothing could come from her to me while he was withheld. She wasn't punishing me. It was impersonal, structural, necessary. If I failed – if he died but she and I survived – then something might be possible between us, if I could stand it. But not while he was alive, not while he was withheld. Until he was established one way or another – rescued living or discovered dead – her soul was on pause. I told myself, obviously, that none of this was coming from her, that all of it was my own projection. My thinking self understood this. It didn't make any difference. Every time our eyes met, there it all was. It ought to have stopped me letting our eyes meet. Instead I couldn't stop. The truth was addictive.

Five days before the winter solstice I woke around four in the morning and knew something wasn't right. The hunger was wide awake, had been waiting for me, jabbering, fidgeting, occasionally lashing out (it doesn't *recognise* sleep, but eventually exhaustion outmatches it and your body crashes), but through my blood's racket the house let me in on a new silence it was holding somewhere. My watch said 4.17 a.m.

Konstantinov's shift.

Oh.

I looked into the bassinet. Zoë was awake, but peaceful. I got out of bed, pulled on jeans, sneakers, a shirt, and without protest from her slipped her into the carrier around me. There was a Springfield and clip under my pillow. I took it.

Walker's door was shut but I knew he wasn't asleep. I could smell scotch, unwashed clothes, his body's misery. Cloquet's door, wide open, revealed him asleep, fully clothed on his front, one arm hanging over the side of the bed, its immediate radius littered with cigarettes, crumpled bills, change, keys. His curtains were half-drawn, showed the plump belly of the moon – waxing gibbous – the clock that didn't tick down but instead fattened-up to Lorcan's death and the end of everything I knew.

'Whatever you're doing, Mikhail, please, stop. Please.'

I was at the head of the basement stairs. Konstantinov was standing over Caleb's bed with his back to me. He had my cell-phone in one hand. On the floor next to him was an unmarked opaque plastic bottle with its cap still on. I couldn't see Caleb's face, but I could tell from the sound of him he'd been gagged. His wrists and ankles were cuffed to the bed – unnecessarily, since we didn't keep him strong enough to get to his feet.

'Mikhail, just wait, please. It's still okay. You still haven't done anything.'

I came down the stairs, the Springfield stuck down the back of my jeans.

'Come on, look at me.'

'It's the only way,' he said. 'It's the only way.'

'Seriously, Mikhail, come on. Look at me.'

He turned. His face was pale and big-pored. His beard had grown. The rims of his eyes were rhubarb-pink. He looked mad-monkish, on the brink of leaving himself behind.

'If you do this,' I said, 'you won't be the same person. You won't be the same person for Natasha. You have to think of

Natasha watching you do this, because she'll watch it in her mind just as clearly as if she was standing here next to you.'

Caleb was watching *me*, through his sickness and fear. I was thinking: if you ever have the chance to intercede for me, please don't forget this.

I moved closer to Konstantinov. 'This is just desperation,' I said. 'This is just the need to do something. I understand. I feel it too. But you know deep down it won't make any difference, except to change you into someone else. Right now you're still the person Natasha knows. Don't turn yourself into someone who'll be a stranger to her.'

He looked down at Caleb. Not with compassion or enmity. With nothing. With the human face's version of the vast mathematical silence.

'Come on,' I said. 'Leave it. It's passed. You don't ever have to go through this again.'

I like to think that was it. I like to think I'd talked him down, that whatever had happened next he wouldn't have poured sulphuric acid on a young boy's face so that the young boy's mother could hear the screams. I like to think that, but there's no way I'll ever know, because what happened next was that the phone in his hand rang.

It was Mia.

She'd found the Disciples.

PART FOUR

LACUNA

'Beware of false prophets, which come to you in sheep's clothing, but inwardly they are ravening wolves.'

Matthew 7:15

54

Konstantinov was checking the weapons when I gave him the news: 'Vampires are walking in daylight.'

'What?'

'I just spoke to Mia. First it was only Remshi. Now there are at least a dozen.'

'It's a trap. Nothing changes. We go tomorrow as planned.'

'I don't think it's a trap.'

'Nothing changes.'

I was holding a half-cup of cold coffee. I threw it at the wall behind his head. It smashed, with a surprisingly loud noise. He put the AK-47 down on the couch and looked at me. Not much shook him. This hadn't either, but it had registered, faintly, on the outside of his obsession.

'Fuck you,' I said, as a hunger cramp gripped my guts. 'I *know* nothing changes. But I'm sick of this tragic Russian shit. Stop going on as if you're the only one who's got something to lose.'

It was just after ten at night. We were in the large lounge of a two-storey villa three miles from the village of Falasarna on the island of Crete. Travertine tiles, limewashed walls, neutral contemporary furniture, odours of sandalwood and the sea. French doors opened onto a verandah with steps leading down to a pool area and olive grove. Our nearest neighbour was half a kilometre away, down a steep gravel road that hairpinned the hillside with barely room for two cars to pass. Cloquet had found the house by accident, attempting to book rooms for twelve people in a hotel in Chania. The manager had lowered his voice and asked if he wouldn't rather take a house. His cousin's. Beach ten-minute walk. Off-season rates.

Konstantinov stared at me. The stare said, without malice: I've got more to lose because I won't survive if mine's dead. You will if yours is. He was right. I already knew Lorcan's death wouldn't kill me. If the price I had to pay for having a future with my daughter was accepting the blame for her brother's death then so be it. We'd have a damaged love with my shame at its core, but it would still be love. That, of course, was partly *why* I'd thrown the coffee cup. That and the cramps, the sweats, the wolf's thorned antics under my skin.

'Tell me about the daylight vampires,' he said.

Sixty hours ago we'd got the call from Mia. The Disciples were on Crete, in the hills east of Ano Sfinari, in a former monastery now ostensibly being turned into a luxury hotel but in fact purchased and adapted by the believers to welcome Remshi back to the waking world. And Remshi, apparently, *was* back. By the time Mia joined up he'd been 'among them' (having appeared on cue with three priests and Jacqueline at midnight on December 12th) for several days, a handsome charismatic vampire who claimed he was 'older than the first utterance of human speech', who'd performed numerous extraordinary feats and produced one show-stopper: film of himself walking the grounds with a couple of familiars in broad daylight. *In broad daylight.* As his strength increased, he promised, he'd be able to give this gift to all of them, in return for loyalty to him and his queen-to-be, none other than our own Madame Jacqueline Delon. So is it him? I'd asked Mia. She'd said: Parlour tricks and bad poetry. But something in her voice conceded it wasn't so clear-cut. I pressed her. There's something here, it's true, she said. Very old. I don't know. This is irrelevant. Don't waste time. Let me speak to my son.

Finding and joining the faithful hadn't been easy for her. The climate of paranoia was dense. Six months ago there had been a raid on a Helios Project lab in Beijing, and though the Disciples had denied any involvement the Fifty Families (having decided enough was enough) were using it as a pretext for prosecution. A judgement had been passed. Vampire death-squads had been dispatched, but by then Jacqueline and her posse were off-radar. A few cult members were found and beheaded in Istanbul, but the leadership and its priestly cabal remained hidden. As they would have remained hidden to Mia, had her brother not been a member. They'd been made vampires together (she wouldn't tell when) by the same immortal. It's not telepathy, she said. But if I decide to find him sooner or later I will. It goes both ways. That's all. Don't ask me any more. If I asked any more I'd be likely to ask if she could be sure her brother believed her motives for joining were genuine; and whatever she said we'd both know it didn't make any difference, because this was the only plan we had.

And so had followed the phone calls, the regroup, the flight, the scramble to get weapons organised. The weapons, of course, had been delayed. We'd lost another forty-eight hours. Konstantinov was ready to go in, suicidally, unarmed. When the boat had at last arrived earlier this evening I'd had to stop him from attacking the people on it. Now (again of course, of *course*) we had no choice: tomorrow night was the full moon. Full moon, winter solstice, lunar eclipse. We'd run, with delirious, yielding inevitability, out of time.

'What's going on?' Trish said, coming in from the verandah with Lucy just behind her. They were both in sweaters and jeans.

341

In December it was cool here. (I hadn't expected Lucy to be part of this. She'd let me know as much, over the weeks. And yet when it had come to it, Trish had got off the phone with her, turned to me and said: Luce is in. For months now I've been going back to bits of my old life like a bloody dog to its vomit, Lucy had told me, in the departures lounge at Heathrow. Last Wednesday I went to my reading group supper. Bloody Carol Shields who thinks you can make setting the table a religious act. And while they're all prattling on about it I'm sitting there thinking about... Well. You know. Anyway something went. The last bit of denial, I suppose. There's no old life for me now.)

'There's been a development,' I said. 'Vampires are walking in daylight.'

We'd judged going in with the sun up, as humans, the lesser of two evils. With Budarin's four guys, Konstantinov, me, Trish, Lucy, Cloquet and Fergus (whom I'd only met for the first time two days ago: a big Irishman with a drink-darkened face and a physique like Baloo the bear) we had an armed force of ten. Walker was here too but had been sick on the flight, in and out of fever ever since. He'd refused to see a doctor. He'd refused to see anyone, except Konstantinov, and for the last twenty-four hours had been in his room in bed. He wasn't likely to be fit for action. If Mia's intelligence was sound there were seventy-nine vampires with a standing guard of twenty human familiars. Ten humans (assuming Walker's absence) against twenty humans was better than ten against seventy-nine vampires, even if four of us were in all our transformed glory. But now, if Mia's story of daylight vampires was true, the odds had worsened.

'How is that possible?' Lucy asked.

'Christ knows,' I said. 'Mia said three times now a group of four vampires have been selected from the congregation to "receive the gift". Remshi takes them to his room. The following night there's filmed footage of these four walking around the place in sunlight. After the first round of scepticism they had themselves filmed next to TVs showing live news to verify the date and time. Tough to fake. These are CNN and BBC news anchors. Any way you slice it we have to figure on a dozen wide-awake vamps in the place tomorrow when we go in.'

'Should be interesting,' Trish said.

Lucy sat down at the table where the guns were piled up. 'Don't we need... You know, wooden stakes or something? Garlic?'

I went out onto the verandah and phoned Madeline.

'She's absolutely fine,' was the greeting. 'Stop worrying.'

The moon was up, low over the sea. Full tomorrow. *Wulf* was big and angular and impatient under my skin. I thought of those cartoons where someone swallows something and becomes the shape of the thing they've swallowed. There was a lovely smell of clean concrete and the pool's chlorine and something like sage or rosemary in the shrubs nearby. All distinct beguiling counterpoints to the hunger's bass throb.

'I want you to know something: I trust you.'

'Yeah yeah yeah. Here, listen to this.' She moved the phone. Rustling, then my daughter's breathing. Steady. Strong. A thousand miles away. 'She's fallen asleep watching a DVD with me.'

'What are you watching?'

'Don't laugh. *The Little Mermaid.*'

'You're a good person.'

'What, apart from killing and eating people?'

'Apart from that, yes.'

'What's going on there, anyway?'

I filled her in. I couldn't ask her what I wanted to ask: Have you sorted out *prey*? Is it safe? Will my daughter be safe? Explicitness died in my throat. The little fey truthful indifferent bit of myself inside said let it go, there's nothing you can do now and you'll most likely be dead tomorrow anyway. Dead and gone to join the vast mathematical silence.

'About the money,' I said. 'If I don't come back—'

'La la la la—'

'Listen, seriously. I've spoken to my lawyer. He's got the codicil. You'll be okay.'

'You've told me all this.'

'I know, I know. Let me listen to her again.'

'Hang on, I'm losing you...'

'Oh wait, I'll move. There's a dead signal spot... Is that better? Can you hear me?'

'Yeah, that's better. Here you go. Don't wake her up!'

I listened, without making a sound. Without making a sound on the outside. Inside I couldn't shut up. I'm sorry, angel. I made a mess of everything. I'm so sorry. This girl I've left you with, she's a little crazy, but her heart's in the right place. If I don't see you again, I think she'll take good care of you. It's what my instinct tells me. We don't have much going for us, but we've got good instincts. I love you. I love you. I love you.

'Okay?' Madeline asked, in a voice that said she'd heard as clearly as if I'd spoken aloud.

'Yes. Thank you. Thank you for doing this incredible thing.'

'Look, don't get maudlin. You'll be home with your boy tomorrow then we can crack open a bottle of Bolly. Okay?'

'Okay.'

'How's Fergus the Lergus?'

'The what?'

'The Lergus. Like the Lergie. How's he behaving himself?'

Fergus had in fact just appeared on the verandah, one hand holding his phone to his ear, the other gripping a scotch and cigarette. 'To make money work for you you've got to have contempt for it,' he'd told me, apropos of nothing, about a minute after we'd been introduced. 'You've got to have contempt for the stupid obedience of money. The problem is, to develop the contempt, you need to acquire quite a lot of money. When you're ready to discuss your fortune, *how* to treat it with the necessary contempt, you let me know.'

'Colourful,' I said to Madeline. 'Weirdly, there's something about him that inspires confidence.'

'Yeah, it's greed. You know that as long as what you're asking him to do will max his profit you can count on him to do it. What about Walker?'

'Still sick. He won't see me.'

'You do know he's in love with you, don't you?'

Pause. Well? Didn't I?

'Are you in love with him?' Madeline asked.

'What, we're going to have this conversation *now*?'

Our connection flickered shadowily over the line. It came to me that she knew what had happened to him while we'd been held prisoner. Something in her tone. Which brought again, whether I wanted it or not, the image, Walker bound and bent double, Tunner jamming the bloody nightstick deep, Murdoch observing glassily while conducting a conversation on his phone.

'You could do a lot worse,' Madeline said.

There's something better than killing the one you love.

'I'm just saying,' Madeline said, 'there aren't that many blokes worth having. But he's one of them. I'm losing you again, babes.'

'I should get back anyway,' I said, as the Hunger sent a shuddering wave through my legs and I staggered. 'I feel like shit.' Madeline, courtesy of the same arbitrariness that ruled the other monthly curse, suffered nothing until a couple of hours before moonrise on transformation day. It was the other reason she'd been the obvious choice to babysit. The primary reason being

345

that Lucy didn't want the responsibility again. 'I'll call you tomorrow,' I said, moving into the darkness of the little olive grove beyond the pool's paving, where for some reason the signal was strong. 'Assuming I'm still alive, obviously.' I saw Konstantinov come out of Walker's room and leave the door open behind him. He was frowning.

'Walker?' he called.

'Don't be daft,' Madeline said.

'Walker?' Konstantinov called a second time. I couldn't see him now but I could hear doors opening and closing. Fergus, live to the shift in the air's character, hung up his call and turned back to the house.

'You still there?' Madeline asked.

'Something's happened.'

'What?'

'I think Walker's gone.'

'Gone? What do you mean?'

'Hang on a second.'

Konstantinov came out onto the verandah.

'Listen,' Madeline said. 'I wasn—'

You always know a split second before. At all the big moments it's as if, for the tiniest fragment of neural time, you realise your whole life's been leading up to this.

A figure didn't spring or leap but seemed to walk very rapidly out of the darkness to my left. I had time. I had mute leisure to notice he was dressed like a cat burglar in close-fitting black, balaclava'd and gloved, leisure to recognise his packed scent, leisure to realise I was no longer visible from the verandah and to wonder where Walker could've gone and what Madeline had been about to say – before the man in black smashed his fist into my face.

I felt my jaw break and my knees flood. My arms seemed

to spend a long time softly churning nothing. Something jabbed me, hard, in my left thigh. I was aware of trying to hold onto the phone as the ground swung up. I tasted cool dust and heard the blood bang once in my head. Then what felt like a paving stone hit the back of my skull, and all my lights went out.

55

My first feeling, on opening my eyes, was relief: the hunger told me I hadn't slept through transformation. It told me via wracking spasms and futile nausea, but still, it told me. Lorcan was alive, though there couldn't (the hunger *also* told me) be more than three or four hours till moonrise.

That was the end of the good news.

I was lying on my back in a bolted-down cage in what I knew within seconds – the ribbed flanks and steel-flavoured cold – was a cargo trailer. My left ankle and left wrist were cuffed to one of the bars, my right mysteriously at liberty. Two brilliant storm lamps hung from hooks outside the cage. I could taste dried sweat on my lips.

'Happy solstice,' Murdoch said.

I struggled up, first onto my side, then with the aid of the bars into a sitting position. You give thanks for small things. I gave thanks that I was wearing jeans, not a skirt. People start trying to kill you, you stop wearing skirts. He moved into the storm lamps' bleaching light and there was the height and the poise and the white crew-cut. He was still in the cat burglar get-up, minus the balaclava and gloves. He'd lost a little weight, but retained the facial expression of a calmly deranged hawk.

'What do you want?' I asked. My throat was sore. Dehydration was a dog doing the same shrill bark repeatedly in my head. *Wulf*, at the end of its patience, was trying to break the rules in my bones. But they were the moon's rules, and by them my bones were condemned to hold their form. Since it was its departmental job a bit of my brain was racing through possibility flowcharts, Jake's despised strings of *ifs* and *thens*, in what the rest of me knew was a pointless exercise. There was no way out. There was no way out because there was nothing Murdoch wanted. Or rather whatever it was he wanted necessarily entailed me having no way out. In spite of which, and aside from the redundant calculations, animal motherhood launched a giant dumb imperative: plead with him. Offer him money. Offer him anything.

'Reinstatement,' he said.

Please, please, please. Motherhood insisted there was some elusive tone that would do it, if only I could discover it. Idiocy at the cellular level. I pushed myself, quivering, to my feet. New sweat needled. *Wulf* breathed hot in my palms and breasts and scalp.

'Do you remember our conversation about the relationship between sex and chaos?' Murdoch asked.

Mentally I was going through the contents of my pockets. Nothing in the jeans, some euros, a tissue, a gum wrapper, fluff. The jacket? It was one I hadn't worn much and didn't particularly like, black canvas, a bit big across the shoulders. In fact it had only survived to Crete by never having been unpacked from the tote bag I'd been using since I left New York what felt like a decade ago. It had only made it out of the bag now because the island had turned out cold and it was the one heavy thing I'd brought. In any case I didn't remember its pockets ever holding a penknife or a corkscrew or a hatpin or a screwdriver or anything that could conceivably serve as a weapon. I'd taken to carrying the Springfield in a shoulder holster, and had been packing it when he'd jumped me, but it had been removed, naturally, along with keys, watch, phone.

'I'm sure you do remember it,' Murdoch continued. 'I said that sex was a rogue force. Let into that arena it would've meant distraction, conflict, insubordination. In a facility like that it's not just an unaffordable luxury, it's a potentially lethal virus.'

The moon was close. Astronomy was counting down via spheres and shadows to my son's murder. All that time – vast bergs of it – since he was snatched, and now here we were down to the last melting lump, barely big enough to stand on. *The death of a loved one brutally vivifies everything*, Jake had written; here was my sickening preview of its truth, the violent still-hereness the world would inflict through its cars and vending machines and weather and TV ads, through my own stubborn body that would need its nails clipped and its bladder emptied and its itches scratched. The world betrayed the dead by continuing without them in it, and you, full of shamefully reliable life, collaborated.

'But we're not at that facility any more,' Murdoch said. The sound of his own voice fascinated him because no matter what he said it bounced around in the vast mathematical silence. He didn't smile or leer, cinematically. Just turned and walked into the darkness beyond the storm lamps' glow. From the slight bounce as he moved I could tell the trailer was still on its truck. Where? How far from the Disciples? Did he even know they were here? He had to. Otherwise too much of a coincidence. But if he was here, who else was? *Reinstatement*. I understood. He'd been demoted or kicked out. We'd escaped on his watch. Our recapture was his only way back in. Herr Direktor, I present, for your consideration, Subject A, Talulla Demetriou, escaped werewolf, nymphomaniac, absent mother—

A cramp jack-knifed me, yanked my cuffed ankle and wrist. Someone had been killed in here before. Not recently, but there was no fooling the burgeoning bitch nose. The moon tugged at my blood. Closer than I'd thought. Maybe two hours. It was impossible to see past the wall of artificial light but a current of air with a flavour of dry grass and pine resin said the trailer door was still open. Since it couldn't possibly make matters worse, I screamed for help as loudly as I could.

Murdoch, hopping back in, didn't bother saying don't bother screaming we're miles from anywhere. It was more satisfying to him to let his silence make it obvious.

He wasn't alone. At his side was a stale-looking, heavily built guy in his mid-forties in a black leather jacket, baggy khaki combats and a string vest. A St Christopher winked in his chest hair. He was full-lipped, in need of a shave, with big, wet, heavy-lidded eyes the colour of prunes. He didn't say anything. Just looked at me with a sort of hopelessness that emptied me of everything except the certainty of what was going to happen. I'd wondered why I'd been left with the use of two limbs. Now I knew. Same reason they'd given Caleb the blood rations before sending him into *his* cage: maximal spectacle. Murdoch didn't want me powerless, he wanted me overpowered, given just enough will to really feel it not being enough.

I thought, while String Vest took off his jacket and unzipped his pants, of all the times I'd heard or read about someone getting raped. *I decided straight away I wasn't going to struggle.* Some rapists liked that. *I decided I was going to fight the sonofabitch with everything I had.* Some rapists liked that. *I fought him at first, but in the end I couldn't stop him.* A lot of rapists seemed to like that. There was no kind of rape there wasn't a rapist for. I had never been raped. Faced with it I felt the ghostly weight of all the women who had been, ranks upon ranks reaching back to the first sad loping

351

female hominids. Incalculable numbers, a wretched sorority only truly visible when you found yourself about to join it. At the same time here again was the terrible aloneness I'd felt when my waters broke. However many hundreds of millions had gone through the experience, when it happened it was only your own version that mattered.

'Here we are then,' Murdoch said, quietly, unlocking the cage door.

I stared at him. 'I'm going to kill you,' I said, also quietly. 'You're going to turn me over to the organisation and I'm going to get out, just like I did before, and I'm—'

'I find I have to do these things,' he said. Which forced a weird pause between the three of us. 'There's a momentum,' he said. 'When I was a child I remember learning that if you gave an object in space just a little shove it would go on for ever. Assuming it didn't hit anything. It would just keep going, for ever.'

String Vest breathed audibly through moist nostrils. I could smell him. The woman in me could smell cigarette smoke and beer and sweat, food fried in old fat. The wolf could smell his thrilled blood and riotous pheromones, stale piss, spiced meat breath and the first ooze of semen. He wanted this raw interim to be over. It was dangerous for him, my personhood like a shimmying or vacillating flame, one moment being the reason he couldn't, the next moment being the reason he couldn't *not*. I said to him: 'Wait. You don't have to do this. You know you don't have to do this.' But I knew it was pointless. The raw interim *was* over. It was over from the first step he took towards me. Now anything I said or did would be provocation. Now the bare fact of me was provocation. That's the nature of rape. His face had thickened slightly, his limbs filled. This was what he'd been waiting for: the illusion of necessity, submission to the force of the dimming drug.

This man is going to rape you.

All the documentaries and articles and silhouetted testimonies. All the little intuitions I'd had about certain women. She has been. She has been. *She* has been. All this flared and billowed like a suffocating cloud around me and I realised that behind all of them was an actual event, an actual man closing actual distance between himself and an actual woman and shoving himself onto her, into her, through her, breaking the physical boundary and dirtily ransacking the soul's house of priceless memories. Behind all those stories were the candid odours and needling palms and legs sick with adrenaline and the universe's indifferent obedience to physics: physics said if you couldn't fight and your thighs were open and the man was determined to put his cock inside you then that's what would happen. Your body would accommodate it because your body was under the same pointless administration as stars and molecules. I'd seen it in my victims, of course, the shocked realisation that a claw applied with the right pressure would open the soft meat of a midriff and there was nothing the universe could do about it. Right, wrong, good, evil, cruelty, compassion... the universe just shrugged: I don't know this stuff. I just know physics. *I'd seen it in my victims.* Let's not forget that. Millions of women could have asked their rapists, legitimately: *How can you do this?* Millions of women who genuinely didn't know. Not me. I knew how he could do it. He could do it because it was good for him if it was bad for me. He could do it because it was only the best for him if it was the worst for me. I knew the equation. The equation had integrity. The equation didn't change. Only my place in it.

That was an option, of course, to take it as poetic justice, a penance earned from my own mortal sins. Aunt Theresa had a big thing about offering your sufferings up to God. I'd overheard my mother arguing with her: What kind of lousy sadist God wants my sufferings? Don't be such a retard, Theresa. A flash of love for my mom went off like a gorgeous firework – and I laughed out loud.

I know how uplifting it would be to say the laugh unnerved my rapist, but it didn't. He was past all that. Laughter might have had a chance in the raw interim, but not now. Now he'd dropped deep into his blood and only outside force could stop him.

He was less than two feet away. His body's heat touched the cold sweat on my face. *Wulf* was outraged at the timing. An hour, maybe two, and she could tear him in half. But that was part of the Murdoch design. He wanted me as close as possible to the Curse's gift of physical strength without being able to use it. Think what you could do to him if only the moon was up! Oh, but it's *not* up. Of course. Shame.

Without warning String Vest slammed into me, hurling me back against the bars. His weight was a momentary eclipse – but shot through by a sudden distinct pain in my left flank, just under the ribs. For a second I thought he'd stabbed me, albeit with an absurdly small and blunt knife. Then I realised: there was something in one of my pockets after all.

I'd stopped wearing make-up when I was pregnant. Not on principle, but because most of the time my skin was so sensitive that dragging cosmetics across it would've been plain masochism. But here, from the days before maternity, was an eyeliner pencil. I remembered. One night in Palm Springs while I was still pretending to feel great about the divorce I'd tripped, drunk on margaritas, getting out of a cab, and half the contents of my purse had ended up on the sidewalk. A friend had handed me the eyeliner pencil I'd missed, and I'd shoved it into my pocket on my way up the steps to the club. It had been there, with its nib stuck in a tiny hole in the lining, ever since.

Don't bother looking for the meaning of it all. There isn't one.

354

No, there wasn't. But I couldn't help thinking of the young Konstantinov and the pencil he'd had in his pocket the night his beloved Daria Petrov was attacked by a vampire. Every now and then life sold you an illusion of design. A coincidence, a parallel, a sledgehammer symbol. The goods were always faulty. You forked over the cash only to discover they'd fallen apart by the time you got home. But life kept at it. Life couldn't help it. Life was a compulsive salesman.

Out of sheer reflex I'd been struggling, without much success, to keep my free hand free. I'd smacked him a couple of times ineffectually on the side of his monumental head, tried kneeing him in the groin, but the cuffs ruined my balance. He only needed his left hand to pin my right. He only needed to lean on my right thigh to keep my legs open.

You know what you have to do, my mom's voice in me said.

He tore my shirt and yanked at the bra until my breasts were exposed. The trailer's air on my bare flesh was a blunt indecency. He made a noise of mild animal approval, as if he'd unwrapped a box of chocolates and, though he was full, was going to eat most of them anyway. My head was hot. He looked me in the eye. He wanted me to see there was no hope. Of course that's what he wanted to see. Who knew better than me? I closed my eyes, turned my face away, and let myself go completely limp. I had a choice: I could let him put it inside me, let him *get going*, so his reaction time would be at its slowest, or I could do what-ever it was I was going to do (you know what you have to do, Lula) before he put it in me, and spare myself the seconds or minutes of – euphemism failed – *being raped*.

His cock was out of his fly, the head of it pressing my abdomen. It was dark, hard and pornographically huge, with an odour of Vaseline and piss. I didn't want it inside me. I really did not want it inside me.

I turned my face back to him, met his eye, then let him see me look down at it, with ambiguous disgust, then back up at him.

'No cheating,' Murdoch said. 'You need to be aware, my friend, that she's got a hist—'

A cellphone rang. Murdoch's. He looked. Had to take it. I heard him say: 'Sir?' then he took a pace back beyond the light.

'Please don't,' I said. 'Please... please...' I let my legs buckle. Slid towards the floor. He hit me, hard, in the mouth. My bottom lip split against my teeth. I cried out. Off-balance, dragged down by trying to hold me up, he let go of my free hand.

The screaming imperative was to make my move right then, but I overrode it, just. 'Oh God,' I whispered, sobbing. 'Oh God, oh God... '

I imagined my mother standing close. Sell him the idea you're not going to fight, angel. Come on, *sell* it. You can do this. This piece of shit doesn't know anything. This piece of shit is a *human.*

He hit me again, a sensation like when I fell going down Lauren's concrete yard steps and smacked my skull on one of the slabs. Lauren had been date-raped when she was twenty-three. We were talking about it and she'd tried to make it sound like a wacky adventure, like a night with a hilariously terrible guy who said and did all the wrong things and even at one point spilled a drink on her – then she'd got up suddenly and run to the bathroom and I'd gone after her and found her throwing up and even then it took ages before she stopped trying to laugh it off as just another of her wild-child escapades and absolutely refused to go and report it to the police.

He was unbuttoning my jeans, and – since I was whimpering and boneless with my face covered in blood and snot – using both hands to do it. He was at a rolling boil of excitement. It was as if there was an audible wordless incantation going on inside him. I remembered reading my mom's copy of *The Female Eunuch*. 'Women have no idea how much men hate them.' That wasn't true any more. My generation had a very good idea. My generation had decided to be cool with it, more or less. Yeah, guys hate women. That's kinda… interesting. *There are only two types of guy,* Lauren had said. *The type who feels lousy about degrading you and the type who doesn't. Which leaves a girl a choice between getting degraded and hating it or finding a way to enjoy getting degraded. Or, obviously, just having nothing to do with guys.*

Very slowly, I put my free hand into my jacket pocket and withdrew the eyeliner. I bent my head forward and sobbed against his damp chest. My forehead touched the St Christopher, evoked the victim at Lucy's, my own back catalogue of carnage. *Wulf* was at stilled attention, intrigued. The ghost jaws moved in mine. The nerves leaped under my nails. My mother said: Be accurate, angel. Believe you can do this, and be accurate. I'm so proud of you.

He'd undone the buttons on my fly and shoved his hot hand into my panties. Calloused palms. I wondered what his hands did, in their other life, if there was another life. Then I wrapped my free leg around his thigh, tightened my grip, rushed one last set of calculations, and said: 'Hey.'

He looked at me.

I thought: big eyes. Good. The left if anything slightly bigger.

So I picked that one.

56

Hard, deep, accurate, fast. Cornea, pupil, lens. Most people would miss. Most people would miss because the concept would defeat them. The concept was nothing to me. Therefore I didn't miss. I hit the back of the socket and pulled out, my free right leg locked around his as if we were posing to simulate the tango. His roar assaulted my face with hot breath that said dehydration, nicotine, coffee, a samosa. Since his reflex pull away was checked by my leg, we found ourselves in a stretched moment, me flushed, him suffering shock's detachment. He stopped mid-scream, as if giving reality a chance to tell him it was kidding, the bitch hadn't *really* just stabbed a pencil through his eyeball. But reality had no such news. His next move would break my leg's hold and take him out of my reach. Both his hands had flown to cup the wrecked eye.

So I jammed the pencil into the healthy one.

Not as clean a hit. It went in under the eyeball, scraping the socket – and snapped as he wrenched himself backwards, fell over my leg, and scurry-dragged himself, blind and screaming, as far away from me as possible. There wasn't much blood, but it was more than enough to get *wulf* in a lather. For a second or two the animal hardened in the muscles of my back, sent the first no-nonsense signals of transformation through sacrum, heel and skull. If there's blood it must be time. *Surely* it must be time? Precipitate lightnings in my leg-bones, elbows, wrists; for a moment I felt the whole giant head shoving up from behind my ribs, an air-starved diver kicking frantically for the surface. I forced myself to keep breathing. Not yet. Not *yet*.

I looked over at Murdoch, who, having finished on the phone, had stepped back into the light. His expression remained undisturbed. The guy on the floor screamed.

'Did you bite him?' Murdoch asked, when the scream withered.

'Tell me what's going on in the big picture and I'll tell you if I bit him.'

He took out a handgun from his side holster. 'Silver this time,' he said – then shot String Vest in the head.

'Now we can stop talking as if you've anything to bargain with,' he said.

'Who's "Sir"?' I asked.

'"Sir" will be here shortly.' He looked at his watch. 'Hopefully within the next... twenty-two minutes. It's a long time since he's seen a live transformation, apparently.'

'Tell me one thing. Do you know what I'm doing here on Crete?'

'You mean are you still *on* Crete?'

'Well? Am I?'

I don't know if he would've answered me. His phone rang again, and he took it, again. The truck's weight-shift said he'd jumped down. The trailer door slammed shut with a boom. Twenty-two minutes to moonrise at (I knew) 21.03. I'd been unconscious for a night and a day. Plenty of time for Murdoch to get me off the island. Or was it? If he'd been fired he wouldn't have choppers and planes at his disposal. Would he risk it by boat? But if WOCOP were in the region surely they'd know about the Disciples, in which case they'd be on Crete themselves and there'd be no *reason* for Murdoch to move me. I decided to assume that, for the time being, since there was nothing to be gained by assuming otherwise.

Which got me nowhere. It didn't make any difference whether I was on Crete or Mars if I couldn't get out of the cage. Twenty-two – make that twenty-one minutes to moonrise: how long would Lorcan have, once he'd changed? And would the others go ahead without me? Konstantinov would, obviously – but the rest of them? For all I knew they thought I was dead. Walker would have accompanied Konstantinov and most likely thrown his life away, but Walker had gone missing, too. Why? I remembered Konstantinov's face, dragged back down from its remote epic agony to the irritatingly mundane here-and-now. He'd looked annoyed; but by now, if Walker really had gone, he'd look desperate.

Meanwhile the bitch was unpacking herself, in the fibres, in the bones. The nerves in my teeth yelped. I had a sudden wrong view from the monster's head-height then snapped back down to my own. Hunger stretched my blood. String Vest would still be warm when I changed. There was food, if nothing else. You live. There's no God and that's His only Commandment. Fifteen minutes. Twelve. Murdoch was still on the phone. The cuffs would either break or lop off my hand and foot. They looked weaker (or at any rate slimmer) than the ones that had held me in the van with Poulsom, a lifetime ago in Beddgelert Forest, and *those* had snapped, eventually, after several seconds of excruciating pain.

I was close. I turned and grabbed the bars of the cage. Something to hold on to, for as long as holding on was possible. Here, they said in the movies, bite down on this.

The door opened. Voices. Murdoch got up into the trailer. Not alone.

'I'm not promising anything, John. I'm one of six. You know this.' Deep, rich, posh English accent.

'I'm aware of that, sir. I know how much ground I've got to make up. This is a start.'

'Well, now, here she is.'

Murdoch's companion — 'Sir' — was a big-bellied, round-shouldered Asian (Indian? Pakistani? Sri Lankan?) in his early sixties with thick, oiled grey and black hair swept back off his brow in a rippled quiff. The sort of heavy-lidded eyes that made me think of the hookah-smoking caterpillar from *Alice*. The face said the body had absorbed excessive pleasure as its birthright. Tailored black three-piece suit, white shirt, blood-red tie. An oblong gold pinky ring set with an enormous flat ruby. Superficial odours of Chanel *pour homme*, cigar smoke and jasmine incense around the deeper stinks of sweat, urine, shit. His flesh was heavy with booze and cholesterol, his sluggish gut packed. He'd had his fingers and face between a woman's legs recently. I hoped it had been with her consent — which thought evoked Madeline. And so Zoë, and so Lorcan, and so time running out.

He walked up to the cage, took stock of String Vest's corpse. 'I suppose I oughtn't ask?' he said.

'Collateral damage, sir,' Murdoch said. 'In any case she'll need to feed.'

'"She" is here, by the way,' I said, shivering. 'If anyone's interested.'

Sir turned to me. 'How are you feeling, Ms Demetriou?' he asked.

I couldn't answer. The penultimate phase was passing. The moon had already connected with whatever it was in the earth. My soles prickled. The first of the half-dozen big cramps hit, bent me as far double as the cuffs would allow. Hot bile rushed up and out. Murdoch lifted a digital camera. My scapulae squeaked, stretched, cracked. I shook my free arm from the jacket while I still could. Sir watched. He looked like God blinking out balefully from a cloud of cosmic boredom. Think of Konstantinov with three werewolves at his back kicking a door in and a crowd of vampires screaming. Hold on, angel. Hold on. They're coming. But what if they weren't? No point thinking that. The seams on my jeans exploded. Sir lit a slim cigar, fish-mouthed a fat smoke-ring that shuddered between the bars and floated towards me like a little spirit of mockery.

'Sir,' Murdoch said, 'I know my opinion's not important—'

'Relevant, John, not *relevant*. You're opinion's always important to me.'

'As you like, but in that case... I have to say... '

Whatever it was he wasn't quite ready for its diplomatic articulation.

'I know, John: the company we're keeping. But you know yourself there's a long tradition of cooperation.'

'But *they're* paying *us*.'

'Handsomely. It's called a global recession for a reason, John.'

'I know, sir. But still.'

'Flexibility, John. We've solved the Breakfast Club mystery, by the way.'

'Sir?'

'Formula's flawed. Lethally. They die sooner or later depending on how many doses.'

'But Remshi? He's still going?'

'He only appears in close-up clearly on the first two films. After that it could be anyone.'

The first two films. They'd seen the footage Mia told us about. The Breakfast Club: vampires who walked in daylight. Which meant they knew the Disciples were here. Which meant almost certainly we were still on the island. Which meant which meant which meant?

Nothing, if I couldn't get out of here.

Pain. Left wrist, left ankle. The cuffs had cut into the flesh. For a moment I had two fiery bracelets. Then the ankle-cuff burst. Sweet relief, though the wound immediately blurted blood.

'It's fine,' Murdoch said. 'They were just for the woman.'

The wrist-cuff went. Another little blossom of eased pain. *Wulf* wriggled up through my shins, detonated in my knees and elbows simultaneously, with a sound of ice snapping dragged my jaws and nose into the muzzle and snout – at which the last of the human seal on smell ruptured and the gloriously stinking world spoke fully and freely again: String Vest's adrenalin binge and cooling sweat; the cigar's rich toxins; the trailer's odour of murder and greased steel; the two living bodies' rhythmic reek of thrilled flesh and blood.

I threw myself at the cage door. No give. The bolts were solid and the bars were a finality. Neither man flinched. I closed my eyes and saw moist turf passing under me, felt my daughter's weight on my back. Farm fields dark and undulant, a moon-silvered stream. Opened them. Suffered the still-warm corpse's pull. Closed them again and saw different ground, dust and shed pine needles *racing* under me at incredible speed, felt a heartbeat in my own and an ignored sixth sense in Murdoch hammering so loudly I couldn't believe he just stood there holding the camera as the head I was inside lifted to see the back of a trailered truck flanked by cedar trees and lit by the risen moon and a lone guard in Hunt fatigues peeing into the shadows, rifle shouldered, and our mouths opened with joy as he I we leaped and felt the tiny rogue details of the air rushing past the hairs on our ears before the sweet impact and the cry my timed howl drowned out, and the night's first taste of blood from the torn-out throat before his giant hands flung the door open and Walker, transformed, stood framed by the moonlit forest.

57

L isten. *I wasn—*

Listen. I wasn't going to tell you, but I bit him. I know why you couldn't. I get it. But it doesn't matter if he ends up hating *me*, does it? It's what he wanted. And don't fret. It was just a bite. No hanky-panky. Like I said, you need all the help you can get, and since I'm on fucking babysitting duty...

SILVER! MURDOCH! PISTOL!

Murdoch was on his way for it when Walker sprang. I saw Murdoch's face. All his boredom vanished like a grace God had suddenly withdrawn, and there, left behind, was the desperate and wholly generic desire not to die. He'd thought he'd come to the end of himself years ago, through violence and the vast mathematical silence. Imminent death made a nonsense of the idea. He might as well have been eight years old.

Reflexes are terrible things. Confronted with the loose were-wolf, reflexes pushed Sir back two paces closer to the caged one.

Two paces were enough.

If his hand hadn't been going into his jacket (for a gun) I might have ended up with *just* the jacket. As it was he couldn't get the arm back quickly enough, though I was impressed that the manoeuvre occurred to him. Instead I hoiked him by his collar off his feet to join me at the bars, where the back of his head struck with such a crack I was amazed he didn't pass out. Panic fast-tracked him to the truth: he was going to die. I got a second of his psyche's race through its heaped contents in the desperate hope there was something, something, *something* there that could save him. But of course there wasn't. There never is. I sank all five blade-nailed fingers of my right hand into his throat, closed quickly, made a slippery fistful of his trachea, oesophagus, larynx, pharynx and thyroid veins, squeezed – and ripped them out.

Walker, meanwhile, had got to Murdoch before Murdoch had got to his piece. Murdoch was on his back, minus the arm that had been going for it. Now the shoulder ended in ragged flesh around the yawning joint, severed veins pumping out blood as if in a hurry to be rid of it, as if they'd been dying to do it for years. The weapon itself lay within my reach. I squeezed the last of the life out of Sir (*there* was a baroque feast, a life full of casual extremes and indulged deviance, but if I started I'd lose myself in it), let him fall then grabbed it. Not easy to pop a clip out with blood-slick werewolf hands – and the silver buzzed in my nerves – but at the third attempt I managed it.

WE DON'T HAVE TIME!

For all you want to do. Please. We have to go.

Murdoch had already spent what attention his system allowed on the lost arm, though the socket still feebly spat blood, now an image of futile ejaculation. His system had the big picture in view. The big picture was death. His face had changed. The bald-eagle glare was still there, but with an appalling tremor. The mouth had gone infantile. Walker, I knew, wanted two things. He wanted Murdoch to recognise him, and he wanted Murdoch to suffer for a very long time before he died.

I KNOW, BUT PLEASE, JUST BE RID OF HIM.

Anti-climax. The moment of revenge always is. It's only the

hunger for revenge that enlivens us. Murdoch not knowing it was him was like a bereavement.

Suddenly Walker lunged, bit and doggishly shook the remaining arm at the shoulder, pulled with concentrated fury. Murdoch's mouth downturned, eyelids fluttering like a coquette's. After a queer, silent, quivering pause – Murdoch trying to disbelieve what he knew was happening – the arm left its socket with an emphatic wet crunch. Murdoch screamed.

PLEASE, WALKER. MY SON. THEY'LL *KILL* HIM.

But it wasn't enough. Of course it wasn't enough. Everything Murdoch had done to him (or had *had* done to him, to show it was minor, delegatable) was back with Walker, in his skin, his blood, his bones, demanding he find an equation of violence to erase it. No such equation existed. Nothing would be enough. He tore down Murdoch's pants and underwear. Murdoch, armless, wriggled and whined. The last lights of his consciousness sputtered. With what looked bizarrely like tenderness Walker put his hand behind Murdoch's head and lifted him, just the way you would a sick man to help him sip a glass of water. Walker's other hand settled around Murdoch's genitals. Murdoch, shivering, wide-eyed, scattered, suddenly focused.

'You?' he whispered.

Walker nodded. Smiled, though human eyes wouldn't have seen it.

Then he tore off Murdoch's cock and balls. Threw back his head. Howled.

58

It took us ten minutes, going flat-out, to reach the monastery. It stood in a valley that was approximately the shape of a ladle, halfway up the bowl end on a broad natural shelf, bounded by white stone wall. The front looked down the long narrow end of the valley; the back was built into the hillside's curve.

The moon was as yet uncomplicatedly full. The eclipse wouldn't begin until 23.04 and would be maximal at 00.42 – according to Mia the sacrificial hour. We had time. For all the good it would do us. The plan, before everything had gone wrong, had been simple. Not simple in that it was likely to succeed, but simple in that it had only three components. The first was us taking out the six perimeter guards, two at each of the three gates in the wall. The second was Konstantinov, Lucy, Fergus and three of the mercenaries getting into the east wing (three guards) and freeing Natasha. The third was me, Cloquet, Walker, Trish and the other mercenaries getting into the west wing where Lorcan was housed (four more guards) and snatching him. All of which was supposed to happen in broad daylight, with zero vampires and liberty to make as much noise as we liked. Mia's news, that a dozen or more vampires *could* be up and taking the noon air, hadn't changed that, though it had reduced what was already risible optimism to plain suicide. Bullets wouldn't kill boochies, obviously, though *enough* bullets would slow them down a little. The weapons choice had been based on combat with human familiars. Konstantinov had ordered a couple of crossbows just in case, and there were three machetes, but it was nowhere near enough.

Yet even those odds had been better than the ones we faced now. As far as Walker and I knew we were a force of two against twenty humans and seventy-nine wide-awake vampires.

A pale dirt track descended the western hillside in a series of switchbacks. We ignored it, cutting instead through the trees' cover. Plane, cypress, oak, and enough evergreen pine to keep the darkness collusively deep. There air was cool and still, the grass surprisingly lush underfoot. Neither of us had fed. Deliberately. Satiation would have slowed us. We were in and out of mutual intuition that bordered telepathy. I could feel his shock at how ravenously, now, he wanted life. In the end lycanthropy hadn't erased what had happened to him but it had forced him to outgrow it. The Curse's brutal gift was that whatever your human horror stories it dwarfed them with the new headline: YOU CHANGE INTO A MONSTER EVERY FULL MOON! He was dizzy from the new perspective, aerial, that showed him the map of himself he'd thought exhaustive was now only a small part of a vast and unknown continent. The bare physical facts were still a tingling sacrilege, in the palms of his hands, the soles of his feet. His body still blared astonishment at its new cellular trick. *Wulf* stretched and snapped in him, lashed out in joyous ownership, sent dark bulletins of the scope of its strength through the mutant nerves. The human self had run and hidden like a cat, now peered out in awe of the new no-nonsense housemate, who would – it was obvious – be satisfied by nothing less than complete fusion. It only had twelve nights a year. For those twelve nights it would demand everything and deny itself nothing.

My heart was thudding from the run. The air was cool enough for visible breath, the cartoon plumes to denote an angry bull. Some tiny pale winter blossoms watched us like fairies in the lower gloom. Hunger flared and writhed in my blood. Another hour and it would be making us reckless. The core of *wulf* was an idiot with a one-word vocabulary: *feed... feed... feed* – until you *do* feed, then the idiot is beatified and gives you in return deep animal peace.

Fifty metres. Forty. Thirty.

According to Mia's smartphoned sketches the monastery was built in the shape of a broad-armed cross. Beyond the wall was a semi-circular courtyard with steps at one end leading up to the main entrance. Through the main doors a hallway offered five choices, two corridors on the left, two on the right and one straight ahead. Straight ahead through a set of double doors was the main chamber, the square at the centre of the cross, a big windowless room with an altar on a dais at the far end. We had detailed directions from there to where Lorcan and Natasha were being held below ground, in Lorcan's case most likely useless now. I'd wondered about Natasha. Specifically, whether she was still alive. Konstantinov had asked Mia for a physical description of his wife. Mia had done better. She'd sent a photograph. It was hard to make out the background, but there was no doubt it was Natasha. Taken with a flash that bleached her, squinting slightly, one hand raised as if to ward the photographer off.

I stopped at the edge of the solid cover. There were only a dozen or so trees between here and the slope leading up to the wall and the gate. Walker stood behind me, put his arms around me. His hands covered my breasts, muzzle nudged. Yes. That was available, in spite of everything. Of course it was. There was urgency in his touch, but sadness too. All the time we'd lost. And now, soon, we'd be dead. I leaned back, pressed myself against him, felt the giant undertow. It would be so sweet to go into it. For a little while there'd be nothing else. The moon wouldn't object. The moon was ready with its blessing. I was about to turn to him – *I know, but I can't, even though nothing matters, even though God hardened Pharaoh's heart—*

We froze. The air had stirred, barely enough to move the fairy petals. He'd smelled it too.

A dead branch snapped and something scurried through the undergrowth.

Then three figures came towards us out of the darkness.

59

Lucy, Fergus, Trish.
     With a bag of hastily-fashioned stakes. I recognised chair- and table-legs from the villa, rudely sharpened. Plus the machetes.

Their story flashed and tumbled, three versions like three sacks of miscellaneous objects emptied down a hill, random distinct details, overall confusion, no time to stop and make order.

Not order, maybe, but sense: Konstantinov and Cloquet had taken the mercenaries and gone in as planned in daylight. They hadn't been seen since. A combination of pragmatism (Fergus), fear (Lucy) and instinct (Trish) had made the werewolves wait.

So the odds had got better and worse. Better because now there were five of us. Worse because the vampires almost certainly knew we were coming.

•

There were only two options. The first was to barrel-in en masse and hope they *didn't* know we were coming. The second was to assume they didn't know how *many* were coming, and try to make that work for us.

WITH YOU.

NO. WITH THEM. PROFESSIONAL.

He knew it made sense. My three couldn't be counted-on on their own. Lucy was on the edge of abandoning us. Trish and Fergus were in, but without leadership would be off-mission – screwing, chasing down vamp familiars – within minutes.

YOU'LL KNOW WHEN.

I KNOW.

For what it was worth we'd stick to the original post-rescue plan: passports, money, first aid and clothes were hidden in the rubble of a derelict farmhouse a mile outside the town of Mesavlia, and two hired vans were parked in the town itself. If we got separated whoever made it to the vehicles would wait till nine a.m. Whoever didn't show by then was on his or her own. From there it was a short drive to the airport at Chania.

SORRY FOR EVERYTHING.

It's always all wrong, the timing, the suddenness with which the only thing to say is goodbye, your disbelieving body forcing itself to turn, walk away, run.

60

The wall around the monastery had three gates. The middle one stood open. There was no one visible, but when I crossed the threshold the stink of vampire dropped me to my hands and knees. I shuddered out bile and saliva. The world offered vivified details, should I want things to waste consciousness on: a moonlit pebble's shadow; a cigarette butt; the coolness of the ground. *You have to get past this. You have to.* The heroic imperative. It meant nothing to my body. My legs, when I wobbled up onto them, were empty. My head hosted a murmuring swarm.

A shift in the light made me look up to my left. A vampire, male, young, tall, blond, wearing a swipe of the ludicrous olfactory-block paste under his nose, stood above the western gate with a gun trained on me. Two more – a middle-aged black male and a female with a scrubbed beaky face and dark, centre-parted hair, appeared – as if they were simply morphing out of nothingness – alongside him, also with the paste moustaches. It was no surprise, when I turned my head to the east gate, to see another two – a Meg Ryanish female and a male with a mohawk and face-piercings – perched opposite their colleagues. All aiming at me, all silent.

'Silver ammunition,' Beaky Face said. 'You're expected. Go on up.'

Assume they don't know about the others, assume they don't

know about the others. Assume they – but if they do we're fucked.

GO UP RIDGE. FIVE ON COURTYARD WALL. COME DOWN FAST.

The building's stone planes were saturated with moonlight. I went, preceded by my rippling shadow, up the half-dozen stairs to the main doors. They were ajar. I pushed them wide open, and the smell that rolled out like the tongue of a dead animal had me on my knees again. I could hear one of the vampires – Meg, I thought – laughing at my back. I got to my feet again, bent, hands on knees, legs fighting their own private delirium. The corridor was high-ceilinged, floored with dark blue marble, lit by soft ivory inset wall lights. As per Mia's intel, two more corridors opened on my left and right.

Breathe. Breathe. Breathe. To conquer a foul odour you drink it in, overdose the receptors, make their report redundant. I straightened, shivering. Thirty paces opposite me double steel doors clunked, popped and hissed six inches open. Colder air. On it, the concentrated stink of the Undead, incense, candle wax, human flesh and blood.

And the scent of my son.

It cleared my head. I felt tired and glowing and calm, as after a day's hard playing when I was a child. In spite of everything the little spirit of honest life was glad to see the last ounces of choice draining away. There were so few things I could do now, it would be easier to do them. I filled my lungs, stretched, stood to my full height and walked towards the doors.

The room beyond was tall, square, white and windowless, with walls covered in sheet glass, and it looked as if all the Disciples (with the exception of my welcome committee outside) were here. A dozen favoured human familiars attended their owners.

374

Lorcan, transformed and radiating misery, lay on his back on the altar, wrists and ankles secured with restraints. He turned his head at my scent and looked at me.

There he was, looking at me.

Everything stopped. He recognised me, knew me, wanted me. It was terrible, his instant willingness to start afresh, to let nothing else matter, to forgive me completely if only if only if only I would come and claim him *now*. Until this moment I hadn't allowed myself to see getting him back as anything other than a problem I'd set myself to solve. I'd never imagined holding him. I'd never imagined settling him down to sleep next to his sister. I'd never imagined the afterwards. Imagining the afterwards would've been provocation to the God who wasn't there to end things in the before. Now, thirty feet away from him, I knew there was something the size of an ocean tilted behind me, waiting to fall. It had been there all along, like death.

DON'T BE AFRAID. I WON'T LEAVE YOU.

How odd to know this was true. I *wouldn't* leave him. It was a surprising gift to my heart. I smiled, though only another werewolf would've seen it.

'Talulla,' Jacqueline said, smiling herself, while the vampires nearest to me backed away, holding their noses despite their ridiculous stripes of paste. 'Welcome. If for no other reason than at least now I know exactly where you are.' She was dressed in tight black suede pants and a black silk blouse. Red hair Hitler-slicked as before. Peppery green eyes and precise, glamorous make-up. Standing next to her was a tall, slim, prettily handsome vampire male. Turned in his early thirties God knew how long ago. Dark hair, shoulder-length, a finely cut, high-cheekboned face – and eyes that stopped you in your tracks: they were pale silvery-green, filled with forgiving omniscience. He could have played Jesus. He was barefoot, dressed in an ivory silk Indian ensemble, long *kurta* with Nehru collar and baggy pajama pants ruched at the ankle. I thought of what Mia had said: *There's something here, it's true. Very old. I don't know.* Very old. I could feel it. Sunlight in a Roman courtyard. The smell of slaves and dust. Big stones going up. A thousand miles of forest. Firelight in the mouth of a cave. Ice, everywhere. *Not many live past a thousand years.* This one had. Remshi.

There were other vampires in a loose horseshoe around the royal couple, holding candles or censers. A small pulpit stood next to the altar, occupied by a short, plump boochie with thick white hair in a basin-cut and a white beard like a stiff paintbrush. He was wearing what looked to me like white work overalls. A large book was open on a lectern in front of him. Two more... priests, I supposed, since they were the only ones uniformly dressed in the absurd overalls, stood at either end of the altar. Their outfits made me think of the movie of *A Clockwork Orange*. Six bare steel columns upheld the roof. Konstantinov, covered in blood, sat cuffed, unconscious (not dead, my nose said) to the base of the one to the left of the altar. Cloquet, as far as I could tell uninjured, stood cuffed to the one on the right.

I was scanning the ranks for Mia. I'd never seen her, but I told myself I'd know her when I did. The logic had to hold: as far as she knew if I didn't get out of here alive she'd never find her son. Ergo, she'd have to make sure I got out of here alive.

'They're all dead,' Cloquet said.

'I'm afraid that's true,' Jacqueline said. 'But you knew that already. Otherwise you wouldn't be here.'

They're all dead. She'd agreed. She didn't know about the others.

'*C'est vrais, n'est pas?*' Jacqueline asked Cloquet. 'She wants to trade?'

NOT YET.

Cloquet looked at me. There was no sign I could give him that I wasn't alone. He'd be wondering if he was ever going to see another sunrise.

'You want to offer yourself in exchange for your son,' Jacqueline said to me.

Lorcan struggled against the cuffs. I felt it in my own wrists and ankles. The effort to keep still was making me dizzy. All my failures formed a close-fitting heat around me. Breathe. Breathe. *Breathe*.

'I don't have children myself,' Jacqueline continued. 'And without intending this personally I must tell you I loathe the idiocy that infects adults the minute they become parents. But of course I understand. It's an instinct.'

'We are not sadists, Ms Demetriou,' Remshi said, smiling. His voice was warm, resonant, gentle, with an accent unlike anything I'd ever heard. It was hard, after the first look exposed you, to meet the silver eyes. I had an image of him standing in a desert alone at night. Icy sand. Stars that came all the way down to the ground. The remote past was here, in the room, centuries made negligible, an effect of appalling compression. It was dreadful to be connected to it, as when I was a kid and my dad had given me the kite string to hold and seeing it up there in the sky so far away but attached to me had made me terrified and sick and I'd started crying. 'The blood of *gammou-jhi* is the blood of *gammou-jhi*,' Remshi continued. 'Yours, your child's, it makes no difference. If you would like to take your son's place, that is acceptable to me.'

'Don't listen to them,' Cloquet said. 'They're going to give you to Helios to get the Families off their backs.'

Remshi laughed, with what seemed genuine amusement. 'Of course,' he said. 'And we shall frequent graveyards and wear black cloaks and twirl our moustaches and say "Ha-*harr*" with great relish of our wickedness.'

Konstantinov, on a rogue current of consciousness, groaned, then fell silent again. Jacqueline looked at him. 'Irony is inexhaustible,' she said. 'We released Natasha last night. She's out there, free as a bird. She's probably on a plane home as we speak.'

I looked at Cloquet. 'Who knows?' he said. 'She's probably dead.'

'I promise you she's very much alive,' Jacqueline said. 'Alive and at liberty, although not quite the woman she was when she came to us.'

The neat, grey-haired vampire from the Alaskan raid handed Jacqueline a syringe. She came around the altar, descended the four steps and walked down the aisle to stand six feet in front of me. She bent, tidily knees together, placed the syringe on the floor, stood. 'A sedative,' she said. 'You understand?'

Yes, I did.

NOW! NOW!

Nothing happened.

I pointed to Lorcan. Him first.

'Talulla,' Jacqueline said. 'Let's be grown-ups. You can either trust us and do exactly as we tell you, in which case there's a chance your child will live, or you can die right here and now, in which case your child will certainly follow you. Look around you, please.'

At least a dozen members of the congregation had weapons trained on me. Silver, my spine said. The ones not holding guns were all carrying copies of a small, red leather-bound book. Naturally. *The Book of Remshi.*

NOW!

Nothing happened.

'It's now or never, Ms Demetriou,' Remshi said. 'We don't have much time. Forgive me if I seem punctilious, but for better or worse there are protocols, and I've been waiting four hundr—'

'Move and this goes through you,' Mia's voice said. 'Don't talk, just do exactly as I say.'

She had been one of the crowd around the altar. Now she had her arm around Remshi's throat.

'Good grief, is that a *stake?*' Remshi said. 'Seriously? You seriously think a stake is going to—'

'Shut up,' Mia said. 'Jacqueline, release the kid.'

'Are you out of your mind?' Jacqueline said.

'Don't speak. Just do it.'

'My lord, for God's sake,' Jacqueline said.

'I'll tell you something,' Remshi said. 'The last time someone tried this was in Florence in twelve eighty—'

I don't know how he did it. The moves were so fast that when they stopped it was as if a chunk of time had just been cut out. One moment Mia was behind him with her arm around his throat, the next she was on the floor, disarmed, with her head bleeding from where it had cracked the side of the altar. He had one knee across her throat and the stake poised at her breast.

'Who *are* you?' he said.

Mia spat in his face. '*Pizda,*' she said

'Charming! Nice talk from a lady.'

A murmur had spread through the congregation. A fair-haired vampire detached himself from the throng and stepped into the aisle. 'Mia,' he said – then followed it with Russian that self-evidently translated to something like: *What the fuck are you doing?* Her brother, I realised. Dimitri. Same glacial eyes and sensual mouth.

Mia answered him in Russian, not with self-evident meaning. I wondered how strong his faith was. No doubt Jacqueline had preached the new messiah would divide loved ones, set husband against wife, brother against sister...

'Let her go,' Dimitri said. His English came with a slight American accent.

'Stand down, Dimi,' Jacqueline said.

'Let her go *now*.'

'Dimi, please.'

He took three paces towards the dais, nostrils tense, hands readying themselves.

'Restrain him!' Jacqueline ordered. Immediately three male vampires from the front row grabbed Dimitri and wrestled him to the floor.

'My lord,' the pulpit priest said, 'we really need to get on. The time is crucial.'

'Is this it?' Mia shouted, eyes closed. 'Is this the best you can do? You fucking useless piece of *shit*.'

She was talking, I realised, to me. Yes, this was the best I could do. Fail. My son would die and so would she, believing I'd killed her boy. If I'd been able to speak I would have told her: It's all right. They'll let him go in a week. But I couldn't speak. She'd die hating me.

'If you wouldn't mind, Talulla,' Jacqueline said. 'The sedative?'

There was nothing left. I bent, ostensibly to pick up the syringe, in fact to get maximum speed and force from a standing jump. I wondered how many I could kill before one of the bullets hit. Jacqueline first. Rip that precisely-lipsticked smile off her precisely self-delighted face. Lorcan looked at me, snapped an appeal with a small sound between a bark and a yap.

I'm sorry, kiddo. Really, I'm so sorry.

'This is taking too long,' Jacqueline said. 'Inject yourself now or they shoot.'

'My brothers and sisters,' Remshi said, arms raised. 'It's been a long wait, but at last a new day is dawning!'

'Horseshit!' a male voice called out from the congregation.

Vampires and familiars, stunned, turned to where the voice had come from.

'Fraud!' the voice called out, apparently from somewhere altogether different.

'Silence!' the pulpit priest shouted. 'Who is that? Who is that speaking?'

'Ask them why they killed Raphael Cavalcanti,' the voice said, from yet another place. 'Go on, ask them why they did away with poor old Vincent Merryn.'

I looked at Mia. Her look back said whatever this was it was nothing to do with her. The part of her look that wasn't filled with hatred for me.

'Jacqueline?' Remshi said, very quietly.

Madame was visibly confused. Her petite fists clenched under her breasts. I knew it was a childhood habit. I had an image of her as a little girl standing just like that in front of her father, being scolded.

'Show yourself,' she called out. 'Show yourself!'

'Show myself? What are you, blind?' the voice said – and there, suddenly, when everyone looked up, was a figure descending feet-first through the air.

61

The silence was dense, seemed synaesthetically to pick out *visual* details: the candle flames; Jacqueline's pearl earrings; the white-gold edging on the priest's book. With the possible exception of my son, everyone in the room was staring at the vampire who now stood – *smoking a cigarette* – at the bottom of the steps leading up to the altar.

Human age would've put him in his early forties, a slim, dark-eyed man of no more than five-eight, with skin the colour of latte and longish dusty black hair. A full-lipped face of chimpish mobility and mischief. Beautiful dark hands, though the fingernails were filthy. He wore a fractured leather flying jacket over a white t-shirt, with pale green combat pants tucked into battered shitkickers. If you found out he'd just completed a thousand-mile motorcycle ride it wouldn't surprise you. It would explain his look of exhaustion, exhilaration and grime.

'You people are ludicrous,' he said. 'Absolutely *ludicrous*.'

I was thinking: He doesn't smell. Impossible. But he doesn't. His accent, like Remshi's, was homeless, but quite different. I could have sworn I'd heard it before.

'Give me that,' he said, approaching a stocky, goatee'd vampire in the front row of the congregation and snatching the little red book out of his hand.

'Who the fuck *is* this guy?' Remshi said.

'Who the fuck is this guy?' the newcomer mimicked, falsetto. 'Well, you should know, Bubbles.'

'It's... He's one of us,' Jacqueline said. 'Marco, what are you doing?'

The vampire in the flying jacket, 'Marco', flicked though the red book, cigarette slotted into the corner of his mouth, eyes narrowed against the sidestream smoke. I looked at Mia. Remshi still had her pinned, but his attention had shifted. She knew. She was getting herself ready.

'I repeat,' Marco said: 'Ask them why they killed Raphael Cavalcanti and Vincent Merryn.'

'Merryn was working for WOCOP,' Jacqueline said. 'Everyone knows that. What can you possibly think—'

'Merryn was working for WOCOP, yes, but that's not all he was doing, and that's not why you killed him, is it, *ma bichette?* Ah, here we are: *Vor klez mych va gargim din gammou-jhi*: "When he drinks the blood of the werewolf." Any scholars in the audience?'

The room remained utterly still, solid with the congregation's focused consciousness. Jacqueline was at the edge of herself. Her face's poise quivered.

'Linguists? Historians? No?'

'The translation is correct,' the priest said, exasperated. '"*Vor klez mych*" is "when he drinks" and "*va gargim*" is "the blood". Everyone here knows what "*gammou-jhi*" is. Really, Madame, this is ridiculous. He must be ejected immediately.'

In a move almost as fast as the one that had subdued her Mia jabbed upwards with the heel of her hand and struck Remshi with incredible force under the chin. We all heard the little *tuk!* of his bottom teeth hitting his top ones. She twisted out from under the stake and before he could react had launched herself through the air away from him – though after only a second she was back on the floor, sucked down, it appeared, by sudden magnetism.

'Stay put, Miss Tourisheva, for God's sake,' Marco said. 'I like your style, but seventy-four to one... or *two*– ' a wink at me – 'are fool's odds. Now, where was I? Yes, the translation.' He took a last drag of the cigarette and tossed it. "*Vor klez mych*", as the padré has pointed out, is indeed "when he drinks". The problem is "*mych*" is an erroneous verb. It's been there for more than four thousand years, but it's wrong. The original had a different verb altogether. Isn't that right, Madame?'

Jacqueline's nostrils flared. She backed towards the altar, where Remshi stood holding his jaw.

'The original word was lost because the original word in the text was obliterated,' Marco said. 'Physically obliterated by an arrowhead, as it happens, but that's another story. Apart from the author of the Book only two people knew what the line read, before its lacuna.'

'Kill him,' Jacqueline said. 'Kill him now.'

At least ten boochies from the congregation leaped forward – then stopped, as in profound confusion. Their mouths opened and closed. Their eyelids fluttered.

'And the guns,' Marco said. The armed vampires all did exactly the same thing: they looked at their weapons, frowned, developed a brief, intense palsy in the hands holding them, made a noise of surprise, then dropped them. One of the pistols went off, and hit a Disciple in the shin. The vampires holding Dimitri barely stirred when he shrugged them off and went to his sister.

'Who *are* you?' Jacqueline repeated.

'And another thing,' Marco said, lowering the book and addressing the faithful. 'This daylight nonsense. Where are they, these credulous cretins who've strolled around in the sunshine?'

'Remshi has given them the gift,' Jacqueline said. 'You've seen it with your own eyes. You've *all* seen it.' A definite note of defence, now. 'Olivia. Olivia? Olivia and Federico, where are you? Step forward. Step forward. There. They walked in sunlight *this morning.*'

Two vampires, a thin, freckled woman in her mid-forties and a young olive-skinned male with all his features a little too close together in the middle of his face, came to the front of the crowd.

'There,' Jacqueline said. 'You saw the film yourself.'

'I certainly did,' Marco said. 'I've seen all the films. They walk, they talk, they smile for the camera, they watch CNN, they stick around for a day or two, then they slip away. Any headaches, Olivia? And Federico, how's that rash on your heel?'

The formula's flawed. Lethally. They die sooner or later depending on how many doses.

Federico and Olivia looked at each other. Then at Jacqueline.

'Headache, rash, fever, coma, death. Anything from forty-eight hours to a week. An improvement on Helios. Their guinea pigs skipped the minor preliminaries and just went straight to death. Usually within twelve hours.' Then to Federico and Olivia: 'Sorry, kids.'

The question was: could I rip Lorcan's restraints from the altar? Once I made my move I'd have maybe two seconds. I couldn't see the fastenings clearly from where I was standing. If I'd had one of the machetes I could have cut off his hands and feet. I could have done that. He'd hate me all over again. But they'd grow back, and I'd make it up to him...

Marco had followed Jacqueline up the steps. Now he stood face to face with Remshi. Visually a ludicrous opposition. Remshi was tall, beautiful, elegantly dressed, had the transcendent eyes and unblemished ivory skin. Marco looked like a road-weary bum.

'The author of *The Book of Remshi*,' Marco said, loudly enough for the whole audience, 'was an erratic and impulsive individual.

He disowned his book, which in any case he claimed he'd concocted as a joke at his own expense. Of the two people who knew the original verb, one didn't care about that sort of thing, but the other made his own copy with the *correct* verb re-inserted. Further copies followed, but none survived – or so it was thought. But Vincent... ' He paused... '*Merryn* – ' On the word 'Merryn' he slapped Remshi's head so hard that the vampire rocked, spent a comical moment on one leg, almost went over, before Jacqueline grabbed his arm to steady him – 'Vincent *Merryn*, God bless his Fabergé egg-head, *found* one. Imagine that! A word-for-word-correct version of the holy book! The living word!'

'Oh my God,' Jacqueline said, quietly, in what sounded like a man's voice. 'Oh my God.'

'Vincent Merryn told Raphael Cavalcanti, and Raphael Cavalcanti, dear spectacular *moron* that he was, told Her would-be Royal Highness, Madame Jacqueline Delon.'

With her brother's help Mia Tourisheva had got to her feet, but with a look of negotiating significant invisible obstruction. A crescent of the pink sweat I'd seen on Caleb showed above her top lip.

'And do you know, my little starvelings,' Marco continued, 'do you know what the missing verb *was*? Can you imagine why it didn't *fit in* with Madame's little scheme? You'll be amazed when I tell you, you really will.'

Palpable Disciple suspense. It wouldn't have surprised me to see walls and ceiling had developed a visible pulse. Jacqueline backed away from Remshi. There was a moist sheen to her mean, pretty face.

'Madame?' Olivia asked, in a tiny voice. 'Is it true? Are we going to die?'

I doubt Jacqueline was going to answer her, but we never got to find out, because at that moment the doors burst open and four blood-covered werewolves crashed into the chamber.

62

THEY DIDN'T SMELL US COMING! For a moment no one moved. It was as if the universe demanded everyone involved take a couple of seconds to absorb the incendiary reality of the situation: confined space; seventy-plus vampires in a state of collective shock; five starving werewolves.

Then Trish flung the Meg Ryanish vamp's severed head at the altar steps, where it struck with an innocently resonant *crack* – and the collective paralysis exploded.

I leaped for my son.

The altar was white granite, refreshingly cool to my palms and soles. Lorcan's restraints were bracelets attached by short cables to panels bolted into the stone: all steel. More than enough to hold a werewolf infant. Not enough to stop an adult. Two, three, four seconds of resistance – then the ring holding the left-hand cable snapped. Instant logical joy: if I could break one I could break four. I had a terrible dizzying vision of myself with my son and daughter in human form (Lorcan's face the human face *wulf* could see even if the rest of me couldn't) snuggled together on a couch in a house by the ocean with a fire going and the TV on, Cloquet making dinner in the background. I had to shut it out. Shut everything out except breaking the cables. Everything but that.

The second cable snapped. I reached for the third. Details from the ambient blur registered whether I wanted them or not. Most of the vampires, rudderless, traumatised by the failed Mass and slapped messiah, were just trying to get out of the chamber, and the few who weren't were feeling the full force of hunger-furious werewolves. But the hunger worked two ways: thwarted it was fuel for rage; confronted with live prey it forgot everything else. Boochies weren't food (blared poison, in fact) but the handful of scurrying human familiars were. For now my will and Lorcan's reek of fear was a frail leash, holding the pack, but there was no guarantee it would last. The air was an orgy of odours, vampire blood and human flesh and our own frank canine stinks. I saw Walker take the head off a Disciple with a single clawed swipe. Fergus jumped to intercept the white-haired priest in mid-flight (a basketball clash), staked him, got his wrist stuck in the ribs, plummeted back to the floor, pulled his arm out gashed by the broken bones.

My hands were bleeding. The cables had left lines of fire in my palms. But there was only one left to break. Suddenly I felt my son's hot hands gripping the fur on my back.

Mother.

Entitlement. Forgiveness. Demand.

Almost there, angel.

A vampire's decapitated body sailed over my head and crashed into Cloquet's steel pillar. Cloquet, hands bound, kicked it away.

My son first. Don't worry. I'll get you out.

Someone was nearby. I looked up.

Marco stood six feet away, lighting another cigarette, watching me. Behind him, Walker had made it to Konstantinov and was in the process of cutting him loose. I had an illusion of sound – the room's slaughterhouse or torture chamber audio track – muting, as if I'd dunked my head under water. Not all the mischief had left Marco's face, but enough to make way for a look of twinkling recognition – part invitation, part provocation – under which I felt peculiarly small and finite and known. Peculiarly *young*. Jacqueline's *Oh my God* recurred, her face's momentary loss of its guiding intelligence.

He indicated with his eyes that I should look to my left just as sound rushed back in – and I turned too late to dodge a huge crew-cut vampire – six-four, maybe two hundred and eighty pounds – who came down on me like an anvil, ripping the cable from my grip (I felt a swatch of skin go from my left palm like someone tearing off the mother of all band-aids) and propelling me with him from the altar down onto the steps. His face was tattooed with a spider's web. Rotten-meat breath and the pigshit-stink of his skin filled my mouth, nose, head, all of me. His nickname was probably Geronimo or Banzai or Mad Dog. He was a grinning moron whose only route to credibility was doing insane stunts. He'd landed on top of me. His left arm was across my windpipe and his right had its fingers buried deep in the flesh of my left breast. He was going to rip it off completely. *Hey, check it out: genuine werewolf tit!* My left side was in singing shock from the fall (the steps had broken three or four ribs) but my right arm was free and in full command of its faculties. I went into the soft part of his flank, hard, with my glass-edged fingers, forced a screw action until I'd got through the muscle into the wet privacy of his mutant organs. I grabbed a handful of whatever he had in there – if it was gut it had the consistency of Vaselined beef jerky – screwed again and yanked as hard as I could. Two seconds of resistance – then it tore, came free in my hand and unplugged a sudden gush of dark blood that smelled of raw sewage. He screamed, lost his will for a moment. Long enough for me to shove my hand back into the hole it had made, push against the spinal column and thrust with my pelvis, to flip him onto his back. I only had a second, but it didn't need more. I closed my jaws around his neck *don't swallow the blood* jammed them together, shoved two fingers into his screaming mouth, then bit, shook and yanked until his big bald head came off.

Sensation was returning to my left side. I got to my feet and raced back to my son.

Because the universe is perverse the fourth cable proved tougher than the other three. My cut palms were burning and slippery with blood, and for what felt like an hour I stood there, braced and straining, hands haemorrhaging, thighs quivering, while around me the sound dropped away again and I imagined being stuck like this for ever, like a scene in a macabre snow-shaker. Walker had freed Konstantinov and slung him, unconscious, over his shoulder. Dozens of vampires had got out (once the silver ammo dropped out of the game, they really didn't want to play) but there were still twenty at least in various states of combat or mutilation. Trish had cut her way to Cloquet and hacked through his bonds with one of the machetes.

Lorcan was now the only one of us still prisoner.

I howled. Vampire hair stood on end.

The cable was grating against bare bone in both hands.

I saw Marco look up and say: 'Visitors. Another time, Mistress.'

Then the steel fibres snapped and the room's cacophony rushed back in – and my son jumped into my arms.

Joy closes your eyes.

But if you're a werewolf, silver opens them.

In this case to see Remshi on the floor, convulsing around one of our homemade stakes, and Jacqueline Delon standing over him, holding one of the discarded guns in a two-handed grip, aiming directly at me.

63

All I wanted time to do was turn and get my body between the bullet and my son. I didn't get even that. I was still midway through the move and the understanding that Jacqueline wasn't going to bother with the Hollywood villain's victory speech but was in fact going to shoot immediately, when an explosion (as if a time bomb had been ticking in Remshi himself) detonated at her feet.

Heat the size of a planet hit us, spun the walls and ceiling and floor. We were airborne, revolving, for hours. Plenty of time at least to see that Marco had disappeared and that there was no sign of Jacqueline. The bottom half of Remshi's corpse was gone. Fergus was feeding on a familiar unchallenged in a corner. Lucy had her jaws around the throat of a female vampire, human age of about seventy, with liver-spotted hands, dangling diamond earrings and what had started the evening as an elaborate silver chignon. Trish had given Cloquet the machete, but the vampires still left in the chamber were more interested in escape than battle.

Lorcan and I hit the ground as a second blast blew a hole in the western wall and let in with the smell of explosives the cool air of Cretan night with its scents of thyme and pine and moist grass. Let in too gunfire and the soulless chatter of helicopters.

My son moved against me.

Alive. He's alive and you've got him.

I knew he was alive because the blast burns were making him whine and the whines were twisting me inside. Somewhere far away Zoë was feeling it too, a scaled-down version of his trauma in her skin. I had to squash a surge of joy at the thought of them lying curled next to each other. Not yet. Not *yet*. Two more explosions, the second of which tore a big piece of the roof out and sent Fergus flying across the aisle to land, dazed and bloody, a few feet from me.

WOCOP. WE GO *NOW*.

Walker, with passed-out Konstantinov slung over his shoulders, was hoiking me up with a hand under my arm.

DON'T KNOW IF SILVER. HAVE TO MOVE FAST.

Fergus was struggling to his feet. Trish and Lucy were half barring the exit, half taking it in turns to feed on an unfortunate familiar who'd fallen there. The remaining vampires were going for the hole in the roof. Blue-white WOCOP chopper search-lights flashed in, wobbled, flashed out again. A vampire hit by at least twenty wooden shafts (the hickory darts of the Hail Mary) screamed and fell from one of the steel uprights.

Next to Mia.

She was conscious, but trapped under a slab of fallen masonry. Her brother had disappeared.

We looked at each other. I knew what she was thinking: *You've got what you want. You leave me here, I die. No one to come looking for you and your kids.* She was resigned and disgusted. Resigned because she didn't live in a world where one appealed to another's better nature. Disgusted because after all the things she'd seen and done (her history floated around her, as if her ghost were rehearsing its departure) here she was about to meet her end ignominiously, helpless, pinned, ready for a WOCOP hot-shot to stake or behead at his leisure, some mortal idiot whose memories stood in relation to hers as a flea to a city.

Vampires are strong – but not like us. Feeling my prompt Lorcan swung around onto my back and clung on, leaving my arms free. Mia's expression didn't change. We understood each other.

If you think this means I won't kill you, you're wrong.

I know. Can you walk?

Her left femur and tibia were broken, the tibia sticking through the milky skin just below the knee. (*Legs that would've been at home in an ad for quality nylons*. Oh God, Jacob, I wish you were here!) However fast she healed it wouldn't be fast enough to get her out before the grunts arrived. A hickory dart hit her in the face, went through her left cheek into her mouth. She plucked it out, spat dark blood. Another two hit the wrecked leg.

I offered her my hand.

Visibly nauseated – nostrils flickering, gorge rising, mouth turned down at the corners – she took it. I wondered if she'd ever touched a werewolf before.

Walker, unable to stand the smell of her so close, put some distance between us.

Between them Trish and Lucy had eaten at least a third of their victim. On my back Lorcan went taut at the scent of it – but not hungry. They'd fed him tonight somehow. Presumably a drugged or idiotic or compelled familiar. Or, as an homage to the movies, a peasant girl with restive breasts and torn skirt, eyes wide, skin wet with sweat. However they'd done it I could feel it in him, the flecks of foreign life, the dirty enrichment. Relieved as I was, *I* was still starving. Walker too. He'd taken Murdoch's life but he hadn't eaten him. I'd thought at the time: he doesn't want him inside him. Not him. Not inside him.

HELP ME WITH HER.

But they couldn't. The smell. The *smell*. Trish took Lorcan instead. He went to her readily enough, once I'd sent him the prompt. My soul tore a little as his weight shifted from me. It always would, now, for as long as we both lived. I hoisted Mia over my shoulder, though I knew it mortified her. I felt her retch, emptily, realised she wasn't wearing the nose-paste; of course: she'd wanted to know when we were coming.

We ran into the courtyard. WOCOP troops weren't on the ground yet, and there were only four choppers. Some of the vampires had taken up positions – armed with machine guns – and were returning fire. The moon, in the first phase of its now religiously redundant eclipse, was a blood-edged peach. Walker, shouldering Konstantinov, was ahead on my left, Fergus on my right. Cloquet (having ditched the machete for an abandoned machine gun) was close by me, running flat-out and looking as if doing so was going to kill him. Lucy and Trish were covering our rear. A sort of giddiness flowed between us. Cloquet wouldn't be able to go at our pace. Would have to suffer the indignity of being carried. Fergus, at my thought, swerved left and scooped him up in a fireman's lift.

The first of the outlying trees was near. Crawling towards it, hilariously exposed, was an injured vampire familiar.

64

We ran until we hit deeper forest, went a quarter of a mile in and stopped to catch our breath. Pines, holly oaks, evergreen maples. Wood-flavoured air and a feeling of sanctuary. WOCOP hadn't followed. I thought I understood: But *they*'re paying *us*, Murdoch had said. The Fifty Families, he'd meant. Unable to locate the Disciples they'd contracted-out to the Hunt. Job done and no vampire blood on vampire hands. And a bonus if you leave the werewolves alive. The Helios Project hadn't given up on lycanthrope genetics holding the key to daylight tolerance.

The moon was almost wholly eclipsed. I'd wondered if it would make any difference. It didn't. If anything *wulf*'s dial was higher. Certainly it hadn't dinted my appetite. We'd torn the vamps' human into portable chunks and Walker and I had gone through our share in two minutes, barely lifting our heads. Trish and Fergus had slunk away to fuck. After a few moments of palpable vacillating, Lucy had followed them. *Anyway, something went*, I remembered her saying. *There is no old life for me now.*

Walker, obviously, was in a state. He wanted me (and knew I wanted him) but he knew I wouldn't leave Lorcan again. Not now.

YOU GO WITH THEM. I WANT YOU TO.

Blurred and dreamy and unlocked with relief, I did want him

to. The thought of him enjoying himself with Trish or Lucy (or Fergus, if the Curse had begun ravaging his other certainties) or all three of them together didn't bother me in the least, because I knew how much good it would do him. Not only did it not bother me, it filled me with quiet benign pleasure. Just at that moment the notion of monogamy seemed grotesque and anti-life and absurd.

NO TIME. MIKE.

Relief on this scale evidently brought idiocy. Of course there was no time. Konstantinov needed treatment. As soon as we'd got our bearings we'd have to move again. The others would either lose themselves or catch us up, but either way *wulf* was done arguing with them.

AND NOT SAFE.

Mia, he meant. Her leg (she'd shoved the tibia back in by hand) was healing who knew how fast, and though there wasn't much she could do to me there were Cloquet and Konstantinov to consider. She was already able to walk, albeit with an obviously excruciating limp.

IT'S OKAY. WATCH.

I tossed a small stick at Cloquet, who was leaning against a tree looking as if he might vomit, to get his attention. I pointed at Mia, then mimed phoning.

'I understand you?' Cloquet asked. 'This is the situation we discussed?'

Mia's eyes watched everything. I nodded: Yes. Do it.

He turned to Mia. 'Caleb is in the basement of a house in the town of Lymington on the south coast of England,' he told her. 'I'm texting you the address now. He's being looked after by a doctor who supplies him with blood when he needs it. Your son is fine, but not at full strength. After you've spoken to him, the doctor will leave him enough blood to recover completely. He'll also leave him money and the phone you're about to speak to him on. You can make whatever arrangements for a rendezvous you like. Is that acceptable?'

Mia looked at me. Like me she'd trained herself to harden her heart. But now here we were, and I could feel the little force field of desperation around her. It was desperation that wanted to be allowed its true form: love.

I gestured to Cloquet to get on with it. He dialled. It couldn't have rung more than once. I pictured Budarin hearing him out: the round, unperturbable face, the body as neat as a well-fed sparrow's). 'Put Caleb on,' Cloquet said, then handed the phone to Mia.

She spoke one word in English: 'Caleb?' then switched to Russian.

It was either a coincidence or testimony to the power of his native tongue that Konstantinov, who'd been unconscious the whole time (I'd thought he was in a coma), coughed, said something in Russian, spat out a gobbet of blood and sat up.

Problems were stacking like air traffic. Since Murdoch had staked out the Falasarna house there was every chance he'd know about the stashed IDs and getaway vans. In the panic of flight we'd come a long way off-course. Mesavlia was now some eight miles north and there wouldn't be cover all the way. Our only practical support was the sketchy weapons contact in Athens and his unreliable buddies in Heraklion. Konstantinov needed water and antibiotics. We had neither.

But I had my son back. Unearned, unjustified, a second chance.

He was curled up in my lap, asleep, I'd thought, but when I looked down I saw he was looking up at me. The giant primary realisation – *mother* – had blazed through him in the stretched seconds and minutes of the rescue and made everything else irrelevant. But now his reflex emotional spend was over, and other information – more inconvenient truth – was reasserting itself. He knew, at a level beneath or beyond articulation, two things. One, I was guilty. Two, he'd suffered. There was a gap between these two known things. Watching me, letting my body's heat meld with his, he was deciding what to do with it, this gap. He was deciding whether to close it with a connection. I had an image of him years from now as a wiry teenager sitting on the edge of the pool in the Los Angeles villa, moving his legs slowly in the sun-marbled water, then glancing up at me with the human version of the look he gave me now, one that knew he had power of judgement over me. It would be like a talisman he could produce at any time, to stop me in the middle of whatever it was I was doing, to stop me in the middle of loving him, probably, if he'd inherited any of his mother's perverseness and cruelty.

We stared at each other now and understood all this, but understood too that there would *be* love to ruin, which was better than no love at all.

He blinked. Gradually let the pieces come apart in his mind – for now. I put my hand on his hot chest and felt his steadying heartbeat. His sister would be what we both loved. We'd meet at her, like rival gang lords on neutral turf.

'*Ya teebya lyubyu, Angel moy*,' Mia said, ending the call. She put the number into her phone, tossed Cloquet's back to him, looked at me. 'We'll meet again,' she said.

'When you do,' Cloquet said, 'remember she saved your life.'

It didn't register. Cloquet didn't count. Humans didn't count. She turned and limped away into the darkness. A few moments after she was out of sight we heard her go up suddenly and noisily through the trees... and a few moments later come down noisily again. She was in no shape for the effort vampire flight required. But she was desperate to see her son.

65

In the end there was nothing for it but to stick with the original out. Even if Murdoch had known about the vans and the hidden IDs, he wouldn't have passed it to WOCOP. It was after all supposed to be his one-man show: single-handed capture of live werewolf for which Helios would pay WOCOP – or now that I thought about it more likely Sir, privately lining his own pockets – handsomely, and in return for which Murdoch would've been reinstated to the Hunt.

All we had to do now was make it across eight miles of patchy cover with an injured man.

Which, incredibly, is exactly what we did. Cloquet called the Athens contact, who promised (drunkenly, it sounded to me) he'd send 'a medical person' to meet us in the airport parking lot. Walker carried Konstantinov, the rest of us took it in turns to let Cloquet hitch a ride. In a forgivable reversion to type, my familiar had brought along a little cocaine in case of celebration. He took a couple of toots when switching from Lucy to Fergus, looked at me and said: 'I feel that we should go to the Caribbean. The water there is like liquid topaz.'

We reached the derelict farm, collected the clothes and IDs, and did what little we could for Konstantinov with the minimal first-aid kit. Cloquet even found a stream nearby, from which, when we carried him there, Konstantinov drank and drank and drank. After that there was nothing to do but wait for moonset. When it came, tacit agreement saw us all seeking our own spots of privacy among the trees, though the air went heavy and active around us when we changed, as if each of us was a separate, confined thunderstorm. We dressed, and Fergus and Lucy went, with the mystery of their human form refreshed (the poignancy of the knees and elbows, the niftiness of the fingers, the unique nudity of the face), to fetch the vans.

Six hours later, Konstantinov having been stitched and medicated by a twenty-two-year-old student, who despite white coat and stethoscope looked like he should have been practising with his band in a garage, we boarded Aegean Airlines flight 341 from Chania to Heathrow, London, England, where Madeline – and my daughter – would be waiting for us.

66

Konstantinov spent forty-eight hours in bed, attended by Budarin, then went missing. Not a word to anyone. No note, no message, no answering his phone when we called.

'It's Natasha,' Walker said. 'He must have heard from her.'

It was around ten in the evening on the third day since Crete; Christmas Eve. We were in the house Madeline had taken for us in the Dart Valley in Devon, a big, detached dampish place half a mile from Dartmouth, on a hill of gorse and feathery pine overlooking (in glimpses through the trees) the river. It smelled of old beds and mould and the ghosts of a thousand meals. We were lucky to get it: a Christmas booking had fallen through at the last minute. Madeline, with Zoë in a new electric-pink carrier, had met us at the airport with rental cars ready and we'd driven south as the first snow was starting to fall. By midnight there was ten inches on the ground, and by morning a little imagination could make you feel snowed-in. Happily snowed-in. With your children. With your lover. With your pack.

'Either that,' Walker said, 'or he's gone off somewhere to kill himself.'

We were in the big sitting room with a garrulous log fire going. (In one of the diaries it said: *Listen carefully to fire's soft babble, its Tourette's cracks and sparks. Listen carefully: Fire speaks in tongues*. Now I had our children with me Jake's absence was renewed, the irreparable brokenness, the unredressable loss. I had images: the twins, aged five or six, listening, rapt, to some preposterous story he made up, or him presenting them with evidence of nefarious activity and saying: And what, exactly, would you say *this* was? Or the two of them making fun of him, riskily, just out of range of a swipe, or the two of them holding his hands walking down a street, feeling utterly secure and oblivious to any danger because there he was and there was the heat and strength of him in his hands and his existence was their freedom to delight in the world, the sunlight, the city, his stories, the moon…) The owners had decked the place out for Christmas, with a big fairy-lit tree and tinsel on the mantelpiece and holly wreaths on the doors. The rooms winked and glimmered and reminded me of being a kid and hurt my heart because I hadn't seen *my* dad for what felt like years, though it was only six months, and he had absolutely no clue what I'd become. Risk or no risk, in the New Year I was going home and introducing him to his grandchildren. As human beings only, for now. One shock at a time. It would first amaze him, then reopen the wound of my mother's death, then begin to delight him, then fill him up with love like brandy saturating a cake. He'd want to see them all the time. It was all going to get more complicated.

'He shouldn't be out of bed,' I said, 'let alone wandering around in the snow.'

'Yeah, well, this is Mike. This is the Russian thing.'

Zoë and Lorcan were asleep side by side in a new (bigger) bassinet close by me. (It was an excusable madness that I literally wouldn't let either of them out of my sight. Temporarily excusable. Soon, if I didn't break the habit, it would turn toxic. Watching them sleep close to each other was an endlessly renewable joy. I'd stand there, transfixed, unutterably happy, happy in my fingernails and teeth and stomach and palms and breasts, then move away to close the curtains or put another log on the fire and when I came back there the same joy was all over again, completely refreshed and brand new and self-incredulous. The beauty of a meaningless universe is that you don't get what you deserve.) Fergus was already back in London, treating his money with profitable contempt for its stupidity. Lucy and Trish were in the kitchen midway through a second bottle of Bordeaux, Trish trying to teach Lucy not just how to smoke, but how to roll her own cigarettes, now that we'd convinced her, Lucy, that unless they were cigarettes containing silver they'd do her no damage. (*If smoking were completely harmless*, Jake wrote, *everyone would smoke*.) Madeline was in the upstairs bathroom making languorous and epic preparation: Cloquet didn't know it yet but tonight he was going to get comprehensively laid. Dangerous, everyone agreed, but we were reckless and giddy after what we'd been through, and Madeline, I knew, felt sorry for him. Besides, she said, I've never done it with a Frenchman. She wouldn't take money. Don't be daft. I probably need it more than he does. It's all right for you, with the big lovey-dovey. In case you forgot, I was babysitting your *sprog* when I should've been you-know-what. Yes, she was. She'd made it all possible – and given me the gift of Walker, too, no strings attached. Do you have any idea what a good person you are? I'd asked her. It had been an odd moment. We were alone in her room, her sitting at the dressing table, me standing by the window with a cup of black coffee, in that peculiar afternoon light you only get from snow outside. I hadn't meant it to come out so seriously, but I'd been thinking of Jake writing he wished he'd kissed her more, and simultaneously got an intimation of a wretched period in her life when she was seventeen or eighteen, new to London, scared, lost. She'd worn a big leather jacket because it felt like a friend she had with her all the time. She'd found herself in wrong situations. Then met people. Then started the Life. And until the Curse she'd lived in perpetual loneliness and boredom and fear. I hadn't meant it to come out so seriously, but Pharaoh's heart, unhardened now, was erratic in its wellings-up. She was just about to dismiss it – Yeah, yeah, fuck *off* – but found she couldn't, because we were looking at each other and she knew I meant it, and no one had ever said that to her and meant it, and suddenly the two of us were nearly in tears, and had to try to laugh it off, but the laughter made it worse, and then we both *did* shed some tears, laughing, and knowing there was nothing to do but just let this moment come into being and pass away. Somewhere in the middle of it she said: It's okay, you know, I don't do it with anyone now unless I want to. Then she laughed again and said: It's just that I want to all the bloody time. Can't lose, really.

I could hear Cloquet now, moving about in his room above us, humming Jacques Brel's 'Amsterdam', thinking he was having an early night. It gave me pleasure to think of the erotic wealth that was coming to his poor neglected body. And because every small good feeling connected to the big one, I got up to look at the twins again.

Walker came to me and put his arms around me from behind. We hadn't had sex yet, but it was close. He was scared he wouldn't be able to, in spite of manifest erections when we kissed and touched each other, and he knew it would get mentally tougher the longer he waited. Like standing at the edge of a diving board, he'd said to me last night, when we'd been fooling around, and he'd got hard, then panicked and retreated, and a silence had expanded between us.

For a while we stood without speaking, pressed against by all the newness. We were afraid, both of us, that now there was nothing to stop us being together we wouldn't want to. We both knew I was attracted to people who were bigger than me – smarter, deeper, less afraid; Jake, most recently and most obviously, but even before him, all the way back to the Very Bad Dirty Filthy Little Girl at college, that was the pattern. Even Richard had been the type, although in his case I'd mistaken vanity and articulate cynicism for depth. But any way you looked at Walker and me, I'd gone ahead, I was waiting for him to catch up.

'How did you do this alone all those months?' he asked.

Madeline, of course, was flamily connected to him, though she did her best to keep out. It wasn't her fault. Turning someone created an unreliable psychic umbilical. She was in him, erratically, whether she wanted it or not. It was, I thought, the real reason she'd decided to give Cloquet the loving-up of his life, to give me as much room as possible with Walker. How Jake had underrated that woman!

'I never really thought I was alone. I always thought... I mean there was the one who Turned me, for a start.'

'And then Jake, eventually.'

'Yes.'

And so it had begun: he'd have to compare himself, have to know who was better. In spite of everything it irritated me. It irritated me because it demonstrated the inevitability of masculine competitiveness and it irritated me because Jake was better and he was dead and I didn't even have his ghost to talk to.

But Jake had had two hundred years to perfect himself. Walker was only four days old.

'Do you feel him, at all?' Walker asked, moving away from me. A glass of Laphroaig stood on the mantel. He picked it up, sipped, tasted, swallowed. 'I mean the dead. That guy we... '

That guy we ate. The victim we'd shared. His debut meal. He

was feeling the first flickers of being inhabited in that way. Tank to the ethereal fish. You think you've felt it all. Then this. (Which thought produced something like déjà vu, for a second or two – then it was gone. The hairs on my skin had a little electrical moment.)

'Not Jake, no,' I said. 'Not my mother, either. But the kills, yes.'

He looked down into his glass. 'It makes us an afterlife,' he said.

I knew what was bothering him. If the dead we ate went into us then the dead we didn't eat had to go somewhere else. If there was a Somewhere Else then anything was possible: God, a scheme of things, morality, consequences. In which case...

'I don't think it's like that,' I said. 'I think it's that their lives don't just flash before *their* eyes, they flash before ours, too. They pass away into nothing, but we're left with the flash, like a snapshot, like an incredibly detailed echo that'll keep sounding in us as long as we live. It's not really them. It's what they were. I don't know.'

'The ultimate download.'

'Yeah, maybe.'

'So you don't think there's anything?'

I remembered the certainty I'd felt looking past Delilah Snow's death into the void that would have swallowed her. I remembered the certainty of nothingness. Last night, in the small hours, I'd begun a journal. *We're alone in the darkness,* I'd written, *so we hold hands and tell stories of good and evil to comfort each other. It works, for a while, for a life, for a civilisation, perhaps for as long as the species survives. But have no illusions: it makes no difference to the darkness. The darkness swallows us all – good and evil alike – with monolithic disinterest.*

An odd beginning, considering I was happy, but I'd put the pen down with a feeling of contentment.

'Don't bother looking for the meaning of it all,' I said. 'There isn't any.'

Not a conversational aphrodisiac. We took the twins' bassinet and went to join Lucy and Trish in the kitchen. It was a big square room with an Aga and spotlights with a lilac tint and gold tinsel on the dresser. Trish and Lucy were at the dining table, an oak slab that looked as if it had been archaeologically unearthed from the days of Roman Britain. The radio, volume low, was playing Christmas carols, currently 'Gloria in Excelsis'. I poured myself a large Hendricks. Zoë and Lorcan wouldn't need milk (they both drank water now and then) for days. *Wulf* kept telling me I was being an idiot about these things, that nothing that didn't harm me could possibly harm them, but enough of my human remained to keep the fires of paranoia going. Not until they're weaned. Another couple of months, according to the internet, although obviously Google was assuming babies who didn't change into monsters once a month and devour live flesh and blood.

'I still can't get over how easy it was,' Trish said. 'I don't know why we didn't make that the plan from the start. They were a bunch of wusses.' She was, as ever in human form, full of compact energy. The green eyes were her face's big treasure, set off punkily by the artfully chopped deep-red hair. She could drink anyone, it had been conceded manfully by Fergus, under the feckin table.

'Yes, but without Mystery Marco we'd have been in trouble,' Lucy said.

We'd gone over it countless times. Whoever he was, 'Marco' had power over the vampires. The armed boochies had dropped their weapons on cue. 'Remshi' – beyond doubt a fraud – had taken his slap like a gimp. Jacqueline had retreated. Even Mia had been compelled to earth apparently at his will.

'Had to be an elder,' Walker said. 'There's no other explanation.'

'Unless he was the real thing,' Lucy said, as one of us always said, sooner or later, every time we talked about it. The possibility excited us. (With the exception of Walker.) *There's something here, it's true*, Mia had reported. *Very old. I don't know.* Of course she would have felt it, and since Jacqueline's male model was being billed as its source, that's where Mia would assume it was coming from. But 'Marco' was there too, as one of the Disciples. It could just as easily have been coming from him. I'd felt it myself, the nearness of a past that should have been remote, the appalling temporal compression. There was the odourlessness too, and the way he'd talked about the book.

There was the look he'd given me, of deep recognition.

'I felt sorry for that Olivia,' Trish said. 'You could see she'd totally believed.'

'At least we know they *can't* walk around in daylight,' Lucy said. 'Or not yet, at any rate.'

Evidently the raid on the Helios lab in Beijing had been the work of the Disciples after all. They'd come away with a flawed formula and administered it to willing zealots as the ultimate Remshi marketing tool. Recipients were shunted out of public view (according to Jacqueline and her puppet messiah, off into the world to enjoy their new daylight freedom), monitored, and killed as soon as they started showing serious side-effects. By which time members of the congregation were queuing up to be given the gift. It was no wonder the Fifty Families had called time: there would be no competing with an outfit that promised its members a release from nocturnality. Jacqueline's gamble was that they'd perfect the formula before the side-effects jig was up, by which time her position as Queen to the magical King would be established beyond question. Also by which time the gift would've stopped being a gift and become a reward, earned only by complete and indefinite submission to the royal will. The old boochie oligarchy would give way to a new monarchy. You had to hand it to Jacqui, as Walker had said: she didn't think small.

'I want to know what the missing verb is,' Lucy said.

Walker didn't, I knew.

'Whatever it was,' Trish said, 'it was enough to get one of their own priests done-in when he found it out.'

'Something blasphemous,' Lucy said.

Walker poured himself another.

'Forget it,' I said. 'The main thing is we all got out in one piece.'

'I'll drink to that,' Trish said, topping up her and Lucy's Bordeaux.

'Cheers.'

'Sláinte!'

'*Stin iya mas*,' Walker said – just as his cellphone rang.

He looked at the number. 'Holy shit,' he said. 'It's Mike.'

67

Walker had known. I'd known myself, ever since Jacqueline had said Natasha was free, *though not quite the woman she was when she came here*. It was Madame's style, to return her to her lover as everything he didn't want.

But she'd underestimated both of them. She'd underestimated love.

'Talulla Demetriou, Natasha Alexandrova,' Mikhail said. 'Without doubt the strangest introduction I've ever made.'

Odour, mutually repellent, was a farcical problem for all of us, though less for me after my time in close quarters with Caleb. I stepped forward and Natasha and I shook hands, forcing ourselves not to hold our noses. She smiled. 'It might not look like it,' she said, with only the slightest trace of a Russian accent, 'but it's an honour to meet you. Mikhail's told me you've been a good friend to him. I'm in your debt.'

We were in the house's big back garden, now a foot and a half deep in snow. Neither Natasha nor Konstantinov would ever feel the cold again. *Not many make it past a thousand years*. These two might.

Trish and Lucy, with a blanket-wrapped and wide-awake twin each, were in the conservatory doorway, looking on. Suddenly Madeline appeared behind them, in a short silk robe over white lingerie. She looked like a porn version of the angel on the Christmas tree. 'Christ, can no one else smell the – oh. Blimey. Right. Fuck.'

'I just wanted you to know,' Konstantinov said. 'This is my choice. This is the only way it could be.'

He was a little paler, of course, but apart from that in perfect health. He'd shaved off the sick-bed stubble and in the nude face his polished black eyes were renewed jewels. On looks alone he and Natasha could've been brother and sister. Their love had a whiff of that, too, a thrilling, incestuous claustrophobia. It wasn't vampirism that made these two transcendently indifferent to any law, it was love. Next to the love, the vampirism was small.

'I'm happy for you,' I said. 'I really am. I owe you so much. Can you... Would you like to come in?'

There was a moment of fraught silence, then all of us laughed.

'We have somewhere to go,' Konstantinov said. 'I just wanted you to meet Natasha, and to apologise for leaving like a thief in the night.'

It was Walker he'd come to see, I knew. And now suddenly between them there were no words.

Konstantinov put out his hand. Walker took it and, after a pause in which I noticed, belatedly, that the sky was giant and clear and crammed with stars, embraced him.

68

In the absolute snow-stillness and silence of the night, long after Madeline had fucked Cloquet and herself into exhaustion, and Lucy and Trish had staggered with slurred goodnights to their beds and been dropped-on by their slabs of sleep, and Walker and I (helped by whiskey and gin and the shock of Konstantinov's transformation) had had hurried and precarious sex – sex to do nothing more than establish that we could do it, that Walker wasn't terminally mangled – and he had fallen, razed by relief, into sleep, long after all this, the twins and I lay awake and restless.

For a while I fought against it, tried half a dozen variations on the sheep-counting theme, but eventually I got up and dressed, quietly, telling myself it was delayed shock: for three months life had reduced to a single purpose. A horror-purpose, yes, but it had relieved me of every other question and uncertainty, all unease and ambivalence and fear. Not any more. The world was open again, and the dizzying fact of four hundred years in it – with children to raise, with enemies to guard against – was reasserting itself. Four hundred years. There was no grasping that. You groped out vaguely through NASA and the Genome Project and special effects but it was pointless. There would be convulsions, revolutions, things of horrible originality, things that if you were to see them now would look like miracles or magic. I'd forgotten the vertigo I got thinking about it. It was just *that* keeping me awake, I told myself, just the sprawling potential of my condition.

No it isn't, *wulf* said.

Zoë and Lorcan blinked up at me in the dark. I stared at them. Joy. Joy is a circularity. There is the joy. Then disbelief that says you must be dreaming. Then the mental pause or step back to give the universe a chance to wake you. Then the return to see if the joy is still there – and there is the joy again, insanely real and undeservedly all yours.

I took the bassinet and my newly-begun journal and crept downstairs.

The fire in the lounge was dead but the kitchen's Aga still radiated heat, so I drew two chairs together in front of it, set the twins on the floor close by me, put my feet up and re-read the paragraph I'd written earlier.

You kill for two reasons. First, because it's kill or die. Second, because it feels good. In the human court of appeal the first reason buys you theoretical mitigation. The second buys you a silver bullet.

The Hendricks bottle had a couple of swigs left in it. I didn't bother with a glass. I wrote, *Become a werewolf and you break up with humanity.*

Or humanity breaks up with you. You can't blame humanity. You can't expect someone to go on loving you once they know you're going to kill them and eat them. Unfortunately it's not a clean break. In fact it's the messiest kind of break. You still live together. You still have sex. You still have the memories. You still, at moments, feel the love. But sooner or later one of you ruins it. Humanity ruins it by reminding you you're a murderer, or you ruin it by

413

murdering someone. Which ought to be it for you and humanity,
one final exchange of carrier bags, fuck you very much, and goodbye.
But no. On it goes, the living together, the sex, the memories, the
ghost of love——

'It's about time you stopped taking Jake's word for everything,' Marco's voice said. 'Although what he'd think of you drinking *gin* at this hour, God only knows.'

I'd started so violently I'd almost fallen off the chair – but jumped to my feet and got my body between him and the twins.

He hadn't moved, except to raise a hand, palm out. He looked exactly as he had at the monastery, except that he'd apparently taken a shower and washed his hair. There was the dark-eyed face of monkeyish mischief, the odourless vibe of weary amusement and inexhaustible energy. He was sitting directly opposite me on one of the kitchen worktops, ankles crossed. My body was still reacting: armpits, scalp, bladder, adrenline-ravished, blood-rich. Not straightforward fear, though fear was the big flavour. Excitement, dread, something like recognition.

'What do you want?' I said.

'Not to harm you or your children or anyone in this house,' he said, 'unless egregiously provoked. I thought we might have a chat.' He pulled out a pack of American Spirits and a brass Zippo, lit up, took a visibly-relished drag. 'I assume you have questions.' He registered me keeping one eye on the bassinet. 'Really, I promise you, you're completely safe. The nippers too.'

'Who are you?'

'Straight in, no foreplay. I like it. Who am I? I think that's one you know the answer to already.'

'Remshi?'

'You yourself say so.'

'What?'

'Tell me something. Do you still believe the universe is a meaningless accident?'

'What?'

'I was thinking of names, you see. Your own, for starters. Talulla Mary Apollonia Demetriou. "Talulla", as you know, is an Anglicised form of the Gaelic name "Tuilelaith", composed of the elements *tuile*, meaning "abundance", and *flaith*, meaning "lady" or "princess". Commonly said to mean "prosperous lady". Then you've got "Mary", with its connotation of miraculous birth – it certainly must have seemed miraculous to you when you found out you were pregnant – "Apollonia" is the feminine form of "Apollonios", meaning "destroyer", and then to cap it all "Demetriou", the root of which is "Demeter", goddess of fertility. So you've got a prosperous lady with a history of miraculous fertility who's also, once a month, a destroyer.'

'Wait. Stop talking. What do you want?'

'I've already answered that: to talk to you. It doesn't stop there, does it? Look at the kids: "Zoë", Greek, meaning "life", and "Lorcan" – this is my favourite – derived from Irish Gaelic *lorcc*, "fierce", combined with a diminutive suffix to give "little fierce one", when practically the first thing he did on entry into the world was bite someone!'

'How do you know that? You were there?'

'Twenty thousand years, you think you've seen it all.'

When he said this, it was as if he were standing right behind me. His breath touched my ear, though I could still see him across the room. The physical sensation was real. I couldn't help spinning around.

'Sorry,' he said. 'Look, I'm right here, sitting still. I shan't move without your permission. No more tedious gimmicks.'

In the monastery I'd had the feeling of having heard his voice before. *Twenty thousand years, you think you've seen it all*. I had heard it before. That night in Alaska when my waters broke, spoken right behind my ear. Twenty thousand years. It was impossible. Except of course it wasn't.

'Someone's awake upstairs,' he said, looking up. 'We'll have commotion if they come down.'

It was Lucy, going unsteadily, barefoot to the bathroom. We listened to her peeing. An absurd suspense.

When her door had closed again, I said: 'You *are* a vampire, right?'

'*The* vampire, you might say.'

'You don't smell.'

'Not at the moment.'

'At the moment?'

'It's a long story. Is that really the one you want to hear?'

'Did you write *The Book of Remshi*?'

'Yes.'

'When?'

'When papyrus was new.'

Vertiginous compression again, the ancient past dragged here into the kitchen. The beautiful hands' unimaginable history of touch. I got glimpses: a small jar made of lapis lazuli; a tooled leather saddle, sun-warmed; an oiled male shoulder, skin the colour of plain chocolate. I thought: I can't. I *can't*. I didn't know what it *was* I couldn't. I was excited and sickened.

'In Egypt?'

'I wasn't in Egypt when I wrote it. I was in China.'

'And you've been asleep?'

'Yes, but I've been up and about since before you were born. You and Jake drove by my house in Big Sur.'

'*What?*'

'There are patterns all over the place. Stories. That's *my* curse.'

'Wait. Please. One thing at a time.'

416

'Apologies. Fire away.'

I looked down at the twins. They were asleep again, Zoë with one arm across her brother. I was aware with a detached part of myself that I should be afraid, making plans, working out if there was anything sharp and wooden I could get to. I was aware of it, but stuck in the state of debilitating sickened excitement, full of useless energy.

'Do you have answers?' I said. '*Does* it mean anything?'

'I have the answer to the missing verb.'

'That'd be "no"', then.'

'God bless Manhattan for breeding the most impatient people on the planet! Manhattan impatience saves the world decades that would otherwise be spent not cutting to the chase.'

'Look, if you've genuinely got— '

'Shshsh! That's Walker.'

Sounds of movement from upstairs. Walker called out: 'Talulla?'

The vampire was silently on his feet. 'I'll have to go. No good for any of us if he comes down and I'm here.'

'Why do you say that?'

'I think you know.'

'No, I don't.'

'He's guessed the missing verb.'

And so, with sudden embarrassment like a sickening roller-coaster drop, had I.

'*Vor klez mych va gargim din gammou-jhi.* "When he drinks the blood of the werewolf." It's not *mych*. It was never *mych*. It was *fanim*. Present tense of the humble little verb *fan*, meaning "to join". *Vor klez fanim va gargim din gammou-jhi.* "When he joins the blood of the werewolf." I'll see you another time.'

Walker was on his feet, moving with purpose. I was seeing

what he was seeing: me gone, the kids too. I could feel him feeling the house keeping a secret. I looked down at the twins. They opened their eyes, simultaneously.

'You haven't told me anything,' I said, looking up – but I was talking to myself. The vampire was gone.

EPILOGUE

TALULLA VICTRIX

'It's old money, Dad, I keep telling you,' I say, quietly. 'His father's side was originally from England. Microelectronics back through steel through coal through cotton through rubber. That's the official family line, but ask Walker and he'll tell you it really began with selling Indian opium to the Chinese.'

'Jesus, I'm not asking him that.'

'Well, stop pestering *me* about it, will you?'

We're in loungers by the pool at a luxury villa in the Napa Valley, just north of Calistoga (south of the Robert Louis Stevenson State Park – Jake would've approved) on a hot, static, blue mid-August day. Sunlight on the water. The smell of clean concrete, lavender, pine trees. We're drinking; a Hendricks with lime on ice for me, a Bushmills and soda for him. Zoë and Lorcan are in a big sunshaded playpen, Zoë with immense frowning concentration pushing different yellow 3-D shapes into their appropriate holes in a red globe, Lorcan sitting cross-legged and sucking catastrophically on a sliver of mango. In two months, they'll celebrate their first birthday.

Walker is indoors getting chips and salsa, since we're mid-cycle and eating regular food like normal people. I've got a whole calendar worked out around this for when my dad can see us.

'Look, you can't expect me to just absorb all this like a... You can't expect me not to be curious.'

'I know, Dad. I get it. But this is *months* now, with the same shit. You're spilling, you're spilling – wait.' He can't stop monkeying with the lounger, and his latest adjustment has lost him half his drink. 'Wait. Let me. There. Okay?'

Cloquet has been sent on a month-long all-expenses-paid vacation around the Caribbean. (You won't need me any more, he'd said, after Crete, once it was apparent Walker was going to be more than a fling. I'll look for something. It's fine. I understand. Rubbish, I told him, my unhardened Pharaonic heart in a sentimental mess. Go if you want to, but not because you think I don't need you. I'll always need you. *Always*. I put my arms around him. We both cried. It was ridiculous. So he stayed with me. Practically, not much has changed anyway: Walker and I don't, technically, live together, nor, with the exception of fuckkilleat, are we sexually monogamous, though we still do it with each other a lot more than we do it with anyone else. So Cloquet's role has remained approximately the same, familiar, logistician, babysitter, friend. The kids adore him.) Anyway, he's off in the Caribbean. Madeline (who told me the sex was 'as a matter of fact fan fucking tastic', and who descends every now and then, fucks Cloquet's brains out, then disappears) will be 'bumping into him' in Barbuda. All planned by yours truly.

'I don't know why you're obsessing about the money, anyway,' I say to my dad. 'Just be glad we've got it.' Since Jake's financial history was spare I put it to use and made it Walker's. My husband's. The father of my children. Lies, lies and lies again, but the old man needs a picture that's safe, secure and sensible. Doubly so after the shock of me presenting him with twin grandchildren eight months ago. 'You worried about money when we had enough,' I tell him. 'Now we've got more than enough and you're still worrying. It's depressing.'

'All right, all right, fine. Jesus. Did you sign a pre-nup at least?'

'Dad, for God's sake. Yes. *Yes*. We divorce, I get a lot. Trust me, more than I'll ever need.'

Walker, tan, lean, wolf-fit, in Bermudas, comes out of the house with the chips and salsa on a tray. 'Nikolai, you look more than ready for a refresher there. Here, let me get that.'

My dad's amazement at Walker's alleged wealth regularly short-circuits his basic social functions and he ends up, as now, gawping at him, as if he expects to see fifties and hundreds sprouting from the man's head.

'Dad!' I say. 'Do you want a refill?'

'What? Oh, sure, sure. Thanks, Robert.'

'Miss D?'

'Hell, yes.'

The afternoon melts away in heat and sun and alcohol and increasingly frank and freeform conversation. The sentence I wrote in my journal last night after Walker had fallen asleep keeps tugging at my brain: *Talulla Demetriou, you have been a Very* (pause) *Bad* (pause) *Girl*. My dad, drunk, cooks lamb with red and green peppers in a rich tomato sauce – *arnaki kokkinisto* – my favourite from when I was small. The sight of him in paunchy, grey-quiffed, long-eyelashed profile at the stove with one shirt tail out, cooking, calm as God, gives me profound pleasure. It's a risk, of course, having contact with him. WOCOP (or SLOW COP, as we've taken to calling them) are lately wise to the existence of a new generation of werewolves (current count is fifty-plus: Fergus found out about the lovebite, and somewhere out there Devaz has been running amok) and Helios remains bent on cracking the daylight magic of the lycanthropic gene. Either organisation could get to me through the old man. But I know if I gave him the choice he'd want to see me and the kids.

So I've made the choice for him. We just have to be careful. Very careful. Jacqueline Delon, rumour has it, survived the raid on the monastery, though with a Fifty Families price on her head she's choosing her friends carefully. Mia hasn't shown her face, but I know she's been close. Sorority says she can't quite bring herself to assassinate the woman who saved her (and her son's) life. *Wulf* says she's taunting me for fun. Something between sorority and *wulf* says that for the time being fascination's sweeter than revenge. That's what it feels like: the death of either of us would be an impoverishment to the other, the subtraction of a bitter but compelling magic.

After dinner Walker takes the kids up for a bath (they still don't leave my sight unless he or Cloquet is with them; if it's neurotic, fine, I'm neurotic) and my dad falls asleep in the recliner in front of the TV. I step outside with a fresh drink for a smoke. I've been dying for one all day, but I can't in front of my dad. Cancer; my mother; sacrilege.

Barefoot, blissful after two drags, I wander down past the pool, across the lawn and out the gate, which opens onto a track that runs a little way uphill between the pines to meet the road above. The sun's down and the air's blue-golden, soft, warm. A cloud of gnats a few feet away in what looks like pointless frenzy.

I'll see you another time.

That was eight months ago, and I haven't seen him since.

I can't pretend I'm not a little disappointed.

Vor klez fanim va gargim din gammou-jhi. When he joins the blood of the werewolf. When he joins. As in… joins. What God hath joined, let no man put asunder…

I almost didn't tell Walker, that night. Five minutes' surreal conversation with a vampire in the kitchen had felt like an unholy infidelity. But I did tell him. For once grace was given to me to do the right thing. Hot-faced, trembling, I blurted out the whole

424

story. If I hadn't, the concealment would've grown into contempt. That's what happens when you keep a secret from someone you love: you start to hate them for allowing you to prove your own willingness to deceive them.

So I told him, but the feeling of infidelity didn't entirely vanish. Hasn't entirely vanished.

I finish the cigarette and walk back to the pool. The patio smells are benign: chlorine; clean stone; sun-tan lotion; lavender. I can hear basketball commentary from indoors.

I'll see you another time.

Eight months. Twenty thousand years.

I can't pretend a part of me isn't still waiting.

In the house I discover Walker has fallen asleep on my bed in his underwear, with a twin nestled (also asleep) in each armpit. I draw the comforter over them and turn out the light. They won't roll off. He won't squash them. Species certainty. Species gravity.

In the lounge, my dad snores, open-mouthed, in the recliner. I cover him with a blanket, mute the TV and set a glass of water on the side table next to him for when he wakes up, parched. I should be sleepy myself, after so much booze and sun and food, but I'm not. I'm alert, restless, vaguely bereaved. It occurs to me that for the first time in a long time I'm not worried about anything.

I hadn't thought peace would feel like this.

It won't last, of course.